Copyright © 2011 Anna El-Eini
ISBN:1456373560

Cover art "BOY" copyright ©1996 Anna El-Eini. Cover photo "Oxon Cove" copyright ©1999 Anna El-Eini. Cover design by Jodi Ferrier.

This is a work of fiction. Names, characters, places, and incidents either are the product of the author's imagination or are used fictitiously. Any resemblance to actual persons, living or dead, events, or locales is entirely coincidental.

Permissions Acknowledgements can be found at the end of the book.

BEATING HEART

a novel

Anna El-Eini

For Jim and Nicholas

*And to Eugene and Tonya
for inviting me to take a walk with them to Oxon Cove*

BEATING HEART

When you crack open the egg of a three-day-old chick embryo you see a network of blood and the yolk below. And you think that there may not be any embryo there at all, until you see a tiny motion—a red circle moving in a rhythm that you begin to understand is that of a heart. You can see the beating heart.

To stop that heart from beating, you have to know why.

OF BEAUTY AND SCARS

But where shall wisdom be found?
And where is the place of understanding?
                                    Job 28:12

I always believed I would save my brother. I never thought I'd mourn instead. I never thought I would lose—not once, but twice. The first time I didn't get to say goodbye; the second time, I was the one who walked away.

I used to have photos on my office wall of those moments in time that seemed to transform the history of the world. A student holding back the tanks in Tiananmen Square. The Berlin wall coming down. Nelson Mandela's inauguration. NATO planes taking off for Kosovo. Rabin and Arafat shaking hands. Children flying kites over Kabul.

I was once deeply inspired by those images; they were proof that the world can change. But I've learnt that some problems cannot be solved; some people don't want to change. And it may just be the ones you care the most about. It's the hardest thing in the world to accept. That nothing you can say or do will make a difference. I've been forced to tally my losses and move on. Now my office wall is filled with new photos. Not the stuff of international peace and unity, but of all that is much closer to home and matters just as much.

The other day I came across the ad for the job that started me out on this path–the one that led me to believe, as the cliché goes, that we can all make a difference in this world. I had recently moved to Washington, D.C., a city that's as good as Mecca for people like me. Except I wasn't on a pilgrimage–I wasn't looking to taste holy waters or kiss a sacred wall and go home again. Maybe it was more like being a young actor, piling into the car and heading west to Hollywood. I was newly married, drunk with love and optimism, and I thought I'd take whatever job came my way and start from there to make my mark on history. The ad stood out from all the others–it read like a lexicon for reinventing the world–full of powerful, fighting words. Recruit. Build. Educate. Organize. Empower. Campaign. Legislate. Change. I wanted to do all of that–I believed I could–and more. Just two days after I mailed my application I received a call, so of course I thought, I have this job in the bag. *Homes First*. The organization's name alone summed up just about everything I believed in. Doesn't everyone deserve a home?

On the morning of the interview, I shuffled sleepily into the kitchen enticed by the smell of fresh coffee.

"Aren't you going to be late?" Ian looked up from his breakfast with concern. "When are you meeting with *Homes First*?"

Seeing him now—tanned from our weekend away, clean-shaven, his thick, dark hair falling softly down to his intense blue-green eyes—I was tempted to lead him back to bed with me. I leaned in and kissed him; I had all day, but he needed to get to work.

"Not until this afternoon and it's not that far. Make me breakfast for good luck?"

He pushed the cereal box and milk towards me, smiling. "Good luck. Here, I'll even pour you a cup of coffee."

"Dinner then? To celebrate?"

"That's my plan. You'll do great, I know it."

After Ian left for work I lingered over the *Post*, reluctant to concede defeat to the crossword puzzle over a quirky black and white movie ingénue whose name I failed to spell correctly. I cleaned and stored the camping gear from our trip to Chincoteague, before at last changing and heading out. Slipping into the moody summer day outside my apartment building, bulky gray clouds nagging the blue sky, I biked slowly across town along the National Mall, glancing back every couple of minutes to make sure that yes, that was truly Lincoln looking over my shoulder. The same Lincoln who once watched over MLK when he spoke out about the *fierce urgency of now*. I was a long way away from San Francisco. For one thing, D.C. was gloriously flat. For another, it was impossible to travel five minutes, my bike crunching its way over the crushed white gravel footpath that framed the mall, without passing one of the monuments or museums I had always dreamed of seeing. In the grand brick building to my left were the *60 Minutes* clock, Dorothy's shoes and the Greensboro lunch counter. I could only glance quickly at the sleek, modern limestone building to my right; I often swung by the museum to wander for an hour or so through the modules, rockets and spacesuits of *The Right Stuff* and lunar landings, always leaving fully reassured that Americans have never been afraid to dream big. I rounded my way slowly past the Capitol, the legendary pearl white rotunda and flag at its pinnacle soaring up to the now silky gray sky. I soon found myself in front of the Supreme Court and coasted to take in the vast quad that serves as its outdoor court of public opinion, the banners, TV trucks and voices of the past filling the stony air. This was a city of change and power and movement and I wanted in that moment, more than anything else I'd ever wanted, to move with it.

I eventually turned south towards the Anacostia Museum to meet Jonathan Steele, the Director of *Homes First*. I was making great time until I somehow missed the turn for the bridge across the Anacostia River. I ended up lost, on a long, broad street closed off from the river by endless blocks of shuttered warehouses and forlorn-looking apartment buildings slung low around gaunt asphalt courtyards; the only sign of life was the colorful laundry splashed over balcony railings. I recognized the government housing placards marking the end of every apartment block. I could have been back in Oakland, in any one of the projects I'd worked in over the years. My surroundings were suddenly all too familiar, unexpectedly, disappointingly so. One wrong turn from the immaculate gardens and historic townhouses of Capitol Hill and here I was, and now the directions I'd been given no longer made sense. I stopped on the sidewalk and leaning on my bike, I looked up the museum in my city guide. *Anacostia Museum*: Off the Map.

Off the Map?

I had no idea what that meant, but I knew I had to be *on* the map, in the museum, in less than twenty minutes. All I could think was—how do I get across the Anacostia River? Where is the bridge? I realized now that the river itself wasn't in my *NEW! COMPLETE! Guide to Washington D.C.* No river, no museum.

I didn't have a clue back then, about what divides us—what drives us apart, what keeps us apart. I do now. It's the lines we choose to cross, the lines we draw and the lines we don't even know we've left behind us. Now, years later, I look at that map of D.C. and it seems wholly unnatural to me, like the stump left behind when a tree is felled. All the life and brilliance is gone. A river and a community and one hundred thousand people cut away by a cartographer's hand.

I pulled out my other map, the one I had picked up at a visitor's center when I first arrived in D.C., and quickly unfolded it. It reached up into Maryland, covered most of northern Virginia, but there was no Anacostia River on this map either. By now I was struggling against the overwhelming sense that something not entirely my fault was at play here. It wasn't just my having lingered most of the morning in my sunlit apartment, or my euphoric, unhurried ride across town; I may have procrastinated and left little time for a wrong turn, but I could never have predicted that a quarter of Washington D.C. could be off the map.

Eventually I hailed a cab, after frantically chaining my bike to a parking meter.

"The Anacostia Museum, please," I said, "Can we make it in fifteen minutes?"

The driver—arm stretched casually across the back of the passenger seat—turned to look at me, and laughed.

"Iss jus' 'cross the bridge, we'll make it."

And then I found myself thinking—although only now, as the car sped over the bridge, leaving the charted world behind me—is this *safe*?

I sighed deeply as I entered the cool, modern museum and read the banner that bore its name. I had made it to the *Smithsonian Center for African American History and Culture*, known locally I now realized, as the Anacostia Museum. It was gorgeous, though far too small for the story it was committed to telling. The United States Congress had been bickering for years about how, when and where to build a real museum in D.C. to display the part of America's history so many Senators and Representatives were hoping might somehow be forgotten instead; likely some might find their own family's ignominious paths to power highlighted in an exhibit.

"You must be Linda."

There he was. Jonathan Steele. Widely known as a personal friend of the Kennedys and the Bushes, patron saint of lost causes and descendant of slaves. I had long-admired him as the first black Housing and Urban Development Secretary, and for having started his own organization to tackle poverty in the nation's capital. The tall, slender man approaching me was fifty or so; he had graying hair, deep lines around his strong smile, and bright, hazel eyes that immediately drew me in as we shook hands.

"No problem finding the museum, I take it? Thought this might make a convenient place to meet. We're still looking for new office space."

"I did get a little side-tracked but I'm here at last. This is beautiful. I'm so glad I made it."

He showed me the way to the conference room; a wall of windows faced part of the parking lot and the grassy hill down to the main road. I could just make out the bridge I'd taken, and found the Capitol on the horizon. The distances seemed oddly distorted, as though we were further away than I knew us to be from the Hill and the Mall.

Jonathan gestured for me to take a seat.

"The materials you requested," I said, handing them to him.

Without even a glance, he set them aside.

"So you've been in Washington for how long exactly?"

"One month. Well, no, nearly two—"

"One month. And you lived where?"

"San Francisco."

"Well, you're a *long* way from California now."

The way he said this made me think of the California that tourists crave. Redwoods, surfing and the Golden Gate Bridge came to mind. Hollywood. Not Oakland though. Definitely not Oakland.

"And you've worked with low-income and homeless adults—white and black?"

I thought, does it matter? They were homeless, or in trouble. I did what I could. Of course it matters.

"Both. Kids too. We took in the runaways. Foster care was such a nightmare. I'm sure you know."

He nodded as though conceding that this was what he wanted to hear. I couldn't gauge what was bothering him though; something else was on his mind. He half-turned away, looking out towards the parking lot, as though preparing his next question. Did it trouble him that I was young? And white?

"I thought I saw a cab pull away."

He was letting me down gently; I knew now he couldn't possibly hire me. I had never crossed the river before; I was a stranger in town. I had no ties to the community, no knowledge of the city at all. Maybe I would have impressed him if I had swooped into the parking lot on my bike and greeted him helmet in hand. Fearless, ready to get to work. But as likely not. Forced to admit it, there would be no celebrating with Ian that night; I'd been in D.C. barely two months, not long enough to claim the right to start making changes around town.

I suddenly found myself asking—I knew it was bold, he might even have taken it the wrong way—"Could we take a drive, or a walk? As you now know, it's my first time here. Would you show me the neighborhoods?"

He was taken aback, but after a moment his expression softened; he looked relieved by the request. He didn't answer at first. But I knew we both understood what I was saying. *I'm not the person you're looking for, but maybe I will be, one day.*

What started as a stroll in Jonathan's neighborhood grew into all the years since with him as my guide. His tips on City Living didn't include where to eat in Georgetown or what parts of town to avoid at night and he didn't need to encourage me to walk or bike. Fear, back then, was an afterthought for me, an orphan emotion I never truly felt was my own, always arriving after the fact, too late to deter me. For about a year after the interview, I took part-time jobs to help pay the rent and mostly spent my time exploring every last neighborhood in D.C. When Jonathan was certain that I had come to see Washington for what it truly was—a city with its beauty and scars all laid out, easy enough to love—he offered me a job at *Homes First*. He coached me closely over the years until we reached a point where, no matter the odds, we mostly won our campaigns. I fell into my work hard and fast. Long hours, I didn't care; I loved what I did. I became the go-to girl for failing campaigns across the city, guaranteed to flip the switch for victory, and one day I woke up and I was the new Director of the Low-Income Housing Program. It was all happening, just as I'd hoped when I first tacked those photos on my office wall and dreamed of altering the course of history.

And then my brother died. Except David didn't die—death didn't come *to* him. He gave up on life. And I just couldn't accept that. Not when I had devoted my whole life to change. What could have been so bad about his life that he couldn't change it? We were cut from the same cloth—how did he fray at the edges and finally unravel completely and I'm still here, intact, barely a thread loose? Recruit. Educate. Organize. Build. Empower. Campaign. Legislate. Change. *What was the point?* David had slammed the exit door in my face and left me behind on this fragile planet, full of people in need, feeling certain that nothing I could say or do mattered anymore. Had it not been for Ian and Jonathan, had it not been for *Richard*—who was by my side every day at *Homes First*, who without knowing it, stepped in to take David's place—I might not have found a way back to my work. It would have been so easy to do something else—work that didn't require me to believe that what I did, day to day, counted for something, or that the lives of others might even depend on whether I cared enough about my job.

As for what happened next with Richard, I feel it more every day, just as the memory of David stubbornly refuses to fall away. David and Richard—my two great losses in life. How to set them aside and keep doing what I do? I'm still working on that.

OF LEARNING TO LOVE AGAIN

For wherever else an American citizen may be a stranger, he should be at home in his nation's capital, Washington, D.C.
                                                             Frederick Douglass

I wanted to arrive early for the meeting at the Windsor Apartments on Oakwood Avenue, to have a chance to speak alone with Anita Douglas, and to avoid the day's heat. But even at eight in the morning, the stifling air hung as though already exhausted, about the tree-lined streets of Anacostia. There were few people about as I walked the long blocks from the bus stop toward a cluster of tall modern apartment buildings that stood high above the trees of Oxon Run Park. Only the occasional passing car or bus, brakes puffing and grinding, fractured the heavy silence. I turned to take a shortcut across a small playground and saw two kids balancing on the edge of their swings, rocking lazily back and forth, and I waved to them.

As I rode the bus on my way here, I felt buoyed, happy, watching the neighborhoods, scenery and landmarks of the nation's capital go by, my work once again taking me across the city, to the other side of the Anacostia River. With expansive views of both riverbanks, there is never enough time to take everything in as the bus speeds over the Douglass Bridge. Anacostia Park to one side, sparkling green despite the haze over the water. To the other side, the recently restored old pump-house, with the sunlight bursting off its giant picture windows; the piles of rubble that are all that remain of the old sand and gravel plant; the vast warehouses and red brick factories of the Southeast Federal Center and Navy Yard. This landscape that I knew so well, would soon be unrecognizable as the new baseball stadium rose up to a chorus of excitement and fear for what would come after it. For a few seconds that morning, I caught a glimpse of Poplar Point, with its spectacular, but now abandoned and overgrown, greenhouses, where the Architect of the Capitol once fussed over flowers and shrubs for the gardens of the United States Congress. I have been inside. I had to break through the chain link fence with wire cutters, but once I did, I was free to wander alone through the enormous, deserted glass buildings. I have been everywhere Jonathan told me to go.

Each time I cross the Anacostia River, it is the same; I find those seconds suspended over the water to be an exhilarating fragment of time. I allow myself to believe during that tiny interval, that it is possible to revive this struggling city. Momentarily, I'm not so much saddened by the brutal neglect of this part of town as brilliantly inspired to hasten its re-birth. *Driven to act.* Then my eyes fall to the water itself, and as always, the surge of hopefulness recedes. The river lays to either side of me—a murky, dull mass flowing cautiously, fatigued, through a careworn, isolated community, carved up and away from the rest of the city by a startling mess of raised highways and bridges fleeing to Maryland. A river so recently sacred and vital, that there are those still alive who remember the baptisms performed in its once sparkling, clear waters. A place so quickly—a matter of years really—violated and degraded, that standing on its banks and watching the brown silt of hurried suburban developments slow its progress, knowing that under its surface even the soil is poisoned, those once christened by its clear waters are left faithless. Unable to believe that such a trauma might ever be healed. Forced to acknowledge that not in their lifetime will the waters of the Anacostia River split light in quite the same way again.

As though to reinforce the hopelessness of the situation, the bus took its turn onto Martin Luther King Jr. Avenue and this once thriving road shook me as it always does, from my childlike dreams of revitalizing Washington. There is a comforting sense of prosperity at first, but it is soon marred by the realization that this grand boulevard has few functioning commercial establishments. I saw once more the old Safeway grocery store, now closed for good, the name still visible as pale gray letters outlined on the dirty façade where neon letters once hung. The empty parking lot before it craved cars, lying ugly and useless in their absence.

"I like lemongrass. Do you like lemongrass?" Jonathan had asked me during our first tour of the neighborhood, after my interview, all those years ago.

"Uh, no, I can't say I do. But if it means I'd get the job, I could start to like it, I'm sure."

His face was tense, not laughing. "That's what this neighborhood is like, if you really want to know. Assumptions are made and they cannot be unmade. Safeway assumes we don't want lemongrass, or fresh carrots, or anything of quality. Because we live here."

"Don't want it or don't know what to do with it?"

He stopped to look intently at me and said, "Yes, you're right, both." Hands in his pockets, he kicked at the ground. "This isn't just a supermarket, and we'll know that for sure when it's gone."

We were standing in the parking lot looking up at the sign—at the time still working—bright red box letters, certain of their message, SAFEWAY. A smaller sign flickered at the window, OPEN.

The store's closing was a blow to the heart of the community. The mediocre, grimy supermarket had long ceased offering the same range of produce available elsewhere in the city and the shabby, empty aisles drove residents to shop across the border in Maryland even before it closed. Just as Jonathan had warned me, its value was measured by its presence. There was necessity, and prosperity enough, to support such a store, to support other stores nearby. But without a supermarket—if Safeway didn't want to stay—it seemed, when other neighborhood businesses faltered or failed, as though no one could make it here.

Soon the bus passed a collection of shining churches and well-kept lawns in front of low-rise apartment buildings and then I saw Players, a bar that is a hotbed of east-of-the-river politics and that sometimes plays the role of MLK's only restaurant. That was where I decided to get off the bus that morning, in front of Players, its dark painted doors and heavily barred windows baking in the morning sun, the heat radiating relentlessly off the boarded up buildings that lined the avenue, from here, all the way to MLK's horizon.

One night, a few months before, I had met Anita Douglas in the back room at Players. I was drunk and celebrating with an exuberant bunch of activists at the end of a campaign to stop a truck fueling station from being built in the neighborhood, so I didn't see her coming at first. But soon the formidable, meticulously dressed woman who was clearly sober was inexplicably bearing down on me.

"You're with *Homes First*, aren't you?" she said, "I've been meaning to give you a call."

I squinted and then stared at the imposing, young African American woman who had singled me out. She held her tall, slender body straight backed, her thick, shiny, black hair swept away from her face, her dark eyes holding my own, and she reached her hand down to me where I sat low in the sagging, balding sofa with my friends crowded around me. I felt unjustifiably honored and foolishly small.

"Hi, hi. Yes, I'm Linda. I didn't stop the trucks! I didn't! My friend here—he stopped the tru-uh-*ck*."

Nothing more but a dry grunt came out. I instinctively placed my hand over my friend's mouth before he said something equally drunken and stupid that would turn Anita away. I tried again, raising an unsteady hand.

"Linda Douglas. Nice to—no, no—*you're* Douglas, *you're* Douglas. I'm, I'm *Linda*—"

She stood nodding at me, as though encouraging me, as though I might just make it. But I lacked faith in the parched croaks that seemed intent on escaping my throat. Somehow I managed to reach into my briefcase, and struggling to prevent all of its contents from spilling out onto the sticky, dark floor below, extracted a business card; I handed it to her.

"I'm sorry—can I—I could call you. We could call—*each other*!" My voice, still thin and gritty, worked at last.

"Don't worry about it," she laughed, and placed my card carefully into her wallet. "Maybe we can celebrate a victory together sometime."

Anita had not called right away. I was pained to think about what an idiot I had made of myself that night. But before the week was up, while sitting in my office reviewing a city Housing Authority list of the buildings slated for demolition and renovation, I had, at last, received a call from her. And I found myself thinking afterwards, this is it. This is something I need to do. *I want to be there for you Anita Douglas.*

One of the kids waved back; the other bashfully leaned her head against the swing, but allowed me a smile. I kept walking along Oakwood

Avenue. As I approached the apartment building I took a moment to find my breath—it was trapped, the humid air forcing it down, the heat making it impossible to inhale deeply and clear my lungs. I looked up and took in the unusually tall, expansive buildings before me. It was clear to me, as I tilted my head backwards, shaded my eyes and looked across the apartments with their shining windows and broad balconies, that this would be an entirely different battle; this was the largest building I had ever visited. I guessed there were four hundred units—as many families at stake—and winning would be an absolute necessity.

The idea hit me then. Maybe I'd be running away from something I shouldn't, but here at last, was something worth running to. I had already sensed it through my drunken blindness that night at Players—Anita would convince me to leave my work at *Homes First* behind and come onboard her campaign to save the Windsor Apartments.

I entered the building and was relieved to feel the cool air of the lobby once the security guard buzzed me in. I noted that the elevator was clean and functioning, and that the ceiling fan worked, as I watched the numbers light up for each floor. I understood the significance of this immediately—this was not a neglected building; the holding company had done well to protect its investment. But as I adjusted my suit, freshened my face and wrists with wipes that I miraculously found in my briefcase, and touched up my lipstick, I put my assessment of the building to the back of my mind. I focused instead on making a good impression on Anita now that she had given me a second chance.

I pushed back the unlocked, slightly ajar door of the apartment. Impressed by this, I simultaneously noticed an alarming array of locks on the door. Anita greeted me warmly and we shared a brief moment of mutual admiration that felt oddly as though we had found each other again after a lengthy, unwanted separation.

"It means a lot to me that you invited me," I told her.

"Hope you're ready to get to work? I have ridiculously high expectations of you."

"Jonathan?"

"Of course."

We laughed.

"Don't believe everything he tells you about me. And you should hear what he says about *you*." The words *young hero* came to mind but I didn't want to embarrass her.

"Come on in. Make yourself at home," she said.

Once inside, I saw the usual assortment of community figures that I'd rubbed shoulders with over the years, but I also didn't recognize several faces in the room. Charlie Boyd, from the Park Service, came over to shake hands, and I noticed Luther Shaw, a local lawyer and activist, nod to me from where he sat in his wheelchair; we had worked together in the past and I wondered at his role here today. I scanned the room once more to assess the turn out, noting who formed the different conversation circles, committing new faces to memory. Jonathan often told me that on this front, I had left him in the dust—the way I discreetly record what I observe and sweep the room for clues that may later help me channel people in directions they never even knew they wanted to take. I instantly liked what I saw, a veritable hive of worker bees ready to go anywhere for their sweet queen Anita.

I moved over to where Anita stood slicing a brightly frosted lemon cake as though there were something to celebrate. Looking around again, it occurred to me that maybe there was; no matter the reason we had all gathered here, the apartment resonated with shoulder-to-shoulder resilience, togetherness. As fast as Anita cut the eerily incandescent pieces of cake they were scooped up and devoured eagerly by all around. There is nothing so delicious with a cup of strong coffee in the morning, and I struggled to resist a second slice. I caught parts of conversation as I ate, and discovered that many of the people around me first heard the news that the Windsor Apartments were being sold, at a community picnic, just days ago. It would have been easy to mistake the jocular cake-eating and banter around me for either capitulation or complacency, but the apprehension broke through in fragments of defiance and disbelief.

"...never moving. No-one is gonna *make* me leave."

"I have nowhere, nowhere to go."

"My Grandma won't leave. How can she? She's eighty-five and this is the only safe place she's ever lived."

"Man, I hated my mother and her apartment. Now I'm getting all sentimental about what? Home ain't nothing but a place you hate when you're there and miss like crazy when you leave."

Suddenly Anita stood beside me; she nudged me as she set out ginger ale alongside the coffee and tea.

"Oh, I *know* its only morning, but I drink the stuff all day long. Sixteen years and counting."

I contemplated this reference to sobriety and recalled the first night I met Anita.

"So, I really made a good impression on you at Players?"

"Go on girl, walk around and take a look at my place. You haven't far to go. Here, take this with you."

I turned down the soda and happily accepted a glass of ice-cold water instead, before leaving to take in the apartment and its views. Anita laughing off my concern, inviting me into her home, it felt good; she had moved us effortlessly from strangers to something else, for us to define together, but already conceived.

I walked from the living room to the two bedrooms, glanced at the bathroom and returned to the living room. A modest display of African art hung in the main bedroom, alongside a set of framed psalms, a portrait of a melancholy, black Jesus with a brilliant golden halo, and a wreath of dried flowers. The second, very pink, very lacy bedroom could only be home to a teenage princess. The larger portrait of Jesus—more modern, square-jawed and blacker still—was draped with beads, friendship bracelets and silk flowers over the edges; it hung not by the bed, but over the desk, where a clutter of textbooks, a computer and a printer all vied for space. Back in the living room, an exceptionally large, original painting of blue irises reigned over the sofa; elsewhere an assortment of framed flower prints and photographs filled in the gaps. The bedrooms were an intense religious experience, the living room a cool summer's day.

In the small hallway near the kitchen, I stopped still in front of a giant painting of a slave girl on an auction block. It was a disturbing image of innocence for sale. The painting depicted the slave girl with her chained hands held in front of her, as though the men and women shopping for slaves could take a good look at the girl's shackles to be certain of the absence of freedom. The girl's skin was shiny, almost oily, and somehow despite the humiliation, she looked—just barely—peaceful. The painting was an original; parts of the canvas were worn and cracked, and I wondered at its age.

"That's my great grandmother's work."

Anita was behind me; I turned to her.

"It's quite a story," Anita said, her tone both welcoming and cautionary, and she gestured for me to return to the meeting. "Some other time, we'll get to it."

During introductions I stood aside slightly, taking some measure of each person present. I turned momentarily towards the balcony in the living room and understood at last—understood completely—why the fight to save the Windsor Apartments, in far southwest Washington, D.C., would be different. The Mayor's office was involved. Someone must have described the view to him. It was once the view that told poor black folk that they had been cast far away from the city where the white people lived, with a river in between to keep them away. But now it was a view of freedom, of African Americans choosing where to make their homes. And of lush green hills, water, and the Capitol of the United States of America. Of prime real estate.

OF ROADBLOCKS AND ONE-WAY STREETS

You took away all the oceans and all the room.
You gave me my shoe-size in earth with bars around it.
Where did it get you? Nowhere.
You left me my lips, and they shape words, even in silence.
                                        Osip Mandelstam

"It's really very simple," Anita told us, "our time has run out." The group of residents and community leaders crammed into Anita's apartment had at last settled down, and her words resonated freely, unchecked by our silence. Every space in the living room and kitchen area was filled. Men and women in work uniforms and suits sat on the floor, a woman nursed her baby in the hallway under Anita's great grandmother's painting, and a group of Metrobus workers—moments earlier boisterous with laughter and small talk, now listening solemnly—leaned hard on the kitchen counter. A cluster of younger residents, clad in mandatory baggy clothes and head-gear, stood bunched together by the door, pretending to be at the meeting against their will; they jostled and joked with each other, but they too paid attention. We had finished the introductions, and I noticed that Luther made certain that the sign-up sheet did not stall as it was passed around; he watched it carefully, a covenant for his community's future.

"We were supposed to find a way to somehow—no matter what—*improve* our lives and then move on. Or better still, get rich. But we haven't, have we? No we haven't. We are still here, and we still need roofs over our heads, and we're still deeply, deeply in trouble."

This is how each campaign begins. Ordinary people in a room slowly gathering their courage, trying to interpret the warning signs, wondering what hazards lie ahead. The particular story that Anita struggled to relate—how her friends and neighbors would soon be forced from their homes, with few options for where to go next—was being played out across the city and across the United States, in neighborhoods just like this one. It could only invoke a conflicting sense of urgency and numbness for those who listened so intently all around her but I tried to remind myself that Anita's story was not new to me. *This is your game.* I steeled myself, prepared myself mentally for the fight ahead. *You know how to play it to win.*

From my work with Jonathan I learnt that the government loans and tax credits of the 1980's, which funded the country's largest affordable rental properties, Windsor Apartments included, had expired. That as a result, many real estate corporations, after gambling with low-income rentals for twenty or more years, were now free and eager to sell or redevelop their properties as middle-income and high-end condos, and that most tenants simply had nowhere to go. I knew this and still, I lowered my eyes. It wasn't easy listening to Anita when the very personal nature of this, her latest effort to defend her community, found its way into her voice, heavy now with her own potential loss and sorrow for her neighbors who had been given notice to move out and leave their homes and their neighborhood behind.

I felt encouraged though, knowing why Anita asked me to join the group today. With my years of tenant buy-out work around the city she hoped I could offer advice on this campaign. Jonathan and I had already made our back-of-the-envelope assessment of a potential tenant bid on the Windsor Apartments; with a stable mix of long-term, low-income and lower middle-income residents we thought it might just work, despite the daunting size and value of the buildings. This news would be well received here. But just as I was about to step forward for Anita to introduce me, she paused and then nodded, as though confirming to herself that she should continue, and instead she introduced Luther.

He wheeled himself forwards, a well built, distinguished-looking African American man in his early forties. He wore impeccably pressed clothes, his shirtsleeves folded back on muscled forearms, deliberately conveying his readiness and ability to take control. He was attractive but his long, narrow face was dominated by the fierceness in his dark eyes; he emananated independence and strength. He took his time to begin, centering himself before the group, holding the room in silence for a moment, and then he spoke. No one in the room was expecting what came next. I couldn't really believe what came next. Luther described a new threat to the community that seemed so absurd, I had a hard time taking it seriously because really, I thought I'd heard it all before.

Community organizers really only survive by learning to swiftly separate rumor from fact. In D.C., there are always stories swirling around about out-of-town real estate moguls buying up South Capitol Street in a dirty deal with the feds; or city recycling trucks illegally emptying their dumpsters into the Anacostia River; or even government plans to build a secret nuclear power facility on MLK. It would be a huge mistake to chase down each of these red herrings and let the foxes, marauding freely around the city, slip by. But I knew Luther from past campaigns. He was astute, cynical—a fearless D.C. native who didn't pay heed to hearsay. He mined hard for facts; the only bedrock he was willing to build on was the truth, and he had no time for whispering games. He had been the community's finest legal defense against many of the injustices heaped on it since the day he graduated Georgetown Law School two days after his thirtieth birthday, just over ten years ago. So for Luther to be presenting this latest threat as a legitimate concern made me realize I needed to listen up.

"We're getting a brand new, state-of-the-art prison in our neighborhood. Not the new supermarket we've all been holding out for. No one's planning to fix Greater Southeast Hospital that I know of. But we are getting a prison." He gestured towards the balcony. "Right there, right on the river. We'll be able to see it from our windows—if we get to stay here, that is."

We all turned to the Potomac River, a broad band of silvery light, glittering over the dark canopy of trees beyond Oakwood Avenue.

"2,500 beds. Less than a quarter mile from all our schools. On National Parkland."

I wanted to believe that Luther had made a mistake. You can't build anything on National Parkland, can you? Luther was a lawyer; he wasn't going to let that slip. So why didn't he dismiss the foolish scheme for what it was? He didn't get a chance. The room shuddered to life. The kids by the door were the first to move in towards him.

"A prison? A *prison*? Instead of a new high school? What're you saying? Are you *messin'* with us?" The kid who spoke was tall, skinny, he threw his hands out as though blocking Luther in a basketball game. "Luther—you're not gonna let this happen!"

Luther didn't give us the answer we were hoping for. "I know you're all thinking, how can this be right? How can they be fixing to build on our parkland? Well I'll tell you how. Because the United States Congress gave our parkland—all 45 acres of it—to a private prison company. This is real, it's happening. That's all I can tell you right now."

"As Luther said, it's a private prison. A *for-profit* prison," Anita added. "And their experts have already decided that every last inmate will likely be black."

Her words reverberated through the soul of every person in that room—I am certain of it; I felt instantly shaken to the core. There could be no misunderstanding what Congress intended by taking such action, no doubt that once again in America, a price had been fixed for a black man's head.

Another resident rose from where he had been sitting on the floor. His face was tight with anger, but his voice arrived calmly. "First we're told to leave our homes, now this? Congress is planning to lock our boys up, and make money off of them, right in our faces? Right *here*, where we all live?"

Luther must have gauged the pressure change in the room; a rush of unanswerable questions would soon follow. "All we know now for sure, is that this prison is headed our way. No one on the City Council seems to know a damn thing about it, or they're playing dumb. I got the call from a friend on the Hill. But I will find out—trust me, we're going to find out how this happened."

One of the women seated on the sofa leaned forwards and spoke as though to herself, as though everyone around her were a part of her. "Well that's just it," she said, "Come on people. Lord knows we've been here before. We know what to do."

While Luther continued to talk, I mulled over the few pieces of information I had to work with. A confidential call from my friend Greg, in the Mayor's office; he had refused to elaborate but warned me that if Anita came calling, I should move fast. Anita seeking me out shortly afterwards. The revelations from this meeting. I glanced over at Anita. It must have seemed to her that she could no longer keep tending to her neighborhood as she had always done, mending its fraying seams, patching over what was laid bare. What Anita knew as her neighborhood would soon be torn away from her. She had set about finding new leaders, with original ideas and a distinctive kind of energy, and she had filled her apartment with people who could maybe do more than stave off these new threats. This time around, Anita was likely hoping for more than restoration; she was holding out for transformation. As I watched her then, standing, listening to Luther carefully, clearly explain the problems they faced, I was reminded, by the way she so quickly took charge of the campaign, finding so many people ready and eager to work for her, that she was a legend in the world of local community organizers. But if she had earned such an accolade, while still so young—she was just thirty-five or so—the notion surfaced that maybe she was ready, even eager, to step back and let others take up the fight, but she couldn't. That such a decision wasn't hers to make.

I turned back to Luther, and I reminded myself that I needed to think this all through, and quickly, if I were to press on and do my part. *The developers wouldn't want a prison next to their property, so maybe that threat alone could convince them to take a tenant buy-out. Easy enough. But we also need to stop the prison. How, if Congress is backing it? And even if we did that, Windsor Inc. would be back in business.* Then it dawned on me that we couldn't play one proposal off the other, we couldn't put off one campaign for now and get to work on the other; we would have to fight both the prison and the Windsor redevelopment at the same time. And only once we'd done that, could the other work continue—the work of improving lives, of stabilizing and rebuilding the neighborhood. I recognized once more the start-stop rhythm by which low-income, minority communities live as they try to move forwards, no matter the detours marked out for them. Start. Stop. Start. Stop. This was the cadence of Anita and Luther's own lives, choosing, as they did, to help steer. I rode along every now and then and I hit the highs and the lows, but I was never really here for the long term. I could now see that this would always be the difference between me and most of the people in this room. I retreated every day to a neighborhood where prisons would never be built on public parkland, where I turned a key each day to open the door to a home that I owned.

Suddenly Anita introduced me and I was expected to speak. I hesitated before using Jonathan's trademark opening line, but they are words that need to be said when there is no visible way through or around what lies ahead.

"You all need to know, we are going to win. We're going to save your homes, and we're going to stop this prison. And if I can borrow your words," I gestured to the woman on the sofa, "We know what we need to do, so let's get started here."

I took off running, fighting hard. This was what I did best; it was what Jonathan had trained me to do and why Anita asked me to be there that day. Fully charged, the anger fresh, I worked the room over and again for suggestions and thoughts about how best to block the prison and prepare a takeover strategy for the Windsor Apartments. I didn't let anyone go unheard. Everyone had a voice; everyone in that room was there for a reason. The kids by the door stepped in towards the living room to participate. We started throwing around possible campaign slogans. Something short, sweet, simple.

A young girl, her breathing strained by the anxiety of speaking out in public said, "We have to say, don't we, that no one would build this prison on a park on the other side of town, so why ours?"

She was right, but then the room broke into an uproar over why Congress had given away the parkland and why they figured it was O.K. to build a prison near the local schools, and I had to take back control. Jonathan taught me early on, that when people take leave from work and school for a meeting, find someone to watch their kids, there is never any time for *how did we get here*? Our job is always to get *there*—past this—because no matter what this is, it's just another roadblock and it either needs to be hauled away or circumvented. There will always be plenty of time later to take a closer look at who put the roadblock there in the first place, and why. So no matter what I was thinking, feeling, no matter that my stomach churned at the thought of what was really at stake here, so many lives, families, kids—*those sweet kids on the swing this morning*—I kept the meeting moving by shutting down the questions and staying with our message.

"The slogan has to be short, it has to say what you're feeling. It's got to say in just a few words, what's wrong, and what's right."

"Schools not prisons." It was the same boy who had spoken before.

Luther looked back from where he had been staring intently out the window the whole time I'd been leading the meeting. "You're right, Theo," he said softly. "You're exactly right."

Just then an elderly gentleman rose to speak and leant forward on a chair in front of him. "I really think we oughtta look into where all the residents is going to go if we has to leave." He shifted his weight as though from a weak hip. "You know, find some places we can start thinking on moving to."

I hesitated before writing down the words, *Go Where*? I was never cut out for that kind of contingency planning or allowing for loss; I was too used to making my way through, too used to winning. Then just as quickly, someone else suggested we find out the average rent in the building, to see if a buy-out was even possible. Not exactly a new idea, but at least we were back on firm ground. None of the suggestions marked on the flip chart, balanced on a chair in Anita's living room, seemed adequate at first. But one by one the sheets were torn off and taped up, filling the walls, growing into our campaign plan. Just an hour later, with people starting to rise to leave, we had already moved from fear to action. That was more than enough for now. After saying a brief goodbye to Anita and Luther, with another meeting to get to, I hurried from the room and tried to shake off the feeling that Luther had not entirely approved of my being there that morning.

OF TIME TAKEN

There were once five and twenty tin soldiers, all brothers, for they were the offspring of the same old tin spoon. All the soldiers were exactly alike with one exception, and he differed from the rest in having only one leg. For he was made last, and there was not quite enough tin left to finish him.

Hans Christian Andersen

"The spinal cord," Rafael told the kids gathered around him, sitting in a circle on the floor of the barn, "Is a source of frustration and wonder to scientists."

He tilted his head and his hands moved rapidly through the air as he spoke. My friend was doing what he loved most of all, capturing imaginations.

"You see, sadly, we never did repair Superman's broken back—but that's only because we didn't figure out how, in time. But we know that one day we should be able to do that kind of thing, to help others like him. Like you."

Rafael chose his words carefully. He did not give false hope. The riding stables' instructors were deluged with frantic calls from mothers after Diane Sawyer interviewed Dana Reeve on TV, and she said everyone believed Christopher would be cured, even up until his sudden death. It was noticed by all the instructors that very few fathers called. The children, all with physical and learning disabilities, were mostly from complicated, difficult home situations. They were all still clinging to the memory of Christopher and Dana Reeve's visit to the stables on one of their lobbying trips to Washington—his confidence, the joy she brought them. Superman was their source of hope, his picture hung in every classroom. What, the mothers had asked, would the children have to believe in now? Then when Dana Reeve passed suddenly, succumbing to cancer so swiftly it seemed she was called to be with her husband, it had seemed urgent, necessary to reassure the children that the research they funded would still go on. Rafael had left the lab where he worked as soon as he heard the news to come down to the stables to talk to the kids. He had called me and asked me to join him.

"Any disease that a scientist like me works on, really it's a puzzle, just like the ones you play with. You've all learnt a little about DNA. So you know that life in many ways comes down to A's, G's C's and T's. Now that makes it seem so easy, doesn't it? We should be able to make people better if we just play with the letters and move them around?"

He looked at me. I knew that he had cracked codes and opened giant biological safes, but that once inside, the work of sifting through and fixing the treasured contents was what really mattered. He shook his head. He had to plunge deeper and it would hurt.

"Eddie, may I talk about you for a moment?"

Eddie nodded. Small and frail, gaunt, he was disappearing from us.

"Eddie is sick because of the roughly 3 billion letters that make up the DNA in his body, nature has mistakenly placed perhaps a *T* for a *C* on one of his breathing genes, and maybe missed a letter on another. So his code is broken, his breathing genes can't make the protein they're supposed to make and so Eddie's lungs fill and he can't keep his lungs—" Rafael seemed to search carefully for the right words. "He cannot keep his lungs open all the time."

He likely knew that one of the children would ask him to fix Eddie, to make him better. As he spoke he drew sand genes on the ground. He was playing God with diseases of dust, editing nature's mistakes, explaining life to desperate and wonderful children.

"It's like a bike lock that won't open so we can't move the bike, not without the right combination." He looked at the children and smiled even though I knew what he was really thinking. It's just a question of time, and time is what Eddie does not have. "We could make it move though, couldn't we, if we try hard enough?"

And then, as though to remind himself that many of his little friends gathered around him were also playing a waiting game, he told them, "The spinal cord will be harder to fix. It needs a lot of care, a lot of respect. Each of you needs our very best. And we are doing our very best. *Really* we are."

When I asked Rafael why it was that we two had become friends out of all the volunteers whom we met our first summer at the therapeutic riding stables in Rock Creek Park, he told me that he knew we would come together the moment he laid eyes on me. He saw that I was able to charm the kids and magically transform their injured spirits, but that I could not do the same for myself. He watched as I fumbled with the saddle buckles and struggled to place the bridle on the horse's head the first morning we were assigned to the same team. Seeing the uncertainty with which another adult performed a task that they were certain of, made him realize, he said. That I was lost in some sort of war. As though I had gone in to fight a good fight and come away confused by what I had done. We came from vastly separate worlds he and I, but we came from the same place. Rafael thought he was pretty much alone the way he felt about life and about himself, but seeing me awakened him to the reality of what had happened. To his life, to mine, to so many like us. What it was that had caused us to drift away from ourselves and forced us to start all over again.

We had worked together all through that summer, either side of every horse and child we taught. In the end, my friends may have carried me through David's death, but from Rafael I learnt how to go on alone.

Rafael finished working with the kids and I helped him walk his horse back to the stable and stow away the tack.

"So, it's good to see you, you dark horse," I said.

"Linda!"

He hugged me and gestured for me to follow him to the staff room. We sat in the sparse, gray office drinking bitter coffee and we played catch up. Nearly a year had passed since we last saw each other. I looked him over. He was ferociously good-looking—his complexion dark and uneven, his thick, straight hair falling in his face, his eyes deep, eager and heavy-lidded—and I thought, damn, I had forgotten how *beautiful* he is. He was grinning at me evidently knowing that this was what I was thinking or maybe he was just exceedingly happy to see me. It had been three years since I volunteered with Rafael. I came after losing my brother, David, to a drug overdose that I somehow managed to blame myself for. Rafael had left his wife, Marguerite, after five years of marriage, for his work. A decision that at the time was hard for me to understand. Really, you'd think a man like this would choose the woman.

"Rafael, you didn't drag me here to catch up. You need something from me. What is it?" I asked.

"I'm getting back together with Marguerite," he told me. "And I really need your help."

"But I thought I was the one who helped you get *over* Marguerite, remember?"

"No, I want you to forget all that. I'm a changed man. Let's have dinner—the four of us—you, Ian, me and my lovely Marguerite."

"I'd love that." *What is he not telling me?* "Are you getting remarried?"

"Maybe, we're not sure yet. But that's not it. That's not why I called you. I'm trying my hand at your business. I need your help, really I do."

I was not sure I entirely understood him, but Rafael was clearly in one of his exceptionally good moods, and instead of explaining what he really wanted from me, he talked for a long time about his newest class of kids in the program at the stables. He spoke of each child as though they were his own and he was funny and moving and passionate and I found myself missing all the antics and chaos of our days volunteering together. But then he let slip that the whole therapeutic center was being moved out to Maryland. There was an uncharacteristic wistfulness about the way he delivered the news; I assumed he would have to give up the kids and the horses. When I asked him if that was what he wanted help with—stopping the move—he waved the suggestion off. "No, it's done. Anyway, it'll be closer to my lab. I can still volunteer, maybe even more often. It'll just be different. The kids from D.C., I'll miss them, you know?"

He started to update me on his lab research but I had to run, no wiser as to why he really wanted to see me, but happy that we had at last caught up with each other. It had been fantastic to step into Rock Creek Park in the middle of the day, and to spend some time with Rafael, the kids and the horses, an unexpected break from my normal routine. But after the meeting at Anita's apartment that morning, it seemed as though my work was fuelled again with an urgency I hadn't known in a long while; I was eager to get back to the office.

A storm thundered across downtown D.C. late in the afternoon, just as I was finishing my presentation for the upcoming *Homes First* board meetings. I was lost in the document that I was editing on the computer, and was unaware of its approach, not hearing the initial rumblings, or noticing the first fierce raindrops against my office window.

At some point, lightheaded from staring at the computer for so long, I took a break and headed to the kitchen. I set up the coffee maker and started to review my mail. A large internal office envelope marked *Private and Confidential,* caught my eye. So late on a stormy Friday afternoon I imagined there was no one else about, yet I instinctively glanced over my shoulder before tearing back the top and pulling out the envelope's contents: a generic memo from the CFO, and a copy of the latest quarterly budget to review for the *Homes First* board meeting. Too boring for now, I moved on to the rest of the mail. I opened a letter from my friend Catherine, with the mailing labels I had requested from her. She included a cartoon of the Mayor in a hard hat, in front of a public housing building being converted into stylish condos. The caption read, *Affordable Housing: Anyone who contributed to my campaign can afford to live here.* I reminded myself to thank her for the labels and to tell her not to be so cynical about our lovely Mayor.

After preparing a mug of coffee and skimming the rest of my mail, I headed back to my office. I heard a noise in Jonathan's office and I stepped inside.

"You're burning the candle at both ends, Jonathan. Go home!" I admonished him.

"Oh, hi Linda," he said, smiling. "You're one to talk. Go on home to your family and get away from this storm."

"Board meeting stuff."

"Me too."

"Want a coffee? I'll get it."

I returned with a cup and placed it next to his *Complete Guide to D.C.* I gave it to him as a little joke between us when I first started working at *Homes First*. No matter how many timed we'd moved offices, it found a way back to his desk—some kind of talisman, I guess. It was at times like this, when we were shooting the breeze with no one else around that I felt as though I were the luckiest person alive to know the man facing me, let alone to work with him every day. After our drive around Anacostia together, I told Jonathan I didn't want the job. It saved him from having to tell me straight out that he couldn't hire me. But he told me that it was mine when I knew I was ready. And then there we were, years later, still going strong. We finished our coffees and he kicked me out, back to my office.

I finished sorting and marking up the mail and returned to the budget document. I had a phone meeting with Richard Foster, the Director of the Homeless Assistance Program, scheduled for ten o'clock on Saturday morning and although I know he would be late, or might even cancel it, I felt compelled to prepare for it. Richard and I had agreed to review the allocation of funds for our programs before the board meeting. The income for the affordable housing program was about to surpass the homeless assistance program for the first time ever. The required shift in priorities for the organization did not sit well with everyone at *Homes First*, least of all Richard.

When I turned to the first page of the budget I discovered that it had already been marked up with a highlighter and that there were handwritten comments in the margins. I don't know why, but I instinctively stood up and closed the door to my office; an uneasy feeling, almost nausea, was rising inside me. I walked to the window and took time to notice the rain. I needed to figure out who sent me the marked-up budget and why. What did they want me to know—now—before the Board meeting?

Still confused, I checked my emails but found nothing that could help me. There was however, a new email from Richard postponing our meeting. Of late he had found it hard to face me, even when work demanded it of him. I turned away from the computer to watch large, plump raindrops explode against the window, their fragmented remains descending in miniature rivulets, and thought about my chance meeting with Richard's wife, Danielle, on the Metro last week. Just the two of us, alone, and for the first time ever, I had allowed myself to see her immense suffering.

I returned again to the budget and found additional documents stapled to the back. I was reluctant to confirm so unexpectedly, this swiftly—and it seemed without any hope of doubt—what I had already suspected for a while. I sat back and tried to make sense of it all. All morning I had struggled with the idea that Anita's campaigns needed me, that I wanted but could never bring myself to leave *Homes First*. Now it seemed as though I had to leave. After all these years. The thought, now fully formed, staggered me; I grew up here, my first job out of graduate school. I had stayed so long with *Homes First* not just for what it stood for—this alone would not have been enough to make it through the financial crises, administrative upheavals and day-to-day drama of the office—but because I had Jonathan to call a friend and mentor. If I allowed myself to leave, I needed to believe Jonathan would understand.

The rain fell harder still over the next half hour. I watched people in the streets below running to avoid the water thundering down on them, some laughing, to be caught out so unexpectedly, giving themselves up to the warm wave washing over them. A Friday afternoon summer storm is the perfect ending to a D.C. workweek, a hand at your back hurrying you home. I finished my coffee and looked for a CD in the filing cabinet by my desk. Well, *there* was something I wouldn't miss about Jonathan—his torturously boring collection of jazz music. He played it all the time, and he insisted on listening to the instrumental stuff only. I comforted myself at the thought of leaving, that I would never have to listen to another sax solo again.

"*Words*! Jonathan, where are the *words*?" I had teased him endlessly.

Damn, I did try. Ian and I lent him all our favorite CDs, dragged him and his family to concerts at the 9:30 Club and even to the safer acts at the Warner theater and the Birchmere, and still he wouldn't relent. This about him I had not changed. And he had changed so much of me. Jonathan was the father I never had, only better, because we had skipped the growing pains and moved straight to the mutual respect phase and our relationship was pretty close to perfect. Nothing would ever threaten that, even if I left.

When I realized that my CDs had been moved around, my other personal items—my bag and keys—none were as I left them, I contained the immediate swell of panic by reminding myself that my research fellows had been in the habit of raiding my music lately. But it was no use. I knew that my unease had nothing at all to do with anxiety over my CDs or anything else I stored in that drawer; it stemmed from the envelope, the one that I was now staring at, trying hard to believe that I placed it there myself. Except for the sticky note addressed to me on the outside, I almost convinced myself. I slipped a newly minted mix into my archaic (did not support iTunes without crashing randomly and repeatedly) non-profit computer and cautiously, as though the contents might physically hurt me, withdrew the documents from the new envelope. Highlighted, disturbing even had it not been torched in bright, neon yellow, was information I could use to bring Richard Foster down.

I had all the evidence laid out in front of me now. Someone at *Homes First* wanted me to be the one to expose what Richard had done and was hoping I would take action in time for the board meeting. I felt as though a part of me was starting to fall away, the place inside me where *Homes First* belonged. The loss was physical; my hand covered my stomach where suddenly I was hollow. I placed all the documents into a file folder, sealed the file in a new envelope and locked it away.

I tried to return to my work at the computer, my heart now pounding. Tens of thousands of dollars…and this was not the first time. How far did this go? Could it even be hundreds of thousands? As I struggled to focus on my report, I mulled over each sentence for too long and read over and again, even out loud, the words in front of me, without seeing them or understanding what I saw. I was forced to admit that I didn't yet really care about what Richard had done—I had suspected as much for a long time. What I could not fathom was who would want me to betray Richard? Worse still, who could believe me *capable* of betraying Richard?

The rain now rushed wildly against the windows, and the thunder broke in frightening roars outside the office. The daylight was forced from the room and I was working in the dark when I suddenly became aware that someone was reaching for my desk-light and turning it on.

"Jonathan, you scared me."

"Why are you working in the dark?"

"I hadn't noticed. I was going to—" And then I heard myself say, as though the words could not possibly be my own, "I'm leaving."

"Good. Get on home."

"No. *Homes First*."

Jonathan seemed to understand immediately and I saw from his face that he had already resolved to disguise how he truly felt. I hoped he would fight for me—even the pretense would have been a comfort. Instead he said simply, as though nothing had passed between us, "I just came to ask you if you wanted to order pizza, or something else—you know, if you'll be working late."

"I will. I mean I have a ton of work tonight. Go ahead, lets order it."

Jonathan leaned over to my phone and called the pizza in.

"What's going on?" he asked me at last.

"I don't know. I mean, I *know—*" I said cautiously. "Did *you* know?"

And we agreed silently, our eyes set intently on each other, that it was Richard who must be protected. And that it was I who must leave. I can't explain it. But there was a silence between us then that I had never known before. Like the silence when an orchestra has finished playing, just before the audience starts clapping; silence of pure gratitude and awe before the crowd gets to its feet to demand more, already knowing that the orchestra's work is done.

He went back to his office and after the pizza arrived he buzzed me to say he'd left the box in the kitchen and I should help myself since he was heading home after all. Jonathan couldn't face me. Likely he was burning up over what all of this meant for his organization and I didn't doubt that he too was trying to figure out who else knew and had demanded of me to expose what Richard had done. Regret filled my heart that night as I closed up the *Homes First* offices and switched off all the lights; it was as yet too little comfort knowing that I had somewhere else to go, another new campaign that needed me.

ANITA ALONE

I love to think of nature as an unlimited broadcasting station, through which God speaks to us every hour, if we will only tune in.

George Washington Carver

Anita returned home to her apartment from the church where she worked, just as the first thunderclaps broke outside. Within moments, the summer rain was thrashing and streaming against her balcony and bedroom windows. She stopped still just inside her front door to watch the storm. Broad yellow streaks of lightning filled the sky as heavy, dark gray clouds gathering from the southeast moved rapidly up the Potomac River. Just beyond Oxon Cove, the storm faltered temporarily before being torn apart as it approached the confluence of the Potomac and Anacostia rivers. Now the rain slowed and the thunder moved on, becoming a hesitant echo of the drum-roll that had moments before filled her small home. She watched in awe as a blacker, more expansive wall of clouds moved swiftly north past the cove and collided with the light haze beyond her apartment building. Thunder exploded once again all around her and the trees outside bent impossibly to the sudden blast of wind that rushed across them. Her throat tightened, her mouth felt parched, as she realized how violent the storm outside was and that just minutes before she had been walking home from the church.

She ventured towards the sliding doors of her living room balcony and looked down below to the parking lot of the Windsor Apartments. She saw a few of her neighbors with newspapers and bent umbrellas over their heads running towards the building, their imagined laughter and screams breaking the safety and peacefulness of the apartment. Thinking of the wetness of their clothes and the cold air passing over them as they entered the air-conditioned foyer, eleven flights below, made her shiver as she watched.

The sky turned to night outside in an instant and as Anita reached for the light switch, she felt suddenly exhilarated, hopeful, even compelled to act bravely in an inexplicably irrational way. The electrically charged mix of emotions grew stronger still as she watched the ferocious storm lash at her windows, the rain coursing downwards and away, leaving her sheltered and untouched. She moved quickly to change out of her clothes, still sticky from the humidity of the morning before the storm broke through. She showered and prepared herself a snack. Now she would have time to think more clearly about the meeting in her apartment this morning. She sat on the sofa near the balcony, and gazed out at the pearl white remnants of clouds strafing the now brilliant blue sky.

With a deepening sense of relief, she began to realize that she had gathered together a remarkable set of leaders to save the Windsor Apartments and stop the prison at Oxon Cove. Luther and Charlie were by her side, counseling her, giving her strength and courage. And Linda, Jonathan's protégée, using his methods to help the group swiftly define the two campaigns, had already motivated a reassuring number of volunteers. Anita's own past victories arose from an intuitive notion of how a good campaign should be run, but what Linda had unfolded was a kind of template, a method by which any campaign could be run and won. Linda had been unconditionally mathematical in her approach, as though it might even be possible to prove that winning was inevitable.

"So we think we need more people to help on the campaign? Not good enough. How *many* people and by *when*? Ten people, or thirty? By tomorrow, or in a week? We have a budget, but how much can we raise, and by when, exactly? Every objective, every step to our big goal, needs a number. How do we tell if we're winning or losing? Look at the numbers."

Every idea was assigned a value; every suggestion was given a place in a ranked list of priorities. The room opened up—the idea of smaller goals with real numbers was a relief, no matter how illusory, from having to fight eviction and a prison—each threat until then had been too immense and devastating. Linda managed to round up the meeting with something close to enthusiasm, even excitement over the work ahead.

"This is great—*great*—what we're doing here. Because Windsor's just the beginning. We all know that. Let's be honest here, everyone wants a piece of your neighborhood now. This campaign, if you play it right, this will be your chance to start fighting for what you want, not against what everyone else wants for you."

Right at that moment, Anita noticed that Luther had moved in closer, wheeling himself directly besides Linda. He had expressed reservations to Anita about recruiting Linda to the campaign, yet he was curious to learn her methods. Anita watched as he leaned heavily on his right arm, head tilted, a sure sign of him giving up his full attention.

"Look at some of the great redevelopment plans out there already—they've been kicking around for years—why haven't they been implemented? What and *who* needs to change? Start now to think beyond these campaigns. Otherwise—" Linda paused. "I'm not telling you anything you don't already know—it'll always be like this, won't it? Decisions being made *for* you, without you, over and over again."

Luther had laughed out loud. Linda was surprised, faltered and looked questioningly at him. He just excused himself and still smiling, nodded at Anita, and told Linda to continue.

Anita knew that Luther hated nothing more than the fact that there were thousands of people just like her in black communities across the country, giving up every free moment of every day to stop the deterioration of their neighborhoods. They both knew from personal experience that anyone with enough determination could win a campaign. But in a community like theirs, victories were short-lived. Campaigns came and went. If Anita, whom he called their neighborhood's own Mary McLeod Bethune, wasn't fighting to stop the construction of a prison next door to the elementary school, she'd be fighting to secure more funding and supplies for the after-school learning center she had founded for bright kids who's schools were failing them—a wildly costly, but successful program. She managed the center in the evenings after work, while campaigning to re-build the decaying and failing high school and trying to force the city to clean up the mountain of trash piling up around the abandoned social services agency building. Of late, she had been consumed by her efforts to shut down the gas station at the corner of South Capitol and Mississippi, for refusing to pump gas while running a thriving drug and handgun business. She sat on the Mayor's community redevelopment board each month and watched, as her proposals were set aside over and again for lack of funding. And now this. The Windsor Apartments. A *private* prison. A company that wanted to make a profit by putting African Americans behind bars. She shook her head in disgust. *No.*

Because Luther did not reach people the way Anita did, he tried hard to advocate his ideas through her and they constantly clashed because of it. He fought with her to ask the most of their neighbors, to push them further. He believed it was time for their community to stop riding out the tides of fate and to start creating their own good fortune.

"Our neighborhood fights against whatever gets sent its way. What do we do? What do we make? What do we define or build?" Luther had demanded of her over and again. "What do we own? What is there—that's truly *ours*?"

He was right. She knew it deep down inside. She was a fighter but she had until now, refused to take on board Luther's convictions that campaigns could be and had to be linked, should be made to force deep and great change within her community. She always believed that people were motivated to act only by the unique issues that personally touched their lives. She believed in asking the least of her neighbors, of keeping them fresh, of not owing too many favors. One by one, she took on the issues, and so she was, for the most part, reacting to what came her way, she would freely admit that. There seemed to be no time, no opportunity, for anything more.

Linda had unknowingly re-ignited a fire when she championed the idea of building a new movement, with Anita at the helm, the very idea that Anita had resisted all along. Anita, already a veteran campaigner at thirty-six, secretly eager to rest from all the fighting, was now personally facing eviction. The looming threat to the Windsor Apartments, the private prison, awoke her to the scale of changes facing her community, and Luther's convictions had started to weigh heavily on her.

She watched as the rain faded away far out across the city. The new faces at today's meeting revived her sense of courage; she did not feel so weary, so certain of defeat. She found herself believing, for the first time since she heard of the plans for the Windsor Apartments, that she could really win this campaign and could even find the strength to take on the prison. She had struggled her whole life for the safety of the walls around her but it was not merely her home that was now under threat. Though she had done well for herself, and she and her daughter would make do elsewhere, she knew she could never leave her neighborhood behind. Somehow Luther, Charlie and Linda, and all the faces in her home today, had helped her, at a moment when she felt as though she could not possibly give anymore, to feel less alone. This campaign, she now promised herself, would be different. Knowing that there were others newly arrived to carry some of the burden would make it easier. Because Luther was right, she had merely been holding her finger to the flood. The dam was breaking, and all that she loved was about to be washed away. She looked down at her notes once more. In the margins she had scribbled a message to herself. *Surely the Lord is in this place*. Of late this seemed impossibly hard to believe.

OF STARTING SLOWLY, SLOWLY TO LET GO

*The future: time's excuse
to frighten us; too vast
a project, too large a morsel
for the heart's mouth.*
                    Rainer Maria Rilke

"Bamboo is for bloody pandas!" Ian said, as he pushed his shovel deep into the dirt and struck hard, unyielding bamboo roots once again. "It does not—" he now set the shovel further back from the enormous, rock-like root ball, "belong in our garden. A place where I hope to sit and drink beer, and read the *Washington—*" he gasped and exhaled a huge grunt as he resorted to pulling with both hands at the roots he had uncovered, "bloody *Post!*"

I laughed as I watched Ian cursing to himself, dressed in mud-smeared shorts and sneakers, shiny, gray sweat pouring from his face and down his lean, bare back. It was another scorching, unforgiving July day in Washington. The steamy air drenched us, making our efforts in the back yard heavy and slow, so Ian's tirade was a happy distraction. When I returned to my job hacking up the giant bamboo stalks that Ian had been endlessly generating all day, a thought suddenly occurred to me. We lived treacherously close to the National Zoo.

"Do you think the bamboo tunneled its way here from the zoo? Because if it did, you're digging an escape route for the lions, my friend."

He turned to me, smiling and desperate. This was what I loved most about him. The way his face could hold laughter and sadness together at once, his eyes full of resolve. His approach to life—his dedicated, profound love for living life any way it came at you—had settled into the lines around his mouth and his eyes; it defined his cheeks, it was what made him attractive, more than handsome. His dark hair, thick but cut tightly back, framed his sunburned face against the backdrop of the garden and as I looked at him then, my heart was almost too full.

"You know we do have another shovel," he said. "Want to try *digging* for a change? I might even let you sit in my garden when we're done."

I really couldn't just stand there staring at him in admiration so I decided to take him up on his offer and was surprised to discover that I enjoyed the formidable effort needed for the job. The sound of the shovel hitting the dirt, and the feeling that came from working the blade into the ground over and over again, leaning into the deeply buried, thickened and hardened roots until they could be freed at last from the earth, was a task at once mesmerizing and compelling. So I continued working. Together Ian and I pulled up root balls as large as softballs bearing roots that were three inches thick, radiating twelve feet out in every direction. We had to haul away paving stones from the garden path, and dig under the gravel bed around the magnolia tree to extricate the whole root system, to be certain that the bamboo jungle that had overtaken our garden could not grow back again. The more we dug and removed the bamboo, the deeper and wider the open trenches that formed across the garden. I had been curious as to why, exactly, clearing bamboo had been occupying all of Ian's spare time since he decided to take on the task of reclaiming our overgrown back garden; now I was filled with admiration for his efforts.

"So *this* is what you've been doing. This is great—I love it!" I said excitedly, as we pulled together and successfully removed another root. The effort threw me backwards to the ground.

"You love it?" he asked, looking down at me as I sat laughing and rubbing the elbow I had fallen on.

"You've got to admit it's satisfying work. Look how much we've pulled out and look how *huge* those roots are!"

"So you think this is it, huh? Lin, we've just started. There are at least another two layers of these bastards under here—I guarantee it. We won't be planting any butterfly bushes or bee balms just yet."

"You're joking." It seemed impossible that there could be any more of these triffid-like monsters lurking in our garden. "Are you sure?"

"Oh, I can assure you, I'm not joking, darling. Still feeling as addicted and invigorated?"

He laughed and approached me as though to hug me. I stepped away from him and fell again, tripping over a hidden root.

"You're disgusting and slimy. Don't come anywhere near me!"

"You're not looking so gorgeous yourself, you know."

He moved in to catch my fall and we kissed. It was the saltiest, dirtiest kiss of my life, and I couldn't decide if I wanted or never wanted to do that again right away. He held me as though we were not really covered in filth and grime—close and strong—and I was ready for what had to come next.

"Anyway I think we need to call it a day," he said, letting me go reluctantly. "I'm taking a plane out tomorrow, I've lots of work to get done before then."

"Not what I was expecting, but O.K., I guess I'll stick around here a while longer."

"Later, I promise." Ian reached back over his shovel and kissed me again. "Go easy on that bamboo, girl. You're a non-native, invasive species, too, you know."

"Yeah, well just don't get any notions about replacing me with sweeter smelling locals," I fired back.

I laughed to myself as Ian stayed on my mind through the rest of the afternoon while I struggled ever harder to fight the bamboo jungle in our garden. It was such a relief, even in the heat, to be gardening outside, away from the cracked walls, leaking toilets and broken tile that awaited our attention inside our house. Ian was determined to turn our yard into a garden, to restore dignity to the rare and precious urban oasis we had longed for when searching for a house before Sandra was born. We had upgraded from an apartment with a once desperately sad little balcony off our bedroom. After Ian and I tiled the balcony floor with exquisite little terra cotta tiles, white washed the brick wall and stripped the eleven-foot glass door back to its original wood, the balcony had come alive. We kept pots of brilliantly colored flowers spilling out onto the floor and climbing the wall, and the balcony had been our heavenly escape for five years. Now we faced a much larger but equally compelling challenge—an overly neglected yard calling out for the loving attention of anyone fool enough to first tame the bamboo then haul away hundreds of pounds of gravel and concrete, before any landscaping could even begin.

Seeing the earth turned all over the yard and smelling the fresh, moist soil gave me hope. I continued to dig well past the time in the evening when I normally would have retreated inside or fired up the citronella lamps to ward off the mosquitoes. I felt driven to keep going, to give Ian the chance to realize his dream garden. By now I was pretty certain that we would, over time, find the right combination of bulbs, perennials, shrubs and trees to fill the rapidly expanding emptiness that was being left behind by the growing absence of the bamboo forest.

At night, Ian and I fell into a deep, hard sleep. It was the end of another day of backbreaking work to reclaim and restore our Washington home. The bedroom was stifling because the ceiling fan had broken again. The heat, combined with the weariness of our day working outside, left me no energy even to hold to my head the cold towel that Ian prepared for me. It fell from my hand, and I dreamed of the shovel scraping, grinding against the roots, of gathering up armfuls of bamboo and of the vastness of the cool, dark, earth left behind.

The following morning a wet kiss from Sandra woke me up, but I discovered that I was unable to move. My back was locked up and my shoulders were too stiff to turn. I looked at the clock. I was due at the *Homes First* board meeting in less than an hour. Sandra walked around to Ian's side of the bed and kissed him.

"Daddy, wake up, Mommy's stuck."

Once Ian opened his eyes and noticed the daylight flooding the bedroom—the blinds had fallen again in the night, something more to fix—he asked me, "Don't you have to go to work today?"

"Yeah, I have to tell them I'm leaving. Can you help me move my left arm so I can sit up?"

But it was Ian who sat up. "You're leaving? *Your job?* Lin—what did you just say?"

I carefully stood and bent slightly, to ease the pain on my lower back. "I can't talk now, we never got around to it yesterday, I have *got* to get to work."

"Well, we have a date this afternoon, when you get back. You, me and the bamboo, and the reason you're leaving the job you love. I can't wait."

I gave him credit for not being angry—just genuinely, understandably taken aback—but I really didn't have the time or head to get into it. It. The grants. The fraud. Richard. Jonathan letting me leave like that. As quickly as I had lost myself for a whole day to the earth and its mystifying order of what grows—what survives and what doesn't—I was back in the real world.

I let the water run over me for a long, long time, ducking my head under again and again, to massage my back, neck and face. Eventually my muscles loosened up, and the weariness seemed to dissipate; still, I reluctantly turned the water off. As I stepped from the shower, the pungent, sweet smell of steamy, warm air and soap filled the bathroom. I loved that Ian and I at last owned our own home, that we had a yard, that Sandra had a place to play with her toys, and that this bathroom, with abundant hot water, was where each day began.

I sailed to work on my bike, the silence of a Sunday morning free of traffic accompanying me as I let my pedals go and swooped down 16th St., with the wind rushing against my face, red lights passing me by. I arrived at work in ten minutes and as I locked my bike against the same parking meter I had used most days for eight years, I can't say why, but this was when it hit me what I was about to do. I was afraid I would lose control right there in the street, with staff and board members arriving any minute. I called my best friend, my co-conspirator in life, my cynical, tough and always brutally honest, Catherine.

"Catherine, it's me."

"Fuck, Lin—do you know what time it is? It is *Sunday*, right? This better be good."

"It's Richard."

"It's *always* Richard. What now?"

Catherine never held a special place in her heart for Richard. She despised him. She would not have been the best person to turn to if I had thought anything could be saved, but right then I was focused on holding myself together, and only she knew how to help me do that. I filled her in on my pending resignation and she was, for once, speechless.

Suddenly, just behind me, the Chair of the Board passed me by and at first, did not recognize me in my bike helmet. She backtracked and beamed me a smile.

"We will start on time, *won't* we? See you inside, Linda."

Catherine heard her over the phone and she laughed.

"Was that *WWW*?"

"We will start on time, *won't* we?" I mimicked back to her.

We had both worked professionally with the Wicked Witch of the West—she was a formidable fundraiser, an impressive meeting facilitator, was in possession of a brilliant mind—we were just not quite sure she was human.

"Listen Catherine, I have to go. Ian is flying out tonight–"

"Yeah, yeah, I'll bring my jammies, talk all night if we have to. But please, spare me the version where you ask me to understand whatever the fuck Richard has gone and done this time." She hesitated briefly, then added, "Lin, I know how much this means to you so you know, if you have to cry, just do it with *dignity*, O.K.?"

I could still hear her laughing as I signed off, already feeling stronger. There would be an opportunity later to deconstruct the dissolution of my life, as I knew it, which was about to unfold as soon as I walked in the door of *Homes First*. Ian and Catherine were lined up for me, my back-up guys. And knowing that was the only reason I could even make it up the six flights of stairs to my office.

OF THE MINUTES LEFT TO US

Oh yes I knew him, I spent years with him
With his golden and stony substance
He was a man who was tired
            Pablo Neruda

"There was no time to tell you," I said to Richard. "I made my decision on Friday. You canceled our Saturday meeting. I could hardly leave you a message–hey, I'm resigning." I was surprisingly relieved to have broken the news to him. "I'm going to work for Anita. It's a great opportunity—I can't pass it up."

He looked away. He was calm, taking his time. I remained standing, he sitting. I watched him slowly cross and uncross his fingers, held up to his chin. This was not for Richard a sign of nervousness; it was merely how he formulated his ideas. As I waited, I took him in as though for the first and last time. His long, elegant face with drawn cheeks and vivid blue eyes, beckoning relentlessly for attention, was more beguiling than handsome; his dark blonde hair was just messy enough to blunt the edges of his otherwise disarming seriousness. He had my attention.

"How long?"

"I'll tell the board today and then, two weeks. It's all I've got. Windsor is heating up and we don't even know how bad this prison thing is."

I was trying hard to control the emotions gathering inside me, but I could feel my face begin to betray my resolve. *Two weeks*? I will walk out of *Homes First*, for good, in two weeks? Richard looked directly at me, waiting for more. He must have suspected—he must have known—there were other reasons for my decision; he needed to hear them from me. I checked my watch.

"We've got to get to the board meeting. I just didn't want to go in there without letting you know first."

He stood up. "Is this about Danielle?"

He had chosen to confront me on territory most familiar to us. We were seasoned negotiators—I recognized his technique, but I didn't know how to fight back. I didn't want to fight at all; I was hoping to leave something of what we were intact. His eyes remained set on me; he would not let me look away.

"No, not Danielle. Windsor is—it's 800 residents, Richard. If that falls, if the wheels start to turn, Anacostia is cooked. The stadium, all that planned development, it's changing everything—you know that. If I can help? I'm honored to have been asked."

He softened his approach.

"Lin, *Homes First* can give you the time you need to work on the campaign." He considered for a moment, how best to package an offer that might appeal to me. "Like a sabbatical."

"It won't work."

I was about to explain the magnitude of the Windsor campaign, the dirty parkland deal, but I stopped myself. Every word I said would afford him time to draw me in again; we were both experts at buying time.

"Thanks, anyway."

I moved towards the door. He reached it first and with his hand on the handle, he leaned towards me, "How much do you know?"

I froze at the sudden closeness between us, the way he bore down on me using his full height as he had never done before, and I struggled to find my words, "*Windsor*? The Mayor's office—it's coming from the top. The prison? The Senate Majority Leader wants it."

He hesitated, probably assessing whether I knew what he had done and I was just protecting myself or if, perhaps, I truly didn't know.

"Linda, come on. Just tell me."

"I'm not sure what you mean."

"Is this to protect you or me? *Why* are you leaving?"

If I don't walk away now, I will tell him everything.

We had known each other and worked together for so many years, we anticipated one another's thoughts and moves, and adapted astonishingly quickly. What was left unsaid was already known, what was said, was understood completely.

"There's this really surly bastard on the team—you remember

Luther—I'm just doing it for the challenge of working with him."

He laughed, acknowledging at last that I wouldn't give in, and he gently moved his hand away, allowing me to pass. But the space I left behind filled with his words, "Let's put off telling the board till we've had a chance to talk more."

"No. I have to tell them today," I said, walking away, knowing from his voice that if I turned around and saw his face at that moment, I would give in. I headed straight for the conference room, where I slipped into idle conversation with our board members, all the while wondering how my years with *Homes First*, with Jonathan and Richard, could possibly have all come down to this.

I returned to my office during the break in the board meeting to reflect on how my news was received. I spent the morning trying to read the faces of those in the room to determine who had provided me with the budget documents the previous Friday. While I was no closer to knowing this, I had seen that Richard was somewhat relieved that I was leaving. He seemed upbeat in the meeting, showering me with cloying praise for my work and fundraising successes. I suspected he wanted to believe that his secrets were safe with me. But he never left anything to chance; he would need some reassurance that whatever I knew was leaving with me. The morning wasn't about convincing me to stay, it was just his first failed attempt to ascertain exactly what I knew, and I anticipated he would try again.

There was a knock at my door. Of course it was Richard. I was taken aback at the rush I felt to see him. It was instinctive. We had been as close as I ever was to my brother, David, and working with Richard every day for all those years had mostly been a thrill, a ride I hoped would never end.

"Look, Lin," he said, "if I've forced you into this decision there are other ways to handle this situation. Let's take some time, take another look, what d'you say?"

I was surprised at how quickly the anger rose inside me, giving me the confidence to confront him.

"*What* situation, Richard? That you've completely fucked with my program budget behind *my* back, or that you've spent the last five years screwing around behind your *wife's* back?"

He froze. I had seen this face before. Richard caught like a hunted animal in the sight of a gun: he elicits the feeling that you are the one who is pulling the trigger, you are the one doing the damage.

"So you do know," he said quietly, and he moved to sit across the room from me on the windowsill, his arms folded across his chest, protecting himself from me. I had never known us like this, so afraid of each other. Recognizing the shift I eased up a little, not wanting us to break apart so soon. It was not in me to be angry with him. My role had always been to take Richard's side, to defend him. To give him time to change my mind and believe in him.

"Is that all you've ever cared about, whether someone else knew?" I asked, with something of generosity in my tone, allowing him to prove me wrong if he could. "Not whether what you were doing was right or wrong, but whether you could get away with it? And what was I to you anyway? Just someone to make it all O.K., no matter what you did?"

"Lin, please—give me a chance to explain what happened."

His few words infuriated me because they were too familiar and inadequate. I had given him so many chances, I was long past too many, and Catherine's words quickly returned: *It's always Richard.* If I controlled my anger and kept my voice level, it was because I knew Richard could only be reached in this way.

"What happened? You mean what you *did*, right? Isn't that what you mean? The work we do here, it's not just some job we do to get by. We change people's lives, for God's sake. We—*you, Richard*—get homeless people off the streets, and give desperate, *desperate* families somewhere to live. How could you do this Richard? How could you screw everything up so completely?"

He knew that I was working myself up to leave. He knew that if he was to stop me he would have to give me more than promises of explanations, but he disappointed me again.

"Please, let's talk about it—just not now. I need time to find a way to explain everything. Especially to you, Lin."

"You don't think after all these years together, I don't already know what you were trying to do? I should never have let you get away with it all. I should never have believed you—every time—that you wanted to get it all right. It's gone beyond me anyway. Other people know."

I unlocked the filing cabinet and opened the envelope. I pulled the file out and handed it to him.

"Here. Take it. I don't need it. Your problem isn't me. Someone else knows everything, and maybe, unlike me, they are not going to just go away."

We were inches apart now. I had breached his defenses.

He took the file from me and briefly skimmed through it. "You're giving this to me?" he said in astonishment, "I don't understand. Why?"

He stood up and we looked directly at each other, regret forcing the anger from us both. This was my cue to secure a reconciliation between us, it was what we were both trained to do, but I decided differently.

"I think what you're doing is so—I—I don't even know what to call it. God, but I know I can't stick around and watch you destroy yourself, and definitely, not—" I turned to my computer, just to gather myself together, and the end was lost to him, it remained with me, "us."

"Please, could you leave?" I told him. "I need to somehow make it through the rest of the board meeting."

He was still for a while; he was no doubt expecting me to fight harder for him, for us, to survive. He walked over to my desk and holding the file in front of me, he leaned in.

"Thank you, for this," he said, barely able to form the words.

With twenty minutes left before the next session of the board meeting, I took the time to call home and tell Ian why I was leaving the job I loved so much. We would not have time to talk later as it turned out; he was catching an earlier flight, and he was waiting until Catherine arrived before heading out. Ian told me that I did the right thing giving Richard the file. He paused.

"How did it go with him?"

"I feel like—I don't know—like I'm leaving him behind, and there's a war out there we need to fight together."

"Well, he's dug a pretty deep hole for himself."

"I love him, Ian. He's been there for me too. *You* know. It wasn't just me watching his back all these years."

"I have to say I love the bastard too, even though he's so messed up. He's going to be a hard habit to kick."

"This is crazy. All this change—how am I going to make it?"

"Darling, you have me, remember. I love you, I believe in you. You're making the right decision. Anita, Luther, your work with them. And Catherine is bringing brownies, although you didn't hear that from me."

Later, when I returned home, I found Catherine waiting nervously by the door. I wasn't sure what she was expecting, for me to collapse into her arms?

"O.K.," she said, before I could even get past her with my bike. "I'm going first. I screwed up. I made brownies, but I left them at home. They're not in my bag, I don't know how it happened."

I was really looking forward to drowning my sorrows in chocolate, but I had to make my friend feel a little less guilty. She was there for me after all.

"Don't worry about it. No surprise, I knew anyway. Ian spilled to cheer me up." I hesitated, not sure that I wanted to hear myself say the words out loud, and then I confirmed for myself, as much as for Catherine, "I resigned."

"Sorry."

"It's O.K. No. It's not."

Catherine threw her arms around me and the tears broke freely. There was not much dignity involved, but it was time to let go. She wheeled my bike away from me and led me to the sofa where we began trying to piece the last few days together. If we laid it all out then, it would have seemed unbearable to me, leaving Jonathan, *Homes First* and losing Richard. But Catherine did something I was not expecting, that allowed me to really believe I would get through. She told me that she believed that Anita and Luther would come to mean the world to me and that Richard, much as she loathed him, mostly because she couldn't really imagine it any other way, would most certainly find his way back to me.

OF THE NEED FOR CLARIFICATION

Men simply copied the realities of their hearts when they built prisons.

Richard Wright

I watched the fax come out of the fax machine as though I were watching a woman giving birth— eager to see the baby but also really scared that it might just get stuck on its way, or that even if it made it out alive, it might be really ugly. I waited with teeth gritted, praying that nothing would go wrong. Page after page from my contact at the National Park Service was grunting its way out of the rollers that temporarily held each one hostage, and then finally, when I had double counted that all twenty-three pages had safely arrived, I began the work of reviewing them. As I looked over the document, I had to wonder at what I discovered.

What was a Senator from *Mississippi* doing introducing an amendment to force the *National Park Service* to give away parkland in *Washington, D.C.*, to a private prison company based in *Ohio?* I found myself thinking, how does that work exactly? Does the prison company CEO write the venerable Senator a hefty campaign check, send him a bottle of the finest single malt, and then call him up to say, "How're you enjoying that Macallan I had sent over to you? Hey, write me an amendment, would ya? Get me some *land*, would ya?"

As it turned out, the deeper I dug, the more faxes I waited for, the more government entities I sent FOIA forms too, the more dirt kept piling up on the whole deal. I might have been a somewhat naïve, non-native Washingtonian but I really did feel compelled to get the facts straight. I discovered that the for-profit prison company from Ohio was not only receiving parkland, but would also be paid federal taxpayers' money to build the prison. I soon determined that the genteel Senators from Maryland and Virginia also had a heavy hand in the deal, along with a strange cohort of congressmen from far-flung states across the country.

The Virginia delegation was peddling the amendment because it was keen to expel the existing prison (also paid for by taxpayers) in Virginia. The members were hoping to turn over the land rights to developers to build high-end gated communities and townhouses on the now desirable and valuable land. No prizes would likely be awarded me for guessing to whom the developers of choice wrote campaign checks in the last election cycle. Meanwhile, the Maryland delegation was delighted that as part of the deal, the National Park Service would be receiving a huge gift of land from the prison company to add to the Maryland park system.

So D.C. stood to lose parkland and gain a for-profit prison? *Hmmm*, this suggested to me that Congress was under the impression that D.C. residents, unlike Maryland and Virginia residents—well, black D.C. residents at least—preferred the indoors to the outdoors. Of course I could not resist filling out even more *Freedom of Information Act* requests to keep flushing this mess out, and as I did this, I made some calls.

I was always a little afraid of contacting D.C.'s very own Congresswoman-in-the-making. She was a force of nature, petite but with a commanding presence, oscillating between fight and flight in her attitude towards D.C.'s woes on the Hill. I steeled myself; I had to talk to her office—her people would be all over this deal. She would be screaming *Representation Now for D.C!* and lamenting all this back door dealing by those who neither represent D.C., nor have its best interests at heart. She would surely have information that could help us. But I discovered from her weary staff that she was unavailable; she was simply too busy horse-trading on other issues, not least of which was how to convince the overlords in Congress that D.C. was worthy of their respect. And if we couldn't have that, their money. I thought it best to leave well alone for now.

Next I called Catherine at work. She would know, I was certain, what to make of the meddling of disparate members of Congress in the prison deal. Catherine had worked for various cause-based non-profits for over fifteen years, helping them to navigate the halls of Congress in their efforts to save the redwood forests, save America's historic main streets, save the oceans—*save, save, save*—as she affectionately called her work. Now Catherine worked for American Farmer, an organization dedicated, just as its name suggested, to saving our most highly endangered species, the independent American farmer. Catherine told me, and I believed her because she had the reports and statistics to back her up, that we were losing 1.2 million acres of American farmland a year and that small, family-owned farms were rapidly disappearing from the landscape. To her, it seemed as though we were hemorrhaging the lifeblood of America with every farm that was ploughed over to make way for the inevitably vile mess of malls and housing developments creeping across the country like an inoperable cancer (her words, not mine).

"Catherine, I am in FOIA heaven. How are you darling?"

"Well, I just discovered that our farmland bill is not quite dead, not quite alive, so I'm happier than most days. What's up?"

"This prison deal is getting weirder and more complicated by the minute. Thought you might be able to help me out." I filled her in on the facts.

"So what do *you* think?" she asked me.

"I think D.C. needs representation in Congress, I think we need statehood," I said innocently.

"That's it—that's all you've got?" She laughed, and in her best Southern accent she told me, "Ah think the *Senata* from Mississippi has the verrra *bess* interess of tha Distrit of Columbia at heart. Ah think he is thinking of tham poor, black folk down tha in Ana-*cost*-ee-ah, and he jus' so *wants* to give tham a nah-iss, new prison as ah token of his lurv."

Laughter broke from deep inside me; she's good, but then it was my turn.

"I propose we build the prison right next to the High School, with a connecting door. Think of all that effort wasted trying to get black kids into college when they could just go straight from school to prison. Oh, and did I tell you? I'm buying shares in the prison company. Black men in jail? I'm going to *retire* on that, darling."

Catherine laughed. "You're vile," she said. "Buy me some shares too?"

We always did this when there were serious matters at hand that were simply too ugly, too brutal, to fully accept. Our well-honed comedy routine served us well to survive the garbage we waded through daily in our work. Catherine decided to take control of the situation.

"Listen, give me some time, I'll dig up the rest of the dirt. That's what I specialize in, remember—good ol' fashioned, fertile, down and dirty, American dirt."

We signed off and I got back to the monumental task of clearing out my office and preparing to leave *Homes First*. I slowly sorted through every file, culling the deadwood, eliminating whole drawers of older case-files and research. This was my life for the past eight years that I was now trying to reduce to the very best, only that which would endure and continue to have meaning in the life of the person who would assume my job. Looking through the technical assistance cases, it seemed as though scarcely a day had gone by when I wasn't filling some request for help. Sometimes all it took was a phone call to the right government bureaucrat, friend of a friend, or council member's assistant to make a difference in someone's life. Other times, I would become deeply involved in the situation and it would consume me for months, even years, at a time. And now I looked at those cases and campaign files and they were simply—for me, at least—the diaries of my days at *Homes First*.

I prepared my office for my successor, deciding to leave my collection of photos and posters on the walls, hoping they would offer comfort and inspiration, and knowing that they covered up the worst plaster cracks and water damage stains. I started making the rounds of goodbyes with the staff. We took long lunches and skipped out for afternoon coffees in the park. It was easy to explain where I was going, harder to accept that I was really leaving. But with all the messages and emails that came in over the final few days with kind thoughts and thanks from friends and colleagues around the city, I felt more prepared to move on at last. These same people would be with me as I started my new work. That the messages come from all over the city, from north, south, east and west, made me realize what I had already achieved. How far and wide my efforts reached.

One morning, in the middle of a meeting with Richard where everything except what had happened to our once unshakable friendship was discussed, the receptionist stopped by to ask Richard to drop in on an impromptu teleconference Jonathan was hosting. I saw him rise with reluctance. He was not looking at me, but I knew what he was thinking, because I was feeling it too. These were our last hours together. That we spent them discussing the details of the organization's short and long-term strategic plans was almost too painful to bear. This was all that remained between us before I left. He stammered awkwardly that he would try to return quickly and he left.

I felt confused and vulnerable with him gone, unsure of what I needed to do next. I quickly took the back exit to the restrooms, washed my face, and headed down the back stairs out into the street for fresh air. I hesitated on the sidewalk as a bus passed by, oddly mesmerized by the strangers' faces that I watched go by me, and not until long after the bus had passed did I head back to my office.

When Richard returned he must have seen in my face that everything had changed between us.

"Could we return to my office so we can finish what we were–" He hesitated, looking away from me. "I'm really sorry, about that interruption."

As soon as we entered his office I realized we had come to the very end, and he felt it too; I could see by the tension around his eyes, the loss of color in his face. I took in the familiar pictures and the clutter, the view of the street from his window and I thought, *here is the opportunity*. For one of us to say that we cannot leave each other like this. Instead, I heard my voice estrange itself from my heart as it announced, "We're making good progress in Ward 6, with input into the Mayor's housing redevelopment plans." We slogged through the rest of our meeting with our minds elsewhere, a place where we once were the best of friends.

Later that day, Greg, my trusty mole in the Mayor's office called me. The news had spread that I was leaving *Homes First*; the question on many people's minds was why. Greg was rooting around for gossip.

"Oh, come on Linda, you didn't just get a conscience over night, you already have the most overdeveloped martyrdom complex of anyone I know. What's the deal?"

"Anita asked me."

"Anita Douglas? Anita-Windsor-Apartments-Douglas?"

"The very same."

"Linda—you didn't tell anyone what I told you did you?"

"Greg. What you told me just confirmed what everyone already suspected. This Mayor wants rich folk in and poor folk out. He wants to build a nice fat tax base, the whiter the better, to make a claim for statehood and go down as the man who made D.C. the 51st state. No one really thinks AOL and Booz Allen are having cocktail receptions on the banks of the Anacostia because they believe in river restoration. It's show-time in Anacostia, Greg, and I'm not going to stand back and let the whole thing blow apart."

"As always Linda darling, beautifully put. Now, come on, gossip time—what'd Richard say?"

Greg deserved some insight into the mess I found myself in, but not now.

"Richard is helping make the decision to leave easier."

"Really? I thought he'd go nuts! You two are like superheroes together."

It was true. Everyone had said it of us. From the moment we paired up to work at *Homes First*, under Jonathan's guidance, Richard and I had been pretty much unstoppable. No campaign was too great or hopeless to take on. We had built a name for ourselves, for *Homes First* being the place to go when people were about to be turned out onto the streets, budget cuts for shelters were proposed, or public housing faced redevelopment. Over the years, as I expanded the affordable housing project, Richard overhauled the homeless assistance program. He had a legendary reputation for magically securing the necessary services needed to support families who struggle to survive without a permanent home, helping to keep them healthy, safe and, if at all possible, happy. We had earned the respect of many of the local community leaders working on redevelopment and housing in the city, and because there could have been no legitimate committee without *Homes First*, Jonathan had been appointed chair of the Mayor's Affordable Housing Committee. That was how I met Greg, my most valuable source of information on the Administration's inside agenda.

The committee's annual report, *Everything You Need to Know About Homelessness*, was the go-to, first-stop source of information for housing policymakers in D.C. Each year we helped to paint an increasingly accurate portrait of the city's homeless. That forty percent are in families, that thirty-three percent of them are children, that between thirty-three and fifty percent of the homeless in the D.C. area are actually employed. Richard and I were relentless in hammering home the simple conclusion of each year's report. That the primary cause of homelessness is a lack of affordable housing. Not criminal behavior, drug addiction, mental illness, inability to work, or laziness—my personal favorite of the oft-quoted causes for destitution. It's just a simple question of math when you get right down to it. How many homes do we need and how many do we have? The solution seems obvious enough until you try to secure the funding for it.

"Listen Greg, I will keep you posted on Windsor. So far, all we have is a group of really angry activists and some good ideas. You know what I like to do in a situation like that."

"Oh, you'll win, I know that, but I already have a bottle of champagne chilling. I'm celebrating you coming East of the River full-time."

I was clearing out the last of my files as we chatted, but now I came off speakerphone and picked up the receiver.

"It's nice of you to say that, Greg. I'm kind of worried that I won't be strong enough for Anita and Luther. I've taken quite a hit here."

This was all I could give up. I was desperate to tell Greg what Richard had done; we were good friends and he deserved to know. But I felt bound to protect *Homes First*.

"You mean Richard?" He paused. "It's impossible to imagine what he could have done?" He waited. "Well, you're going to love working with Anita, even Luther. Just give him time—and space—and run when you see him coming. No really, good luck, girl. Really, this is great news!"

"Thanks, Greg. But I can't do it without you. Keep those insider calls coming."

It was time to say goodbye to Jonathan. I could not resist preparing him one last CD of music that I thought was impossible not to love. He saw me enter and he laughed—he had spotted the shiny case in my hand.

"You never give up do you?"

"I believe that's what makes me such an outstanding organizer."

"What is it this time?"

"Well, I did some research, and every track has an instrumental solo, there just happens to be some singing involved too."

"I'll give it a try," he said, smiling, but his voice rattled low, disguising very little of the emotion in the moment. "I have a CD for you too."

"Right, well I need to leave *now*," I said, backing up to the door before he could make me take it from him. Please God, not more of Jonathan's ghastly jazz music.

"Come back here. It's *not* music."

"It's not?"

"No. It's the application for our database. I trust you will do some good with it, and besides you're the one who pounded the streets of the city to make most of these contacts over the years."

"Well, I had the fear of you at my back. I had to do a good job." I joked. Then before I knew that I would admit to this, I added, "Richard should take some credit too—he used to be out there."

Jonathan acknowledged what I had said, even before I recognized that this was something that had long been troubling me.

"I'm going to get him back out there, don't worry. He needs to get out of the office and back in the community, I know that. Mean time, go east young lady, and feel free to share updates on that database with us anytime."

We stood to take a long look at each other and then we were in a long embrace filled with gratitude and hopefulness. I knew that we are both thinking of that drive we took together, it was the instant that this friendship was born.

Finally Jonathan told me, "My door is always open."

OF WHAT WE CHOOSE TO SEE

I, being poor, have only my dreams. I have spread my dreams under your feet; tread softly because you tread on my dreams.
William Butler Yeats

I took time out from my last day at *Homes First* to sit in the park outside my office building. The Civil War general on his horse at the center of the exquisitely landscaped gardens cast a cooling, somber shadow across the lawn below, where I sat to take in the place I had walked by nearly every day for eight years. I watched the homeless men shuffling around the benches, engaged in conversations together, some laughing, others arguing, some set apart, some incoherent and gesticulating randomly, like actors warming up for Shakespeare in the Park.

And this their only chance at life. They could have been comedians or astronauts or carpenters. Instead they were Homeless. I was reminded that my daughter Sandra, at four years, was more confident in her ability to be someone someday than these grown men. I watched strangers passing by the homeless men and women with oblivion, pity or disgust playing on their sunlit faces. Pity found its way in the coins tossed into a cup, even a few moments taken to exchange encouraging words. It seemed from where I sat, that it was the very notion of homelessness—that perhaps it could happen to any of us—that initiated the most instinctive reactions from passers-by. Quickened steps, heads lowered in shame (or defiant heads held high) but always a certainty of direction. Such busy lives we lead, and so meaningful, and theirs—so evidently empty and wasted. It occurred to me that only in places such as this park were we really forced to blend nonetheless. Here the hungry and homeless were allowed to momentarily court those sheltered all day in cool, gray offices who came to the park to escape. Even the name we have given the homeless defines them not by who they are but by what they lack. And what they lack we have. We are always two steps ahead because of it, no matter the character of any of us. But like unnerving, unwanted guests at a fantastic party, the homeless are not leaving, not until they have secured a parting gift for the road, even if it is merely an acknowledgement of their existence. Here, in this park, they inhabit other people's lives momentarily, forcing us to encounter one another, briefly enough to cause an exchange of emotion.

Downtown remained the last place for such miniature gatherings of opposite people. Yet, as Richard had taken great pains to demonstrate, under the current city administration, the homeless were slowly but surely being eliminated from Downtown, from the Golden Triangle of commerce. The city's actions allowed us to dream that we were improving as a society; instead we had merely made it easier to avoid running the gauntlet of the once ubiquitous, dirty and wretched looking people—the most desperate of the homeless, the ones who were most visible—who might trouble us on our way to work. We cursed them for filling the pit of our stomachs with guilt by exiling most beyond the city center. But they were still among us.

Years ago, Richard helped stage a mild revolution amongst the homeless men and women in D.C. He encouraged them to start showing up at hearings and council votes, arranged meetings for them with council members and even called press conferences on benches in the park. Some of them took to advocacy like naturals and they became a force to be reckoned with. There were numerous non-profits still angry with Richard for carving them out of the action—so used to representing the homeless, it had never occurred to them to let the homeless speak for themselves. He had brow beaten one of the activists working with him to run for office on the city council. Re-writing the rules, he organized voter registration drives across the city, and those who didn't know him shunned him, thinking he was too young, too new and definitely too white to handle such a campaign. By the time word got out that he was here to stay, he was able to secure serious funding to keep the drives going. That year, his campaign nearly succeeded in getting a new At-Large council member elected, and every election year since then, he had organized massive voter drives across the city.

From the first, I knew that Richard's motivation was pure and earnest. If he made a mistake, he was like a child breaking a glass by accident and wanting to help clean up—hoping the broken glass would be forgotten and everyone would remember how well he swept up the dangerous shards. If people got hurt along the way, he would find a way to make amends. But after a while it became habit for him to take shortcuts, bend the rules, to manipulate the people who trusted him, to break what was precious to those who loved him and he grew careless with the shards. I lived in a world of Richards. They were all I knew. People who worked hard to right the wrongs in the world. The wrongs, which were so obvious and painful, that my four-year old was already able to determine for herself, that there is an illogical imbalance in the world.

"Mommy," she said, one day, on the way to school, "why do some people have two houses and some people have none?"

In Washington, people either work for a cause-based non-profit, a lobbying firm, a lobbying firm disguised as a law firm, the government, congress, the administration, or some other permutation of a job that allows you to believe that you are Making a Difference. Even when the difference is the kind that ruins lives along the way. And no matter the genuine good he had done, Richard had already ruined his fair share of lives.

My cell phone rang. I was distracted from people watching by its optimistic trill. Looking down I saw Richard's number.

"Yes." I waited, unable to stop myself from hoping that he would want to talk about us.

"I wanted to know if you could go over some more work with me, before you leave."

"I think I've gone over enough work with you Richard," I said, surprised at the hostility in my voice. "I've done enough for you."

He seemed to realize how tenuous his hold was on me now.

"I can accept that. Hey, I'm sorry to have asked."

I switched the phone off and returned to my lunch; looking at it, I saw for the first time how grossly over-sized the field greens salad was that I had purchased. The large plastic shell *urging* me to waste in the face of need. Even if I saved the rest of the salad for another meal, that the unnecessarily gigantic container would end up in the garbage seemed suddenly disgusting to me. Such extremities of waste and need right there in that beautiful park, on a spectacular summer day. Unwanted freshly baked bread (came free with the salads), unfinished burritos, half sandwiches, unopened potato chip bags, all sitting buried in the garbage can, or if guilt surged unexpectedly, maybe someone found the grace to leave their unwanted food visible, in the hopes it would not go wasted. Not stopping to wonder what degradation of the human spirit and soul must occur for a person to reach for the trash of another person to eat and call their own.

For Richard and me, our work was always a mad rush to keep such desperation at bay. I worked with people who had roofs over their heads, had access to bathrooms and running water but who were steps, moments, a court order, away from their friend or realtive's pull-out sofas, or worse, the streets; he worked with the homeless, those already out on the streets, with nowhere else to go.

I saw my first eviction as a student in college. I was living in a five-story apartment building with a doorman and night security. When I biked home from a party late one night I saw a huge pile of clothes, furniture, books, pots, pans and photographs strewn across the sidewalk in front of my building. I assumed the worst, that there had been a fire. The security guard saw me arrive and he opened the door for me. He greeted me as though nothing had happened, asked me about the party, asked if I wanted help getting my bike into the elevator. When I asked him if the fire had done any damage, he looked confused. Then I discovered that as quick as a blazing fire can destroy a home, a person can be turned out onto the street, with no place to go, their belongings on display for the whole world to wonder at their failure to pay a rent check. Later I realized that the neighbor that the building had chosen to evict was in her seventies, something had gone wrong with her pension checks, she had no relatives and no place to go. I remember thinking I couldn't live in a building where that sort of thing could happen and then discovering it wasn't just the building bending the law, it was a whole collection of people from the government on down to me, choosing to look away. The lady was a civil rights activist, she had worked for thirty-five years as a school teacher and the thought of her out there in the world alone has haunted me ever since. Even now, the memory of that night chills me, the fear that rose in my throat when I thought that my apartment was burnt down, and my belongings lost, the greater loss that came of knowing that someone that I might have helped was gone instead.

When I first met Richard, early in our careers as community organizers, it seemed as though we were destined to end homelessness in our lifetime. We moved from victory to victory—his work improving access to social services and mine, keeping low-income housing a priority of the first two administrations we had worked with. The change arrived with the new Mayor. He came in promising to create new housing in the city, and he did, except that very little of it turned out to be affordable and the waiting lists grew rapidly. In various disguises he had tried to propose opening shelters in forgotten parts of southeast Washington to remove and consolidate the undesirables harbored in dilapidated properties sitting on suddenly desirable lots in downtown D.C. He had gone so far as to say repeatedly in public that Washington didn't need any more poor people, and that Maryland and Virginia should shoulder their fair share of them. Luckily for me, my campaigns had surged ahead, donations and funding flooding in, as a response to the new Mayor's policies. Curiously enough though, Richard's funding had suffered. There was a consensus in the funders' circles that maintaining and creating permanent affordable housing needed to take priority over homeless services for the moment. If the new housing wasn't acquired now, in the current building boom, there would be nothing but new developments across D.C., and no turning back the forced exodus of African American residents from their homes. Providing food, clothing, health services, counseling, rehab—these were expensive, labor and capital intensive services, and they needed to wait. It didn't help that the city's efforts to eliminate the homeless from the downtown Golden Triangle of commerce, was having the desired effect of allowing investors and new residents to be comforted by the belief that all those troubled, ragged-looking people who used to clutter the streets had, at long last, gone away.

It had been a surprise to all just how quickly Richard's program funding had started to dry up, but causes are fads, like diets or self-help manuals. As Catherine liked to remind me, ozone had been huge in the 70's and the environmental movement was flush with money to save the world from the great hole in the sky; once the hole became smaller, the world celebrated and forgot about the problem. Even though the ozone hole grows larger each year because international chlorofluorocarbon agreements are not being enforced, you now can't scrape two pennies together to work on the issue. Once affordable housing became the *cause du jour*, the more service-intensive homeless folk somehow got second shrift. Jonathan and I had agreed to share some of my unrestricted funds with Richard's program and it was generally acknowledged that this had saved his staff at *Homes First*. But he had gone further and plundered other program funding to sustain his own. I could imagine what he'd say now, the way he'd justify his actions. "What does it matter what the fucking *funders* think when the work we do is essential? Come on Lin, come on, you know I'm right?"

I called Richard back. The work he did was essential—this was what motivated him; despite myself, I still believed in him.

"What did you need help with?"

There was relief in Richard's voice. "I just need an hour to go over the latest draft of the strategic plan we prepared. Jonathan just gave me his edits back."

Always another hour. We had always found another hour for each other and it had led us from success to success. For the people in this park, for Jonathan, for *Homes First*, maybe even for Richard himself, I gave him one last hour.

OF POINTS OF INTEREST

While men in dark suits commute in limousine. Landfills and incinerators abound. As if we had the only land in town.
                                                        Bunyan Bryant

"Sometimes I think it's the pollution that will save us," said Anita. "Either that or the crime."

A murmur of laughter, tainted by wistfulness, floated across Luther's apartment where a small inner core of volunteers, who made up the newly formed campaign organizing committee, had gathered. We stood around the kitchen table reviewing a large map depicting the entire park system for the east of the Anacostia river region. The map was marked up and annotated to identify every location where a crime had been committed during the past two years. With us was the head of the city's newly revamped *Environmental Crimes Unit*, Charlie Boyd.

"This should help you understand what you're getting yourselves into," he said.

Charlie arrived dressed in his National Parks Service uniform, maps and reports under his arm, eager to get to work briefing the group. He was a life-long resident of Anacostia, and a 28-year veteran fighter against illegal dumping, artifact theft from historic sites, drug dealing, murder and the numerous other offenses that plagued the area. He told us that he had even fought against well-respected, local diagnostic labs for repeatedly dumping hazardous medical waste in the local parks. He read the amazement in our faces and smiled.

"Easy to get those guys," he chuckled. "Soil samples tell us everything we need to know. Always call in the TV crews myself. Slap the labs with big fines and shut them down—at least for a while."

He leaned in over the kitchen table.

"Those are the murders," he said softly, tapping on the map, to show us. "Not as many now, but still."

A little blue dot for every life lost, like a really tacky, inadequate highway memorial—plastic flowers and hand-written signs washed out by the rain—to a child who died when a drunk driver hit and ran. We all of us contemplated the loss and the grief concentrated in each tiny dot. There were no blue stickers on Oxon Cove Park, the site of the proposed prison; this was something of a relief.

Charlie stepped back and gave us some time to take the map in. It was difficult to believe that for most of his time spent as an NPS officer east of the river, he had worked in a cramped trailer office off of I-295, with staff and support for his work ebbing and flowing wildly with each new Mayor, NPS Director, and D.C. Environmental Crimes Unit Director that came and went. As bad as the situation was, it could clearly be worse. He had single-handedly closed many of his cases over the years, driven by his evident abundant love for each and every one of the local parks, and the crime rate had been steadily falling. He explained to us why, he believed, it was easy for Oxon Cove to have been traded away overnight.

"You neglect a piece of land like that for long enough, let the trash and debris pile up, you turn down every request for money for rangers, to maintain the trails—makes it real easy for the government to call the park *underutilized* and to treat it like excess inventory. It's bad for the Park Service everywhere, especially here, east of the river, but we never stood a chance with Oxon Cove." He shook his head. "What you all are trying to do is nice, it's good, you've just come thirty years too late."

I stepped forward to present a copy of a satellite map from the local Conservation Club that showed pollution hotspots in the neighborhood. There was no mistaking the concentration of unwanted—what realtors like to call undesirable—facilities east of the river. Each was identified by a red arrow; the satellite map was covered with red arrows. Together with an assortment of local civic groups, the Club had taken legal action against the city and federal government for lack of enforcement on several of the sites. Many were new to me, but most were well known to the residents around the room. Anita couldn't have put it more bluntly. We were hoping that the information from these two maps, and the others like it that we spent the morning reviewing, would force the developers to re-assess the market value of the Windsor Apartments, take a tenant bid, and then hightail it back to their headquarters in Georgia. The prison company would likely take persuasion of an entirely different nature to back away from building their state-of-the-art cages at Oxon Cove.

Charlie's interest was peaked suddenly and he came around to take a closer look at the Conservation Club map.

"Look at this. This map is great. These apartment buildings—*here, see*? Look, right here, the owners are repeat offenders for pumping raw sewage into the ground. We've been fighting them for years. A lot of the buildings are only partly occupied because of the state they're in. These are the ones they should be tearing down and re-developing for their fancy condos. But we don't stand a chance, they're Roland buildings."

At the mention of Roland, the sound of whispered curses skimmed across the room. I had had my own share of run-ins with him and his cronies over the years. Jonathan was always there to watch my back. I reluctantly acknowledged that there were some political games that only D.C. natives with long, complicated histories—like Roland and Jonathan— ever get to play. W.J. Roland was a local African American businessman who made his fortune in the 80's, building substandard affordable housing with HUD and D.C. government loans. He was a powerful force in local government affairs, had the Mayor's ear, and was eager to re-invent himself as a mixed-use real estate developer east of the river.

"Roland's not going to sell his land until he can get top dollar. The banks won't give him a dime to re-develop, not with his history. So for now he's just biding his time, allowing his properties to fall apart, until he can sell the land. People living like only animals should. The city should have shut Roland down years ago." Charlie seemed energized to be with us; perhaps he was passing on the torch at long last. "And look at this, the impoundment lot. Has to be in Ward 8, does it? Used all the time for illegal dumping."

"Well, maybe no one will want to live near the sewage treatment plant," Anita said, pointing to an enormous area highlighted on the map, the Blue Plains Water Treatment Facility. Will you look at all these red arrows? And here's Oxon Run, you can see all the trash running right through the neighborhood. How can you take a stream and put it into that concrete thing? We could have had benches and landscaping. The city said it would help control the trash."

Charlie laughed. "Oh, I remember that, we fought that too."

The revelations that came from the maps started to fall like heavy rain around us, making it difficult to see through to what needed to be done. This feeling was so familiar to me; the facts come too hard, too fast, and the room starts to fill with a mounting sense of despair. We needed clarity about our purpose, and I was contemplating how best to re-direct the group, when one of the residents spoke up.

"So why's Windsor already working so hard to throw us out? Don't look like a place white folk would want to live."

"Not yet, anyway," Luther said. "Not yet."

Luther's low, composed voice seemed to awaken us all from contemplation and now he commanded our attention. He spoke with a carefully muted sense of outrage, his emotions impounded—only to be drawn on when absolutely necessary. I knew enough about Luther's past to understand that he had been forced to lay his anger down many times in his life. Because you expected anger, perhaps even an edge of violence, but he showed none, at all times he seemed entirely in control, and unassailably sincere. Often his words didn't seem to emerge from any kind of feeling at all, only from what he understood absolutely. He gathered and retained information relentlessly—this was his weapon of choice as he fought—only ever speaking once he had the chance to fully process what he had learned.

"Only on the surface is this neighborhood as damaged and undesirable as you have portrayed it," he said. "We all need to understand what is happening to Washington, what is happening to historically *black* Washington, especially over here. We're losing a fight half the residents don't even know has begun. The baseball stadium has put us on the map. Just down the road from here, St. Elizabeth's? A tinderbox about to blow. Right there on Martin Luther King Jr. Avenue. What do you think should become of it? If you haven't thought about that yet, then we're all in trouble."

St. Elizabeth's, where John Hinckley, the man who attempted to assassinate President Reagan, was confined with a handful of mentally ill patients left over from years long gone, was already being bitterly fought over. This was one of the first places that I visited with Jonathan. We shimmied in past the security guards without any kind of authorization. Jonathan simply nodded and they let us in.

"Are you crazy?" I asked him, only half joking.

"Come on, relax. We're not here to visit the patients."

And then I saw for myself why there was such intense speculation over what would happen to St. E.'s. This was not just an old, neglected hospital. Magnificent brick buildings—an enormous campus—glowing carmine red in the setting sun; vibrant, landscaped gardens; vast expanses of beautifully kept lawns, all stretched out before us. We looked down on the Potomac River, and towards the most beautiful views of Northern Virginia and Washington D.C., that I have ever seen, even to this day.

"Jonathan. This is —"

"Yes it is."

We didn't need to say more. We simply watched the sun finish setting over the river, bathing St. E.'s in a wash of gold and violet light and took in the redolent summer air soaked in the fragrances of the flower gardens and lawns. We remained this way until we were looking out into the dark night sky and D.C. glittering in the distance.

"I used to come here as a kid to watch the 4th of July fireworks. We all did. Lay our picnics out on the lawn over there, families together. I can tell you Linda, no one is picnicking at St. E.'s these days."

I brought Ian there. Jonathan gave me some magic password for the security guards and we were allowed in. Ian took one look around after passing through the gate and he simply grabbed my hand and we ran. We ran laughing through the campus like college freshmen. We found a beautiful little contemplation garden down by the river, and we lay down in the grass and we kissed and laughed, our hearts still pounding from running. I can't explain it, what it felt like. Except to say that it felt like the first time we saw our run-down house. A beauty laid low. And we had joked about how all she needed was some lipstick and rouge. St. E.'s didn't even really need the makeup; it simply needed to open its gates back up again to the people, to let them back in where they belonged. A belief came alive as we lay there talking and laughing, that this place could offer a park, homes, education, endless possibilities, dignity to people who lived their lives on housing waiting lists. This was the wild and crazy hope that had made us laugh so long and so hard. After sunset,

Ian and I walked back to the Anacostia Metro station and as we passed a group of kids loitering around the escalators, one of them shouted to us, "Yo! What the *fuck* are you so happy about?"

According to Luther, despite St. E.'s having long inspired dread as a decaying, remote enclave for the mentally ill, set inside a violent, black world, it was now seen as irresistible real estate. Congress was planning to close the hospital as quickly as possible. Developers and city officials were seeking special permits from the hospital's authorities to host business partners at elegant dinners on the campus lawn, complete with guided walks along the Potomac River. A Mayoral task force was already in frantic negotiations with the federal government to transfer ownership of the property back to D.C., and the city's delegate to Congress was fighting—with a mix of desperation and dignity unique to Members with no voting rights—for local residents to have a place at the table. Whatever the outcome, the Windsor Apartments would fit perfectly into this new world, offering a vast number of newly renovated residences for the rebirth of this previously feared and forgotten part of Washington D.C.

"With Homeland Security on MLK already, it's just a matter of time before the high-tech government leeches will want to set up shop at St. E.'s. Don't believe the training program hype—we've heard it before. The contractors and consultants will take over the rest of MLK and they'll want to house their young, hip, white techies in brand new apartments nearby. That's when you'll see the city get real serious, real quickly about cleaning this place up. Fixing the parks, letting the Run go again, and chasing Roland out of town and to hell where he belongs for what he's done to his own people."

Luther finished, simmering but still far from boiling over. I looked across at him and wondered if I was supposed to take offense that he had classified the enemy—the very people who would take up residence here in Luther and Linda and Charlie's apartments—as white. I struggled with this every day in my work. *Is it a class issue or a race issue, a race issue or a class issue? Is it both? Can I doubt that those who come will, as Luther says, be mostly white?* Because I did not doubt that they would be of substantial means when compared to the residents of Anacostia, where thirty-six percent of the residents lived below the poverty line. On some level though, wasn't this exactly what Luther wanted—to re-build the neighborhood economy, bring new businesses, people and ideas in? But how do you do that without moving the current residents out? For all the urban planning books and all the conferences and workshops on the subject, very few neighborhoods have ever improved by moving their residents up instead of out. Especially when the stakes were as high as they were in Anacostia.

My thoughts were interrupted by Damien, one of the high-school kids from the first meeting, who was taking part in a civics honor program at his school and had chosen the Windsor and prison campaigns for his independent study project. If you saw him on the street you would certainly take note of him. Well-built, muscular and markedly tall, he likely weighed 250 pounds already. He wore gigantically baggy clothes and a skin-tight do-rag, bore a scary looking tattoo of a knife on his right forearm, and had been chain-smoking menthols on Luther's balcony for the past hour.

"I lived in this city ma whole life. An' I'm mo' afraid now for ma community than I've *eva* been. Because iss not jus' whites tellin' blacks where to live anymo'. You can motivate people aroun' tha'. Iss not jus' white men in power decidin' where their buddies git to build stadiums and apartment buildin's and which projects git teared down. Iss way mo' complicated than tha'. Our own Mayor, from our neighborhood, got busted wiv crack an' prostitutes! Insteada workin' fo' the people who believed in him, an' stood by him, fo' thirty fuckin' years. You spec me to believe in him *again*? I don', I fuckin' don'. An' who even knows the name of our new council member? She's like nowhere to be seen? What'd she git? Twelve thousand votes and suddenly she represents me?"

Damien pulled himself away from the balcony railing and threw his cigarette down to the ground. He crushed the butt completely, leaning in with all his weight and then he moved into the living room and braced himself against the doorframe.

"What I *do* know is tha' Anacostia ain't goin' to change so tha' poor black people can still live here and *their lives* can change instea'. Tha's too messy. Iss people wiv money comin' our way an' some o' them wiv money is *black*. An' they need us *gone*. *I mean gone*. So how we gonna convince *blacks* to fight tha'?"

We all held still. I wondered how long Damien had been waiting for a chance to voice his fears about the seismic shift that was about to tear up his neighborhood. He looked around slowly, waiting for one of us to respond, unafraid to look us in the eye, daring us to take him on. Luther slowly wheeled himself over to Damien—a boy about the same age as Luther when he was shot. He was perhaps wondering that he did not have this clarity of mind when he was Damien's age. Not until *after* he was shot.

"You're right. You're *right*. This is different. That's why we need you and your friends to get involved, Damien. This time around, it's your lives on the line. They're going after you and your friends, and measuring beds in that prison, just for you. They're tossing you out of your homes just to make sure you have nowhere else to go."

I caught Anita's eye; she encouraged me to step in.

"Seems like we have our work cut out for us," I said, trying hard not to keep staring, as everyone else seemed to be doing, at Damien and Luther as they conferred together out on the balcony. I handed out assignments while reflecting on how much I evidently still had to learn about this community that I prided myself on knowing so well. After the volunteers had a chance to skim through their responsibilities and groan about what they were getting themselves into, Anita made an announcement.

"Fundraising for both campaigns falls to Linda. Any questions about your budgets, ask Linda."

If I were new to this game I would have been flattered. People who hold the purse strings hold the power—isn't that what they say? Nonsense. Both Anita and Luther made it perfectly clear to me that they loathed grant writing and fundraising. I did too, even though I'd had a lot of practice over the years; it's like trudging through a desert with no water or food and not even a mirage for comfort—you have to do anything necessary to survive, even when you're tired and burnt and eager to give up. "You know you love it," Anita had said, with a delicious smile—part mockery, part relief—knowing I wouldn't say no to her, knowing that the part of me that loved to win always pushed me forwards, no matter what, and that somehow, I would deliver the goods.

When I was done with my overview of our goals, Luther came over to tell me that he was assigning Damien to me. I was surprised, relieved, touched. It was a sign of his deepening trust in me. I knew that he wanted me to see his decision as nothing less.

Anita began to speak. She was emotional; it had already been a long road for her, all these campaigns, all these years. She was old enough for her parents to have lived through segregation and she suffered terribly from growing up poor, but she had risen up, only to witness her neighborhood implode once drugs, guns, and the violence that came with them, took hold of the streets she once walked without fear. She was young enough and strong enough to have made mistakes, survived, and made a good life for herself and for her daughter. Now she spoke in that melancholy voice of hers—rich, strong, resonating with a powerful mix of wisdom that she had been forced to acquire and wisdom that she tenaciously sought out.

"We will create our own compilation of the threats and opportunities in the neighborhoods east of the river. It will be our way of fighting back. We will familiarize ourselves with our adversaries—we need to do that. But I think, more than that, as Luther has long been advocating, we have to define our own hopes and plans for our neighborhood. Let's not stray on these two campaigns and forget that work, because it will matter the most in the end."

She shifted in her seat at Luther's kitchen table. She looked thoughtfully around at each of us. She drew her words out; she wanted us to feel their power.

"We will identify the assets in the community. They exist, in abundance—all those contact lists I've been keeping to myself, Luther! We do have people ready to serve and fully believing that they can help. The prison company, the real estate developers, they've all paid consultants to make maps and plan, and to talk about how they know what our neighborhood needs. But we will ask, who are the people in this neighborhood? What are their lives like now and what will happen to their lives if they are forced to leave? How can we help them to stay instead, and improve their lives? And as for the prison?" She paused, arching her back, allowing the anger in. "Locking up black boys who have never been given a real chance at life is not about *profits* for corporations. It is for us to save our sons and our brothers and our fathers. What we are trying to do, what we need to do, is to stop this prison—yes—but we also need to give our kids hope, not condemn them to hell."

Luther stared at Anita. He seemed awash with relief; he fell back against his chair, as though stunned. I had never seen his face so lit up, open, his eyes glistening.

Damien got up to go after we exchanged numbers. He slapped me on the back and I barely managed to stop myself from falling forwards from the impact.

"Call me," he said. "I ain't kiddin'."

I said my goodbyes and walked back to the Metro station. *If all this changes*, I thought, as I took a detour through some streets off of South Capitol, and watched residents out and about, *where will these people go?*

OF SELF-EVIDENT TRUTHS

Is there no way
That I may sight and check that speeding bark
Which out of sight and sound is passing, passing?
                                        Paul Laurence Dunbar

I was in the kitchen at home with the documents that Catherine sent to me sprawled out on every surface. I had a lot to learn about the prison company, *Reform and Corrections Inc.*, and their connection to the signatures on the land swap amendment. But my attention was now on a collection of reports that Luther had just messengered over to me. I figured I had a long night of research ahead, so I pulled out half a bottle of wine left over from dinner, a box of stone-ground wheat crackers and the last of some exquisitely sharp, dry, Irish cheddar to sustain me. I poured myself a glass of wine and before I began to read, I took a moment to contemplate Luther. He was starting to grow on me; I was learning to accept and work around his habitual surliness and it had, of course, been great fodder for jokes for Catherine and me. Anita told me she thought I was a making an impression on Luther, but she wouldn't commit to what kind of an impression that might be. These were still the early stages of our relationship and I hoped one day to look back down the long path that led us to a great and everlasting friendship; all I saw now though, were insurmountable hurdles, not the least of which was proving to Luther I was the right person to help him win this campaign. I felt certain that I could not underestimate what he expected of me.

I started to make my way through the first batch of reports concerning the demographics of the prison population in America, incarceration rates in African American communities across the country, and a newly released overview of crime and law enforcement in the District of Columbia. First off, I needed to learn not to be alarmed that there was such a thing as a *prison population*—a term that to me, sounded absolute, permanent, too well accepted. As I read, I grew more and more agitated. The statistics piled up before me until I sat back, overwhelmed. How could all of this be happening right here in the town I lived in, the place I called home, the place I was raising a family in? I was out there on the streets every day; how could entire neighborhoods across Washington be failing completely—inside, out—and I didn't know, even with all the work I'd already done at *Homes First*?

I was trying to stop a prison from being built on a park in Ward 8, home to the city's poorest and most troubled neighborhoods, and I had been thinking all along that this was a good thing—the right thing—to do. But what I now knew was that there were thousands of residents of Ward 8 and the rest of D.C. already in prison, and *destined* to be incarcerated, and it suddenly seemed no longer true to say that we didn't need a new prison. I didn't even know where to put that feeling—how to take on board the idea that what I was working for might be flawed, or even wrong. I had to set it aside. What stayed with me instead, what stunned me—no, *paralyzed* me—was the prediction, made over and over again by a disparate assortment of independent watchdog organizations, police commission reports, victims' rights organizations, prison family advocate groups and Justice Department studies.

FORTY ONE PERCENT OF AFRICAN AMERICAN MALES BETWEEN THE AGES OF 18-35 LIVING IN THE NATION'S CAPITOL WILL BE INCARCERATED AT SOME POINT IN THEIR LIVES.

I had come to this campaign to stop a prison and to save an apartment building and suddenly I was facing the much bigger issue of what in God's name were we going to do about this vast and unforgivable waste of lives that we had come to accept as a statistical certainty in our society? As I read on, I drank too much and I knew it, but I could not stop. I was feeling something of what was in Luther's voice when he called me to tell me he was sending me the reports. I couldn't discern what it was then; I simply took note it was there, and it had been enough to make me put Catherine's research aside and take up the package from Luther.

"Babe, what are you doing?" It was Ian. He had come in half-asleep to check up on me. Neither of us sleeps well alone. "It's three in the morning. Come to bed. What are you doing?"

"I don't know," I told him. "This is—so—fucked—*up*."

"What? What? We can't talk about this now, just come to bed."

I looked at him as though he were a stranger to me, because really, it didn't seem to me that anything would be the same after this. I had suddenly, definitively, been drawn into a world I had merely been tiptoeing around the edges of for too long. A world most of us prefer to deny exists—the imperfect America that has not made amends for its past.

"I don't feel like I can stop or win *this*," I said, holding up one of the reports. "You should read it, really. It makes for a great bed-time story."

I saw him glance at the second bottle of wine and my glass.

"You're drunk, Lin." He took the bottle away and sat next to me. "What, babe? What is it?"

"There are two million people in prison in this country. Two million people sitting behind bars, and you know what I just discovered, Ian? Forty-six percent of them are black. Nine hundred thousand African Americans in jail. How can that be? I thought we, you know, *ended* the whole slavery thing."

"Lin come on, it's the middle of the night."

I stood up and leant on the kitchen counter for support. "No, see, this is the thing. It turns out D.C. does its fair share of contributing to that prison population. There is actually a term for all those people rotting in jail—the *prison population*. So this isn't about stopping a prison. It's—I don't know what the fuck it is—but it's not about stopping this prison. And you're going to say what? Nothing? Go to bed?"

Ian looked at me as though he was about to give up and leave. Instead he pulled me back down to sit next to him and he turned me towards him.

"You know what? You're just scared. And that's O.K. Ever since you started doing this work, every campaign you've worked on ended up being tied to something bigger that you expected. You always end up fighting a bunch of scary, evil, self-serving developers, council members, or some sold-out old bastard on the Hill. It's always the same. You always find a way to take them on and win. This is just your new thing, Lin, and it's even bigger than you thought, that's all. You and Anita, and Luther, you'll find a way to take this on and do the right thing. I know you will." He kissed me, held me tight for a moment, just long enough to make me want him to stay and then he got up. "I'll see you in the morning."

Before he left he took the last of the wine, threw it out, and poured me a glass of water. His leaving made me feel chilled and alone and I was too drunk to sit up reading at the kitchen table. I took a small pile of work into the living room with me and it was not long before I fell asleep. Nine hundred thousand African Americans will sleep behind bars tonight.

Catherine called me early the next morning. At some point in the night, I had dragged myself upstairs and I was curled up against Ian when the sound of the phone ruptured our sleep.

"Get up! It's *gorgeous* out and I want to go to Oxon Cove."

My head was pounding and I knew Ian would be unbearable later if I talked to Catherine in bed while he tried to sleep on. I reluctantly agreed to call her back momentarily. Once downstairs, I alternated between coffee and water, coffee and water, as we made our plans for the day. I had, of course, completely forgotten that I had promised to take her to Oxon Cove, to see for herself what all the fuss was about; she wouldn't admit to being more than curious to meet Luther, Anita and Damien. At her urging, I organized a field trip of sorts. Ian was joining us too, as soon as he could drag himself from bed. Damien was bringing some of his friends. Luther and Anita would meet us there.

"What does that mean, they'll meet us there?" she asked, "I thought you said, it's huge and there are no trails, and it's all overgrown. And we're just going to find each other? I'm not Hansel and Greteling my way back home you know."

I let this one go. She would soon see for herself. We picked up pastries and coffee on 14th Street at one of the now ubiquitous, trendy new cafe's that had sprung up overnight and we drove to Oxon Cove. The only place to park was at the Police Training Academy nearby the park entrance. The police officers there were, by now, intimately familiar with my blatant violation of their *No Parking* signs, and likely had my license plate memorized; the two officers getting out of their patrol car as we arrived actually nodded to us in approval. Ian and Catherine were very impressed.

"Well, here it is," I told them.

They looked around at the barren expanse of concrete, and the chicken wire fence up ahead, and no longer seemed quite so impressed.

"Trust me, it gets better."

We walked through the gate and started along a paved path that within moments was bordered on both sides by grassland and wildflowers—a chaotic mix of daisies, firey red and yellow salvia, pumpkin-orange butterfly weed and dandelions—with three or four different kinds of butterflies hovering over them. On one side, the grassy verge rose up to a forested hillside, dense with maples, ash trees and poplars. Catherine and Ian look around in disbelief. I couldn't help but smile. This was the same magic that Luther and Anita worked on me the first time I came here with them.

"This is beautiful, it's like being in the countryside," Ian said, and he reached his arm around my waist to draw me in, smiling, laughing, his eyes lit up, as though I had thrown him a fantastic surprise party. "I can't believe I'm in Washington."

Catherine ran on ahead to the picture-perfect, stone bridge over Oxon Cove. "It's *ridiculously* beautiful!" she said, laughing. Ian and I joined her, and from there we looked out over the clear, slow-moving water and were entertained by a great blue heron wading and feeding. Suddenly noticing us, the bird swooped up and away toward the Potomac River on giant, almost prehistoric-looking wings. Catherine pointed to a small box turtle swimming under the bridge and Ian noticed two catfish skimming the banks of the cove not far from where we stood. I was delighted that the cove was putting on its best show for us, although so far, in all my visits there, I had not failed to see a bald eagle and I was holding out for another one today. I led them on across the little bridge and we stepped into Prince George's County, Maryland.

"Just like that we're in Maryland?" Ian asked.

"For real?" Catherine said.

This amused them for a while; they ran back and forth across the bridge like three-year-olds, shouting, *Maryland! D.C! Maryland! D.C! I can vote! Now I can't! I can vote! Now I can't!* We walked on and talked about Oxon Hill Farm and its museum—the beautifully preserved land that bordered Oxon Cove on the Maryland side—that was as well-serviced as Oxon Cove Park, in D.C., was over-run and neglected. I found the sandbar where the bald eagle often rested and my heart racing in anticipation, I tried to casually suggest we walk to the water's edge for a closer look at the cove. As we brushed past a low-lying branch of cottonwood we caught a glimpse of the water and then Ian saw the eagle first.

"Oh—my—God." He breathed the words out, filled with awe. We stood ten feet from a bald eagle on the sandbar, doing nothing more it seemed, than watching the world go by. Catherine squeezed my hand, afraid to breathe and scare the bird away. We watched until he took off, gathering his wings and effortlessly lifting himself up into the blue sky; the beat of his wings could be heard across the silence that filled the cove.

"I'm thinking let's put the prison right there—right across from baldy's patch—what do you think?" Catherine said, apparently unable to bear the perfect experience any longer.

She was joking, but now it was time for me to tell them that along the water, where a forest now stood, its trees rustling through the stillness of the cove, was exactly where the prison would be built.

Ian had not yet turned away from the water when he said, "you have to stop this."

Catherine seemed eager to press the point home. "Yeah, no offense Lin, but do *not* fuck this one up."

We walked back to the bridge and Damien and his buddies greeted us there, along with Luther and Anita; this path was the only part of the 45 acres that was even remotely accessible, let alone for wheelchairs. We exchanged introductions and Damien and Catherine immediately fell into an intense discourse on music. Catherine liked to think of herself as black, even though she was as white as the snow-capped peaks of Montana, her home state. But since she liked and knew black music—all black music, including jazz, where she lost me, of course—owned a cart to haul her groceries and lived in the Trinidad neighborhood of D.C., she considered herself somewhat black. In an honorary degree sort of way. Poor deluded Rocky Mountain girl, what can I say? Sure enough though, I heard her sharing this notion of her inner black woman with Damien and his friend Theo, and they were having a good laugh together over it. Ian, meanwhile, was excitedly telling the others about the bald eagle we had just seen, when the bird passed over us again. We gasped and squealed delightedly, little children again, as we watched the creature glide through the air, its distinct, bold colors—the dark brown body, white hood, golden beak—blurring as it rose up past the creek and over the trees, disappearing. Damien pointed up to the sky to trace the arc of the bird's flight. "Did you see tha'?! Did you see tha'?! A bald eagle! I neva seen one before!" There was a giddy, charged feeling in the air—for me, somewhat intensified by my hangover—a sense of connection between us, and all that surrounded us, on that calm, beautiful, summer day.

After everyone had explored the Maryland side of the cove, we crossed back to the D.C. side and followed the fence up to the official park entrance. Anita wanted everyone to see the place, the ground itself, where the prison would be built. I looked up along the path, and I was surprised to see Jonathan with his wife, heading our way. I ran to greet them not knowing until then, just how much I had missed him. We embraced and feeling now like I wanted to share this place and its story with the whole world, I brought everyone around to the park entrance. A small, sad, battered National Park Service sign reassured us that at least for now, this was public property.

"Sorry, Luther, looks like wheelchairs not welcome, but don't feel bad, looks like we're not exactly welcome either," Catherine said, standing before the densely overgrown path ahead of us.

Luther smiled lightly and tipped his head to her, but Damien burst out laughing. Ian must have seen the look on Jonathan's wife's face.

"Catherine, why don't you go *first*?" he said.

We had to bushwhack our way for twenty minutes, through a mess of shrubs and grasses that were scratchy and coarse, often snagging our clothes, before we were able to reach the cove. In bleak contrast to the Maryland side with its pristine trails, trash lay scattered about all around us—it was caught up in the bushes, strewn across the path; in places we could see huge piles of garbage that had been deliberately dumped under the trees or brush. Catherine provided the running commentary. "Well we can't go this way, definitely don't want to go that way, back up here, people..."

The water's edge rose steeply above this side of the creek and in the absence of trails, approaching from above, we were forced to slide down the bank, crouching low, to reach the shore. We all stood together on a long sandbar while Theo sat on a rock, slightly apart from us, digging into the sand with a twig.

"If I'da known there was a park here, I'd come. You know, I would. All you think's here is the Impoundment Lot, an' the Police Academy an' that, cos this is all fenced off. We never even knew there was water here and birds, an' all of this." He dug deeper, scraping hard at the sand. "My Mom used to *love* stuff like this, family picnics an' all. We always'd go to Anacostia Park, but this is like, at the bottom of my street! You clear all this trash out, put trails in, I mean—look at this place!"

"Iss the difference between tha' and this," Damien said, looking out to the Maryland side. "They have a park and we have this."

When Anita suggested we should get back to Luther, we turned to clamber back up the bank, and it was hard going all the way. I stopped to check my footing and noticed that Jonathan had stayed back and was standing, arms around his wife, looking out at the water as an osprey swooped past and several ducks swam by.

"Lord, but this is beautiful," I heard him say. "The third day. And God saw that it was good." He paused. "That anyone would want to destroy this is beyond me."

Back with the rest of the group, Ian commented that there was something downright un-American about the whole sordid affair and he and Catherine, with their inimitable manner of dissecting a scandal to its finest parts, had the group roaring with laughter. We spent some time talking about the morning and what we had seen, what we felt ought to be done. I was happy to have opened up my new world to Ian and Catherine, and to have had the unexpected chance to share the cove with Jonathan and his wife. We were all preparing to leave when Luther pulled me aside. He asked if we could meet, just the two of us, for a strategy meeting.

"Sure," I said, "Oh, and by the way, thanks for all that happy reading material you sent me. Keep that up, you'll make an alcoholic out of me."

He laughed. I liked the sound—natural, without the usual sarcasm—it was new to me.

"Just wanted you to know what you're getting yourself into."

"Here's one for you," I told him. "Guess who's representing *Reform and Corrections*? Raymond Weaver."

Anita, Jonathan, Damien, Theo, Ian, Catherine, everyone around us, turned to where I stood next to Luther.

"Fu—*ck*," whispered Catherine.

"Thank you, Catherine, for that insight," Ian said, scowling at her and gesturing towards the high school kids in our midst.

"Tha' lil bastard's in bed wiv Roland," Damien said; his fury was palpable, menacing, if he weren't on our side.

Luther turned to Damien with respect and admiration glowing in his face.

"So that's what we're up against. Raymond Weaver," Luther said, and I detected both rage and excitement in his voice. "*Raymond Weaver.*"

RAFAEL ALONE

So they made the tin soldier to stand firmly on one leg, and this caused him to be very remarkable.
                              Hans Christian Andersen

Rafael kept two photos of Lance Armstrong on his desk. One showed Lance, lying barely alive in his hospital bed, about to start his next round of chemotherapy sessions. His eyes say it all—*I'm in your hands now*. The other photo—the Blue Train powering up the Alps two years later, Mont Ventoux looming ahead, a mere mountain, nothing more when compared to cancer.

Rafael knew that his colleagues thought he was a sentimental fool. He accepted their good-hearted teasing and bluster and eagerly participated in heated debates, over drinks after work, about whether science existed for the public good or to satisfy the curiosity of brilliant minds. His friends were mining the depths of science for the fun and thrill of it all; he often wondered at, even envied, their detachment from the world outside the lab. For him, there was always the question of Lance, and all the others relying on researchers like him not to goof off, to step up to the plate and hit cancer out of the park. He sometimes listened to Lance's satellite radio show while working, and it seemed to him that this was the sound of life itself. A man having a laugh on the radio, playing his favorite tunes, seven Tour de France wins in him, a whole future ahead of him. And cancer behind him.

Sometimes Rafael felt like a poster boy for science—the rugged loner working late into the night curing cancer. Other times, most of the time, he was a man with a team of scientists methodically, meticulously revisiting over and over again, *what do we know, what do we need to know*. He was developing a new kind of *in vitro* proliferation assay, looking for the dose-dependent, growth-inhibitory effects of different chemical agents on his line of lung cancer cells. He was hoping to discover why this particular form of cancer spread so rapidly and efficiently by observing which chemicals applied to cancer cells grown in the lab, could speed up or slow down the cells' development into cancerous masses. His work was tedious, repetitive; every minute detail mattered. His yardstick for progress was measured in nanovictories that built one on the other for years and years, long years. Until one day there might be a little pill or a bottle of liquid that could be administered to a very sick person to turn their life around. Rafael had found that he looked to Lance for inspiration—the irony was delicious—to understand what kind of perseverance is needed to win when a victory seems so far away. Lance didn't just ascend the Alps and cruise through seven Tours so effortlessly after all. He had to do a lot of repeating too. Maybe not the twelve or fourteen hours a day that Rafael regularly devoted to his lab, but the six hours every day riding his bike over and over again. Rafael often thought, *we are not so different after all, Lance and I*. And yet they fell at either end of the cancer spectrum.

Tonight Rafael was eager to check up on his latest round of cell cultures. He had been hoping to see slower growth of the cancer cells after administering a series of promising new agents that promoted differentiation and inhibited cell division in normal cell lines. Lung cancer, he knew, did not lend itself well to typical cancer therapies because the cytotoxic drugs often wreaked havoc on the healthy cells in the body before they even had a chance to reach the target cells. Clinical trials of cancer drugs, as horrific as it seemed to the outside world, centered on the balance between toxicity and efficacy. Do we kill the patient or the cancer? How close can we come to killing the patient and how exactly do we control that? Rafael hoped to come at lung cancer in a different way—he was searching for a way to slow the cancer cells but not kill them. Make them act the way they were supposed to all along. A kind of *lets not give up on these rogue cells, lets try to make them like us* approach. Then the million-dollar (likely multi-million, for that matter) question still remained—how do we get to the cancer cells and avoid harming the healthy cells in the patient? He would leave that particularly enormous problem for others to solve; his job was to identify a candidate drug and pass it along. Somewhat reluctantly he recognized his limitations.

He removed his cell cultures from their warming oven and carefully started his observations through the microscope. He laughed. *I am such a cliché. I am a scientist with a microscope.* He settled in for the evening. It would be a long while, counting cells, observing morphological changes, carefully noting down his results. The dull hum of the hood extractor, the harsh fluorescent lights, the Petri dishes and culture flasks—some with lurid pink solutions inside, others colorless—an assortment of carefully labeled bottles and pipette boxes, all this kept him company as he worked. He was as comfortable in this world as Lance Armstrong gliding effortlessly up Mont Ventoux.

OF WHAT CAN BE LOST IN A MOMENT

I will show you fear in a handful of dust.
                                        T.S.Eliot

Whenever I called Rafael at work, I always had the sense he was on the verge of curing cancer in that very moment and that I needed to be brief.

"Rafael, dinner, remember? And you wanted my help with something?"

"Linda, I am—"

"Let me guess—in the middle of a very important experiment?"

"Exactly!"

"Sunday night, two weeks from now. Mind if I invite some other friends?"

"Done."

"Good night. Oh, you do know it's past eleven?"

Marguerite's enemy—the lab—still had its hold on him, no matter their reconciliation.

"I know that *you* are calling me from the bus after one of your meetings in Anacostia, so please, you're not one to judge."

"How did you know?"

"Screechy brakes. It's a giveaway. Good night, Linda—see you in two weeks."

Laughing, I turned to pick up today's copy of the *Express* on the seat next to me. I had not heard about the man walking his dog. All day, working the campaign, I was too busy to even graze the paper beyond the national headlines. Now as I read about him I could feel the fear inside me ascending, icing my limbs as it rose, reaching my mouth as a peculiar, dry taste that made me swallow again and again. I looked around the bus—three men and me, the only woman on the bus. The young guy sitting across from me with his Nationals baseball hat, was suddenly a Young Latino Male. The man reading his pamphlet from the DCDOH about prostate cancer was suddenly now a White Male, mid-40's. There was no one else on the bus except Don, the driver who always worked this shift and made jokes about me coming home so late. African American Male, early 50's, but I knew him well, so he was O.K. Just two more stops to the end of the line. I started to panic at the thought of getting off the bus. *A six-foot man with a German shepherd dog.* What chance does anyone have? I looked deliberately at the young Latino man and forcing myself to smile, I asked him the time, in Spanish. Just to feel a connection, to feel less afraid. Don heard me and made another joke about my working so late, how I should get myself a watch, then I'd know I should have been home hours ago with my little baby. We had known each other since I was pregnant with Sandra, who would somehow forever be a baby to Don. I always sat—facing sideways, usually reading a book or the paper—in a seat at the front of the bus so that I could casually exchange comments with him. I relaxed a moment at his words, something inside me instinctively joked back, "You know she's in college now?"

The young Latino man leaned in and showed me his watch. 11:48. Twelve minutes earlier, last night—just over twenty-four hours ago—a man walking his dog had been shot dead a block away from my bus-stop. I walked past the same house where the killing took place each time I stopped to buy something from one of the stores on the main street, and occasionally on my way to and from work. I rose to get off the bus feeling lightheaded. Don caught my eye and I knew that he had read me. This was the moment when we might have said something. It would mean giving recognition to the connection that existed between us, just from knowing each other's names, recognizing each other's faces, from having exchanged conversations about this and that. He might have said, "Are you OK?" I might have said, "Did you hear? It's so sad, isn't it?" But it was impossible to voice whatever it was we were feeling just then, and in a split second Don had turned his eyes back to the road and pulled the bus to the stop.

"Goodnight, Don," I found myself saying, his name feeling like water to my dry mouth; like safety, human kindness, friendship—all the things that can expel fear. Just for a second, as I stepped off the bus, I was unafraid, and then as my foot touched the ground, the terror of the empty, unknown night outside returned. I was running before I had decided to run, my laptop bag full of files, banging against my side, shifting around uncomfortably. Suddenly, I reached the house but I could not run past. I stopped still in front of the heartbreaking shrine of flowers and bears, photos, cards and melted candles. As I looked at the photos of the man—unbearably young, smiling at life—and his dog, I forced myself to be angry instead of afraid. I made myself *wait* there a moment, to look around and take the scene in on my own time, pay silent respect to the victim. Only then did I walk, walk, walk slowly home. Remembering that every alley was a place where kids played, not where unknown terror waited. I walked, my heart pounding against my chest, the three blocks to my house. This was my neighborhood, my street, my home, and I told myself that nothing was going to make me feel so helpless and undone, again.

I thought about how unforgivable it was—*the Young Latino Male, the White Male*—my seeing them so differently in an instant of fear, feeling suddenly like a woman alone and vulnerable. I only ever noted gender the way I did tonight, when I was scared. I only ever deliberated color and race when I was afraid. Each time it was because something happened to trigger my prejudice—being lost somewhere new without a map late at night, hearing about some meaningless death like this. It had taken me my whole life to understand that it is prejudice itself, if you let it in at times like this that feeds the fear, and not the other way around.

I recognized that in my neighborhood an unknown assailant likely would be male, definitely young, probably black, and maybe Latino. There weren't too many muggings or car break-ins carried out by old men, women, or white people around here. If I lived in Texas, all bets would be off, it seemed that white people—women and men—were shooting each other to pieces or beating their kids to pulp every day.

But how I survived, how I lived in this city, was by choosing not to use that information to walk around suspecting any man I passed on the street the way I did tonight. I had worked hard to place trust before fear. I had learnt to talk to someone new before they talked to me. This was what I did for a living, every day. I believed in people even before, even after, they showed me who they really were, handing out abundant second chances if they screwed up the first few times. Not just so I could do my work, not just to get by; so that I could believe in myself. Because we all deserve that chance, not to be judged too harshly in a moment of rash ignorance.

That night my terror had been different though, it had won over my carefully, painstakingly cultivated sense of blended fearlessness and rationality. Although the man had been shot dead, nothing was taken—neither his wallet, nor his watch; even the dog had been spared. His family and friends, the police, were hurt and confused by what was left behind. Nothing was taken from the Young White Male except his life.

"What's wrong?" Ian asked as soon as he saw me walk in. "Did something happen to you?" He got up from where he had been watching TV.

"I was just there, where the man with his dog was shot."

"I didn't know if you knew."

"I was so scared, and I don't even know what of."

"I know," he said, "I felt that too."

As we stepped closer and held each other we both silently acknowledged what had been shared between us; what it is to be a man walking alone, what it is to be a woman walking alone. What fears, what prejudices, if you allow them in, can stalk a person alone. I looked out past Ian to our neighbors' houses across the street where the street lamps cast silver pools of light on the sidewalks, and I was relieved that I had walked, not run, home to Ian in the late, still night.

OF THE LINES WE CHOOSE TO CROSS

It is not light that we need, but fire; it is not the gentle shower, but thunder. We need the storm, the whirlwind, and the earthquake.

Frederick Douglass

As I headed up to the Metro to meet Luther at his apartment, I reflected on the paralyzing fear that took hold of me just nights before, walking this same street. I looked around and reluctantly acknowledged that the recent murder here was not hanging in the air, it had not slowed the pace of the neighborhood. Enduring sorrow was a burden known only by the victim's family and friends. Life for the rest of us would go on just as before, even though we were one less as a community, and we now knew for certain that a murderer lived amongst us. I learnt long ago to set my worst fears aside, to take Washington as it is and to believe that whatever happens here, the city has a good heart. It was the only way I could ever have traveled so far and wide. And so other than a creeping tiredness that was starting to set in, I allowed myself that I was actually feeling pretty good tonight about having a chance to turn all the research I'd done recently into action on Oxon Cove.

The rain was falling as I left the Anacostia Metro station, surrounded by commuters and children on their way home from work and school; a sea of black faces, black umbrellas. When I got to Luther's apartment, I hesitated, willing myself to knock but unable to move. I knew what was at stake here; I was no fool. If I walked through the door, there was no going back, not with someone like Luther.

When I finally tapped lightly on his door, he was there in moments to open it.

"Come in, meet my nephew, Kumar."

Kumar—about two years old, still chubby-legged and pouty-lipped, my favorite age for any kid—and Anita were playing with building blocks on the floor of the living room.

"Anita, hi, I didn't know you'd be here tonight. Hello little guy, you are very cute."

"Oh, hi Linda. We can head out now, Luther," Anita said, as she started to gather up Kumar's toys. I helped him tip some last few blocks into his toy truck then taking him by the hand, I led him slowly to the door while Anita leant down to give Luther a kiss. "See you later."

I looked at Luther but he was giving nothing away so I took a second to stow my umbrella and glance around. The walls of the living room were still covered with the butcher-block paper from our most recent organizing session. I had turned all the ideas that came out of that meeting into an updated campaign blueprint, which I now handed to Luther. As he read over it, he confirmed that the ideas were all there and one by one, tore down the huge sheets of paper.

"You are—going to recycle those?" I told him, as I watched him head for the kitchen trash.

"Yeah. Yeah, of course." He stopped still, and awkwardly laid the crumpled sheets on the kitchen counter.

"Sorry to be so pious—it's second nature. Recycling, I mean, not—uh—piety."

Luther nodded, smiling. "So what else have you got?"

We sat at the kitchen table together and we carefully reviewed our campaign strategy. We had clearly identified key targets, a timeline for each of our objectives, a core group of volunteers with duties assigned, and I had prepared a detailed budget, that I now shared with him. A large part of my time this week was occupied by grant writing and making calls to old donor friends to see if we couldn't infuse the campaign with cash. Anita's organization that she founded many years ago, The Concerned Citizens Group, was now my official employer. I had not yet found the courage to suggest to Anita that they needed a more exciting name if they ever hoped to raise any serious money. The group could scarcely afford to handle the Windsor Apartments campaign, let alone the prison fight and I had been unpaid since I came on board. Since I needed to raise the funds for the campaigns and for my own salary, as tedious as fundraising was, it had become somewhat personal. The organization did receive a check from Jonathan and his wife last week, for

$300, but I hadn't deposited it yet—I was hoping we never needed to—I regarded it as a good luck totem, to be shredded one happy day when we would be flush with cash. The check was stapled to the budget and Luther spotted it.

"Aren't you going to deposit that? It's got to be half your salary at least."

"Very funny. Anyway, so how do you think I'm doing—do I meet your standards?"

Luther was unexpectedly quiet.

"You're not even paying me," I joked, but he didn't take the bait. I hadn't felt this way, so eager to get it right with someone, since I first met Jonathan, years ago. What was driving me was knowing, just as I had with Jonathan, that this unique human connection, if we could piece it together, nurture it, hold onto it, had the potential to both improve and meld our lives' once incongruent paths.

"I've already started on the lobby packet," I said, shifting the silence aside, returning to the work in hand. I handed him a very rough draft copy. "And here's a first shot at a Council resolution. I'm sure your legal eyes will be all over that."

"Well, good. This is all excellent work."

"So what now?"

"I think the group's first instincts were good—we have to go all out to kill this prison in Zoning. Some of the council members have too much at stake to get involved, even if this is a D.C. Statehood plum ripe for the picking. It's going to be hard to get the resolution passed—we should still try—but our focus is the Zoning Commission."

Luther was right of course. We were facing a team of giants in Congress who had, for their own personal reasons, chosen to rally around this really mediocre backwater cause. There were scarcely any D.C. council members with the ability or desire to stand up to the Senate Majority Leader and his cronies. Then there was the issue of the prison itself. It would get built; no one doubted that. If we kicked it out of Ward 8, there were other city wards, notably 5, 6 and 7, their demographics almost as suitable—black and poor—where the prison could still be built. The council members for these wards would be reluctant to open a debate about where a new prison should be built, even if it meant defying

Congress and giving D.C. voters the right to decide. For them, a prison in Ward 8, as dictated by Congress, was better than risking having the prison built in their own backyards.

I gave Luther a summary of all the documents that I had reviewed over the past few weeks and he turned away after he ran his eyes down the full list of Members of Congress who conspired on the land swap amendment. As though still trying to parse the full meaning of what he had learned, when he spoke again his voice was hollowed out with disgust.

"It's amazing how green the waters in America really are, when you think about it. Money flows from every direction all the way to Congress and baptizes even the toughest nonbelievers, who born again, rise up to support—what? Just about anything that pays well enough. Why else this? Why else a private prison, *here*?"

I shrugged. My anger was days old, already stale. I had come to accept what Catherine had argued all along. That America is just a giant, irresistible, apple pie. Congress carves it into tinier and tinier slices, every year. Sweet little slithers served into the mouths of whoever writes the biggest check.

Luther held the amendment up to me. "This is so wrong. *So wrong.*"

We didn't want to take on Congress, and as it turned out it was too late anyway. The amendment had already passed and the land deal was already in motion. We could, however, target the private prison corporation directly and challenge them at the Zoning Commission hearings that were required before the company could break ground. We were hoping and praying that no commissioner in their right minds would give approval for a private prison to be built on public parkland, on a river, in one of the most economically depressed black communities in America. But the prison corporation was likely ready for the fight, especially after having secured the land so effortlessly.

"Are you ready to take on Randy Weaver?" Luther asked me.

Like countless players in D.C. politics, Randy Weaver was a figure who engendered both admiration and horror and who loved the smell of money. His so-called law firm, a lobby firm that worked the D.C. council, the suburban Maryland and Virginia councils, and Congress, touted itself as the only minority-run firm, *of its kind*. Weaver never defined what kind that was, on any of his advertising materials or anyplace else, so I always assumed he meant the *sleazy and self-serving kind*, because there were plenty of honorable minority-owned law firms in town. He lobbied on behalf of a whole range of shady individuals and businesses looking to fleece the local and federal governments at any given opportunity. This campaign, if nothing else, was going to be a thrill of a ride.

"Looking forward to it. Bring him on. He'll be a lightning rod for activists for our campaign."

"You really enjoy this don't you?"

"Hey, I just like an enemy who's you know, unambiguously, unequivocally, a total bastard. A person who's even a little bit likeable has always been my downfall."

Luther laughed. "Go home. This is good work. We're done for tonight."

"Can't—what about the elephant in the room?"

He threw his hands up and glanced around as though to say, *I don't see any elephant here.*

"Luther, I *have* to defer to you on this. What are we going to do about the prisoners? How do we make sure the prison doesn't end up in Ohio or Minnesota or some other place no one will ever visit them again?"

Luther nodded as though to reassure me that I was right to have brought the subject up. He must have known this was where he might lose me. When he spoke, his voice was different, as though he knew he needed to reach and lift me up gently, to bring me back on board.

"We keep to our story, Linda, that's all. D.C. has the right to decide, for itself, if it wants a prison, and where it should go. Without interference from Congress. No private prisons. And that this is an environmental justice issue. They wouldn't pull this kind of stunt in a white neighborhood, so don't do it here. Parkland not prisons. Schools not jails."

I heard him, knowing that everything he said was right, but still unconvinced.

"You and I both know that for the prisoners to have a hope in hell of ever getting out and leading a normal life, they *need* to be close to family. We need to embrace that idea at least and explore what it means for our campaign. Otherwise we're going to lose half the community's support—and I think we'll have failed to get this right, even if we win."

Luther shook his head. "There are four schools within a mile of that site. We stop this prison. We focus on the next generation *before* they get locked up. This generation—" He was reluctant or unable to finish his thought.

In so many ways I knew he was right. This was a neighborhood that had seen too much crime already and that really didn't need a brand new state-of-the-art prison looming over its dilapidated, failing schools. I stood up to leave.

"Hey, Linda, we have some serious coalition building to do, O.K? The prisoners' families will be part of that, I promise you. And I'll get to work finding out what the community in P.G. County is thinking. This prison will be close to them too."

"This has been good, thanks," I said, but before I could let myself out, he wheeled himself over to me to shake hands. I was uncomfortable looking down at him. At the stables, I used to get down to eye level with the disabled kids; it meant the world to them. Now as I looked down at Luther, I saw his wheelchair for the first time. *Really* saw it—past the commanding, invulnerable man that Luther was—and I allowed myself to wonder what life must be like for him. Every day. What the first time he saw the wheelchair must have felt like, knowing he would never again be without it.

"Promise me one thing," Luther said, with a tone of voice that made me imagine him in that moment when he was seventeen, caught out by stray bullets in a random act of horrific violence. His voice was soft, serious, hoarse, uneven. I can recall it at any moment and it will elicit the same emotion—awe for how human beings go on when life demands of them to give up. "You'll stick this out."

He had laid down the gauntlet, as I knew he would. I was not sure what kind of promise I could make just then—campaigns can drag on for months, even years—but I knew what Luther was asking from me was only fair, what he was really asking of me.

"I will. You can't get rid of me now."

"Good, *go.*"

On the Metro home from Luther's apartment, there was an ocean of black faces all around me again. Not a single white person other than me, to be seen. You can only think two things in a moment like that.
1. Ununited States of America.
2. What difference can I possibly hope to make?

OF A BOY WHO SAYS YES TO LIFE

your wit and
nervous laughter,

bouquets for the rainy winters
of your friends

                                            Reuben Jackson

Having made progress with Luther on the prison campaign, I knew it was time to meet with Anita about our Windsor Apartments strategy. But first, I had an important promise to keep. I arranged to meet Damien at a cafe in Eastern Market after school one day. Ever since my first time here all those years ago, horribly lost, late for my interview, the neighborhood had held a special place in my heart. The picturesque, mostly well-preserved townhouses and storefronts, many with carefully tended flower-boxes spilling mounds of gorgeous colors out into the tree-lined streets and sidewalk cafes, made up the kind of neighborhood many people look for when they live in a historic city like Washington. So far, its revival had not chased away all of its original residents; I knew of many low-income families still living in their original townhomes throughout the neighborhood, fifty years behind them, and no sign as yet of being forced out by the tides of change. It could be done, it seemed. Restoration of heart, soul, and all that is manmade at once. The romantic in me couldn't help but hope for a similar sense of place and good health to be restored to each and every one of Washington's distinct neighborhoods, no matter their current wounds and gaunt forms. I sat drinking my coffee waiting for Damien and noticed that all around me were faces of every color out on the sidewalks; something inside of me hummed to see this, like everything in the world was right at last and the sound and rhythm of it was just perfect.

    Damien had been ecstatic to hear from me, eager to get to work. We chose to meet at a popular, little restaurant with local artists' work hanging on the original, exposed brick walls. I noticed a black and white photo of a Safeway grocery bag, full of produce, sitting on a weathered doorstep, with a full-color bunch of flowers lying beside it. It had been six years since Ward 8's only grocery store closed; I wondered how many people had seen the photo and thought, 'Oh, cool.'

When Damien arrived at the cafe, his book bag was open, and he pulled some files out as he approached, seeming to fill the place up immediately. He was smiling and cracking jokes with the waiter, as he sat down.

"Linda, what you got fo' me?" he said, sliding his huge frame into the suddenly tiny wooden chair opposite me. He dumped his schoolwork on the table and got to work before I had a chance to answer him.

"I'm listenin'. Don't worry."

He filled out math worksheets, sweeping effortlessly across and down the page, and after he finished each section, he stopped to place his forefinger on each answer while he checked it over. I watched a while and then, when he looked up frowning, expecting me to start, I ran him briefly through the meeting with Luther, and suggested to him that he and his friends could get going on the publicity for the campaign.

"You mean design fliers an' all? Tha's cool. Theo's into that—he's really good."

He asked me to hold on a sec as he finished his third and final page of math and then, pushing the work aside, he took the list of upcoming events we had planned for the campaign and read it over: a series of open meetings, a community walk to Oxon Cove, and a big family picnic to be held just before the Zoning Hearings. We discussed the campaign message, talking points, we drafted a list of sound bites, and we brainstormed about graphics that could be incorporated into all our materials.

"Tha' bridge at Oxon Cove—I'm tellin' you, tha's our logo."

"Why? Are we *building bridges in the community*?" I teased him. "That's just *cheese*, Damien. But I love it."

"Iss not cheesy, iss cool. We're buildin' bridges and the other side's buildin' prisons. Who'd you vote for?"

I couldn't argue with that.

"You know I'm only in this 'cos of Luther, right? He said this campaign is abou' rebuildin' the community. Helpin' it heal. Makin' it strong. I'm in. If this was just another one o' them help stop this or tha' trainwreck comin' our way, I wouldn' be sittin' in Eastern market wiv a white chick right now." He grinned. "I'd be hangin' wiv Theo."

"Offense taken. No problem."

"You know what sellin' short is?"

"What, you mean like stocks?"

"Yeah, we're learnin' about it in finance class. One of my teachers, he's *mad* abou' money—checks his stocks all day in school. He taught us about it. You know wha' it means?"

"No, sorry, I have no clue. I'm hopeless at math. And if it's stocks, it's got to be math."

"Well, we're not goin' to do it, iss all I'm sayin'. We're not sellin' short. We're not stoppin' after the prison's dead and we've saved Windsor Apartments. *Tha's not enough*. Understand what I'm sayin?"

I could listen to Damien all day, really I could, and I'd be a believer. He had his own agenda, which was great—it would keep him motivated. He volunteered his friends to spend time on the weekends handing out materials at the Metro and bus stations, library, community center, local churches; he was overflowing with enthusiasm and ideas.

"This is good," he said, sitting back, satisfied that we had made so much progress. "Weaver ain't gonna ge' away wiv this. We gonna kick his ass."

I could see now that I wouldn't be calling Damien every day to remind him what he needed to do; he embraced his campaign responsibilities and his energy was magnetic. As I smiled to myself at what a pleasure it was to work with him, he leaned in and knocked on the table.

"So Linda, what *you* gonna' be doin' in the meantime? What we payin' you fo' anyway?"

We both laughed. The kid was unstoppable.

"Oh, I'll be sitting here drinking lattes while you and your friends do all the work," I told him, and just to emphasize the point, I ordered another coffee.

"No, fo' real? I wanna see the whole picture."

I told Damien about the outreach work I was planning and how I'd be working to sign up as many people as possible to testify at the Zoning Commission hearings.

"What 'bout the lobbyin'? The resolution?"

"Luther and I are going to help a cross-section of community residents to prepare for council member visits—" Suddenly I saw where he was going with this. "You want to *join us*?! Damien, you could be the *voice of the youth*. That would be fantastic!"

"Wha' d'ya mean, could be? I *am* the voice of the youth!" he said indignantly, smiling nonetheless. "Iss my fallin' apar' school they gittin' ready to build that fancy prison next to. Iss my statistical ass they gittin' ready to lock up."

He laughed. He had gotten what he came for—to be a part of something bigger.

"I'm working on the lobby packets already, but hey, you want to be Mr. Lobbyist, you need to help. You need to know, start to finish, what it takes."

"Sign me up. I'm here."

I pulled out the draft lobby kit I had prepared and I started to talk him through it, but he interrupted me.

"We need letters—righ' up fron' in the packet—we gotta get people to write they think this prison's a bad idea. I'll write one. I'll get a bunch of folks to."

He was a step behind me; I had already started gathering letters in opposition to the prison. For once, the Mayor was making our lives easier. Greg had already secured a promise from him that he would send us a letter opposing the prison in Ward 8. No great surprise; we all knew a prison did not exactly fit in with the Mayor's grand scheme for east of the river, but useful nonetheless.

I nodded to Damien and gave nothing away. He was *thinking* like a professional organizer, best to let his ideas flow, even if they were not entirely novel. It was fantastic to watch. I only wished Luther were there to see it. Damien was *this generation*—the one Luther was talking about the other night. And if he was a sign of things to come, then things were definitely looking up. I decided to put him to the test. We talked about the prisoners' families and what he thought a good outreach strategy should be. Damien didn't hesitate. He got straight to the heart of the matter. We need to keep the prisoners close to home, he said, but D.C. should decide where the prison gets built, not Congress.

"An' definitely not on Oxon Cove. Tha's jus' the dumbest idea I eva heard!" He leaned back. "I been back there with Theo. Seen that eagle again. An' turtles. I ain't neva seen turtles like tha' in the Anacostia. The water must be betta in the creek. Tha's somethin'."

After a while we talked about ourselves, and I learned that Damien was seeing a girl called Sheryl, that Theo was his best friend, and that he was trying for a scholarship to college. He wanted to learn about water, how to clean up rivers and make the oceans healthy again.

"I grown up by the Anacostia. Issa mess, iss jus' a sad mess. It'd be nice if we could clean it up, I mean *really* clean it up."

It was refreshing to hear him talk so self-assuredly of the possibilities that awaited him outside of school. I told him more about Ian and Sandra and what I'd been doing for the past eight years since I moved to D.C. Then the thought occurred to me that there were some people Damien ought to meet; I would put off telling him until I had spoken with them. There was no door that I wouldn't open for him, if I possibly could. He was on a journey of self-discovery well beyond his years and he had both the ability and the desire to take others along with him.

I realized it was time for me to go home to my family. I hadn't tucked Sandra into bed all week. I had seen her briefly in the mornings, before school, and she was asleep by the time I returned from work each night. Someone must have been doing right by Damien for him to be this great a kid. It was time for me to do right by Sandra.

"See you, Damien. I've got to go home and find out what selling short means. Make sure you don't do it to me when I'm not looking."

He slapped me hard on the back and I slammed both hands on the table to stop myself from falling.

"You're not going to stop doing that are you?"

"Nope," he said, with that great big smile of his, shining with eagerness and confidence, the smile of a born leader.

OF ALL THAT NEEDS TENDING TO

For I am my mother's daughter, and the drums of Africa still beat in my heart. They will not let me rest while there is a single Negro boy or girl without a chance to prove his worth.
                                            Mary McLeod Bethune

I arranged to meet Anita at the church on South Capitol where she worked. She greeted me at the side entrance and we followed a long, dull pink corridor, with chronically peeling paint and noticeboards crammed with fliers, towards her office. The church was struggling to survive but it had a loyal and historic following and whatever funds they were able to raise were evidently turned back into the community where the money was needed most. I could smell lunch being prepared in the kitchen down in the basement, and we passed several rooms with clothes, diapers, toys and books stacked and stored waiting for distribution. I heard Bach coming from somewhere in the building, the music floated over us, uplifting and melancholy all at once. We arrived at Anita's office; it was cramped and cluttered, not at all what I would expect of her.

"Excuse the mess," she said. "We're changing all the offices around. Mine is being repainted at last and we're about to receive a donation of refurbished furniture from a local law office."

"I knew this wasn't your style," I said.

She looked at me and smiled; I suspected, like me, she was wondering at the natural familiarity that had existed between us from the first.

"How did your meeting with Luther go?"

"Very well, excellent in fact. Damien too. He gets MVP already. Don't worry about the prison. We have no intention of letting Randy Weaver win. Anyway, looks like you have enough work to do here."

Anita told me more about her job. She was the intake coordinator, interviewing people who came in off the streets asking for help. She worked hard to find them the help and information that they needed, trying to set lives that had been severely derailed back on course. I did a similar job once, for a couple of years, as a volunteer in college. After I saw the woman evicted from my building, I found a job at a local community center doing intake in the evenings. I had no idea how bad it was out there for people in my own neighborhood until I sat, hour after hour, watching and listening to people unravel their life stories in front of me. And when they were done, they would ask me for my help and I learnt to draw on strengths I never even knew I had. I never knew how clever and kind and determined I could really be, until I started working relentlessly to make sure that I did not fail the people who walked in that door. I came to understand, as I sat alone in the office at night after everyone had left, and carefully reviewed those harrowing case files, that the still, silent pool of hope from which I had drawn my whole life had been forever made turbulent. Hope was no longer a place for comfort and contemplation; it had become an engine for action and driven me on and on, relentlessly, ever since.

Anita and I got to work reviewing the Windsor Apartment campaign strategy. Anita had put together a group of volunteers who had agreed to canvas the building to find out who lived in each apartment, what their circumstances were, their financial status, and prospects for finding a new home if the building was redeveloped.

"I'm quite looking forward to it," Anita said. "It'll be an opportunity to meet more of my neighbors, and to let them know what's going on. Of course we'll talk to them about the prison too."

"Listen, Anita." I hesitated. "When you do the interviews—you need to—you're going to have to find out about past convictions, fraud, bad credit. Anything like that."

A frown settled across her soft face; it suited her poorly. Her dark eyes glanced away; she looked angry.

"I've—I've been down this road before. If we end up using any form of public financing to save the building—which granted, we may not—but if we do pull off a tenant takeover, there can be problems. With felony convictions especially, but also credit status, personal bankruptcies, fraud. There are many ways to make a whole lot of people who will have nowhere to go ineligible to stay, and we have to try at least, to prevent that." She did not answer. I needed to make it sound as though we had more control. "We just have to be prepared to fight for all the tenants and we can't—we just can't—have any surprises when it comes time to negotiate."

"Just *hazard* a guess," Anita said, "what percentage of my building do you think have served time, have gotten themselves into debt, have bad credit ratings?"

"I can't say. I have some idea. I mean, I could guess."

This wasn't entirely truthful; the statistics were etched on my heart. *Thirty-six percent of Ward 8 below the poverty line. $19,000 average income for a family of four. Forty-one percent of African American men, ages 18-35 destined for incarceration. Fifteen percent owner-occupied homes. Forty percent of kids don't graduate high school...*

"You'd better be prepared to go to the mat on this Linda, because trust me, there'll be a lot of people to, as you say, *fight* for."

"You bet," I told her, my voice soft and reassuring. "That's what I'm here for."

Inside I felt strangely hollow though, I had no upbeat happy endings playing out in my head. If I allowed myself to think on the numbers, the numbers confounded me. Jonathan had taught me to see past the numbers—to see individual potential, the unshakable sense of belonging, the desire and capability for renaissance, and the immeasurable spirit that resided in his community. But if I did allow myself to stop and look at the numbers, I saw a community awash in waste, failure and profound, abiding pain. Anita simply wanted us to fight for a lucky few. I could do that. Of course I would. But then what?

Walking away from the church to the bus stop, I watched people pass me by, a blur of black faces, and I wondered if it had at last started to happen. I think I have always feared that the potent mix of disquiet and hope that drive my work might eventually start to dissolve and disappear. I'd just grow tired of fighting and worrying, or worse, I'd stop believing that anything was ever really going to change and if it did, it wouldn't be because of anything I had done. I'd start to doubt that I could be useful or effective anymore, and I'd retreat back into a much simpler world on the other side of the river. A place where school events and playdates,

Ian's schedule and where to go on vacation, what new movies are out and what to do on the weekends, would suddenly seem so much more important than the work I did. Maybe it was because Luther told me we must focus on the next generation, and Anita believed you must not give up on this one, maybe it was because I was so damn tired today, I headed home listening to the silence in my head. No great ideas of where to go from here came to me.

At home, Sandra, who had been busy making cookies with the babysitter, greeted me with her best, "*Mm-o-mm-eee!*" She came running to hug me and pummeled me with a barrage of sweet, sticky, chocolate kisses. I turned to the babysitter and I spoke too harshly, but I couldn't help it, I just wanted her out of my house; I wanted my child and my house to myself.

"You can go now. Thanks, I'm home for the afternoon."

She didn't seem to catch my tone and she seemed happy to leave early. Maybe because I paid her anyway for the hours she was supposed to have worked today, or maybe because she saw Sandra's joy and ignored my rudeness.

Sandra was clinging to my leg as I closed the front door behind the babysitter.

"Mommy," she said, and that was enough.

We headed back to the kitchen where Sandra brought me up to speed on the situation. They had not finished mixing the ingredients. I could take over. I could be Mommy and make cookies with my daughter and I was so delighted I swept Sandra up and we danced together while the cookies baked in the oven.

Ian came home and was surprised to see me. We hardly ever saw each other before nine—he traveled, I had meetings, he had meetings—and yet there we were, at six thirty, and we were all together, the three of us. The day had cooled off and Ian decided to light a fire, summer be damned, and we had chocolate chip cookies for dinner. When Luther called me later I told him what we were doing and he laughed. I could hear him hesitate, about to ask something of me, but then he said, "Just calling to say hi."

Ian and I tucked Sandra into bed after reading her a pile of books and then we headed downstairs to clean up the mess in the kitchen. But we could not wait a moment longer, so we left the dishes and we made love instead, and when we were done, we laughed and kissed and held each other and the night seemed as though it would truly, just this one time, last forever.

OF THE SENTRIES AT THE GATES

That Justice is a blind goddess
Is a thing to which we black are wise;
Her bandage hides two festering sores
That once perhaps were eyes.
                            Langston Hughes

But the night didn't last forever. The sunlight crept into the bedroom around six o'clock, finding its way under, through and around the window-blinds. Not enough to wake me, enough for me to begin to leave my dreams behind. A slight breeze wisped the blinds forward and away from the windowpanes; the pure morning light, warm and soft, now fell directly on my face, my eyes filled with its glow. The sound of sparrows, in the eaves above the bedroom, started to escalate. Brighter and brighter, bold and golden, the light now played on the walls as I drifted through the last remnants of sleep—startling, vivid images of Sandra and Ian chasing the surf at a beach. It didn't seem possible that none of it was real, that I could be slumbering through the roar of the ocean and the rush of salty wind over my skin. I could feel my own happiness even as I watched myself, running beside them, in my dreams.

I was smiling into the sun, still not quite awake, when I became aware of a weight, a heavy ball on my stomach and I lifted my head up from its perfect rest, for a while dreaming what I thought I saw, then imagining what I saw, and finally seeing what I could see: my little girl sleeping with her head on my stomach, her feet resting across her father's legs.

A nascent sense of responsibility forced me to look away and read the blurry numbers on the clock. While I recognized the individual characters I hesitated to put the final result together. I laid my head back down on the pillow and placed a hand under Sandra's head to slightly shift the weight on my bladder—anything to delay leaving this place. I closed my eyes and felt full sunlight and warm air flowing through the open window. No more the cool breezes of night and the intangible sun of early dawn, it was the already breathing light and air of a working morning that now fell on me and I knew I had to get up.

Saturday mornings were now unprotected. Once the sacred meeting place for Ian and I, a place no one else dare enter or disturb, Saturday mornings were now scheduled into my calendar as regularly as any day of the workweek. I tried to show discretion in sacrificing them, but I was losing the fight to save them. I showered myself awake and then tiptoed around the bedroom looking for my clothes and jewelry. I stopped at the bed and lightly kissed Ian. As I leaned across him to kiss Sandra, my little girl startled me by sitting upright and asking sleepily yet excitedly, if she could have breakfast with me, as though she had surprised herself by remembering to wake up in time.

I lazily prepared breakfast for the two of us, taking my time, delaying my departure. Sandra asked me questions about everything I was doing; she too was extending our time together. She didn't offer to set the table as usual, or ask to help, leaving all the preparations to me; she knew this would mean more time together. The unspoken understanding was to own the morning. She was clever; she asked for eggs and oatmeal—the stovetop kind, not the overly sweet, instant packages that she and Ian both like. I knew Sandra's game because she asked me for toast too, even though she really liked her eggs on soft, white bread. We were stretching out the morning together and it was a perfect, secret respite from the day that lay ahead for me.

Sandra lifted her knee to her chin and played with her sandal strap.

"Don't worry about me and Daddy, Mommy. We're going to do lots of fun stuff."

"What have you two decided to do?"

"Daddy said he's going to, um, take me, to the, to the—*playground*!"

The destination burst from my daughter's lips like a rocket launched into a limitless sky.

"Really? You are such a lucky girl."

"And he said we'd work on the garden too! I can help him! And I can use his tools—*all* Daddy's tools!"

"*All* his tools?"

"Um-hmm. And he's going to take me to the hardware store, which means we have to go to the bakery! I haven't decided, but I think I may get the sugar cookie this time. Or a lemon square. But Daddy always gets a lemon square, so I could just have some of his...I wonder if he'll take me to the library?"

The rocket howled wildly upwards now, with the whole world below it. Ian and Sandra's day ahead roared away from me, with everything that was good and vital and perfect in life on board.

Then, before leaving, the still surprising, eagerly anticipated, round of *I Love You*. Heartfelt, burning, *I Love You*'s, chanted over and over again, that until now I didn't even know could be said with so much pain and joy, blended like two primary colors, into an entirely different emotion altogether.

"Mommy, I love you."

"I love you too, little one."

"Oh, but Mama, I *really* love you."

"And I *really* love you too."

And hugs that were astonishing for their strength. Little hands locked around the back of my neck. Tiny arms clasped around my back and squeezed tight. Kisses everywhere—kisses on bellies and feet and eyes. And all the while, *I Love You* poured into my ears, drenching my heart with joy. Madness, really, how much love there is in the world. How much togetherness and how much loneliness. If Sandra's innocence, her perfect love, could be sprinkled over the earth like magic dust how quickly the world's troubles would disappear. *Just-one-more-hug* and *just-one-more-kiss*. P-lease Mommy.

I left the house, walked up the still-quiet street and descended into the cool, dark underground Metro station. The escalating rumble of the approaching train, the eerie yellow flashing floor-lights, and the chimes of the doors opening, cued me to think again of my work—that it had value, that it was worthy of being torn away from a warm Saturday morning in a sunlit bedroom—and my regrets diminished. I stepped onto the train and there were weary faces all around me. Saturday work was no stranger here; the warm beds left behind for jobs in suburban malls and museums and grocery stores, libraries and hotels could be seen in the half-open eyes and the tired, swaying shoulders unable to resist the motion of the train. I pulled out my meeting notes and thought no more of Ian and Sandra.

The room was packed, standing room only. We were in the basement of Anita's church, and we were about to start our first large-scale open meeting on the Oxon Cove and Windsor campaigns. Damien and his friends did a monumental job with the publicity for the event and it had paid off. Word of the private prison spread like wildfire through the community and people were here looking for information and answers. You could feel the energy thickening the air in the room, the anticipation and excitement rising as Anita opened the meeting.

This is the defining moment in any campaign, when a community that until recently was unaware of the enemy at the gates, is given the grave news. The moment when the sentries, the small group of individuals who make it their business to protect those gates, must relay the situation back to the people and hope that they will rise up to defend themselves and their neighborhood.

Luther and Anita presented the facts, as we knew them. There were gasps and shaking heads all around the room. There were '*Lord have mercy*'s, '*That ain't right!*'s and '*nnn-nnn*'s. I sat on the little stage at the front of the room and I watched the news sink in. And it is sickeningly cliché and exposes my persistent naiveté, but it happened again. Nina Simone was there in my head. *I wish I knew how it would feel to be free. I wish I could live like I'm longing to live*. The words that define the madness of the never-ending African American experience—the freedom that isn't truly free, the equality that isn't really equal, the opportunities that when you look closely aren't, weren't ever, really there. It was, as Luther said, *so wrong* that the people in this room had to give up another minute, another hour, another day of their lives, to fight to be free, that the fight is always so petty and weighty at the same time. That so much energy had to be tapped from the people here, to fight a proposal that should never have seen the light of day, that the prison had to be fought and stopped just so they could face the next threat head-on, and the next one after that. And always, the threat of losing their homes hanging over them: the ultimate failure, the ultimate loss, the ultimate humiliation—*to have nowhere to go*.

I stood to give my presentation and I remembered that I was one of the lucky ones. I got to talk about all the things that could be done to instill hope instead of fear, to make it seem as though it would all be O.K., after all. My language was the language of action, of doing, of resistance, of change, of never giving up. I saw the trust rise in the eyes of the people around the room as I talked of all the things we had done already, all that we were planning to do, to stop the prison and save their homes.

"Why is she here?"

The question soared across the room, stopping me mid-sentence. I looked at Anita, and then at Luther; Anita smiled, Luther nodded lightly. They were closing ranks around me.

"Anita, I don't mean any disrespect to the lady but she doesn't live here, and she's not *known* to me. How do we know that—that the Zoning Commission is the best place to fight this prison?"

There were murmurs around the room, but no signs yet of this being common dissent. Best not to say anything, best let this man get it all out.

"I want to be in on these meetings you've been having and I want to have my say in how we go about this whole thing."

I weighed the speaker up, getting ready to respond. The man could be one of only two kinds of activist. Years ago, Richard and I came reeling out of a terrible meeting, where we were attacked from every side for not having involved the community in the decision making process for a campaign we had only just initiated. We had called the meeting to bring the community in, and yet we had been accused of not bringing the community in. It was a terrifying, surreal experience and we'd both been shaken up by it. We found solace in a night's worth of tequila shots that had me throwing up and sick to my stomach for days. But we had successfully defined that there are only two kinds of activist in the world: the *eagle*, and the *yellow-bellied sapsucker*.

The eagle is the hard-working volunteer who when pointed in the right direction, will soar to great heights, putting all their energy into helping win a campaign. The yellow-bellied sapsucker is the person who is eager to criticize what everyone else is doing, but who will never actually help out or show their support. They peck away at the campaign, sucking at its sap, but underneath they're too scared to take action. Unchecked, a sapsucker can overtake a meeting in moments, their negativity draining the energy from a room as they push to invalidate work already done. One minute we can all be having a productive discussion about priorities and assigning responsibilities and the next, the debate shifts to *inclusion* and *transparency* and *authority* and *representation*, all very meaningful, except that this doesn't win campaigns. A sapsucker never does the work that does win campaigns—they never volunteer, they'll never be seen working a phone-bank or handing out fliers at the Metro on a Saturday morning—but they'll flutter regularly into meetings, eager for the sweet sap that rises in a room full of dedicated volunteers who are hard at work. To risk derailing our campaign for someone like that, well I just couldn't let it happen. Tricky part is though, you can't presume to know if someone's an eagle or a sapsucker until you challenge the person to take action.

So here I go.

"Sir, thank you for your comments. We'd love you to join us at our regular Metro events—handing out flyers, 9-2, every Saturday? We could really use your help."

The man was still standing. Everyone awaited his response.

"Oh—err—Saturdays you say," he mumbled. "No, I don't think I'll be able to make those."

"How about evenings?" Luther offered kindly, his tone encouraging and open. "We need help with mailings and phone calls too—any week night—here at the church?"

The man shuffled his feet. "No, I don't think so, timing's a little difficult."

"Call me?" Anita generously put the man out of his misery and he sat back down.

Yellow-bellied sapsucker he is then. And as if I needed confirmation, Damien, proven eagle, stood to present his work on the publicity for the campaign, and to ask for volunteers to help get the word out about our next strategy meeting with the Prince George's community.

At the end of the meeting, there was a surge of energy in the room as people rose to sign up for the work that lay ahead of us. I slowly made my way across the room, shaking hands and greeting people, as I sought out the man who spoke earlier. I introduced myself again and I asked him if there was any part of the campaign he would like to assist us on. Defying reason and instinct, I am pathological in my insistence that everyone deserves another chance. As an organizer, I was born of a second chance. He looked me over and I thought I saw a smile break—his eyes gave it away.

"No, young lady. I think you and Anita and Luther and Charlie," he paused, "and that young man over there," he nodded in Damien's direction, "have this under control for now."

OF HOME

The ache for home lives in all of us. The safe place where we can go as we are and not be questioned.
              Maya Angelou

The next morning I slept in while Ian and Sandra went to the hardware store. When they returned, I discovered that Ian had decided that it was time for me to re-tile the kitchen floor. He had no illusions about how draining campaigns could be and he had seen me fall heavily into my work over the past few weeks, so this, he insisted, would be good for me.

"Come on," he said, "your chance to finish something, beginning to end."

Having tiled many floors in the past, I knew exactly what I was getting myself into, and I stared at the boxes stacked in the dining room with a mixture of disappointment and pleasure. There was always a plus side to working on the house on a solitary project like this: I could listen to my music, as loud as I wanted to. Ian read my mind; he had already set up the iPod dock at the kitchen door. I had to smile at his ingenuity and my vulnerability.

"O.K., I guess I'm tiling the kitchen floor today."

Ian and Sandra would have offered to help except they knew they would either be in my way or they'd go deaf listening to the music. This was where *family as team* ended. Ian had other plans for them anyway, as it turned out. They would be taking on the toilets, changing toilet seats and replacing the flappers. It was going to be a delightful Sunday all around.

I hit shuffle on the iPod and got to work measuring the floor. Ian had for the most part prepped the surface, but here and there I found stubborn chunks of the old linoleum floor that I struggled to remove. When this was done, I lined up the tiles, put the spacers in a bucket where I could easily reach them, mixed my mortar, and the next thing I knew, I was tiling. It was an infinitely satisfying task. The illogical, fresh mix of music that the iPod came up with made the work fly by. I had a rhythm going, repetitive and swift, and the old kitchen floor soon disappeared beneath the tide of red stone rapidly forcing me back towards the door. It took me no more than two hours; there were thankfully very few cuts to make, and then I was done.

I stood up and surveyed my work. The kitchen felt newly welcoming and warm; I wanted to eat off the floor. God, if only life were always this simple. From upstairs, I heard Ian and Sandra laughing, sounding suspiciously as though they were having too much fun and I went to investigate. Sandra had her arms in the toilet tank and was trying to line up the flapper with Ian's encouragement. Apparently, they were not taking the task very seriously—Playmobil people floated happily around in the tank.

"Aren't you supposed to drain the tank before you do that?" I asked, not wanting to break up the fun, but curious nonetheless.

"Daddy let me," Sandra said, with the unassailable logic of a four-year old.

"Let me what?" I asked Ian.

"Oh, you know..."

I picked up Sandra's toy sailboat from the bathtub and dropped it in the tank.

"Just in case one of those little guys needs rescuing. Come see the kitchen when you're, you know, finished *working* here."

"It's done? Can we see?" Ian pulled himself up, grabbed Sandra's hand and they went running downstairs. We admired the floor and then Ian gave me a kiss. "Great work. Happy someone got something done today. Come on, let's go out. Looks like our kitchen is closed."

It was a glorious summer day in Washington; there was no hint of the usual humidity and we decided to walk to Georgetown along Rock Creek. It seemed as though the whole city was out in the park; bikers and joggers regularly swished past us on the trail as Ian and I walked lazily hand-in-hand with Sandra running on ahead. Ian asked me how I was doing. We hadn't really taken stock of all the changes that had taken place in our lives over the past few months, especially with my work. I realized as we talked that I was really very content with where I was. That I had been able to establish an effective, satisfying working relationship with the leaders of both campaigns meant the world to me. But I admitted to Ian that I needed to find a better balance with my work and not push so hard; I didn't like feeling the way I did when I left Anita last week, after the meeting in her office. In my line of work, doubt is poison—corrosive, even deadly—if you let it in. And it usually stemmed from tiredness, plain and simple.

"And what about working alone?" he asked me, "I worry that you're not getting your daily dose of water-cooler gossip."

He teased and probed simultaneously and as usual, he got to the heart of the matter; extracting the truth from me was light work for him.

"I miss *Homes First*, I really do. It's not been easy to leave everyone behind. I even miss all the drama—not about Richard—but the other stuff. Even the board breathing down our necks every two seconds demanding to see *progress*. It made for good laughs. You know WWW called to ask if she could help me with fundraising? She offered to put me in touch with some of her contacts. That made me feel good—like she might actually care about what happens to me now, after all those years of pandering to her every whim."

Ian said nothing; he ran his fingers through mine then held my hand again.

"I haven't really allowed myself to think about what I miss. I love spending so much time across the river though."

I only now realized how true this was; with so many meetings there, I had taken time to wander the neighborhoods, and I found myself often at Oxon Cove. I liked to sit on the bank just below the bridge and listen to and observe the abundant birds, watch the turtles trail their miniature wakes on the water, and breathe the air of hours spent outside instead of indoors. I often biked over to Anacostia Park and had lunch with the river and the city spread out before me. These were freedoms I wasn't expecting and now cherished.

"And what about Richard?"

"Haven't spoken to him." I drew Ian close to me.

"It's a shame," he said.

After a while we reached Georgetown and Sandra was tired, hungry and ornery. She had done a terrific job of walking all the way and allowing Ian and I the freedom to talk, so I bent to her every wish, starting with ice-cream at Thomas Sweets, despite having to wait in the long line that reached out the door and around the corner. We had a very late lunch at a cafe on Wisconsin Avenue and watched the crowds dipping in and out of the chic little boutiques that lined both sides of the streets. I couldn't help thinking that we were a million miles away from Anacostia, and yet just a few miles away.

It took us nearly two hours to walk back home. We played Pooh sticks at every bridge on the creek, and there were many, and Sandra and Ian insisted on trying out every dilapidated piece of equipment on the *Life Circuit* course. Sandra almost pulled her shoulder out hanging from the high bar, too afraid to jump, until Ian came to her rescue. Then they challenged each other to twenty sit-ups each and I watched in amazement as Sandra effortlessly knocked hers off, never stopping to rest. They are such clowns, Ian and Sandra, their energy and silliness a deliciously intoxicating kind of happiness to be around. Just as the sunlight began to soften, we took the trail around the back of the zoo and unexpectedly found Amazonia still open. We slipped in through the exit just as some tourists were leaving and suddenly we were in the rainforest. Cackling cappucin monkeys sat on low branches to either side of us and we watched brilliantly colored birds swoop past and disappear into the kapok trees. I picked Sandra up so that she could get a better look at the bale of hay in the treetops that she was amazed to discover, was really a sloth.

"He looks tired," she said, as she yawned and placed her head on my shoulder.

"All systems shutting down over here," I whispered to Ian, and he reluctantly left the macaw he was watching to hold the door open for me so that I could take Sandra outside. We carried Sandra the rest of the way home and then after getting her to bed, we split off in separate directions to get ready for the week ahead. Ian had a presentation to finish and I had to prep for our upcoming council member visits. I went to the kitchen for water and realized that I couldn't enter because the tile was still setting.

Tomorrow night, I told myself, I will grout the floor and we will use the kitchen again on Wednesday. Now that's the kind of campaign I like. Short, sweet and lots of good music.

OF ROLLING WITH THE PUNCHES

And since you know you cannot see yourself
So well as by reflection, I, your glass,
Will modestly discover to yourself
That of yourself which you yet know not of.
　　　　　　　　　　　　William Shakespeare

Damien stood outside the City Council building, dressed like an Armani model. He had on a midnight blue suit, crisp white button-down shirt and red tie, and had even forgone his precious sneakers for some sharp looking dress shoes. Luther carefully looked him up and down, and just for effect, wheeled around him, whistling a long, slow note of approval.

"So is everyone ready?" I asked.

My role today was part shepherd, part firefighter. I confirmed and coordinated the visits, got everyone to the right offices on time, and then I was supposed to sit back and watch. If the meeting started to go up in flames—someone sidetracked, the council member tried to cut the meeting short, or someone offended the council member—I would do what I could to douse the fire. I would get everyone back on point by throwing in some ready-prepared salient and indisputable facts. Other than that, I observed and took notes as the local residents, whose lives were truly on the line, spoke with the council members.

We had gathered together an impressive crew for the day's lobby visits. Apart from Damien and Luther, two mothers of elementary school children and a retired policeman from the Oxon Cove neighborhood, would be joining us. Each would make their case as to why the prison must be stopped; each had a compelling story to tell.

We kicked off the day in the Ward 5 council member's office. Council member Pryor was the self-appointed king of the minority business community in D.C. We had unexpectedly found success with him in the past on some of our issues but he had also disappointed us with his intractable stand on housing code enforcement and tenant evictions. I knew it was considered ill advised to hold personal opinions about key targets, but I liked Pryor. He had a genuine, honest disposition—no airs and graces, no condescension. If he was somewhat aggressive in trying to establish himself as the minority entrepreneur's council member, well at least he was open and direct about it. My read on him was that he would oppose our resolution. Wards 5 and 6 were the two most likely locations for the prison if it didn't get built in 8. Both these wards had vast tracts of land situated in depressed minority neighborhoods that might be made available for the prison. Nonetheless, Pryor was black, a native son of Washington, an ardent D.C. statehood advocate, and I was certain that he understood what was at stake here.

Damien did a little opening piece about why we requested the meeting, how the youth of Anacostia deserved better than this prison, how he'd taken time out of school to come because it was such an important issue. He was nervous and stumbled over his words but this had the effect of making him all the more endearing and believable. Pryor—his dark, kind face smooth and round, with curiously fine lips that made his smile look like a nearly perfect straight line—sat back in his chair and relaxed, but he never took his deep brown eyes off Damien. He listened attentively, encouraging Damien to go on whenever he faltered. Luther caught my eye; we smiled acknowledgement of this incredibly sweet and satisfying moment to each other.

Next up was Mrs. Jasmine Garrett. Her story was heartbreaking. Her husband was killed in a car accident just over a year before and she described the struggle to raise her three kids ever since. The one thing that made it easier for her to survive was the children's school. The teachers were dedicated and committed and she believed that against all odds, her children were being taught to believe in themselves.

"Now how can they believe in themselves if they walk out of school everyday and see a prison?" She asked this directly of Pryor—matter-of-factly—the absurdity of the situation filling her voice.

Pryor simply nodded, and offered a hushed, "I understand. Thank you for taking the time to come today, Mrs. Garrett."

And so it went on. Very little was said by Pryor, while our team did a stellar job of covering all the arguments against the prison. Luther presented a refined and forceful wrap and then directly asked the council member for his support on the resolution opposing the prison. Pryor didn't disappoint in one way at least—his anticipated honesty.

"I can't possibly support your resolution Luther," he said. "And I think you already knew that."

Luther did not flinch.

"Alan, we know this resolution is going nowhere. We'll defeat the prison anyway. This resolution is your chance to look good on statehood. Your signature on it is a registered protest against Congress' interference with D.C.'s governance and it gives us a better chance of getting our parkland back. That's all we're asking for."

Pryor smiled his approval. "We'll talk again," he said, "*after* you've spoken to Sheila."

We huddled outside in the corridor for a quick de-brief before our next meeting with Sheila Worthington, the Ward 8 council member.

"What jus' *happened* in there?" Damien demanded angrily. "Why d'you tell him we know the resolution won' pass?"

Luther didn't answer right away; we were acutely aware of how important today was for Damien. It would be so easy to both underestimate and overwhelm him.

"Damien, Pryor *wants* to oppose the prison, for all the reasons you gave him. But he can't risk it being built in his ward when he's staked his whole political career on redeveloping Ward 5 and giving minority businesses a leg-up. D'you understand?"

Damien nodded, but I could see he was processing the information, fitting the pieces together. "So why d'you ask him again?"

"Because I wanted him to know that the resolution wasn't going to stop the prison, we're counting on Zoning to do that. He has nothing to lose. We only need his support to tell Congress to stay out of D.C.'s business and Pryor can never resist an opportunity to do that."

"So the resolution ain't really to *stop* the prison?" Damien said, his eyes eager to trust us. "Why are we here then? *Why?*"

I looked at Luther and decided to do some unexpected firefighting.

"Look, the council members are all playing dead, pretending this prison thing isn't happening. They don't want to touch it. Congress is bullying them and Ward 8 is kind of irrelevant to them. We're here to put them on notice. *You* are here to tell them that Ward 8 isn't to be messed with and you're going to stop the prison even if they're too chicken to do the right thing."

Damien looked at me with relief spreading across his face.

"You mean this is like a D.C. statehood resolution, *disguised* as a prison resolution?"

"Exactly," Luther said. "It's just part of the strategy to build momentum against the prison, but it's also a way of telling Congress to back off and to get our land back."

"Cool. Tha's cool," Damien said. "Because we wou'n't *be* in this mess in the first place if we had our *own* fuckin' state and those thieves on the hill ha'n't stolen our park."

Sheila Worthington was Ward 8's own worst nightmare. With the ward having the lowest voter turn out in the city, she had sailed to two consecutive terms in office by having no agenda other than to get herself elected and to enjoy an $80,000 annual paycheck as her reward. As Greg once explained to me over a long night spent editing and re-editing one of the Mayor's Housing Committee reports—we had to cut thirty pages by the morning—Ward 8's voter turn-out was so low that the Ward had never broken fifty percent. When I didn't believe him, he pulled out his Blackberry, where he stored all the city's election results for the past ten years, and showed me. Worthington was elected by 22,000 votes, total, out of 80,000. As long as Edgar Brooks—the Ward's long-suffering former council member and former D.C. Mayor—wasn't running, anyone could pick up the Ward 8 seat with a few handshakes and a few hundred yard signs. Of course having W.J. Roland on your side helps. A lot. And in Worthington's case his support had legally or otherwise bought her the election.

Pryor knew Sheila Worthington was in between a rock and a hard place. And we knew it too. As we gathered ourselves to walk into her office, we understood that we were about to go head to head with a woman who was about to have a 2,500 bed prison, as dictated by Congress, built in her neighborhood right next door to four schools, but she could not even dream of opposing it. Because she had made certain promises to W.J. Roland, who'd made certain promises to Randy Weaver, counsel and chief lobbyist for *Reform and Corrections Inc.*, builders of the Ward 8 prison.

"Well if nothing else, this should be interesting," I whispered to Luther, as we waited to be called in by the council member's assistant.

"You are a piece of work," he said softly back, laughing.

"Ah come on, it's days like this—make this job worth it."

"She's an embarrassment to Ward 8."

"She's an embarrassment to herself."

"We aren't going to get anywhere with her."

"Let's just make her squirm. I'll buy you a beer if you get her to say she'll *consider* our proposal."

"Buy you a beer if I don't."

"Here we go."

"Here we go."

The moment we entered, the Council member's discomfort was embarrassingly evident by the way she shifted in her seat and abstractly shuffled papers on her desk. Known for her elegant suits and fashionable hair, neither could help disguise the trouble in her soft, dark face. She *had* to take this meeting. We would have made ground meat out of her in the community and in the press if she declined to even talk about the prison proposal. But now she needed her out and she looked at her phone. I had to laugh. If she tried to pull that trick off, I'd shut her down faster than she could pick up the phone. Luther read my mind—no time to lose with Worthington—and he quickly introduced Damien.

For Damien this was a life-altering moment. Here he was, a seventeen year-old kid, face to face for the first time with *the* elected official who should have had his best interests at heart. And he could not even make eye contact with her. I saw the confusion in his face as he started to relate his well rehearsed but heartfelt story and then realized she was barely paying attention.

"Excuse me?" Damien said.

She looked up.

"Are you *listenin'* to me?"

Worthington fixed her eyes on Damien and it was obvious to us all that she now saw him clearly for the first time. She took in the effort he had made to be here today, to shed his childish concerns and come to her as a young man. She noted his suit and tie, and she asked him, her voice full of regret, to please continue. She listened fully thereafter to Damien and to every one of the residents.

When Luther wrapped up, he wheeled in close.

"Sheila, we were wondering, we know the resolution may not be worded the way you'd like it, is there anything you'd change?"

I was impressed with his tack—he had her on a course that would only allow her to either support the resolution, or to outright oppose it. He had eliminated any option in between by offering to make any changes she required. Worthington looked shell-shocked; she knew she could do neither.

"Look, I have prisoners' families telling me this may not be such a bad idea—" she started to say. She was smart to use this argument, but I was ready with the comeback.

"If you notice," I said, handing her a highlighted copy of the resolution, "the resolution clearly states that, *If the D.C. government determines that it is in the best interests of both the city and the prisoners' long-term chances for rehabilitation, that the prison should be built in the city, then that site shall be chosen by the D.C. government.*"

"We're jus' askin' for you an' the council to get to choose. It should be *your* decision," Damien said, only too happy to hammer the point home.

Sheila Worthington looked as though she was ready to blow.

"I have other meetings to take," she said, with such affected self-importance that even Luther couldn't stop himself from sighing softly. He relaxed his shoulders; I saw them drop with relief. He had decided to talk freely and leave the politics behind.

"Sheila, you've known me my *whole* life, you were a friend to my Mom when—when we—" He paused. "Just tell us—are you going to help us stop this prison?"

Worthington, her eyes fixed on him, replied, "I'd really like to take another look at this. I promise you Luther, it will have my full consideration."

We didn't know it then, but this would be the last meeting that the Ward 8 council member ever took on the prison issue, in private or publicly. Forever after when asked about why she didn't take a stand on the single most important crisis that faced her ward under her watch, she would say, "Well, I found that I really had to consider both sides of the argument."

Damien was almost inconsolable when he realized that he had not been able to convince his own council member of the urgency of the situation.

"We need our *leaders* to fuckin' *lead* us!" he exploded, as soon as we were standing outside Worthington's office. "That woman ain't nothin' but a high-paid sell-out. How can she let 'em build that fuckin' thing next to my school?"

"If only she had heard *that*," Luther said.

I nodded towards the door where Sheila Worthington had just moments before been standing wringing her hands and listening to us. Ordinarily, right at that moment, I should have given Damien a long lecture about watching what he says before and after meetings, how he can never be too sure who might overhear him. But somehow it seemed only fair that if Damien was to be introduced so harshly to the reality and vagaries of the political system that he be allowed to let off steam. Otherwise he would build up such resentment and discontent for the whole process that he might just choose to believe that he had no power to shape the future of his community. And he might just give up trying. So I told myself, it was O.K. for now, if Sheila Worthington heard that a seventeen year-old kid in her neighborhood had cottoned on to the fact that she didn't have what it takes to be a leader and to do right by her community.

"Well, we just lost council member Pryor," Mrs. Garrett said.

"Not really," Luther told her, "we never had him in the first place. He knew Sheila would cave. It made it easier for him to say no."

She frowned and seemed to shrink away from Luther, as though he almost frightened her, the way he so readily navigated the messy political waters we were in. Even though we were achieving our objective of getting the prison issue on the council members' radar screens, Luther and I could tell that this was not satisfaction enough for the rest of our team, and we decided we definitely needed to cheer them up. After a few phone calls, I rearranged our schedule and I got us in with the Ward 1 council member, Darrell Baucus.

Ward 1 was home to an eclectic mix of income, age, race and color, and the council member had carved out a niche for himself as champion of all the little guys—to the residents of D.C. and small business owners, his door was always open. He had gained respect citywide for passionately seeking reconciliation and compromise in the toughest of situations. Baucus liked to say, "The Distance between Ward 1 and 8 is tiny, a matter of miles. What's in the interests of Ward 8 is in the interests of Ward 1. We're all in this together." He was a fantastically energetic man who towered over most people but was never intimidating; he had a warm, reassuring manner about him. His pale pink, slightly worn grandfatherly face with honest, dark green eyes told you for certain that there was no hidden agenda with him. I respected him profoundly for taking his own notes during meetings so that when he said he'd get back to you, he always did. He and Greg were good friends and I had already heard from Greg that Baucus had agreed to sponsor our resolution.

When we arrived, Baucus was delighted to take the meeting; he ordered coffees and sodas for everyone and then immediately focused his attention on Damien. He was so encouraging and thoughtful that Damien visibly relaxed; he sat back and shared jokes with the council member, and the two fell into deep conversation. After the drinks arrived, we sat around Baucus' meeting table and we chatted and laughed about the absurdity of the whole proposal. Baucus insisted on hearing the personal stories that each of the residents had come to share with him, and his response was heartfelt; he assured us that he had made the prison issue a top priority for his team. He offered us advice on how to frame our arguments for the Zoning Commission, and we had a lengthy discussion on the implications of the proposal for the city's comprehensive plan. Damien, grinning, shot me a look to say, *now this I like*.

We left Baucus' office with just enough time to grab a bite to eat and drop in on a committee hearing in council chambers before our last meeting of the day. Even though we were there only briefly, I could see that Damien was not entirely impressed by what he observed—an almost empty room and a technical and tedious discussion on replacing street lamps in the city. Government at its least thrilling. I promised to take Damien to one of the more controversial council meetings, where the room is completely packed and people line up out the door to testify, all the council members are present, and the press are elbowing each other out of the way to get the best shots. Luther joked that in the meantime, Damien had better brace himself, because we were about to encounter a full-force Category 6 hurricane. Damien looked puzzled.

"Is there even a Category 6?" Mrs. Garrett asked.

They would soon find out. Our last meeting of the day was with the Ward 6 council member. Stephen Brightwood—for his reputation, a surprisingly short and stocky man, with a grayish white face and opaque blue eyes—was something of a brute to many activists in the city. A man who exuded nothing but carefully cultivated hostility whenever you met with him, he always started a meeting by pretending not to remember your name, no matter how many times you'd met with him before. He then took every opportunity he could to remind you that Ward 6—*his* Ward—was really all that mattered to him.

"And who are you?"

"And what Ward are you from?"

"And why should this concern Ward 6?"

"And how will this impact Ward 6?"

"And you're from what Ward did you say?"

"And so you're not from Ward 6?"

And on and on. Brightwood's litany of questions was exquisitely honed to prevent any real discourse. Over the years he had banked all the information he gathered and although he pretended not to remember anyone, he was forever referencing his mental database to ascertain a resident's status in the pecking order of D.C. politics. The fewer years you had on the ground in Ward 6, the more quickly you were invalidated. Not only that, but Brightwood had developed a list (Greg had seen it) to rank anyone requesting a meeting with him. He granted full access to donors and anyone with even the vaguest ties to Congress, brief meetings to Ward 6 constituents, and would only sit with D.C. residents from outside of Ward 6 if they had enough local pull to cause trouble if they were ignored. Everyone else had to fight to be heard, let alone helped.

Meeting with Brightwood on the prison was unlike any other meeting that day. Rumors were rampant that Ward 6 was the back-up location for a prison in D.C. With the troubled D.C. Jail and an abundance of shelters and drug treatment facilities already located throughout his ward, Brightwood was clearly going to do everything in his power to support the Ward 8 prison. In fact he was the only council member quite happy to openly state that he supported it. He may have talked bravely in the past about statehood for D.C., but most people knew that he was secretly willing to accept whatever Congress dictated to the city. Especially since the very Capitol of the United States was situated right in the middle of Ward 6, and many Members of Congress were his neighbors. If Congress wanted a prison in D.C., in Ward 8, then Congress should get a prison in Ward 8.

"Isn't Ward 8, after all, where most of the felons came from, Damien?" he said, interrupting Damien in mid-sentence.

Damien was stunned into silence. Luther looked at me and I looked back at him and nodded. We had planned to pin Brightwood up against the wall all along—now was our chance.

"So how would you feel if the prison were built in Ward 2? On the Georgetown waterfront? Not too far for the families of all those Ward 8 felons to travel? " Luther asked.

"Just the same," Brightwood said, without hesitation, "I'd still support it."

Of course he would. How foolish of us. But he knew and we knew that would never happen; hell would freeze over before anyone would propose building a prison in Ward 2.

We went through the motions for the rest of our meeting with Brightwood. Damien tried to make the council member feel as uncomfortable as possible and I let this slide; Brightwood didn't need my protection. This was just a routine call on our part anyway. We were merely checking him off our list, so that when the time came, we could say we had done our due diligence and met with all the council members. Luther and I were also quite happy to have exposed Damien to D.C.'s most unforgivably self-serving council member in all his naked glory. It would toughen Damien up, and he could always take pride in knowing he had gone head to head with Brightwood and tried his best to soften his fossilized heart.

The rest of the week was consumed with even more visits. The Ward 7 council member, even though he was black, and had a large constituency likely to oppose the prison, decided to secretly champion the Ward 8 location for fear of the prison landing on his doorstep. Over at the Ward 2 and Ward 3 offices, we found a generosity of spirit regarding the campaign to stop the prison, and we gained our second and third sponsors for the resolution. After all, there wasn't a chance that the prison would ever be built on parkland near any of D.C.'s benevolent, predominantly white, millionaires who were happily clustered in these wards. For Wards 2 and 3, expelling the prison from Ward 8, in fact from all of D.C., could only be a good thing. The further away the better. That the council members for these wards might also pick up another checkmark on their statehood voting record by supporting the resolution was an obvious added bonus, and it made their commitment to the cause all the more fervent.

Lastly, we took on the At-Large Council members and there was an almost festive atmosphere in these offices. Being an At-Large Council member means you have to care about the whole city. The prison was an obvious no-go to these four council members. Not until the D.C. Government and the D.C. Government alone, decided where it should be built. What better platform to jump off, right into the deep end of the fight for representation for D.C. in Congress? But still, we picked up only one more signature for the resolution. The shadowy, slippery alliances of council members amongst themselves were evidently too precious to forgo even for this issue, and the other three At-Largers, though sympathetic, took a bow when it came time to sign.

So the resolution didn't shape up to be a *D.C. Council vs. Congress* knockout fight after all, as Damien and others less familiar with D.C. politics, might have expected. Congress had successfully, likely to the glee of those who opposed statehood for the city, exposed Washington's underbelly and shown how divided we really are. If nothing else, the week of lobby visits made it clearer than ever that we had chosen the right target for our fight; the Zoning Commission was now firmly in our sights. No ward lines, a place where the interests of the city as a whole, come first. Damien, Mrs. Garrett and all of our activists, were excited to get to work on their testimonies for the upcoming hearings.

After their experience with the D.C. Council they were looking forward to being listened to in a truly relevant forum.

As we said our goodbyes on the steps of the council building on our last day of lobbying, and I observed the residents' renewed optimism, I couldn't help wishing that the council experience had been different for them; I wished they had witnessed a deep unity with Ward 8, instead of near complete abandonment.

OF A BROKEN-HEARTED RIVER

All your better deeds shall be in water writ.
                                        Francis Beaumont and John Fletcher

It was five-thirty on a Saturday morning, and I was bound by tides to wake Ian, get out of bed, wake Sandra, and get everyone down to the river by 6:45. I elicited a grunt from Ian as I shook him.

"What. What is it?"

"Come on," I whispered, "We're going to the river, we can't miss the boat."

"Oh *G-o-d*," he said, clearing his throat. He raised his head heavily and reluctantly. "The *cleanup*?"

I think I knew how he was feeling. We were about to voluntarily wake our sleeping child, drive across the city and dig through mud and garbage on the banks of the Anacostia River. After the last cleanup, we all came home filthy and exhausted and the acrid smell and taste of the river lingered with us for days. Ian slumped back on his pillow and turned away.

"You keep sleeping for now. I'll wake you again in a little while."

I entered the kitchen, perpetually icy cold whatever the season, no matter the heat of a D.C. summer outside, and looked out at the awakening day. I saw two black squirrels chasing each other, scurrying along the back fence, and noticed a pair of cardinals up in the magnolia tree, awaiting their chance at the birdfeeder. Sparrows commanded the feeder for now, squawking viciously and fighting amongst themselves; an abundance of mourning doves and one cautious gray squirrel carefully pecked away at the discarded sunflower seeds on the patio. Nothing went to waste; no trash left behind. It was all very impressive considering what I would be doing with the rest of my day—picking up other people's garbage. I prepared some oatmeal for myself and ate quickly to warm up, while watching the battle outside in the garden. A blue jay suddenly laid claim to the feeder and the other birds, and even the doves and the squirrel, reluctantly retreated to the fences to watch and wait. I would never have put my money on the elegant, lithe blue jay; I thought surely the multitude of sparrows would best him, but power often resides in the most unlikely places, this much I have learnt in life.

I made cinnamon toast for Sandra and Ian, to sweeten the blow of getting ready to leave. I took their food upstairs and scooping Sandra up from where she was fast asleep in her bed, carried her into Ian's arms. Slowly, but surely, they woke up and I sat with them as they breakfasted together in bed. With food inside them, they were more pliable and slightly more agreeable, and they dressed and washed quickly, stopping only to comically glare and scowl at me as I gathered the boots, sunscreen and rain gear we would all need for the day ahead.

A warm, humid haze lay over the city as we drove through the quiet streets of Washington towards the river. Over the years, Ian and I failed to select any one route as the quickest to the Anacostia River. Sometimes H Street and the Benning Road Bridge led us there, other times Rock Creek Parkway to Memorial Bridge and the freeway. That the different bridges serve the purpose of reaching particular neighborhoods on the other side of the river is a fact that never affected our decision on the best way to go on any given day. This allowed us to discover parts of the city we might never otherwise have known and being in a rush always seemed to make our irrational decision-making all the more chronic. There was the added challenge of going the wrong way, figuring out how to go the right way, and getting wherever we needed to be *on time*. Ian took Fourteenth Street, swung left on U St., and passed the massive warehouse that we liked to call the 'world's cheapest place to get cereal,' near the meat market on Florida, before continuing on to Gallaudet University. At Eighth, he turned down what Sandra called her tree street, because of the gigantic old oaks that linked arms above it, turned onto Pennsylvania Avenue, and drove straight over the Sousa Bridge. Try crossing the Sousa Bridge without thinking of trumpets, trombones and clashing cymbals. Can't be done. In any case, Ian's chosen route made no sense for the day's destination, Kennilworth Gardens, but it was pretty and we hadn't been this way in a while. As we crossed the bridge, I strained to look over the barriers to see the milky mist receding from the river. The light of day was gathering its strength and shimmered over Anacostia Park, verdant and pure in its morning christening gown.

We arrived at the designated cleanup site where we unexpectedly found Damien sitting behind a long folding table, signing up volunteers for the day and handing out T-shirts. He told me he had been helping to organize the cleanups since he was a kid.

"Anyway, shoul'n't you be hangin' with your whitey friends today?" He grinned. "I heard Luther gave you the day off."

Ian laughed and took a T-shirt from Damien. It was a lurid, lime green color. "It's a bit bright," he said. "Gross, in fact."

"I like it Daddy," Sandra said. "It makes you look like a clown." And then without hesitating she turned to ask Damien if she could please have some coloring crayons to decorate her nametag.

Damien invited us to join him and his girlfriend, Sheryl, on their volunteer boat. After waiting a while on the shore, we boarded a beaten-up old powerboat that looked and sounded as though it would have great difficulty making it down the river in one piece. Ian and I exchanged glances and he pointed at me and mouthed, *You're the one...* I laughed and mouthed back, *Sorry*. Ian teased Sandra, telling her she could have been asleep or having tea with her bear right at that moment. I looked around at the other passengers on the boat—a mixed crew of high-school students and D.C. government employees—local residents, all volunteers, like us. Our own friends who were supposed to join us were nowhere to be seen. This did not surprise me. It took a certain kind of madness to leave a Saturday morning bed to attempt to clean the banks of a river this desperate and grim. Catherine called to say she had accidentally slept in too late to join us and I told her that of course, she would pay dearly for that some other time.

As the boat hummed along I started to relax. I had been working hard and spending too much time away from Ian and Sandra, and even if we were going to be mucking about in the dirt today, at least we would be together. I made a silent promise to myself that after the cleanup I would devote more time to my family and friends. After many postponements,

Rafael and Marguerite were coming for dinner tomorrow night; it would be a good way to turn over a new leaf. I sat back and watched the birds at the water's edge wading and skimming over the river and then glanced back at the churning waters behind us. The river ran smooth and dark up ahead, but we trailed an angry, white surf behind us. *Passing through*, I thought. We are all just passing through.

At the cleanup site we stepped out onto the muddy shore and were issued ten trash bags each. This seemed absurd to Ian and I the first time we did a cleanup but now we were inclined to ask for more. We gratefully took the bags and pulled on the heavy-duty kitchen gloves that I had packed for us.

"I'm sinking," Ian said, suddenly, "I can't move." Before I could step forward to help, little Sandra had leaned over to heave Ian from the mud, but she succumbed to fits of laughter at the sight of the thick, dark Anacostia River mud oozing out from the tops of Ian's sneakers. As I leaned in to help pull him away from the water's edge, I couldn't resist reminding him that I had set out his boots for him to wear this morning, but he insisted on taking the sneakers instead. Damien smiled and gave Ian a friendly shove and said, "Tha' was *really stupid*, brother. You any idea what's in this mud?" Then the smile faded and he said softly, "Iss real bad, you know."

Ian looked miserable. He was, I suspected, unashamedly worrying about the vile and evil pollutants that were likely now concentrated in his shoes. We had taken a guided Riverkeeper tour of the river, and knew what Damien was talking about, how badly polluted the water was. But to his credit, Ian pulled himself together and took vengeance on the ubiquitous trash awaiting us on the riverbank; he squelched over to the brush and got right to work filling up the garbage bags. As Sandra and I tugged at grocery bags choking the saplings that had recently been planted by schoolchildren as part of a citywide project to help restore the river, I saw Ian talking with Damien as they worked side by side, and I wondered, what is there to say at a time like this?

After a while, Sandra and I joined Damien, Sheryl and Ian as they worked on a steep bank further downstream that was covered with shredded pieces of clothing. We bent over again and again to retrieve each scrap of cloth and bag it. Soon we tired of this and tried to work on larger objects, an old drum from a washing machine, a hair dryer, a shopping cart and finally a truck tire. The tire, lodged deep in the sticky mud, refused to budge, no matter how hard we all pulled on it. Sandra slipped and fell from the effort and landed awkwardly. She held up a brown plastic horse as though it were a trophy and gleefully put it in her pocket to take it home.

"It'll remind me of today," she said, smiling and proudly holding her head high.

We had just finished hauling the tire to the water's edge when Sheryl pointed to a dead fish riddled with tumors all over its body. Ian and I had never given a second thought to Sandra joining us today, but now we were jolted by panic at the sight of the fish lying still on the ground. I could feel the fear rise inside me; I could see it in Ian's eyes. He leaned over to me and whispered, "Should Sandra even be here? I think I should get her back."

But there was no going back yet and we all knew it—not until the garbage barge arrived in an hour or so, to collect the trash bags and possibly some weary volunteers. The other boats wouldn't be back for a while.

"Come over here, sweetheart," Ian said, and they give each other arms-only hugs, keeping their mucky hands away from each other. "Why don't you and I work together?"

I was shaken to my core at the sight of the two of them laboring side by side, collecting the awful garbage that had come to the river from all over Maryland and Washington, their thoughtfulness battling the overwhelming thoughtlessness of those who treated this river like a dump. Raw pain clawed at my heart as I watched them slowly, methodically fill up a trash bag together, their low, sweet voices floating like a healing balm through the air.

Hours went by and a rainstorm slowly passed over us, leaving us uncomfortably wet and dirty. Word reached us that the main garbage barge and one of the motorboats had broken down; we were left on the rapidly receding riverbank to wait until one of the remaining passenger boats, already busy retrieving volunteers up and down the river, could come back and collect us. Garbage bags and all the large objects that we had retrieved but couldn't bag—tires, computers, car batteries, shopping carts and even a fridge door with the egg tray and condiment shelves still attached—lay gathered around us, as though a tornado had lifted them up and dropped them down suddenly. As the filthy water lapped at our feet and the trash bags all around us, I felt tears, conjured from deep within me, streak down my cheeks.

Suddenly Sandra ran towards the water and jumped in; she splashed about and called to us to join her. Ian and Damien both turned and ran to her; they lifted her up together and Ian carried her ashore.

"Keep her out of there," Damien said angrily. "You gotta keep her *outta* there."

Damien and I ended up canoeing back to the park while the others were rescued by powerboat. We spoke very little to each other as we paddled slowly along the murky water, but when we did, it was to share what lay heavily on both our minds—the sense of disgrace and burning shame; how it was that humans had so thoroughly wrecked the order and simplicity of the natural world, degrading the air, the land and the water.

By the time we got back to the park, the volunteer picnic was almost over and we saw that a fire truck had pulled up and a firefighter was dousing someone's car engine that had overheated. The firefighter finished work on the car and offered a welcome public service, washing down and cooling the volunteers. Damien and I stood in front of the water blasting over us and laughed out loud.

"We did good today!" he shouted.

"Oh, *yeah*!" I said, arms raised, fully drenched.

"You all did good today!" the firefighter yelled, and he cranked the pressure valve and waved the hose away from the crowd; the water shot upwards, a pure, white fury raging against the hazy, gray sky.

After wandering through the thinning crowd of tired volunteers, I finally spotted Ian and Sandra and saw that they had managed to improvise a change of clothes. I headed over to them and wearily foraged for leftover food, settling for warm coleslaw and a hamburger bun—the burgers were long gone. As we said our goodbyes to Damien and Sheryl and made plans to head home, a trembling gasp arose from the crowd. One of the garbage barges went by and the volunteers could now see the spoils of the day piled thirty feet high and ninety feet across; we watched silently as the formidable mountain of garbage bags, tires and other junk that we had all collected from just one, short stretch of the river, passed by and made its way steadily through the water. Long past four o'clock, we said our goodbyes again and we made our way back across the river and home to hot baths, clean clothes and beds.

For nights afterwards whenever Ian, Sandra and I closed our eyes or slept, we pictured plastic bottles, straws, plastic grocery bags, tires, Styrofoam, cigarette butts; we saw the dead fish. These images fiercely haunted us at first—sometimes I woke in the night, disoriented and afraid for Sandra—and then they slowly subsided, our dreams restored. The river stayed with us.

DAMIEN ALONE

All water has perfect memory and is forever trying to get back to where it was.

Toni Morrison

"Son, if you could see it now. Sunlight split into a thousand beams o' light. There'd be dancing diamonds all the way out over the water."

My Nana and I sat on her porch overlooking the river. The sun rested above the cottonwood and poplar trees sending long shadows shifting across the garden. The river slipped by, muddy and slow. I closed my eyes and tried to picture sunlight dancing on clear, glassy water.

"Now look it. Sunlight falls down dead, got nowhere to go."

Nana's lived in the same house that my great grandfather built over a hundred years ago. One of the few places people like us were allowed to live. She was baptized here, on the riverbank at the end of the garden path. She grew up running around the garden, helping her Daddy with his vegetable patch and swimming in the river every day she could. I tell you though, she's been left pretty much faithless by what's happened to this river in the past fifty years.

"It ain't never gonna be like that again. Sweet boy, maybe in your lifetime, but not in mine."

Nana grew tired of hoping she'd ever see the water again the way she remembers it. Sometimes she takes her rocker into the house and reads inside because she can't bear to look out at what's become of her river. On a bad day, when she sees an old shopping cart or a tire dragged along by the river, she even turns the chair to face away from the window. I asked her once why she didn't move someplace else.

"I know we allowed to live other places now. But I also know they got us racked and stacked in buildings high up as the sky. No, son, I won't ever be movin'."

Since the water first changed color and all the light went out of it, she hasn't once walked down to the riverbank. In the eighteen years I've been on this earth, we've never stood together by the water, my Nana and me. But I never knew the river any other way. I never knew it when it splintered sunlight and fell like cool raindrops all over the children who played in it. So I'm always wondering, what was it like then? I stand at the edge of the river sometimes, I watch the birds wading like delicate old ladies and flying around like they have important meetings to get to, and the old men fishing because they always have, and I think to myself, there's a heron trying to be a heron over there—are there really fish trying to be fish in that dark, dirty water too?

I'll tell you how it happened, how come this river all but died. People like my Nana remember how the munitions factory poisoned the water in just the few years it took to get ready for and finish the Second World War. And I've seen for myself how the land that's being cleared for development, faster than a rabbit can dig a hole, is washing into the river and making it narrow as a piece of string. I know there's sewage flows into the river every time it rains—that's partly how come my Nana won't go near it. But I also know it's the fault of regular people, too. All that stuff we buy and the things we eat and the things we drink. I know because I've seen it all, strung along the riverbank like a cheap pawnshop necklace.

I came here to tell Nana the news. I'm going to college in California next year, to study water. Full scholarship. If it weren't so far from Nana, I'd be the happiest kid on the planet right now. She just about raised me with my Mom and Dad working so hard my whole life.

"Why d'you have to go so far away? Thought your Mr. Lowe wanted you to go to North Carolina?"

This is true. My science teacher wanted me to apply to all the Carolina colleges. "Son, they have just about a million, million hogs and chickens crapping into their rivers down there," he said. "You want to study water and how to clean it up, that's the place."

But I had my heart set on the West Coast. The college I'm going to is practically sitting on the beach. One day I'm going to take a road trip all the way up that coast, and any place I can, I'm going to get out and put my feet in the clear, blue ocean.

"You gonna forget us, son. I'm so scared we'll lose you."

I put my arm around her strong shoulders, and held her tight. Her slender, dark face was lined and furrowed from living out her sixty years but her skin was still soft against mine. Her deep, hazel eyes glossed with tears that I knew she'd cry only after I left.

"No, Nana, never. I'm going so I can come back."

The Anacostia River has a way of making you come back. Even on days when you stand staring out at the dull water and shake your head at the trash curled up like a whole lot of unwanted stray cats along its banks, you just know you're going to be back here soon. That's what I've done my whole life, no matter that Nana always told me never to go near the water. When I got my first job, stocking shelves at the shabby little grocery store on my street corner, I saved so I could buy myself a pair of the big waders just like the ones you see on the fishing shows on TV. I've been going down to the river ever since to dig. I pull up trash and haul it into a big trash bag and when that one's full, I get to work on another one. Sometimes Nana lets me shower at her place afterwards and she fixes me a big dinner and tells me she's proud of me. Other times, she shakes her head, and says, no. Not today. It makes her too sad to see me muddy and tired, hauling trash that she knows came out of the river she was supposed to have found God in.

It was getting cold out on the porch but Nana and I took our time getting up to go inside. With me leaving at the end of the school year, we weighed and counted every one of those evenings together. The next day was going to be a big day for me—one of my favorite days of the year—and I needed to get some rest, but I liked the way we just sat there, the two of us, and let the cold come to us off the river and neither of us complained about it. I had to be up really early for Cleanup Day, but I didn't mind it. It's one of the days I don't feel so foolish and alone, when hundreds and hundreds of people come out and work all day to clean up the river. Every year I meet some nice people. Every year I leave feeling like we're never ever going to give up because this river, I tell you, it has a way of making you come back.

The next morning, I got to the cleanup event early and helped set up for all the volunteers we were expecting. They came in a big swarm, like they always do, all around the same time, all hoping to get to the boats on time, but not lose too much sleep over it. I was at the sign-in table, giving out T-shirts, when I saw Linda's family. I never met them before. The girl was little; she couldn't be more than five.

"These are for you," I said, handing them each a T-shirt and a nametag.

The dad, Ian, complained that the T-shirt was too bright.

"Good, you'll be easier to spot when you fall in," Linda said, and the little girl laughed and took her daddy's hand like he wasn't even safe on land.

I liked her family, they're funny like Linda, at least when she's not kicking someone's ass to get what she wants. The little girl wrote her name, *Sandra*, in cute, girly letters and she asked me for crayons so she could draw some butterflies and flowers around it.

"You guys are with me, and my girlfriend, Sheryl," I decided aloud.

When I was done with sign-in, I rounded up my group of volunteers and we went down to the dock to take a boat to the cleanup site.

"So, three hours till high tide," I told them all. "Ready to get to work?"

"Three hours," Ian said, yawning. Sandra yawned too and looked around sleepily. Her Mom hugged and nuzzled her. I wondered what made them come, this family? We always get a lot of white volunteers, but they're usually from along the west side of the river—Capitol Hill, Eastern Market—not too far to come, and close enough to the river to care about it. I knew Linda lived on the other side of town and she spent enough time over here as it was, especially on the weekends with all our meetings, so I guess I was just surprised when they showed up together like that.

We waited a long time for a boat to arrive and when it did, I was kind of embarrassed. It was a battered, shaky, old thing. I wasn't even sure we were allowed to take this many folk on it, because the motor ran pretty angry. But the good thing was, it woke Sandra right up and she started laughing and goofing off with her Dad. I watched the light of the new day wash across the sky. I sat back and looked around at the few swallows and gulls that weren't traumatized by the violent noise of the engine, and I was pretty much mesmerized by the smoky, churning water behind us.

When we got to the cleanup site I handed out trash bags to the volunteers.

"So you guys know what you're doing?"

"Oh, yeah, we come here every year—don't ask me, *why*?" Ian said, laughing, but then his face went funny. "Shoot! I'm sinking. I can't move."

Sheryl laughed, pointing to where Ian's feet were rapidly disappearing into the thick muck at the water's edge.

Sandra giggled. "Look at the mud coming out of my Daddy's shoes!"

"Should have worn boots," I said, laughing too, because now the mud had kind of oozed half way up Ian's legs and it looked like he stepped in paint. I got to say, though, Ian looked miserable. And now that I stopped to think about it, I didn't blame him. If it was me, I'd be worrying too. I know this river's nothing but a toxic soup, and now he had it all in his shoes. He was right to worry. I'd seen the three-eyed fish and the tumors on all of them dead animals and birds the old fishermen in my Nana's neighborhood pulled out just about every other day. I couldn't believe that man, Ian, though. He just pulled himself together and next thing, he's gone up the bank, I guess to take his anger out on the trash. He got right to work collecting the mountains of Styrofoam scraps, old pens, plastic bottles, diapers, tennis balls, and what looked like all the straws in the world, lying about everywhere. Linda and Sandra worked upstream of us, trying to pull down all the plastic grocery bags suffocating the scrappy, little tree saplings, and clearing the trash around the roots. As I watched that little girl, I realized I wasn't too happy she had come with us. There's deadly bacteria, all kinds of chemicals, human waste and animal waste deep in the mud, and in the water itself. This much I know. Toxic soup, like I said. All the reasons why my Nana knows the damage done to this river can't be fixed anytime soon.

I worked alongside Ian; I filled up my bags one after another, like I always do. He looked up suddenly and said, "Look at this place, Damien. What the hell happened?" And I swear I saw tears in the man's eyes.

He wandered off to work alone and Sandra joined her mom, Sheryl and me, as we walked on down to an area that looked like a suitcase exploded all over it. Clothes were everywhere—torn and shredded in pieces, caught on every twig and rock, trapped in the roots of the trees rising off the bank. There were tires that must have been lifted at high tide to the top of the embankment, a leaf blower, a hair dryer, thousands and thousands more straws, disposable pens and cigarette ends. I tell you, it was hard, backbreaking work to free all of it from the mud and get it into the garbage bags.

Linda, Sheryl and I pulled together on a stubborn tire, buried deep in the mud. We were all cursing and laughing loud and having a whole lot of trouble putting our best effort into the job.

I called over to Sandra. "*Come on girl*—what are you standing around for? We need all the hands we can get to move this slimy ol' tire!"

As she stepped forward bravely to join in, she slipped and fell on her backside. She landed on something—a brown plastic horse—and wiped it off.

"Is it O.K. to keep this, Mommy?"

Her Mom nodded. It's probably the only thing of any interest that sweet, little girl found all morning.

The rain had come and gone, and you should have seen us. We were all soaked, hot and muddy, waiting for our boat to rescue us. You should have seen what we had. Seventy or more full garbage bags, a bunch of tires, car batteries, three shopping carts, a fridge door, an old dryer drum, eight broken TVs, two laptops, a bag full of cell phones, all piled together. The tide was working its mischief and we didn't have a whole lot of shore to stand on now. That little Sandra, the closer the water got, the more excited she was about getting soaked by the river. She didn't know what mercury does to soft tissues. Before anyone could stop her, she ran and soaked herself, splashing about and giggling like crazy.

"It's so *muddy*! But it's not cold. It's *warm*!" she shouted to us.

Ian and I were on her in a second, pulling her out as though she was getting ready to drown. I saw the fear in the eyes of the adults lined up along the shore. She must have seen it too because she said, laughing, "I'm O.K. I'm just *wet*!"

I wanted to say to her, *oh, sweet girl, you sweet thing, you're not O.K.* This river is not O.K. It's not a place to splash, glide and swim on a hot summer's day. As Ian and Linda worried over their girl, I pictured in my mind for the first time ever, my Nana as a little girl, playing in the river, just like Sandra—only the water is clear and pure. There she goes, ducking and diving. And then the picture disappeared, and it hurt to let it go. I mourn for that child.

The boat came at last but it could only take a few passengers, so Ian went back with Sandra and Sheryl. Linda and I were getting ready to give up being rescued when another boat came by, with a canoe tied behind it.

"Do we get in the boat or the canoe?" Linda asked.

The driver untied the canoe and pushed it toward us. "We've got two motors down and volunteers up and down the river to rescue. Count yourself lucky."

I didn't feel very lucky. We were tired, wet and really filthy.

"Come on then, Damien, I guess it's this or we swim for it."

We'd already shared all the life stories you can talk about, all the times we'd worked together, so we shifted to what was around us as we paddled. She pointed out a red-tailed hawk flying overhead and a great blue heron feeding after the rain. I spotted a raccoon and an osprey nest. The osprey with its little fledglings, all chirpy and eager, just about broke me up inside after the morning we'd had. Animals that beautiful don't belong on a river like this. I lay my oar on my lap and trailed my hand in the murky water, forgetting that I shouldn't. Linda sat up front of me. She moved the oar up and down, smooth and slow.

"Aren't you supposed to see through water?" she said. "See fish and rocks and grass? Don't you think sometimes, it's like the river is just trying to breathe?"

We turned together to look at the water and we drifted silently with the tide. After a while, she lifted her arm up and pointed downstream.

"The river's widening up here. Is this where we turn?"

I told her yes, but I couldn't help feeling as though the river had opened up to embrace us, begging our love.

I sat with Sheryl, waiting for my Nana to bring dinner out onto the porch. While we showered and changed, she made my favorite chicken and peas and she even baked a rhubarb and strawberry pie.

"How come we're eating out here tonight?"

"Wasn't just you today."

"So you're happy?"

"No son, not happy. Just a little touched, is all."

"Touched by what?"

"I saw them boats go by piled high as the heavens. Heard 'em first, they so loud. I saw what you all did today. You eat up. Both of you must be bone-tired and hungry."

It was hard to stay awake as we ate, and I fell happily into bed as soon as I dragged myself upstairs. The little toy horse that Sandra found stood by the lamp, on the nightstand. She gave it to me when we said goodbye, and I washed it and scrubbed it clean. That girl has been baptized in the Anacostia River and now it's in her heart. When I closed my eyes that night, all I could see were straws, cigarettes, BiC pens, Styrofoam, soda cans, plastic grocery bags, shopping carts, tires, clothes and plastic bottles. I saw all the trash of modern life that litters and chokes the banks and waters of the Anacostia River. But when I dreamed, I saw diamonds dancing on the river and a little girl diving and rising up out of the water, her pigtails dripping clear drops of sunlight onto her smooth, black shoulders.

OF FAVORS FOR FRIENDS

Life's most persistent and urgent question is, "What are you doing for others?"

Dr. Martin Luther King, Jr.

The next morning, I decided it was time to get Catherine back for skipping out on the cleanup. When I called her, she sounded sleepy and not entirely happy to hear from me.

"So, where were you yesterday?"

"Sleeping. Which is what I was doing just now. You know, like normal people do on the weekend."

"Well get up, get the papers and bagels and come on over. We're working on the garden and need some entertainment."

"God, you never stop."

"Come on, we've got about a million plants to put in today before they get fried by the heat. We've already left it too long."

"And I should care why?"

"Because no one who works for a cause-based non-profit should ever have both Saturday and Sunday to themselves. You bailed yesterday, so get up and make yourself useful today."

"Alright, alright but we're starting with the society page."

"Yeah, yeah, I'll warn Ian."

Catherine slumped into the swing in the back garden and dumped the bag of bagels and pastries on the old crate that acted as our patio table. She surveyed the garden slowly, and shook her head.

"I don't know how you guys did it. What happened to the urban jungle?"

"Blood, sweat and tears," Ian said. "Come on, read to us."

He was busy turning over fifty pounds of soil conditioner into the barren earth we hoped soon to call a flowerbed. We had already carted away three full wheelbarrows of gravel and packed clay that morning and were now prepping the soil for the army of thirsty perennials, sitting wilting in their pots, waiting to be planted.

Catherine opened the *New York Times* with a great flourish and proceeded to read from the society pages. She had a practiced air about her, lingering on the salacious revelations about prior marriages and tactful references to abundant wealth for each of the happy couples. Ian always protested when she inflicted this part of the *Times* on us at our somewhat ritualized Sunday paper reading sessions. But he laughed as loud as the rest of us at the indulgent self-aggrandizement of that unique brand of American that is the New Yorker. After she had thoroughly exhausted the society page, she moved onto the obituaries and we commented on, mourned and celebrated the peculiar achievements of people we didn't even know: inventors of inventions we had never heard of, parents to children we never met, and painters of art we had never seen. Then it was time to see what was going on in the real world outside and she presented the *A Section* like an oral exam, testing our knowledge of national and world events. Finally, the big bang, the Arts Section and Book Reviews, and we mourned again, all the books we would never have time to read, all the plays and all the movies we would never have time to see. We selected a choice few of each that sounded so outstanding that we made a pledge amongst ourselves to *make* time for these—the one book we would read, the one movie we would absolutely see, the one play, if it ever opened in Washington, that we would attend.

Then as Ian and I worked diligently, the flowerbed slowly but surely filling with a mixture of brightly colored plants and winsome looking saplings, Catherine moved onto the *Washington Post* and we repeated the exercise. Only now the characters were more familiar, even intimately known to us and we laughed harder still—incredulous at the incongruous couplings of some of Washington's elite—cheered for a colleague who had managed to get an Op-Ed piece published, and groaned at the requisite weekly rant about traffic in the Washington region. All in all, this made the time spent digging holes, mixing soil, planting and mulching go by quickly and agreeably. And when we were done, she offered to stick around to help make dinner for Rafael and Marguerite and our other friends who were coming that night.

"You're our guest, go home and come back later," I told her, but she looked at me as if to say, *don't waste your breath*.

Ian disappeared inside with Sandra to go and hang some pictures on the abundant bare walls of our house, and so after I had cleaned up, Catherine and I set to work cooking. We were always happy to spend the day together like this, and it was a mystery how the two of us never seemed to run out of things to say to each other. Ian often expressed bewilderment at our incessant conversation, but knew to tread carefully around us when we were wielding kitchen knives and yelling at each other because we had found something we disagreed about to discuss. Today he steered clear of us because he knew I would be busy humiliating Catherine for bailing on the river cleanup. We were deep into prepping all the food when we turned to our favorite subject, the secret lives of friends.

"So, what's the deal?' Catherine asked me, "Are Rafael and Marguerite getting remarried?"

"Well, that's the million dollar question. Are we unknowingly preparing an engagement feast for tonight?"

"I can't imagine ever getting re-married to someone. Rafael is a mystery to me—how he gets so excited about a bunch of test tubes. I don't even know what he does really. Do you understand what he does?"

"Well, yeah, he's trying to stop lung cancer from eating up people's bodies. No more insane and unattainable a goal than say, trying to save America's farms from this land-eating nation. I'd have thought *you'd* understand perfectly what Rafael does."

"And how's that prison thing coming along? How many signatures did you get again, just *four*, right, out of *thirteen*?"

This was why Catherine and I loved each other so much. Someone has to be able to mock you relentlessly in your life and not let you take yourself too seriously, especially in Washington where everything we do, we do with such earnestness, such *gravitas*.

"Just peel the carrots and remember, I was the one slogging through muck down by the river yesterday while you slept in."

She sniffed the air. "Hmmm, what is that *smell*? Could it be a martyr burning?" she said, and we collapsed into laughter.

After a few hours of cooking and cleaning, Catherine took off to spend the afternoon with her *Boyfriend du Jour* and to get ready for dinner. I found I had an hour or so to spare and returned to the novel I recently started reading. The house was unusually calm and quiet; I wasn't even sure where Ian and Sandra were. One glorious hour spent alone with a book and I was happier than ever and ready to entertain. I selected a beautiful, palm-print halter-neck dress and some insanely delicate sandals I picked up on sale a few weeks before, and I quickly showered and got ready for dinner. When Ian and Sandra returned they were soaking wet.

"Stop by another cleanup?"

"Mommy, we went to the zoo and played in the misters!" Sandra told me, her face lit up with joy.

"We had a blast," Ian confirmed. "You should have come."

"And dinner would have been prepared how?" I asked him, and suddenly he was sniffing the air.

"Time to get ready," I told them, but not before I leaned into Ian and whispered, "this martyr just spent an entire, delicious, *whole hour* reading a book."

"Good for you, *good* for you," he replied, and without missing a beat, "just tell me when you actually ever get to finish a book."

Rafael and Marguerite arrived at our door looking like movie stars. Rafael had taken Latin charm to new heights with his hair tucked back slightly, allowing a sufficiently boyish amount to tumble forwards over his face; he wore a perfectly pressed white cotton shirt over khaki pants and he had one hand casually in his pocket as he leaned in to kiss us hello. Marguerite, her hair loosely tied away from her pretty, round face, wore a white tiered skirt and the most exquisite little lace jacket I had ever seen, tied tight around her waist. While Ian and I, admittedly, had both cleaned up quite nicely, these guys blew us out of the water. Because something was going on with them—they radiated happiness. I hoped Catherine knew what she was up against, and that *Boyfriend Du Jour* was not last week's grunge-king biker dude. Thankfully our other guests did not disappoint. The effort that had gone into tonight's wardrobe told me that all around there was an expectation of a big announcement in the air. When Catherine showed up, last to arrive of course, I had to say something—she looked divine.

"Where'd Catherine go, and who are you?"

"Hello to you too. Are the happy couple here yet?"

"Happy doesn't even begin to describe it. Come see for yourself. And are you going to introduce us?"

BDJ was a hill staffer, who, like all hill staffers, was overworked and underpaid and ridiculously enthusiastic and energetic when he talked about his work. This didn't stop him from giving Catherine a run for her money in the general cynicism department—altogether a perfect BDJ for tonight.

We headed to the dining room and despite the many courses Catherine and I had prepared, dinner seemed to fly by; we were all lost in conversation, for the most part with our nearest neighbors. It was not until after the dessert came out, that the table opened up for group discussion, precipitated in large part by Ian. He could not wait any longer; he had to go in for the kill.

"A toast to Rafael and Marguerite. It's *lovely* to see you *both* again."

We all drank to that, and then Rafael said, "Well, it's good to see you guys too, after so long. My work has kept me away from you, but I think this is true, a little, for all of us?"

"What is it you do?" BDJ asked, and I threw Catherine a warning glance.

Rafael, when asked about his work, was unstoppable. But he was also endearing and fascinating to listen to and I, for one, was settling back in my chair in anticipation of his little speech I had heard so often before.

"I work on lung cancer," he said. "I'm trying to understand why lung cancer cells grow so well. It's one of the most aggressive cancers, relentless. I've cultured some lung cells in little dishes so I can watch them grow. I add different chemicals to the cells, and I watch what happens. I take away other chemicals, that they need to survive, and I watch what happens. On/Off—that's it. How can we turn the normal pathway back on and stop the cells from dividing?"

One of Ian's friends, Marcus, a financial wizard who had made a hefty fortune advising others on what to do with their money—and who had long been contemplating a more meaningful way of earning a living—was so impressed, he hardly got his words out.

"That's *fantastic*. That's really important work. I've been thinking about going back to research. It's what I did before I got my MBA."

Marguerite smiled and looked at Rafael; she took his hand. "I moved from research to finance too, but I'd never go back. Rafael and I could n't survive with us both in the lab. I'm sticking to finance."

Rafael, eager to continue talking about his work, was nonetheless the perfect gentleman, and he asked Ian's friend, and others around the table, and then finally BDJ, what kind of work they each did. BDJ happily reeled off a list of issues he was working on for his Congressman, from land conservation to gun control.

I mouthed, "*Save, save, save*," to Catherine and she had to turn away to stop herself from laughing out loud.

"Well then," Rafael told him, "you have, like many of us here, made a decision." He was suddenly serious; he leaned in a little more. "To live a life of service, for the good of others. There is a price you'll pay for that. You shouldn't kid yourself."

BDJ was clearly enthralled by the opportunity to pursue this idea. As a newly appointed Legislative Assistant on the Hill, he was a fledgling public servant, likely still wild with notions of saving the world; he hung on Rafael's every word. I imagined that as a graduate student in Wisconsin, he probably dreamed of having weighty, thoughtful conversations like this once he moved to Washington. Rafael did not disappoint, he was an open book, always unfailingly urgent, utterly uninhibited.

"I have to tell you, losing Marguerite made me realize that we are fools to think we can do what we do without hurting the people around us. Without making decisions we never ever thought we'd make in life."

He shifted in his chair. He carefully observed the guests around the table and since it was evident that he had our full attention, he pressed on.

"When I was a graduate student, my very first day in the lab, my supervisor told me it was time to start preparing DNA for our experiments."

Catherine looked at me as though to say, here we go—we're in for a long night.

"He led me to a room where there were all these eggs lined up on a bench. And the next thing I knew, I was pulling these tiny, tiny chick embryos out of their shells. One by one, I killed them to extract their DNA. These little, tiny birds. So beautiful. So completely perfect. I had never killed anything in my life. Nothing."

Now even Catherine had lost her appetite for mockery and was listening.

"Then, my professor said that it was time to sacrifice—that's what he called it—some 21 day old embryos. These are the ones that are ready to hatch, fully formed. I break open the shell, I pull out the baby bird, and its first look at the world, if it could open its eyes, would be the scalpel, in my hand. The first time that bird flaps its wings, it has no head attached because I have removed it. The head is lying there trying to chirp and the body is lying there trying to fly. And there were sixty, seventy of these embryos. My first day. My PhD took five years. I crossed over on that first day, and there was never any chance of going back to the person I was before that."

As Rafael spoke it was as though he had opened up a key-card security door into his research lab, and we were standing, naive, young students, around his bench and he was teaching us. He was teaching us what it means to believe in what you do. I couldn't help recalling how it was that Rafael came to be the person who helped me to see past my brother's death. He told me that I had to find something that I could believe in again, believe in enough to overcome the paralyzing sense of failure that came of having lost David. When I responded by challenging Rafael for leaving Marguerite, he told me with his signature brand of blistering honesty, "There are those who have cancer and there are those who work 14 hours a day to cure cancer. And still, it's not enough, because cancer—*cancer*—is working 24 hours a day to kill."

For Rafael the choice had seemed so simple. Only now, years later, had he allowed himself to admit that he needed Marguerite, and the life that came of being with her, that perhaps she was his best ally in his Herculean fight against cancer. And so he had begun to take steps to make amends. He told his story as I had heard it many times before, only now—because Marguerite was back at his side—I wondered that it had not found even greater significance.

"When you crack open the egg of a three-day-old chick embryo you see a network of blood and the yolk below. And you think, maybe there's no embryo there at all, until you see a tiny motion, a red circle moving in a rhythm that you begin to understand is a heart. You can *see* the beating heart."

He sat back and took a deep breath. "To *stop* that heart from beating, you have to know why. Otherwise, you'll learn to shut out your doubt just long enough to end that little embryo's life with a splash of ice-cold solution, just like this," Rafael gestured with his hands to show us, "and to place it floating in a tiny tube that you carefully labeled earlier that morning. But once that perfect little embryo, that looks really like its just sleeping, is stored in the fridge, *then* all your doubts, even pain, will come flooding back, and gnaw at you, and churn inside you. All the way through the weeks of research experiments that follow, you'll be thinking *why am I doing this*? And by then, all that's left of that little embryo, and its life-blood beating through it, will be microscope slides of the finest slices of its brain, spinal cord, lungs, eyes and heart. And you'll not know what to do next; you will have *no idea* how to do the work you need to do next, because you're still back there at that moment when the thrill of seeing that little heart hit you. You're still wondering, *why*? To stop that heart from beating, you have to know why."

In the silence that grew from imagining what Rafael had described, he needed no encouragement to go on.

"So many of us, we've made a decision not to live for ourselves, but to live for our work, to live for others. Why should I spend my life in the lab so Lance Armstrong can ride his bike in the mountains? Why should you spend your life in meetings and dreary offices so that other people have a roof over their heads, so that there are fewer guns on the streets, so that *polar bears* can be saved?

But we're the lucky ones, really we are. We know why we do what we do; some of us even love our work, but let's not kid ourselves. What have we given up? The part that says, go out and enjoy life, just live life—forget about everybody else. *Me, kill*? I never would have thought it. Now I have a whole floor—thousands—of transgenic mice, that I breed, just to kill." Rafael paused, his voice soft. "I gave up my *wife*. And I didn't even realize why, until it was too late. What part of you have you given up? Think about it. And don't take it out on the people whom you love, and who love you. That's what I wanted to say, tonight especially."

We were all still; I suspected we were each reflecting on our work, how it had changed us, why it was that no matter what we did, our efforts never seemed to be enough. I, for one, wanted Rafael to go on. But BDJ was shaking his head.

"No, it's not that simple," he said. That's *just*—I can't accept that. How do you know if what you're doing is *right*? You're trying to save lives that this planet can't even afford to sustain any more. No offense, but I don't really understand why we're investing so much, why you're personally sacrificing so much, saving *Lance Armstrong,* when we're dealing with a world population of six billion, with millions dying every year just from hunger, not from fancy, incurable diseases. There are whole mountains, forests and rivers being destroyed so we can extract ten years worth of lumber, or coal or oil, whole oceans are being polluted to a point we can't even begin to reverse because the pollutants are so persistent and indestructible. We are trashing the *entire planet* and you're worried about *cancer*? We need to do more for the world we live in, that God gave us to protect, I might add, otherwise no matter how dedicated we are, we're—we're just wasting our time."

I looked over at Catherine who was uncharacteristically quiet and simply shrugged, as though to say she couldn't argue with that. BDJ would, no doubt, either learn to modulate his opinion or become even more entrenched in his world-view after a few more years in Washington, but for now, no one was offended by his earnestness. I had to hand it to BDJ; he acted quickly to try to limit the damage from his incendiary, little speech.

"Look, all I'm trying to say is—no, it's great what you do, what we all do, it's just not enough, maybe that's it—it's just not enough."

"*What?*" Catherine asked, fooling me once again; she had merely been waiting for the perfect moment to humiliate us all. "You guys really believe *we're it?!* We're the great hope for the world? You guys are more desperate and pathetic than I ever thought you were! Personally, I'd like to toast Ian, Marcus, and Marguerite, for bailing on science—for being *bold* enough to be the only ones here who do what they do *just* for the cold cash. They're the ones who have it all figured out!"

Silence. Catherine had, as usual, brought us crashing down from our high horses. Rafael may have been contemplating whether to take BDJ's bait and continue the debate, but instead he took Catherine's cue to move on, and a wicked, mischievous grin, spread across his face. He looked at Marguerite and without turning away from her, he said, "I think we've kept you waiting long enough. It's true. Marguerite and I are getting remarried. *This* time I won't let her go."

My eyes fell on Ian, just as he was looking over at me. He smiled and I think I saw in his eyes what rose in my heart; we had done well to stay together and to find a way to love each other more as the years went by. The next moment, we were, all of us, out of our seats and rushing to Rafael and Marguerite, to congratulate them, as though *this had to be*—these two people who belonged together having found a way back to each other. As I hugged Marguerite, Rafael turned to me.

"And *you*, I haven't even told you what I need of you."

"Really Rafael, I'm not that good at flower arranging, could you please find someone else?"

He shook his head, laughing, "Come on, let's talk."

We all wandered out into the garden where Catherine and BDJ lit the citronella candles and votives that were sprinkled throughout the garden and we sat, half in light, half in shadow, the conversations now hushed and intimate. Rafael got straight to the point; he wanted to know if I was aware that the council bill to prevent childhood lead poisoning had stalled in committee, and whether I might be able to help shake it loose.

"Where's this coming from? Rafael, the *activist?*" I teased him, but he didn't answer.

He had told me he wanted to try his hand at my work; I was curious why he had chosen this issue, in particular. I knew from my *Homes First* work that childhood lead poisoning was a threat to Latino kids because of the old and poorly maintained housing stock in many of their neighborhoods. Even so, why should Rafael want to get involved now?

"What's going on Rafael? What aren't you telling me?"

"My niece, she has lead poisoning." Rafael did not look at me as he said this. "She'll be OK, we're hopeful. It's not the worst it could have been. But it could have been prevented. So I want to stop it. That's all."

Rafael was helpless at asking for help. He was a doctor, a research scientist, he was a Latino man who prided himself on being in control, on tackling enormous, seemingly unsolvable problems like cancer—so why not take on lead too? Unlucky for him, he had picked another somewhat unsolvable problem. I already knew that the Childhood Lead Poisoning Prevention bill was stalled for many reasons, not least of which was that Sheila Worthington was chair of the Health and Human Services Committee. She was not going to let the bill see the light of day. Not while the Justice Department was busy handing down indictments to her buddy, W.J. Roland, for violating federal lead abatement standards in several of his rental properties in Ward 8. I knew all of this because Baucus was the author of the bill and he sought our help at *Homes First* to mobilize tenants to get the bill moving. Had I stayed, I would likely be working on the bill now. I would have to talk to Jonathan to see if anything more could be done, but I had my doubts; I kept these from Rafael.

Favors for friends, with the power to save and change lives. Rafael had painted us as people who worked for the good of others. BDJ insisted we were not doing enough. Whatever we were, that we so naturally, so readily, got down to work like this after dinner, made me wonder if we were perhaps merely compulsive problem solvers, scientists all, just like Rafael.

Greg called me the next morning, as I sat drinking coffee and reading the novel I started the day before. I was taking half an hour to lose myself to another time, another place, people I could live with or without; it was a perfect way to clear my head for the day's work ahead of me. I was reluctant to put my book away so I tried to read while I talked to him; hopefully we would just shoot the breeze.

"Guess who called me?"

"Who?"

"Pryor."

"Pryor called you and you're calling me—why?"

"Because he wanted me to call you."

"Pryor wanted *you* to call *me*?"

"Aah, I *knew* that'd get your attention. Stop reading—I know when you're reading."

"How do you know? OK. I'm all ears." I pushed the book aside but

I held my page open with my free hand.

"He wants in on Windsor."

"You've lost me already." Greg didn't answer. He gave me time to figure it out for myself, without his help. I dropped my book as the realization hit me. "Wait, he wants to help finance Windsor?"

"Exactly. But he can't let anyone know until he's sure he can identify some banks that have the finances and ability to take it on. He wants a black business success story, not a well-intentioned failure."

"This is great news! I think. Is this entirely legal?"

"It's all very secret and sordid, but it's all on the up and up. Pryor isn't *giving* this to anyone; he's just helping to spread the word. He's talking to black-owned businesses and banks to encourage them to submit applications to cover the tenant loans. You know the score. You can cast your net as wide as you like, he's just going to make sure the minority banks have time to prepare their paperwork and financing to get a real shot at this one."

"God this is—Pryor needs this politically. He needs this just badly enough that he can't fail."

"Oh, he's not going to fail, not with his track record. We're in good hands. By the way, he was very impressed with you and Luther."

I laughed. "He heard about Worthington?"

"Not just Worthington. How you and Luther orchestrated all those meetings, with that phony prison resolution, just to embarrass the council for being such little chickens. *Two foxes partying in a hen house.* That's how he put it!"

"Luther and I had a blast putting Sheila up against the wall. You know, I've always liked Pryor, he's very—"

"*Ah, ah, ah*, Linda, you're starting to show your soft side. Don't do that, it'll mess up your game."

I hesitated. "So how do I get in touch with Pryor? I mean are we down to chalk marks on the mailboxes and newspaper drops or what?"

"I'm your man, Linda."

"Can I at least tell *Luther*? I have to talk to Luther. He's already done the math to get the dollar amounts the applicants will need."

"Pryor doesn't want Luther to know yet, or Anita."

"Why?"

"It's too much, everything so tied up in the community. You know he's a rulebook man. He won't allow a bank near Windsor unless they're 100 percent following the rules." He laughed. "And he just wants to make *you* the fall guy if it blows up in his face and some whitey bank outbids on Windsor, or the tenants end up being evicted—let's just be honest here."

"Hey, I was planning on winning Windsor anyway, only because many hundred people's lives depend on it. But now that I know my new career and my hard-earned reputation are on the line, I'll just, you know, make *double* sure of that."

"Exactly. I think he's counting on you to do that."

"So, I'm being played, and I should be grateful or pissed?"

"Both, of course."

"Greg, you mover and shaker, you." Now I drew my words out, fully believing them, "We're going to *win* this, aren't we?"

"Like I said, Pryor can't afford to lose, you can't afford to lose; I just have to sit back and watch. My job here is done. Adios, Linda, time to get back to work."

"Before you go. You do know *why* Pryor is helping his brothers across the river."

"Pryor for Mayor. What do you think, this time or next time around?"

"I suspect he'll wait this one out, to build his minority business success story and take it to the polls. I'd vote for him, if he stays on track."

"I'm going to pretend I didn't hear you say that. But yeah, I'd vote for him too."

"Well, well—Greg's soft side."

"I'm out of here, Linda," he said again, sternly, but I knew he was shaking his head and laughing as he put the phone down.

I loved days like this. I lived for days like this. I cranked the music in the kitchen and made a fresh pot of coffee to get to work. All I could think was, I *love* days like this. And then it occurred to me, instinctively, that Richard would have loved this too. We always knew how to unlock the council together, how to pull all the right levers; he would revel in the intricacy and delicacy of the situation. We would be laughing in my office right now and we'd break open the beers, and we'd relish the chance to make Pryor look good, hand a victory to black businesses, keep hundreds of people in their homes, and have a council member who would forever after owe us big time.

But I couldn't tell anyone, not a soul. I had to keep the delicious secret all to myself. Or maybe? I left Ian and Catherine messages on their cell phones.

"Call me. It's urgent—and I can't even tell you what it is."

Catherine called me right back and she was delighted to hear from me; urgent is always exciting—full of possibilities, bad or good, it doesn't matter, urgent never disappoints.

"Tell me everything."

"First you have to swear on your first edition *Silent Spring* that you will never tell another living soul."

"My *signed*, first edition copy?"

"Catherine."

"O.K., O.K. I swear."

I told her about the lobby visits and the call from Greg. She was disconcertingly speechless.

"Catherine? Are you *there*?"

"Sweet, fucking unbelievable—I don't even know what to call it."

"Exactly."

"Pryor is going to look like God when he's done."

"Eight hundred tenants can keep their homes."

"Wow, your sweet butt is really on the line this time."

"Thanks for your support and encouragement. How could I live without it?"

"I can't believe we can't tell anyone."

"Not a soul."

Catherine was quiet for a moment.

"Richard would be all over this. We should all be tearing up Adams Morgan, celebrating, right now."

"Yeah, I know." But I couldn't go there now; I was too happy. "Anita's not going to be much fun to celebrate with—ginger ale doesn't quite do it for me—but you and me girl, we're going to take 18th Street!"

I knew in my heart that Windsor was safe. No one handed me an opportunity like this without me delivering. This was what I lived for.

OF THOSE WE TRUST TO TELL OUR STORY

Don't tell me the moon is shining; show me the glint of light on broken glass.

Anton Chekhov

We could avoid the press no longer. It was time to pitch the story, to craft a narrative that would convince the media that ours was a tale that had to be told. *Hmm...Reporters.* I definitely have mixed feelings towards them. Love them. Hate them. They are all so different, striving to tell each story in their own, unique way, with an ending they might well have a role in shaping, just by choosing to tell it at all. But that's the risk we had to take: to find and trust reporters to tell our story well.

Anita, Luther and I had talked for hours about this. We shared our carefully cultivated personal databases of press contacts and we narrowed our first round picks down to our three most reliable contacts: one each at the *Post*, the local *Fox TV* affiliate, and the weekly D.C. politics radio show, on *NPR*. We went back and forth on whether to pitch the Oxon Cove and Windsor Apartment stories as a package or separately. Anita was adamant that the prison story should stand alone, and on this, I was inclined to agree with her. No journalist in his or her right mind could pass on this classic tale of environmental injustice. The Bad Guys were Powerful, Wealthy and White, the Good Guys were Poor and Black; the setting was a beautiful park on the river. Luther was worried that the Windsor story would be lost if compared to, or separated from the prison issue. As always, he wanted to sell the *Anacostia under siege* angle.

We were sitting in Anita's apartment and as I looked out at the city, across the river, I found that I was actually enjoying the slightly absurd conversation we were having about how best to sell our story. Knowing that my home was where my gaze rested, out on the horizon, and that this was not truly my story after all, perhaps I now tasted what it might be like to be a reporter, with the ability to observe, record and walk away.

Always to walk away.

Luther hesitated before sharing the news with us that two inmates had recently been brutally murdered in a *Reform and Corrections* prison, in Ohio. As appealing as this nugget of information would have been to most journalists—the old cliché that refuses to die, *if it bleeds it leads*, came to mind—we agreed that this particular turn of events complicated our story, and ultimately did not help our cause. We needed to stay on message: *Parkland not prisons; Schools not jails; Congress doesn't get to decide where to put the prison*. Blood and gore—although the recognized currency of modern journalism—would be a distraction from the real story, the story we were focused on selling. Environmental justice, or less elegantly, more truthfully put, environmental racism: blacks don't need parks, but do deserve prisons. Not to mention, at least for now, the dark cloud of homelessness that hung over eight hundred residents of Anacostia.

My cell phone rang. A welcome break.

"Linda, it's Jonathan."

A *very* welcome break.

"Guess who I have on the other line? Kadija Drummond, the Conservation Club's new Environmental Justice Coordinator."

"You're meeting with the *Conservation Club*? Are they branching out into housing these days or are you going green, at long last?"

"Could say a bit of both. She's a firecracker, and she has a great proposal for you."

Jonathan called back again and together he and Kadija worked some magic and we were all suddenly connected across the city, via speakerphones. After introductions, Kadija made us an offer we couldn't refuse. The Conservation Club was organizing a walking tour and boat ride for the local press to highlight urgent environmental and urban revitalization issues in the neighborhood. They wanted Oxon Cove and the Windsor Apartments to be part of the tour, and Kadija invited us all to go along to brief the journalists. She had already signed up an impressive list of reporters from all the major print, TV and radio outlets.

Luther, his eyebrows raised with genuine surprise, nodded his approval, because his wish had been granted to keep the two campaigns together. Anita smiled in agreement since the journalists would get to see Oxon Cove for themselves.

"I think we have a green light at our end, Jonathan. Thanks for thinking of us," Anita said.

I heard Luther mutter *green light* under his breath.

Kadija's relief reached us as a wisp of exhaled air. She was new. We all understood what it was like to be new and to want your first success story.

After we signed off, Luther smiled mischievously. "You whities are really starting to impress me."

"Ah, come on, Luther, the Conservation Club has been a good friend to the black community for a long time now—give it some credit."

"Yeah, but how many *Kadija*'s have you called your own?"

"You? What do you mean, *you*?

"We know you're a card-carrying member," Anita said, joining in the fun.

"Proud of it," I said, with a little bow. "Those GIS maps were a fantastic help to us, not to mention all the legislation the Club helped pass to kick the government's ass into cleaning up their act on the river. Please admit it."

They both laughed and faux clapped.

"Anyway, we have to start somewhere. A toast to Kadija. May there be many more."

"*To Kadija*," Luther said, raising his coffee mug.

Anita happily raised her glass of ginger ale and took a sip. I looked at my mug before drinking. I could not *believe* I was drinking lukewarm coffee to celebrate this perfect moment instead of a nice, cold beer. And then it occurred to me that I really needed to stop celebrating every tiny moment in life. It had become an obsession ever since David died. Celebrate the moment. Live the moment. Don't let the moment pass you by. It's what you're told to do when a loved one passes away; it's what you instinctively do—you try to capture every second of every day and hold onto it, and you lean in closer to the ones you love, the ones who have not left you behind. Something inside of me welled up. There would be other moments like this one with Anita and Luther. Many more, I was now certain of it. And I didn't need to mark them; I no longer needed to convince myself to stay the course. I had taken a long walk through the pouring rain and the rain had finally stopped. Quiet. All I could hear now was the sound of Luther and Anita typing on their laptops.

Later that afternoon, I was working on the first incarnation of a press kit, when the phone rang; I expected a call from my Mom, so I ran to pick it up.

"Mom, *hi*! Are you coming this weekend?"

"Linda, it's me."

Richard. His voice. It never waits to be welcomed; it just goes right ahead and takes hold of my heart.

"I'm calling to say congratulations. You got the Beckerman grant. 150K. Nice work."

"Thanks."

I didn't know what else to say, but it immediately occurred to me—*how* did he know this? I only found out from the program officer this morning. How did Richard know already?

"How did you—" I started, but he cut me off.

"Why d'you go against us, Lin?"

"What? This is why you called?"

"Slight conflict of interest, don't you think. You knew *Homes First* was applying to Beckerman when you left."

"That's not your strongest area Richard, you know, these days—conflict—is it?" *God, I'm such a bitch*. Where did that come from? From missing my friend; from aching to see him again.

He deflected my attack. "We were counting on that money, you know that."

I hesitated; I wanted him to know I still cared. "I think they just liked the Windsor project. Look, it's a seed grant, a one off, we'll go elsewhere next year and you can always apply again."

I was trying to open up, hoping he would discover the field of emotions lying in the shadow of my anger. But he didn't respond; he waited. He often used silence to disarm his adversary. At this moment, as former friends, the silence merely amplified the loss of faith and fellowship between us.

"You called Richard," I told him, not trusting myself to say more.

He readily returned to his true agenda.

"This is going to look really bad to our other funders. You know they take their cue from Beckerman. At least let me see your proposal."

"You know I can't do that."

"I'm not going to do anything with it. I just want to know what made yours better than ours."

"The limited amount of money available for good deeds in this world, don't you think?" I joked, pushing away thoughts of what he would really do with our proposal, and then, because I was still not used to being anywhere else but on Richard's side, I reassured him. "They would have funded us both if they could have, I'm sure of it."

"That's nice, but not true. You kicked my ass."

I'm just going to go for it. What do I have to lose? I thought I would never give him another chance. But what if he was trying to get back to us again—if talking about the grant was his way of getting there?

"How've you been, Richard? How's Danielle?"

"Linda—."

"Please tell me that you didn't really call about the Beckerman grant? That you called because we owe it to each other? I'm ready Richard. I am ready to listen."

He laughed awkwardly. "Danielle left. She *left*, you know. Is that what you wanted to hear? Are you going to tell me I deserve that?"

This isn't what I wanted to hear. I wanted to hear that he and Danielle had worked it out, negotiated a new peace, despite all that he had done. Instead, he had lost Danielle and I wanted to be there for him; it's where I would have been, had he not already forced me away.

"I've got to go," I said, "I have to pick up Sandra from school, and I have a meeting tonight to prepare for. Look, I'm sorry about Beckerman, I really am—and Danielle."

"I shouldn't have said that to you. I'm sorry."

"Richard, I have to go." *I have to go.*

Fuck. He was back. Not buried away, deep, where I could forget him for a while. *Richard. David.* My two great losses, my two great failures in life. Back to haunt me when I had others that needed me now, whom I couldn't fail. I moved quickly through the living room, gathering up

Sandra's toys and getting myself ready to leave the house. As I sat on the bus to Sandra's school, my iPod roared so loud my ears hurt, but I had to shut them out, both of them—David and Richard—the brothers I never really had and will always love.

OF MOVING EVER CLOSER TO THE FINISH LINE

You can be told you have a 90 percent chance or a 50 percent chance or a 1 percent chance, but you have to believe, and you have to fight.

Lance Armstrong

"*A Textbook Case of Environmental Injustice.* I like that. How d'you come up with that?"

I had gone to see Jonathan in his office to revel in the all media hits we garnered from the media tour. The Conservation Club event was a huge success. We landed a front-page *Washington Post* article and a generous online version of the story, leading stories on two news channels and numerous local papers picked up the story and ran photos from the tour. There was no scoop to be had, we had sold the story to a whole boatload of reporters but they liked it nonetheless. Many of them ran headlines with our message lifted right from the press packs, *A Textbook Case of Environmental Injustice*. I coined the phrase while riding my bike through the clog of rush-hour traffic on the way back from Anita's place one evening. The tour made it easy I suppose, for the reporters to find their story. We didn't need to feed it, or pitch it to them, they didn't need to go digging; they just needed to see for themselves. By taking them out on the river, showing them the Cove and walking the neighborhood, we needed to do little more to meet their criteria for newsworthiness. Even the ospreys and eagles out on the Potomac had obliged and worked their magic on the hardened hearts of the local press corps. In the meantime, Kadija had landed herself firmly on the map as the go-to girl on environmental justice issues, her number now speed-dialed into many a journalist's cell-phone. She was excited and eager to keep working with us on the two campaigns in any way she could, and had already committed to signing up activists to testify at the Zoning Hearings. But the star of the show was undoubtedly Damien. The cameras loved him.

His face—sometimes smiling, sometimes stern or thoughtful—appeared in every one of the print articles and on both the TV spots. I gave a few interviews myself—always a thrill and you never really get over the fun of sending the press clips to your Mom. Damien, meanwhile, had tasted fame and loved it.

Jonathan shuffled through the news articles on his desk and laughed at the prospect of Sheila Worthington doing the same thing in her office, cringing at all the Ward 8 coverage that barely mentioned her name. She had declined our offer to join us on the press tour. Those journalists diligent enough to call her office for comments were turned away and tacitly concluded that Worthington not only supported the Ward 8 prison, she had also dropped the ball on saving long-time, local residents from being forced out of their homes. One of the TV reporters unearthed proof that Worthington had received—as Luther had long suspected—several campaign contributions, in the last election cycle, from *Reform and Corrections*.

"Probably best if she lies low right now," I said, sympathetically.

"She must be mighty angry," Jonathan replied, with a broad smile and satisfaction barely concealed in his voice, but he reflected further, and the smile was soon gone. "If she weren't my council member, I'd be celebrating her downfall right now. But this is really kind of sad and embarrassing. Edgar Brooks was our *hero*—he earned that accolade. Before he threw it all away. But Worthington, she's just not worthy of the office she holds."

"Listen," I said, not feeling up to yet another depressing conversation about disappointing politicians, "that *Post* reporter, James Hadid—crime, metro—called me. He said he's dug up some dirt that I might want to talk to him about. Know what he might be onto?"

"James? He's a good reporter."

"I don't know him at all. He must be angling in on the prisoners' families—looking for their story, I bet. I'm going to get eaten alive. Why'd he ask me, why not big, bad Luther?"

"You're a grown girl, you can handle it."

"That's your advice?" I laughed. "Thanks. So, now let's talk about Damien."

"Quite the rising star."

"Will you take him on? I was hoping you could work your charm on him. Take him to the White House, have lunch with him and some of your Washington cronies at Old Ebbitt—blow him away, give him a taste of the power out there."

"You mean all the things I never did for you?"

"Hey, I sucked your marrow dry learning about this city, I didn't need the glamorous stuff to make me want to do this job."

"And you think Damien does?"

"Well he *lives* in the neighborhood I was trying to understand. He needs to know that he belongs in that other world too."

"What do you have in mind?"

"An internship, maybe a fellowship, a couple hours a week. But he works with you directly, so he can see what you do."

Jonathan shook his head. "I should have kicked you back across the other side of the river eight years ago. I had no idea what trouble you'd be." He sat back and laughed. "Of course I'll take Damien on. Someone has to take over my job some day, and God knows, it won't be you!"

"How do you know that?"

"Because Luther and Anita *own* you now, that's why!"

"You think I'm that easy?"

"Easier. I got eight years work out of you just for driving you around my neighborhood."

"So you'll take Damien?"

"He's an exceptional young man. Of course I'll take him."

For me, this was my chance to open a whole new world to Damien, to give a great kid a chance to dream big. For Jonathan, taking any intern under his wing was about nothing less than creating a new generation of African American leaders.

"Hey, Jonathan," I said, as I headed out, "One other thing. Could you please *pay* him? Don't pull that *Washington Intern/Be Grateful For The Work Experience* BS on him. Make him work long hours—I know you will—but please, *pay* him."

Jonathan refused to dignify me with a response and merely waved me from his office.

I biked across town to the next community meeting about the Windsor Apartments, happy to have seen Jonathan but almost dreading seeing Anita and Luther.

"What's *up* with you?" Anita asked, as soon as I arrived. She moved briskly across the little stage, heading straight towards me. Despite my best efforts, I suspected that I was inadvertently broadcasting to the entire room that I was the keeper of a most delicious secret. As of that morning, Pryor informed me by way of Greg, that we had at least three, possibly as many as five or six, minority-owned businesses seriously interested in investing in Windsor and preparing their applications. One was a national bank that had just celebrated its entrance onto the Fortune 500 list, with over four billion dollars in revenue. I could tell by the way Anita trained her gleaming eyes on me, and mockingly arched her eyebrows, that I had already failed in my personal goal for today—to act as naturally as possible. Now she employed a tactic that felt disconcertingly familiar; Ian was a proven expert at utilizing the technique to extract information from me. She leaned in ever so slightly, touched my arm just above my elbow and as though skillfully maneuvering the tiller on a light and swift day sailer, brought me around to a perfect landing face to face with her, our eyes locked.

"Linda?" She leveled her question directly at me, so that it became something nearly overpowering.

Nonetheless, I couldn't breathe a word, even though this would likely instantly transform her from determined inquisitor back into trusting ally. I imagined us dancing around this drab, old room together the way I did, when I received the news. I could even picture us embracing and laughing and opening our arms out to whoever happened to be nearest to us, maybe a tenant with whom we'd immediately share the wonderful news. *Arms locked together, a latticework of strangers swelling around us, drawing on the spread of good news to grow, until all the people here in this room would be bound together...* But I had to tear myself away from the imaginary festivities and deflect Anita's persistent inquiries by suggesting that we get the meeting rolling. Just for good measure, I added that I thought she looked simply gorgeous, as ever, today.

"Anyway," I reassured her, "I'm pretty certain Luther is the one with the big news everyone has been waiting for."

This temporarily satisfied Anita's curiosity; a long, slow smile spread across her face, erasing the fierce battle lines, and she turned to greet some residents as they entered the room.

It was true, I tried to convince myself, I didn't lie; I told a fraction of the story perhaps, but I didn't lie to Anita. Luther planned to announce today, at this meeting, just exactly how much money each tenant would have to pay to help buy the Windsor apartments. Just then, as if on cue, he wheeled over to me.

"*Something* is up with you. You're acting like you know something I don't know and as you know, I make it my business to know *everything* there is to know."

"I think I got that. Let's see—I know something you don't know? Luther, how can that possibly be? The outsider bests the insider? Impossible."

Luther laughed and moved in closer.

"Come on, spill. I can keep a secret."

"Nothing," I told him, my voice chirpy and false. "Just happy to be here."

"Yeah, nowhere else you'd rather be on a Saturday morning then this place. What is *up* with you?"

"Shall we start?" I prompted him.

"I'm going to find out. One way or another, *I'm going to find out*," he warned me and then wheeling around to the front of the stage he opened the meeting.

While Luther talked, I had time to reflect on the people whom we aimed to help. I observed the tenants who had packed the room, a sea of attentive faces, their eyes filled with anticipation; so many sat bearing themselves forwards in an agitated state, the fear and excitement likely clenching their hearts. To those who have never tried, it would seem, at first glance, that a tenant buy-out is an admirable yet unattainable dream. Especially with the construction party currently sweeping across D.C. *Luxury downtown living / Urban one-bedroom lofts from the upper 400's*. Everyone invited except the poor.

An unattainable dream—that was certainly how I felt about the prospect of ever succeeding when I began work on my first buy-out, years ago, under Jonathan's tutelage. If it hadn't been for his constant encouragement and his persistent and methodical approach to solving every problem we encountered, I would never have believed that a group of poor tenants could ever be handed the keys to their own castle. Luther didn't like it when I used that word—*poor*. He had made it perfectly clear that there were plenty of working professionals, like himself, living in the Windsor Apartments, who didn't have adjusted rents and who would do just fine elsewhere; they simply didn't want to leave their community. He refused to engender pity for anyone in his community—or some such noble bullshit—but I didn't have a problem talking about the *poor*. I simply believed that if you don't use that word, often and deliberately, it just makes it easier to pretend that the poor don't really exist. Even the government has to set standards for poverty, and by these standards, which are anything but generous, a third of the people in Luther's community are poor. People who can't even afford a subsidized, low-income apartment, are poor. They may not be living out of grocery carts or sleeping on park benches, but they're working two jobs to barely survive, their kids are in failing, unworthy schools and the chances of anyone in the family ever graduating high school or going to college are slim to nonexistent. They're definitely not taking family vacations to Disneyland either. So they're not exactly living the American Dream.

So why would anyone believe that the unique group of residents, gathered in that stifling basement meeting room that day, enduring the unforgiving heat and the saturated, sweaty closeness of the air, stood a chance against the re-development juggernaut coming their way? Because sometimes, if the man in the moon winks his approval, if all the stars are aligned, if whatever God you believe in decides to shine down on you, it is possible to make dreams come true. Jonathan taught me this; Luther believed this too. He was hoping beyond hope to be a dream-maker for his friends and neighbors. We had already talked the figures over. They weren't the worst I'd seen or the best; I'd helped maneuver tenant buy-outs with tougher financial constraints. But that was easy for me to say. I wasn't one of those working day and night to try to save money that disappeared into rent payments the moment my paychecks cleared.

Luther opened the meeting by describing how profoundly life had changed in the past five years for tenants in Washington. He presented his talk using an overhead projector and a series of graphs and tables, printed on acetates. I couldn't help thinking to myself, you don't see many of those anymore; the golden, mellow light from the light-table added a kind of quaint and earnest touch to the whole meeting. Now, as I watched him scribble on the plastic sheets while he talked, it struck me that it was really impressive technology—the ability to get your thoughts directly on a screen, instantaneously like that. Powerpoint had its place, but this was the real thing, not pixilated or approximated. So there it was—in it's purest form—the news we'd been waiting for.

By Luther's calculation, having analyzed comparable properties and current market predictions, the units that now rented for about $400 a month in the Windsor Apartments, would, after extensive renovation, rent for at least $1,300 a month—a direct consequence, we had been informed, of the building's views, proximity to the new Homeland Security Offices, the river and the new baseball stadium. Our independent analysts had apparently scoffed at the market impact of all those major problems in the neighborhood that we had so painstakingly catalogued. Baseball alone they assured us, would embolden people to bravely go where they never dared go before. We had been forewarned that this was a conservative estimate, based on the expectation that the rest of the development coming soon East of the River might further increase the value of the apartments, in which case rents could even approach $1600-$1800, a month. As I surveyed the room and took in the devastation wreaked by these figures—faces marked with distress and disappointment—I knew Luther would move swiftly onto the good news.

At times like this, you know what the difference is between the poor and the rest of us. Ian and I could scrounge $3000 together in no time for the deposit on an apartment. Not easily, but we could do it; we'd dip into savings here and there, raid retirement accounts, call upon the good graces of relatives and we'd have the first two months rent in hand, ready to sign a new lease agreement. We might have to struggle to keep up with rent, but no more than we do now to meet our monthly mortgage payment. Maybe I'd get a real job, in the private sector, and use all my carefully honed fundraising skills to make up for what other qualifications I lacked from never having worked anywhere beyond cause-based, non-profits. The transition would likely pay off with some real money and I wouldn't regret having to give up, once and for all, the salary scale of the do-gooder. So somehow, Ian and I could certainly make it work. But for what? We'd been there already. When we decided to save every penny we owned and earned to buy our first apartment, it was because we had made a sobering and astonishing calculation. In the years since we each left home, Ian and I collectively, had spent more than $175,000 on rent—to be at the mercy of an assortment of lousy property managers and absentee owners. So we begged, borrowed and changed jobs, but we did it, we got out of the rental business and became homeowners, and hard and terrifying as that can be sometimes, this had made all the difference in our lives; we were no longer merely throwing our money away, year after year after year after year. The whole experience evolved into a new way of life for us. It was a shock, a source of paralyzing disillusionment, to learn, at first, what a pathetic contribution a mortgage payment really makes towards paying off the actual bank loan on a home, how much of our hard-earned money would be devoured as interest. But still we learned to save, or maybe we just grew up. It is probably silly, but never a day goes by, ten years on, that I don't give my keys a little shake in my hands in the morning, just after I lock the door, as I head out to work. *My keys. My house. My home.* All it took was a decent education, help from our friends and family, and two good jobs. All it took was the opportunity denied most of the people in that room.

Right before Luther switched acetates, a thought suddenly struck me. The people in this room didn't know yet—they had no idea that their dream was slowly taking on a life of its own, becoming real. Even after they heard what Luther had to tell them, they would not know that Pryor, Greg and a cohort of other powerful people were feverishly working away to make this deal happen. And the Windsor tenants had something else going for them. The building and the apartments, for the most part, were in good shape—I noticed this the first time I visited Anita—the lights in the hallway worked, the elevators functioned properly, the plaster and paintwork were sound and there was even central AC. Inside the apartments I had visited, the walls were intact, the appliances weren't great, but they worked; even the balconies were re-done in the past ten years. The owners of the Windsor Apartments had been smart over the years, to both protect their investment and treat their tenants with the respect they deserved. Roland could have done better to take a page out of their book. So there wouldn't be a need for extensive renovations after purchase. Luther had taken this into account. We always looked at the state of the building, even before making our first back-of-the-envelope predictions. Luther, his face illuminated and glowing from the light of the projector, from knowing he was in control, looked up and around the room.

"Here it is," he said softly, placing the new acetate down carefully, and he opened up a world of possibilities none of the people in the room could previously have truly imagined.

"I think, first off, that we need to understand that we all have to work real hard to make sure the majority of residents are able to find the downpayment money. We're going to need $2500 from each family, each unit. The more people buy in, the less the rest have to pay. The monthly mortgage payment for each of you will be very close to your current rent. But look, here's how I got to that number, and I think it may come down from there, if we're willing to sell some unoccupied units off with the purchase."

I noticed Luther didn't talk in millions. He didn't explain the purchase price and financial plan for the buildings right away; he kept it real, kept it small. I made that mistake once—I presented the financials as I'd predicted them, and I lost the room to a tide of panic. When you start talking about $18 million, when you really only need each family to raise $2500, it's a losing battle to win people back, to help them believe they can possibly have a part in owning $18 million worth of property, when they live on $18 thousand a year.

$2500. And you get to keep your home. Sounds easy, doesn't it? But the number sat heavily with so many in the room—their dream ostensibly close, yet still impracticable.

"I don' think I can ever raise that kind of money," an elderly lady at the back of the room said, as she stood leaning heavily on her neighbor's chair. "Not now, not at my age."

A well-dressed, tall, wiry man, probably in his early fifties, rose from his chair and said, "There'll be a collection box at my store." He abruptly sat back down.

An enormously large lady, who sat across two folding chairs, shifted her weight and spoke out. "Will they be mo'?" she asked. "Afta this? Will they be proper doctors, in a library, in decent schools? So we kin start changing uss lives once in for all?"

Damien stood up and quieted the room. "Listen up," he said. "Listen to wha' Anita has to say. No one gits left behind. You understan' me? Not this time around. No one gits left behind."

Anita was the fixer, the organizer, the miracle-worker; the people in her community knew, loved and trusted her. So when she stepped up and presented her schemes and plans that would help each and every family raise the necessary money—two thousand, five hundred dollars—to own their future in the Windsor Apartments, the people in the room likely believed, for the very first time in their lives, that they could be homeowners. It went without saying that there would be bake-sales and cookouts, raffles and car washes, the community mobilizing to help its own, as it always had. But Anita had even bigger and better plans this time around. We had solicited substantial grants for a medical office with a part-time doctor, dentist and counselors, a small library, and a daycare and after-school program—all on-site—to service the Windsor Apartment families.

"Linda, is there anything you would like to add?" Anita said unexpectedly, fangs back out, with a cute smile nonetheless.

Oh no. What do I say now? I was a walking sinner just aching to confess my deepest, though not necessarily evil, secrets to whoever would listen. In this case, a roomful of people who would love nothing more than to hear what I had to tell.

"No, nothing. I think you and Luther covered everything, very nicely," I croaked. *Who said that?* Was that my voice squeaking its way through my throat and out into the open?

"We did?" Luther could not resist the opportunity to join in whatever game Anita was playing.

"Anyone have any questions?" I said, loudly, full of confidence— back in fighting mode. I thought people in wheelchairs were supposed to be nice. Reliable. Understanding.

"Yes, I have a question about the financing." Right out the starting gate, some very smart individual decided to pipe up and, of course, ask the question that was begging to be asked. "Luther said we're looking for investors. Have you thought about asking black-owned businesses to help?"

I lost it. I knew I did because the temperature of my face suddenly surpassed the temperature in the room. I was probably close to cranberry color right now, so I stared at the floor, hands held under me, feet swiftly relegated to the darkest reaches under my chair, shutting down all communications systems, voluntary or otherwise. Both Anita and Luther were staring at me. But then I saw the understanding emerge across Luther's face as it lit up. His smile was *huge*—all shining, white teeth and half-moon creases around his mouth and eyes, like an awakening, a re-birth—Luther winning.

After the meeting he called me over. "I'm onto your game. When will we know?"

I laughed. No point even trying anymore. "Soon. We have a shortlist of three. I've worked with two of them before, but we still have some background checks to do."

"How'm I going to find out anything, if I don't know their *names*?"

I leaned down pretending to start folding one of the meeting chairs and whispered in his ear.

"All very Woodward and Bernstein," Luther said. "Why couldn't you just tell me? Or Anita?" Anita didn't need to reiterate this question; her arms folded across her chest and her stony face said enough.

"Well I *could*, but just not to the whole room. Not yet. And if I told you before the meeting and it got out—"

By the look in his eyes, Luther's mind was turning over so fast I couldn't even try to anticipate what he would ask me next.

"Pryor, isn't it?"

Luther, I was learning, was beyond good. Cranberry is not my best color. There are reasons I don't wear cranberry. Right now, I guessed, that was the exact color of my face.

"So, I'm right. Well, this is the best news I've heard in a long time, other than the proof that Worthington took prison money, of course."

"No wonder you looked so happy when you came in," Anita laughed. "You know, Luther said he thought you were pregnant, but you didn't want to tell anyone. That was his theory."

"What was yours?"

"You won the lottery and were feeling guilty because you were taking the money and running."

"This is better," I said, because it was. What a relief to have told someone. Well, other than Ian and Catherine. And Jonathan. To have at last told Anita and Luther my secret. Much better than winning say, twenty million dollars, and hotfooting it off to a life of sunsets and cocktails in the Caribbean.

I was helping stow the last of the chairs away and beginning to contemplate what I might do when I got home to Ian and Sandra, when Greg surprised me with a hug and a hefty jab in the ribs.

"You were here this morning?" I asked him.

How did *Greg* escape my finely tuned radar? I must have swept the room twenty times over the course of the meeting, from my vantage point on the stage.

"Of course I came—wouldn't miss this, are you kidding? So you didn't detect any alien life forms? Alex from Planning was here too. We sat together."

Alex? I missed flaming red-haired, whisper as loud as a car horn, Alex?

"Where were you sitting? It's impossible that I wouldn't have seen you both."

"Well O.K., we weren't exactly here, we were there—sitting in the corridor by the open doors, spying on you. Mayor's Office and Planning. Might have looked like we were somehow involved with this meeting. Might have been taken the wrong way."

"So my radar didn't fail me. I just need to extend its range in future to include subversives from the Administration hiding out in corridors. Good to know."

"What did you think of the meeting?" Luther asked.

"Never saw anyone turn so red in my life," Greg laughed. "Wish I had my camera! But $2500—that's not bad. If Pryor comes through, this buy-out is looking like it might fly."

"I told them *afterwards*. Right, Luther, Anita? I can be trusted, see? Anyway what you and Pryor have done is fantastic, Greg. Shame the

Mayor doesn't share your commitment to keeping roofs over these people's heads."

"Don't be too hard on the Mayor, his heart is in the right place."

"What place would that be? Ward 3, or is it Ward 2 these days? And how are those plans for that Mayor's mansion on ten acres in *Foxhall* coming along?"

Greg shook his head; he decided not to take my bait. The proposed Mayoral mansion—now *that's* one for a cold pint of beer if we're to stay friends.

"Come on Linda," he said, acknowledging that we had agreed to set aside our differences for now, "we've got to win him over on this tenant takeover. Jonathan, Anita, Luther, you, me, we can make him back this. City backing will make this whole buy-out go a whole lot easier."

"Spill, Greg."

"He knows. I told him. What Anita's trying to do. I told him if he opposes the prison but doesn't give his backing to the buy-out it will look like he really is trying to clean up Ward 8 and get it all ready for whitey invasion. He's already hurting East of the River, he knows he needs to make a big move to win back some of the ground he's lost here. I'm close to convincing him this might just be it."

"Just tell him to follow his heart," I said, and I was surprised by the conviction I felt as I said it. Perhaps it came from stating the obvious—the pure, unadulterated, obvious sentiments that are not reiterated enough in the cold, forbidding world of politics.

Greg acknowledged this with a nod. He knew what I was saying. He was one of those political advisors who had devoted his whole life to guiding people in power to stay the course they set out for themselves *before* they were elected. The Mayor had needed a great deal of guidance of late, having been caught up in the giddy rush of development sweeping across town. Greg persevered, despite the odds against him, in his efforts to redirect the Mayor's energy where it was needed most. As he put it, sweet and simple—the greater the ward number, the greater the need. Save of course for Ward 1—it was just its own little world of eclectic challenges—wealth and poverty, cheek by jowl. As an advisor, his work went unheralded, anonymity was his greatest asset; the acclaim flowed directly to the person he worked for. When I wanted to tease Greg, I accused him of having no accountability and far too much power for an unelected official. He joked once that the voters really did elect him; the ballots were simply misprinted with the Mayor's name—a quote I threaten to leak whenever Greg bugs me. If we did manage to win the Mayor over, if the city did step up to the plate to help in the Windsor buy-out, little recognition would ever come to Greg, outside of his inner circle.

"I tell him that all the time," he reassured me, "and I know people find this hard to believe, but the Mayor is *trying* to do follow his heart. I wouldn't work for him otherwise."

"It'll be interesting to see who tries to take the credit, Pryor or the Mayor?" I said.

He laughed. "Joint press conference? Mayor speaks first."

"Reading a joint statement?"

"Something like that. I'm sure we can work it out."

"Listen to the two of you!" Luther admonished us. "We don't even have an investor yet and you're planning the press conference?"

"Come on in and join the fun," Greg said giving Luther a lightning fast left hook to the ribs. Luther coughed his disapproval to successfully disguise his retaliation, landing a hit on Greg's chest that knocked him back a step. They had known each other since elementary school; there was an ease about them that was endearing, that I instantly recognized. I had moved around so much my whole life that I had very few friends who spanned back to my early years, but the ones that did were unfathomably dear to me. Ian often joked that he couldn't keep up with me whenever I was around these friends, and now I understood what he meant. Luther and Greg had launched into catch up mode and their world and the people in it, was a mystery to me, so I slinked off and made my way back to the Metro station.

As I rode the Metro, I reflected on the morning and what I might otherwise have done had I not been at a meeting East of the River. I think I would have taken a long walk through Rock Creek Park. The sun was warm and fresh earlier that morning when I biked downtown to see Jonathan and even now, hours later, it had not boiled up into an oppressive summer day. There was a cooling breeze at my back as I biked home from the Metro and I decided I would take that walk now. The hard part would be finding Ian and Sandra. To my dismay they weren't home when I walked in the door and I found Ian's Blackberry lying useless on the kitchen table. I decided to head to the park anyway. As I disappeared up into the woods, leaving the road behind, I followed a new trail, and before long I thought I saw a pair of goldfinches dart in front of me. I was startled to realize that in all the years I had been coming here, this was the first time that I had seen a goldfinch in the park. One of the birds stopped on a laurel branch just ahead of me and I observed it close up. As though seeing a goldfinch for the first time, I was touched by the startling beauty of the little creature—its brilliant golden yellow body, the strident black and white bar across its wings, its compact, gleaming beak. After the pair had taken their leave, I pressed on and briefly glimpsed a deer feeding down by a little stream that split off from the main creek up near Pierce Mill. And then the thought occurred to me that soccer-crazy Sandra and her Dad would be at the Pierce Mill field playing pick-up soccer with the kids who gathered there on the weekends. I picked up the pace, stopping only to admire a red-headed woodpecker making a racket at the top of a dead poplar tree, and then I came out into the opening just across the street from the mill. And there they were, Ian and Sandra. A whole day behind me already, I ran towards them, a whole new day ahead of me.

ANITA ALONE

And a man shall be as an hiding place from the wind, and a covert from the tempest; as rivers of water in a dry place, as the shadow of a great rock in a weary land.

Isaiah 32:2

Anita returned home, relieved that the weekend still felt whole and free, as though starting off from having slept in late on a Saturday morning. As soon as she entered her apartment she eagerly kicked off her shoes, poured herself an iced tea and settled in before the TV. She watched an old episode of Law and Order while sorting her mail, paying her bills and calling her friends. She was more than content to be at home alone with nothing much to do but prepare dinner for when Luther came over later. After finishing with the mail, she flipped through a recipe book, keen to find something new to prepare. As she turned the pages, a recipe Linda had given her fell from the book and suddenly she remembered something Luther said earlier that day, at the end of the meeting.

It was a joke, Anita was sure of that, but it stayed with her and only now did she consider what he might really have meant. *Our uptown girl's really coming through for us, isn't she?* She realized that after all this time working together, she had no idea where Linda lived, or where she went each time she said goodbye and headed off on her bike. Yet Linda had been to Anita's home many times, was comfortable enough by now to help herself to ice and soda, or to fix coffee or tea, or even to take her shoes off and stretch out with her feet on the coffee table. Now Anita found herself trying to imagine Linda's house. It would take a trip across the river, across 16th Street to get there; she had some sense of the neighborhood, but that was all; she had so far, declined Linda's many offers to visit. She hadn't anticipated the camaraderie borne of the unlikely union of Luther, Linda and herself—how readily they laughed together and made their work go by easily; she wasn't entirely sure what to make of it. Of late, she found herself looking forward to the meetings, simply because it meant they would again have a chance to spend time together. They had made a habit of staying late after the strategy meetings at Luther's place, just the three of them, serious discussion and hilarity whisked together and all sense of time and place cast aside. She recollected the night she met Linda at Players—how silly, drunk and happy Linda had been to be celebrating a victory for Anita's neighborhood. And what struck her then, when she looked at her watch, after leaving the bar—what she still could not entirely fathom—was the ease with which Linda traveled back and forth across the river. Fearless or careless—of course she worried for her—it didn't matter, she now realized. It was something she was holding onto as their friendship grew. How easily a dividing line can shift. Black, white. East, west. North, south. Just a line until it becomes a wall. Just a line until you cross it. There had been a slow erasing of the line. For Linda. For Anita and Luther.

Anita had thought long and hard about the lines that divide us. Black from white. Rich from poor. One religion from another. Men from women. How prejudice can be mass-produced, packaged and marketed just as though it were a can of beans. Finding its way into people's homes to sit on a pantry shelf, ignored for a long, long time, until stocks are down and suddenly it seems like the only thing left to reach for. That was what prejudice was really like, she thought; it never, ever truly goes away. It may be hidden away in the back of people's minds, but it is there, easy to access when necessary. She had explored an abundance of documentaries and writings on the why and how of Hitler, and had found herself returning to the same question over and again. How did one man convince so many people, so quickly, to turn towards hate? To choose hate. Without anyone taking action to stop him right away, at the very base of the Nazi growth curve. It seemed to her that if she could answer that one question she could answer all the others, she could believe again in the opposite of prejudice, the opposite of hate. But the more she studied, the more she understood the simple truth that if people need to, if they want to, they will believe anything you tell them. Lies, fabrications, half-truths, none of it matters. Certain people, if it suits them well enough, believe what they want to believe. The truth can be staring them in the face, beckoning them to stand by its side, but they'll simply look away, hold hands with the devil and follow his path.

She had taken to sharing her thoughts with Luther; the two of them were circling ever closer together it seemed, and she needed him to help her make sense of her concerns. Through her reading and research, she recently stumbled on the information that during the Second World War, when the Nazis wanted to organize and keep track of the mass destruction of Jews in Europe, they had turned to an American company for assistance.

"*IBM?*" Luther asked her, when they were discussing the subject one day, while sitting in the park with Kumar. "Are you sure it was *IBM*? Were they even around then?"

There it was—a cold, uncomfortable fact hanging in the air between them—she thought. Waiting to be believed or dismissed—take your choice. That IBM had readily, eagerly designed a record keeping system for the Nazis to accomplish their Final Solution. The Nazis couldn't have been that efficient and thorough and meticulous, without the American company holding regular meetings throughout the war on how best to improve and perfect their accounting system for each and every human life destroyed. A system routinely optimized to keep track of the millions upon millions of people—Jews, the physically or mentally disabled, homosexuals, resistance fighters—who perished because Adolf Hitler had successfully turned his own insecurities into a widely consumed package of fear and hatred.

"Can you imagine?" Luther had said, and it had passed as perfectly understood between them—what might have been achieved by those who orchestrated the slave trade had they had access to the same technology and equipment as the Nazis. It seemed to Anita that bad enough could always be made worse, when humans put their minds to it.

As Anita pressed on in her research, she shifted her focus to original documents. "There's something about seeing the real pieces of paper," she told Luther, "but it doesn't make it easier you know, it makes it even harder to understand it all."

Luther shook his head, as though he couldn't possibly take anymore on board. "What is there to understand?"

She knew what he was saying. What hadn't they seen in their own neighborhood? What more could Luther himself possibly lose to make him understand any more clearly the evil that resides in human beings, side by side with goodness. But she felt compelled to press on. He was uncomfortable, distressed even, but she couldn't bring herself to stop.

"It took architects to build the gas chambers. Plumbers, electricians. There are blueprints—just like for a house—you can look at them and hold them. How do you go from building houses, schools, I don't know, libraries, to—to that?"

There were other handwritten documents that she had sought out also. She wanted to see for herself what level of determination and organization was necessary to maintain the steady flow, for over four hundred years, of more than ten million human beings forcibly transported from West Africa to the sub-Saharan region, or shipped across the high seas to the Western world and the colonies. Many of the surviving records of the unfathomably massive slave trade were those written by human hands. Her own hands trembled as she held original documents and read the handwritten names of slaves traded in public markets, taverns, outside churches and in warehouses, all over the country.

At the park one day, as Anita and Luther sat together, she had turned their hands over—first hers, and then his. She looked down at her hands and she considered them carefully, intently. Long, straight fingers; dark, smooth skin. Only the finest of pores and the barest hint of tiny, soft hairs here and there. Small, barely etched palms. Elegantly rounded, pale pink nails. Healthy, fine-looking hands. His were so much larger, his fingers broad at the tips; she smiled to herself. He too had fine, healthy-looking hands.

"What kind of person writes that stuff down?" Luther finally broke the silence. He too had been observing their hands. "I mean, as you write, you have a chance to *think* on what you're doing."

Anita considered how harshly these questions would forever hang about them, how they would continue to taunt and demand answers. How could anyone keep meticulous handwritten tax records of the slaves they owned, their names and ages, and then assign each—even the babies—a value in dollars? When searching for her own family's history, she discovered logs from South Carolina, describing men, women and children traded to settle bankruptcies, poker debts, bets, and lawsuits. She read British merchants' letters describing the challenges they faced to keep their cargo intact on the perilous oceans, as they imported and exported beef, butter, cheese, beer, salt and slaves; in letters home they lamented the financial cost if their human cargo was lost to sickness and death before delivery could be made. Why, thought Anita, did their hearts not strain, ache, compel them to change their course? These were people who believed in God, who loved *Jesus*—a man of enduring compassion, who urged his followers to *turn from their selfish ways*; they wore his cross with devotion and pride. What of their faith? Did they truly believe that sweetening the pastries of their own, white children with the sugar made of black children's suffering was what God wanted of them? Did those others—all the ordinary people, with no uniform to blame later for their crimes, who willingly made the Nazi machine so successful and efficient—truly believe that every last Jew on earth did not even deserve so much as to live? Or did each person who had a hand in writing such evil histories simply learn to silence the pleadings of their own heart? How did the Ku Klux Klan, marauding through the country in absurd-looking bed sheets, brutally murdering black men, women and children, come to bear Jesus' cross? How did a man who pleaded for mercy *in Jesus' name*, come to be murdered *in Jesus' name,* by men who first slung him naked, by his neck, from a tree, and then set him on fire? As Anita tried to whittle down her confusion, as she tried to answer the questions she compulsively asked herself, she came back to this—if one human being turns his heart against another's, how does he convince others to do the same?

"You shouldn't be reading all that stuff," her closest friend told her once, as they closed up the church after Sunday worship. "It's not healthy. We all know *enough*. Move on."

She was not the only one of Anita's friends to tell her this, but still she studied, holding a magnifying glass up to the past. Anita monitored a class given at American University on the Yugoslav wars in the 1990's. Today people sit in cafes in Bosnia, Croatia, Serbia and Kosovo, where just a few years ago, more than one hundred thousand people lost their lives. The past is not past, she told herself. She delved deeply into the conflicts of black against black. Rwanda—the summer of 1994—all it took was ninety days to massacre 800,000 people. Hutus making lists, careful hand-written lists, of their Tutsi neighbors and within days, hacking whole villages to death with machetes. Hands that wrote names one day were hands that killed the next. Like a wildfire hatred spread, like a wildfire it turned farmers into murderers, neighbors into enemies, teachers into leaders of death squads. She moved on to discover that religious fundamentalism continued to rage across borders, with no end in sight. In Uganda, Christian fundamentalists had recently widened the gates to hell on earth, and in Sudan and elsewhere, Islamic fundamentalists, proud of their terror, eager for all the world to see their work, busily fanned hell's flames, so that slavery and genocide were neither shuttered nor isolated by the comfort of time passed.

As a woman of God, Anita struggled most to understand religious fundamentalism and its erratic path of destruction across the world. Prejudice under the banner of God—different religions, different nations, but always the same terror—now boiling over in merely a few of the places where it simmers and spits, ready to explode. Prejudice, as superbly well organized as ever, alive and well in the present. How could she reconcile her faith in God with all that was being done in his name? As she waded her way through the unending upheavals throughout human history, she sought out a single point of refuge. That refuge was her belief that God's work could only be done, not through war, or by force, but by healing the physical world one person, one neighborhood, at a time. She felt compelled to boldly try to lift her neighborhood up from the wreckage of slavery, segregation and poverty, into a new future. But she had not always felt this way. She was forced to acknowledge that it had been Luther, despite his own fierce rejection of God, who had allowed her to see that securing her neighborhood's future was her calling, her way of doing God's work. One night, when he had pleaded with her once again to leave her job at the church to help build the leadership movement East of the River, he gave her the Martin Luther King quote that was now tacked to her refrigerator door.

> I refuse to accept the view that mankind is so tragically bound to the starless midnight of racism and war, that the bright daybreak of peace and brotherhood can never become reality.
>
> I believe that unarmed truth and unconditional love will have the final word.   - MLK

She read these words over and over again, and ached with love for him, knowing that despite their having followed very different paths, she and Luther had found themselves at the same point of understanding. For Luther, God had no role in this world other than to divide us, make enemies of those who would otherwise be brothers—each new religion evolving to assert increasingly ludicrous and intolerant claims over God's love. For Anita, her service of God was what motivated her, each day, to keep going—each day and every day; no matter the challenges. But they no longer disagreed about the work that needed to be done.

"I have something new for you to read," Luther told Anita that night, as he entered her apartment. He handed her a worn, tattered paperback copy of *The Persians* by Aeschylus.

"Well, it's not new. It's the oldest surviving play in the world. I've read it, oh, I don't know how many times. My mentor gave it to me years ago, after—I suppose he wanted me to find some kind of peace. I don't know, maybe even forgiveness." He looked away and then turned back to her smiling, as though he had successfully pushed away the painful memories. "Well, you'll see for yourself."

Anita was used to his faltering attempts to share with her what had happened to him. She knew to take these offerings and to wait patiently for more as they steadily learned to inhabit each other's worlds more readily, as these worlds at last began to merge. She turned the book over, then looked through its pages.

"Luther, you've underlined practically every line in here! How'm I supposed to read this?!"

"You'll see why I'm giving to you. You'll see why it's like that—trust me. It's about the suffering of the defeated side in the war between the Greeks and the Persians. The Greeks *won*. Aeschylus was Greek. He should have written about the glory of victory. Instead, he wrote about the blood and suffering of the enemy—the hated and feared Persians—and of the horror of war. Like I said, the oldest surviving play. And look at what it teaches us." He held his hand over the book and seemed to hesitate a moment. "Both sides believed God was with them. The messenger's speeches alone will make you see that *God* must have little role to play in mending this world. Only we can do that."

He was so eager for Anita to start reading the play that he left immediately after dinner. She was disappointed, hoping he would have stayed a while longer, but she understood. He had given her other books to read, and she liked knowing that as she read, he was waiting for her to finish. She liked knowing that when she was finished, he would be back; the book, and all they would have to say to each other about it, would bring them still nearer to one another.

She had found the play difficult to get through; the old English used in the translation from the ancient Greek, weighed heavily on her tongue even when she tried reading it out aloud. But she persisted and it was not long before she understood why Luther told her to read the play. The sheer weight of witnessing such a massive loss of human life had driven Aeschylus to write of his defeated enemy with feelings and compassion that might have been reserved only for his own people. What did it matter what the two sides believed—whether God had chosen one over the other? It would have been so easy to say the Persians deserved the defeat; the Greeks had been the underdogs, they had won against all odds— David against Goliath. She realized after seeing the play through to its end, that thousands of years after it was written, all that mattered now was that one man, Aeschylus, chose to record a brutal reminder of what we as humans do to each other.

"What will save us is not our love of God—different Gods we will never, ever agree on," Luther told her when they were together again, and discussed the play. "It's a whole lot easier than that. It's belief in one other." If Anita were entirely honest with herself, she would have to admit that her difficult, dark journeys through the history of humankind could only confirm this sentiment.

Tonight, as she did every night before going to sleep, she turned to her Bible. Given to her by her mother and father, her constant companion for over twenty years, its fine, opaque pages were in places worn through from use. She didn't have the heart to replace it. Not yet. She feared giving this one up and never again finding comfort in a cold, new, unmarked copy. As she leafed through the book, she lingered on highlighted passages that once inspired her profound devotion and faith in God, no matter her circumstances in life. She knew that she must work hard to restore her once perfect faith, and that only in these pages might she begin to heal her relationship with God. But as she read, the words seemed fatigued by failure—her failure, or His, she couldn't be certain—to change what needed so badly to be changed. She thought she might even know already, what it must feel like to have greater devotion to God's work than love for God himself. Anita found the passage she had been looking for. It had been troubling her a great deal of late—the one turn of phrase, repeating itself in her mind.

If there be among you a needy person, one of your kin, within any of your gates in your land which the Lord your God gives you, do not harden your heart and do not shut your hand from your needy neighbor... For the poor shall never cease from the midst of the land... Open your hand to your neighbor, to your poor, to your destitute in your land.

For the poor shall *never cease* from the midst of the land. What did that mean exactly? Anita asked herself this again and again. Would there always be need amongst us? Then how are we chosen—does God choose? Those who live life without need—who could drown in their abundant wealth—from those who have nothing?

Anita placed her Bible on her bedside table and closed her eyes. She had, her whole life, even of late with her mind so occupied with the fate of her neighborhood, talked to God before sleeping at night, and wholly believed that He was listening. Tonight she thought she would pray to God for the strength to be closer to Him again. But instead, before knowing the words would form on her lips, she asked God to watch over the tenants of the Windsor Apartment building. She said their names out loud, known to her now from all the meetings and interviews—strangers no more. Whether or not God listened, she recorded their names in her heart.

OF THE MILES THAT LIE BETWEEN US

Stealing things is easy. Putting them back again is much harder.
                                                     Mikhail Bulgakov

"Fuck this city!" Ian exploded, as we looked at the empty back seat of our car, sprinkled with shining beads of broken glass.

We had nearly one thousand miles to cover in the next two days, and now we had a broken car window and no car seat.

I had heard the commotion the previous night, but I didn't get up; I slept on through. I awoke in the early morning hours, as I often do when there is a car break-in on our street, to the distinctive *thuck, thuck, thuck* of someone working a jimmy on a car door. Occasionally when the jimmy fails, or the burglar is a blundering fool, I hear the desperate breaking of glass—it sounds so strange in the silence of the night—reminding me of the noise Sandra makes when she pulls open the lid of her Lego box and tips all the pieces out onto the floor. First the pop, as the glass is smashed, and then comes the falling, showering down of beads of auto glass; and then silence. I always try to call it in. I drag myself out of bed, look out of the window as far as I can see down either side of my street, try to figure out which car has been hit, and then I call the police. Often it is just as I am falling asleep again that the police arrive—*woop, woop, beewoop*; soft red, white and blue lights strobing across the bedroom walls—and I get up once more and watch as their flashlights sweep through the car briefly, an officer notes down the license plate number, and the patrol car slowly crawls away again.

But last night I was beat, and I didn't get up when I heard the familiar sound, just across the street. If another neighbor called the police, I must have slept through their arrival too. I think I meant to get up, but I just fell right back asleep instead. And now here we were, our car broken into for the third time, and our third car seat gone.

"Fuck—this—city." Ian breathed the words this time, as he set up the extension cord and shop vac to clean up the glass, and I called auto glass repair stores on I-95; we hoped to find one just off the highway, on our way north, and stop there for the repair. I had already secured a loaner car seat from a neighbor.

"Fuck this city," Ian said again, when he found empty SlimJim wrappers on the floor of the car. The smell of them was so strong it floated over to where I sat on the front step with Sandra, who was watching her father intently.

"Daddy, I heard that," she said.

"I'm sorry baby, Daddy is very angry right now."

"How did it get broken?" she asked.

Ian stopped what he was doing—taping cardboard across the gaping hole in the window with duct tape. We looked at each other. Neither of us wanted to take this one.

"Hang on a sec," I said, "I'll just go get *What to Expect When You're Not Expecting Your Car to Get Broken Into On The Day You Leave for Vacation*. Maybe that'll help us figure out what to tell her."

"Mommy?" Sandra said, looking at me with a fierce frown on her sweet, little face, "Why did our car get broken *into*?" She stood up as her own words started to sink in and she approached the car. "Dadda, where's my car seat?"

Ian looked at me—*you* explain.

"Someone wanted your car seat because they had no money," I told her lamely. "They needed money, and they took it so they can sell it to have money."

Ian looked as though he would boil over, or disintegrate, if I said another word. He was in no mood for social discourse. Sandra was mulling my words over and I stayed resolutely quiet for fear of Ian's wrath.

"So it's just like we donated it, right Dadda?" she said, as though she had only just discovered that $1 + 1 = 2$.

Ian was shaking his head but I saw a smile beginning to break across his face.

"Sure, babe. It's just like we donated it."

"But. But. Why'd they *break* the window?" she persisted. I had once again underestimated her. She turned to me for the explanation.

"The door was stuck? I guess that's what happened."

Ian had had just about enough. He picked up the grocery bag of glass and trash and walked inside. "I'm going in to have my breakfast and then I'd like to go on vacation. Anyone want to join me?"

"I am so there, baby." The thought of bailing this town right then and there was fantastic—all I needed was a good, strong coffee for the road and to have my family around me.

"Did you call it in?" I asked Ian, as we pulled away from the house.

"You know what, I just want to leave D.C. behind us, right now," he said. And then he turned the music up and I knew he was lost in his own thoughts. We were likely thinking of the same thing—the price we pay to live in the city, the effect it must be having on our daughter to know already, at four, that what she owns is not safe. That it can be taken from her. I hoped she didn't think that she was not safe, that anyone would want to harm her. Then Ian surprised me.

"When we get back, remind me to split the *coreopsis* in front of the house. It needs more room."

It was his way of saying, we move on.

After a week spent hiking in New Hampshire and Maine, we arrived back in D.C. to the sight and smell of the lavender bush by our front door, in full bloom.

"I never thought it'd make it,' Ian said, handing me some flowers.

I crushed them between my fingertips to release their cloying, sweet scent. The smell of my childhood: my mother's garden—my brother, sister, and me.

"It looked pretty doomed. Well done to you, for not giving up on it. "

Ian took the crumbled flowers from me and sprinkled them over my head. "Come on," he said laughing, "Let's get Sandra to bed."

It was past midnight. We had driven all day and Sandra was still asleep in the car. I carried her in, tucked her into bed, and after retrieving the last of our luggage from the car, I sunk into the sofa. Ian handed me a glass of wine and we sat, legs tucked into each other, and talked. We held onto the vacation and the closeness of spending a whole week together, and prolonged the silliness and fun of being away from the real world, away from the city. We drank more wine and shifted closer, eager to show our love, as though acknowledging we may not soon again have time to tend so carefully to each other. As I lay next to Ian afterwards, with my head on his chest, I fell asleep to the absolute stillness of the night. When I awoke, Ian was still sound asleep next to me on the sofa. Something had woken me up though. What was it? I heard a slow motion playback of the sound in my head: *thu-ck... thu-ck... thu-ck*. Not again! But I looked around now, fully awake, and I saw that the living room was filled with light. I got up and moved cautiously towards the sound near my front door. Could it be? There it was—a yellow-bellied sapsucker attacking the dead tree in my neighbor's front yard. I burst out laughing. This city! I watched the little bird whacking away at the tree a while longer and then still drowsy, I slipped under the blanket to fall back asleep beside Ian.

That morning I somehow got Sandra off to school, and made it to the Metro in time to get over to my meetings on the Hill. Before I knew it, *there it was*. I couldn't help it. Tears slipped from my eyes. Whenever I see the United States flag floating, snapping, wilting, floating again, high above the Capitol, against a cloudless blue sky—a shudder, a shiver, ripples through me at the sight of that flag. From deep within my heart, love ascended, for this glorious, magnificent country. No matter how many times I had stood there like that, it was always the same.

We gathered on the steps of the Senate Russell building, the same group who took on the D.C. Council, only this time, Damien and Mrs. Garrett were understandably all the more nervous. Never before having crossed the threshold of the United States Capitol, with the prospect of face to face meetings with several Members of Congress ahead of them, they were, I suspected, likely even terrified. Anita had joined us today and she attempted to reassure Damien that he would do just fine. I knew how he felt; that kind of feverish mixture of fear and excitement is not easily dispelled.

The very first time I came to Capitol Hill to lobby, I was so thrilled that I rushed straight to the elevators reserved for the Senators and before I realized my mistake, I rode up six flights with one of the one hundred most powerful people in the United States. I knew him immediately of course: Billy Volger, the Senate Resources Committee Chair, from

Alaska. Individually responsible for *gutting* the Clean Air Act. As an asthmatic, I took that personally. As a mother, I thought he should rot in jail for the rest of his life for not protecting the air our children breathe. I could have used my time to berate him or cleverly plead the case for clean air. Lobbyists have paid serious money to be able to spend a minute alone with Billy Volger. But instead, I took my minute or so to study him intently, silently and to see that he was really nothing more than a man in an elevator. A middle-aged man in a nice suit who had left his wife for his intern only to divorce her to marry his long-suffering chief of staff. Only to cheat on her with his new intern. What would be his legacy? An ugly twelve-lane highway named after him, lined with the trash of careless drivers and decorated on either side by the gas stations and fast-food joints he helped to subsidize. Maybe a fancy library too, if he's lucky, but the story it would tell would be grim—even the cleaned up version. At his funeral would be the posse of oil, mineral and coal executives he used to call his friends, with whom he drank and smoked his way to death. Nothing but a massive trail of human and environmental devastation in his wake. A mere nothing of a man when you really stripped him down to the bare elements. He would decompose in his grave one day, just like the rest of us but in his case, really, the world would truly be better for it. So much better for Billy Volger having been forever stopped and silenced. We might all breath more easily again, if it's not too late, by then, to clean up his Dirty Air Act. These were my thoughts; so no, I didn't say a word in that elevator, not until he addressed me directly.

"Press six for me, would you?" he said suddenly, just short of barking the order at me, as though only now realizing that his floor had not already been called for him.

I looked at the control panels in the elevator—one in front of me, one in front of him; I pressed the button on my side, with a smile.

"My pleasure, Senator Volger," I said. A little human kindness and a little respect. Necessary to survive the longest minute of my life with one of the most unkind, disrespectful men in the USA.

As I walked the marble floors of Congress for years after that, as I sat in an assortment of grand and cramped offices and negotiated my way through countless meetings, I remembered Billy Volger. Every time I went to the Hill, he was on my mind. When he helped ensure the passage of a new Clean Water Act, affectionately known around town as the Dirty Volger Act, I knew then, for certain, that you cannot count on Congress to do right by this country. But you can't just give up on the 535 Senators and Members of Congress either, or allow yourself to *ever* believe that you're wasting your time—that nothing can be done, that the situation is hopeless. Whatever happens, you can't ever give up trying to get the message across that *America deserves better.* Lobbying Congress was the most heartbreaking and frustrating work I'd ever done. It was hard to watch Volger, and his kind, despoil and loot this country—its people and its land, its water and its air—year after year. But sometimes when we won, even though victories on the Hill seemed of late, to be both exasperating and scarce, it was worth both the anguish and the effort.

Of course today, for us—this little delegation of concerned citizens from Washington, D.C.—our efforts had to be doubled and redoubled because we were citizen taxpayers without representation in Congress. We came to the Hill to talk to some key Senators, very few of whom really cared about the District's predicament, as well as the three Representatives who made up the D.C. Oversight Committee—Representatives chosen by others, not by the residents of D.C., to rule over the city. Nothing like a lack of representation in government to make a United States citizen visiting the Capitol feel like a serf who's trudging, muddy-shoed and bent-backed, across private property to meet with his landlord. We would of course try to present our case with every ounce of dignity and grace we possessed, not betraying for one moment how much we resented the disadvantage imposed on us.

We made our way through security and headed over to the elevators for our first visit of the day. Before speaking to the staffer in the Senator's office, I gathered the group close around me, just outside the door, to review one last time the issues we needed to raise in the meeting.

Luther touched my arm.

"Just a second," he said. "I want to say something before we go in."

He raised his hand as though to quiet us, though none of us was speaking.

"I know what you're all feeling. Like we maybe have no place here, that you're not sure we're really welcome here."

Damien was clenching and unclenching his fists; his nervousness was building visibly. Luther turned to him, addressed him directly.

"But you know what? My uncle used to lobby these same guys thirty years ago, to get us the right to vote in D.C., and I'll tell you what he told me. When any citizen of the United States comes to meet with their Members of Congress, they hold their head up high and they go in and ask for whatever it is they need help with. Just like that. But when a citizen of the District of Columbia comes up to the Hill to meet with the people that we never elected to represent us, but who have the right to tell us what to do and when to do it, we're crawling up the steps of the Capitol on our knees and by the time we get to the doors of these offices, we're flat out begging. Well, we're not gonna go in there and *beg*, you understand me? All we're asking for is what never should have been taken from us in the first place. Let's go."

The secretary was already ushering us into the Senator from Virginia's office before I noticed that Damien had taken a moment to review a set of talking points on little note cards, which he now stowed away in his backpack.

We had a difficult road ahead of us: we needed to convince the Members of Congress to reverse the land swap deal and return the parkland to D.C., and we had to ask them to restore the city's funding levels for low-income housing development. The city's painstakingly balanced budget, which had already been approved by both the Mayor and Council, had arrived on the Hill only to be viciously raked through by the Congressional D.C. Oversight Committee. Having been a negotiator for *Homes First* through this annual ritual of D.C. budget appropriations, I was on firm ground here, and Luther had many years of Hill visits behind him. Neither of us was particularly nervous or hopeful. Anita and Damien, I suspected, felt both honored and heavily burdened by their responsibility; undoubtedly their hopes were high.

Just as we did with the Council, we presented a coherent, united argument against the Oxon Cove land swap deal. Damien appeared so natural and charming in his presentation, that he gave nothing away of his true nervousness. The Senator, a large, grandmotherly figure in a blue suit with a red and white kerchief tucked, just so, into the collar, listened attentively. Her wrinkled, round face and wavy white hair spoke more of wisdom than of age; her gray eyes sparkled with interest. I had heard that she was opposed to what her predecessor had done, and was eager to reverse the land swap, but she was new to Congress and would soon learn the value of vote-trading—if she needed the Senate majority leader to advance any of her interests, she couldn't afford to cross him on his private prison deal. Now she peppered Damien with questions and he eagerly responded, happy to demonstrate how hard he had worked to prepare for today. The Senator's scheduler warned her more than once that we were running over time. But she insisted we stay to cover the city's housing budget. All in all a great first meeting.

Outside, after a quick debriefing before heading to the next meeting, Luther said to me quietly, "I don't think she was referring to you, when she said how nice it was to meet the people who are *really impacted* by the outcome of the budget."

These days, he made a habit of blissfully mocking me; I tried to keep up, I really did.

"Luther," I told him, my voice serious and grave, "I'm just here to keep the black man racked and stacked in the projects, you know that."

"There aren't many people who can answer back to *Luther* like that," Anita said, taking my arm. "Good for you."

"Anyway," I said, "if you and Anita get to be homeowners—you know, rushing off to Crate and Barrel for your kitchenware—what'll happen to your street cred then, huh?"

Our laughter echoed happily down the corridors of the Russell building.

"Rememba people, we're holdin' our heads *high*," Damien said, catching the spirit as we made our way out of the building like the lion, the tin man, the scarecrow and Dorothy, towards the office of the esteemed gentleman from Georgia, chair of the D.C. Oversight Committee.

Damien burst out laughing when we arrived and the receptionist offered us all Cokes.

"Is this fo' real?" he asked.

"*Georgia*, baby—they say Coke comes out of the faucets," Luther told him.

Damien and I happily accepted one each and we chinked our cans to the good times. He slapped me on the back and sent my soda flying across the rug in the reception area. As I frantically wiped the mess up, the Chief of Staff walked in.

"Lin-da?" he asked, looking around.

"Right here," I said pulling myself up, "just retrieving my dignity from your—wait, that is a *reproduction*, antique rug? Doug, how are you?"

Doug gave me a gigantic bear hug and I tried to hold onto what was left of my Coke, so that it didn't spill down the back of his very expensive looking shirt. Over his shoulder I could see Luther shaking his head at me.

"O.K. Doug. So look, we'll move fast as always, I promise. Is he in a good mood today? Please say *yes*," I whispered, as we entered the Member's office.

"Oh, he's in ah *goo-od mood*—he's jus' not here." Doug's southern accent rolled softly through the air around us like a sweet, morning mist. He gestured for us to sit down. "So *ah'm* takin' the *meetin'*."

"Doug, come on."

"Nope, ah kid you not. He's makin' breakfast for the kids and takin' tham to school, because his wahf's likely goin' into labor soon. You know what he's lahk. Don't you jus' hate those devoted Dad types?"

Exuding all the charm of a true Southerner, in part because of the delicious manner in which he emphasized nearly every other word, Doug proceeded to make up for our disappointment by taking a long meeting with us. I knew he was with us. Doug was a man with a heart a mile wide and twenty miles deep. He loved America in that old-fashioned way—pure and simply—because it is a land of purple majesty and amber fields of grain.

"The Congressman was *bl-ah-ndsided* by the *lan'swap* deal. I want y'all to *know* that. It neva would have passed if he had been Chair. And we are goin' to do what we can to get it reversed. We're gonna need some *help* now, with the rest of the Committee, I'm sure ya'll know that."

"Give us some clues, Doug," Luther asked. "How do we get to them?"

"Oh. Ah think you're *raht* on track," Doug reassured him, "they're hoppin' *mad* about all the great press you got already. Not the way they lahk to see their names in the paper. Keep it up, is all."

Damien leaned forward. "Can I ask you a question?" he said. " How d'you get to be here, you know, workin' fo' a Congressman?"

Doug smiled. "Young man, ah would love to tell y'all about that. Come on back sometime and ah'll give you a tour and we can talk. Only don't you come after my job, OK?"

As Damien and Doug exchanged emails and we got ready to leave, Doug pulled me aside.

"Honey, this land deal ain't over, not by a *long* shot, and we are gonna do what we can to fix it. You keep it up. Whateva we can do to help. About that other—what was it? The housing budget? You jus' call me, O.K?"

After a long day of meetings, most of which were considerably shorter and some discreetly hostile, we wrapped up and I headed home. Waiting for me was a fax from Jonathan—a confidential document showing which member of the D.C. Oversight Committee had first moved to slash the housing funding from the city's budget. I stared in disbelief at the unmistakable scrawl of Doug's hand across the page. A friend is sometimes only so much of a friend on the Hill. While we now stood a good chance of reversing the land swap deal, the city's housing funding allocation was in jeopardy. This was not the news we had hoped for—to discover that the Committee Chair wanted the housing budget cut.

I called Greg right away to warn him.

"Well this isn't exactly a first, you know that," he told me, calm and resolute as ever. "We're up against Congress every year to give it's blessing to our budget."

"Yeah, but Greg, he was *our guy*," I insisted.

"No, no, it's O.K., really. He's just looking to bargain on something else. Come on Linda, you know the game. They'll put the funding back if we back down on needle exchange or birth control programs."

"Will you?'

"Exchange needles for housing? What do you think? These are not people who care about real lives. They're out to make a point. We're at their mercy."

"What about Windsor?" I asked, hating to sound as though I didn't care about the bigger picture, but right then it was looking as though we were going to need public financing to help the deal go through.

"It'll come out of last years approps anyway, I thought you knew that. As long as the bank comes through, Windsor is probably going to make it. Right now we're trying to save next year's budget."

Of course I knew this. I just wanted to hear it from someone I could trust.

"What's really eating you?" Greg asked me finally. "I'm sitting here explaining Budget Negotiations 101 to *you*, Linda? What's really up?"

"That's just the thing, Greg. It's the same bullshit every year."

Greg sighed into the phone. I could tell he was about to quote scripture to me; I admired the courage he drew from it really, but it would fall on deaf ears. But he surprised me.

"Doug really got to you didn't he?"

"Yes, he did," I admitted reluctantly. "And Catherine called, just before I called you."

"What'd she say?"

"Vile Billy Volger just derailed the farmland conservation bill."

"Great day on the Hill, huh?"

"Just another day in paradise."

"You know it says in Matthew 6: *Therefore do not worry about tomorrow, for tomorrow will worry about itself. Each day has enough troubles of its own.*"

"Well, Jesus, you can say that again," I thought, but instead, I told Greg, "Thanks, Greg, let's just keep on that budget, before there's nothing left."

I called Catherine back. She was frantic; her swat team of farmland advocates was in emergency session. She patched me into the conference call so I could get a sense of what was going on. I discovered that the funding incentive she had been working so hard on, to help preserve small family farms as open space into perpetuity, was being re-routed into one of the many, impenetrable agri-business subsidies. I listened to the ideas firing back and forth; no one had time to think, they had to act on pure instinct. The energy in the room transmitted through the phone— I could feel it—the urgency, the enormity of what was at stake. Catherine commanded the situation well, more angry than afraid. I could hear it in her voice. She was suppressing the sentiment likely troubling her the most right now. It was not fear for all that would be lost if she failed. It was the knowledge that even if she won, this was where she would be in exactly one year's time. Deep in battle over the budget once again. It was the life cycle by which we lived. We rarely won, we rarely lost. We merely persisted in trying to save what diminished year after year.

I had to get back to my own work. Knowing that the Oxon Cove land deal might be reversed was something to hold onto for now. Enough to make me crack open my files and start digging for information to use in testimonies at the Zoning Hearings. Just the thought of the hearings definitely lightened my mood. Kadija had faxed me the latest list of people already signed up to testify. Randy Weaver was likely reviewing this list too right now, and was probably—I was just guessing here—livid. I couldn't help but think how strange the whole situation was. *I am here at home, he is there in his office on K Street*. Both of us in the same town, working on the same issue, one that he supports and I oppose. *Only we both feel certain that we are doing the right thing.* Could I really dismiss him as being motivated merely by money and politics? Was my conscience so clear that I was not perhaps betraying the prisoners and their families by opposing the Ward 8 prison? Maybe Randy Weaver *could* justify what he was doing because of them. Maybe that's how he lived with what he did. I couldn't help but think about Billy Volger again, but I couldn't look out from his side, no matter how hard I tried. What makes a man like him believe that he has the right to filthy the air we breathe, pollute the waters we live by, and bulldoze away the farmland that feeds us? What makes him so convinced that he has the *right* to do that? If I were to sit back and enter his world for a moment, would I start to see that these things don't matter as much as they seem to? If I stood in his shoes, would I *want* what he *wants*? *But I just couldn't see.* How he didn't mind how ugly he made this world. Playing God with appropriations and amendments and riders and closed door committee meetings. Billy Volger. And to think that the flag that I love so much, flies above his head every day. And that Billy Volger will tell you he loves it just the same.

Still deep in thought about Randy Weaver and Billy Volger, I took a call from Luther.

"We're on," he said.

"On what?"

"Delegate Marlowe."

"She deigns to meet with us?"

"She deigns to meet with us."

"How d'you score that?"

"She's not exactly happy we were wandering the halls of Congress, talking about *D.C.* today and we didn't meet with her first."

"She wouldn't *take* a meeting with us! We *tried*!"

"Irrelevant details, Linda. Come on. You should know better than that."

"Let me just drop everything I'm doing and..."

"*Atta* girl."

So the very next day I was back on the Hill; it didn't matter what other meetings I had planned, the Delegate wanted to see us at last, and everything else had to go.

Delegate Rose Marlow greeted us in her charming office—very bold, traditional décor with original oil paintings of MLK and Justice Thurgood Marshall on either side of her gigantic leather chair, behind her solid, walnut desk. Predictable, elegant, nothing controversial, except for a gigantic banner reading *No Taxation Without Representation*, hanging across the entire length of one wall of the office.

"Delegate Marlowe," I said, shaking her hand. "Always a pl—"

"There's one thing you *must* understand," she said. She carefully tucked the back of her pencil skirt in before sitting. She was tall and thin, her black hair curled at her shoulders to frame her sepia colored face and kind, green eyes; she was full of purpose, graceful, easy to like. "I cannot and *will not* take a position on the prison. It's for the City *Council* to decide where it goes. Not for me, not for *Congress*, to decide."

"Well, I couldn't agree more. It's just—"

"As for the *parkland*, that's federal property. That is *my* business. That amendment never should have seen the light of day without my input. I may not have the right to vote on it, but the Members know better than to pull that kind of stunt."

But they did pull that kind of stunt, I was thinking. In fact they pull that kind of stunt all the time. Reiterating this to Delegate Marlowe would be somewhat pointless, of course, since she bore the brunt of the Hill's capricious attitude towards D.C., so I pulled back and Luther jumped in.

"That's why we need representation, Rose," Luther said, soft as butter, not at all becoming to him.

Anita and I looked at each other. *Where did our attack dog go and who is this lap dog that just took his place?*

"But until we get that, we're hoping to crush the Members who passed this without your consent, by getting the land *back*."

Anita nodded at me as if to say, everything's good, he's back.

"You let them steamroll you on this, you *know* what's next Rose. There's a whole lot worse coming after this."

"Luther, of course I know. That's exactly why I intend to fight this, but I'll do it privately, behind closed doors and let you get the mud on your face if it gets nasty. You're on the right track with the media work you've done—it's put a spotlight on this—you've made my task easier. But I have my back to the wall here, on the budget negotiations going on right now. I can reverse the land swap and gain ground on appropriations as long as I *don't* try to shove this in anyone's faces."

She took a moment to catch up personally with Anita and Luther, and then she turned to me. "Linda, how is Sandra getting on? She must be four, now? And Ian?"

"Sandra is—oh, she's amazing."

She always asks. It blew me away how she did this. And yet she was neither friend nor foe. She was simply good at what she did. Or her LD was good at prepping her for what she did. I, on the other hand, had never been good at small talk with Delegate Marlowe. She unnerved me in ways that more famous and powerful Members of Congress did not. Perhaps it was her courageous record on civil rights. She was of the MLK generation, John Lewis, the giants, the greats—an era of blood in the streets, burning crosses, lace gloves and wide brimmed hats. She was the first black woman to head up a government agency. The first to serve a President as Chief Counsel in the White House. She had somehow managed to bring dignity to the position of non-voting Delegate to Congress, something that was originally meant as nothing more than a mockery of representation for D.C. Perhaps it was because I admired, was in awe of, her relentless fight for the African American community, the country and the city, that I found it difficult to ask, *so how's your grandson doing at Yale?*

She eyed me, I swear, as if to say, *my grandson's doing fine, and I know you came to talk about something else.*

"Great. What else?"

"The housing budget."

"Tell me," she said, opening a file on her desk and slowly sorting through its contents, "I'm listening."

Not long afterwards we found out that those few moments we stole with Delegate Marlowe were merely a fortunate lull in her soon-to-be deluged schedule. Seconds after we left her office, Marlowe's Chief of Staff came running in to warn the Delegate that the House had agreed to take up the vote to repeal D.C.'s longstanding gun control law. Later we heard that the vote passed the House, and that the D.C. Court of Appeals struck down the law that had so successfully reduced the number of weapons on the streets. D.C. under attack on all fronts. We were in Luther's apartment after a long meeting, when we saw coverage of the verdict on TV. Luther reacted to the news with uncharacteristically morose defeat in his voice, as though the fall of the gun laws was finally, too much for him to bear.

"How do two teenage boys, sitting on a wall, eating ice cream on a summer's day, protect themselves when they're shot by a *drive-by* twenty-year old, using a legally purchased gun? And the four-year old that was shot dead—same gun—right after I was hit? She was sitting by herself on the porch, while her grandma fixed up lemonade in the kitchen. You tell me how any gun, legal or otherwise would have helped any of us that day? He's still out there now; he was never caught. And he's probably still exercising his right to bear arms. I can tell you that if that 20-year old hadn't walked into a gun shop in Virginia, and bought a gun, like it was an ice cream, my brother would still be here today, I wouldn't be in this chair, and that little girl would be 29 years old."

Anita and I stayed still, allowing for Luther to say more, but he turned away and went to his room, leaving us alone in his kitchen. As I left that night I could feel Anita's whole body trembling against mine. She whispered to me to *stay safe*, the only time I recall her ever telling me that. I felt shaken, hollowed out, as I walked to the Metro; something had been taken from us all the day the gun law fell. Something had been stolen. The D.C. law had stood for nearly three decades, until the NRA's lock on Congress was so strong they could take out any gun control law in their sights, starting with repealing the assault weapon ban, because every American needs an AK-47 or two, and on down to us—Washington, D.C., no representation in Congress—a sitting duck. What an easy shot to take.

Luther, Anita and I careened out of the Delegate's office shell-shocked.

"That was good. She's on it. Great. But I *really* need to go home," I told Luther and Anita. "I have a conference call with W times 3 scheduled for this afternoon. She's recommending us to some funders. I'll keep you posted."

"Who's *W times 3*?" Luther asked, but I rode away on my bike, leaving Anita to explain, and I heard him break out into a loud, deep, roar of laughter. And then as I turned back to wave, I saw him slip his arm around Anita's waist as she leaned down for him to kiss her.

Such delicious gossip and I couldn't even share it with Catherine because she was still in damage control mode. No calls allowed unless it was to tell her I could deliver some votes. While I would love to help, WWW was waiting on me. As I pedalled madly along Florida Ave., I called Ian, who informed me that he thought it was pretty obvious Luther and Anita would hook up.

"Not to me," I protested, "Luther's all business—*serious* business."

"Exactly, that's why he gets what he wants."

So I called Greg and he just burst out laughing.

"Linda, you *are* getting soft. You didn't know?"

I swerved to avoid an even more reckless biker than me and yelled back at Greg,

"Next time, tell me, O.K?"

I was getting another call so I told Greg to hang on. It was WWW, urging me to start the meeting early, right away. I couldn't take a funding conference call on my bike—although of course I hadn't told her that I was on my bike. WWW tended to think of bike riding as a leisure activity—akin to truancy—rather than a legitimate mode of transport to and from meetings. I switched back to Greg, and without a word, I ended the call. He would understand, I was sure. Back on with WWW I told her that I needed an extra ten minutes to get back to my office.

"But everyone is here," she said. "We're *all* on this call, waiting for you."

Another call came in from Greg; I couldn't ignore it—we had an unspoken agreement to always take each other's call, in case it was urgent. When I finally shook him off, WWW was no longer connected. As I now settled into the long haul up 16th street, I decided I would play the *bad signal* card. And I happily ignored her many attempts to get me back on the phone as I pushed past Malcolm X Park and pressed on home. When I got there my phone was already ringing. *WWW.* I threw my bike down, tore upstairs to my office, pulled out the files I would need, and called her back.

"*Lin-da*, so *good* of you to call back. We're all—*still* here."

Time to make some money. As I gave my pitch, I was aware that I was talking to a new cadre of funders—not those buoyed by old-school wealth, but the kind that seemed to have sprung up overnight—a few good hedge fund deals, one hot product, or real estate wisely flipped. They had more money than they knew what to do with and WWW to guide them. She had hand picked some of her choicest contacts for our conference call. As excited and eager as I was to infuse Anita's organization with some real money that would allow her to start planning beyond the current campaigns, I couldn't help the feeling of unease that nipped at my confidence as I described our work. I tried to quarantine the sentiment—I couldn't even define it yet. Was it distrust or resentment? I moved on, the facts and figures readily dispelling the questions I fielded during my presentation. WWW followed up, and she positively gushed about my work. I could tell she had already convinced her friends to pull out their checkbooks. *Such effortless success*. The uneasy feeling now gathered speed and hunted me down as I signed off from the conference call and sat back. *What just happened there?* But I forced the doubt away for now as I settled into my work. I had some serious research to do that I'd put off for far too long and the deadline had arrived. The next day I was meeting with James Hadid.

OF ALL THAT MAY FALL AND RISE
IN A SINGLE DAY

Every betrayal contains a perfect moment, a coin stamped heads or tails with salvation on the other side.
                                                    Barbara Kingsolver

The *Washington Post* reporter arrived forty minutes late for our meeting. I wouldn't have stuck around ordinarily—I had a mountain of work waiting for me back at home, and I had learned to appreciate punctuality after so many years in Washington. But I needed to find out why James Hadid was so insistent that we meet in person. I had searched the *Homes First* database and discovered numerous clues in his contact history to explain why he was so interested in the Oxon Cove campaign. A web search confirmed that James was one of the *Post*'s lead writers on crime in the metro region; he seemed to have covered a truly horrendous array of homicides, burglaries and violent assaults, but I had not been able to guess his motives for our meeting. He evidently held a strong opinion on the Ward 8 prison but I suspected he might go either way. With his experience he could be tough on crime—the more prisons the better—but he could just as easily believe in keeping the prisoners close to home, to give them a fighting chance at rehab. Then again, he was a strong advocate of representation for D.C., so he was likely angry that Congress was forcing the prison on Ward 8. I discovered that he grew up in Ward 8 and had stuck around, choosing to work in his hometown and live in his old neighborhood. It occurred to me that he might even prove to be an ally, not a word I tended to use about reporters, but it would have been invaluable to us if the campaign had a friend at the *Post*. As hard as I tried though, I couldn't figure him out.

"Linda, hi! I'm *so* sorry!" James said, as he dragged the chair next to me towards him and slumped into it. "I just need a minute to catch my breath."

I took the time to observe his appearance. He was in his late forties, and likely once attractive, but he had allowed himself to sag and age too quickly. He was too heavy for his fine features, a strikingly elegant face seemed buried under loose, worn cheeks, and the table barely hid the large belly that protruded awkwardly from below. His dark skin appeared prematurely coarse and wrinkled for a man his age. I noticed that he was clad almost entirely in gray; the color drained the light from his eyes and made him appear older still. I couldn't help but wonder if it was his line of work that was to be blamed for all of this—he was altogether the opposite of the file photos on the web. I was contemplating reassessing my approach to our meeting—wary of the evident breadth of his life experiences compared to my own—when he interrupted my thoughts,

"The DMV—they *failed* my car! I had to go home and get some paperwork to show them that I'd just had the brakes fixed. Some factory recall bullshit going on. Guy took one look at the manufacturer's notice and suddenly, bam! They're scraping the failed sticker off and gracing me with a two-year pass to drive my car and do my damn *job*. Hours of my life wasted."

When I didn't reply, he acknowledged that this was time out of my life wasted too. Not a good start for him, but maybe I could play this to my advantage.

"Look, I'm not the enemy here, OK? I'm just—what the hell—look at this and tell me what you think."

He handed me a set of pages stapled together—a council resolution, signed by every one of the thirteen council members. Right away the document seized my attention—this was *last* session's council, not the current one—and that particular set of saints and bandits never reached a consensus on anything. Except this apparently: a resolution calling on the *United States Congress* to help locate a *new prison in the District of Columbia*. I couldn't believe we didn't unearth this sooner. This could help us or sink us, and right then I was leaning more towards—we were *fucked*.

"Crap for you, right? Don't worry, five pages and all it says is what you already know. We need a new prison. Please keep the prisoners close to home. But what it doesn't doesn't do is give Congress license to steal Ward 8 parkland, or lock our boys up to make a sweet profit off of them."

"I—uh—" I stopped myself from giving him a juicy little quote to pass on to whichever colleague he owed a favor to right now. I couldn't help but mistrust him.

"Look, let's order—my treat for standing you up."

"No way. Then I'll owe you twice over."

"A terrible debt to have to pay back, huh?" he said, laughing.

With some journalists there was a mutual understanding and respect that we drink from the same water, and so we come to rely on, and even trust one other. But still it was best never to get too personal. If anything happened to poison the well you could find yourself having to look real fast for somewhere else to drink.

"Don't sweat, I'm not here to get the goods on your campaign, I'll do all the talking."

We ordered and chatted about our kids and the tragic state of D.C.'s schools, while we waited for our food. James seemed to have fewer reservations than me about getting personal; he had found the perfect summer camp for his two kids and he jotted down the website for me, then cautioned me to make the reservations early because the programs filled up really fast. He was softening me up and I was succumbing to his compulsive personality, eventually revealing a little about myself, and my life. At least at first, we didn't mention Oxon Cove. Until the drinks arrived. Sparkling water for me, beer for him.

"I went out there. Took a quick drive after I was blessed by the DMV. Yeah, that's partly why I'm so late. Unbelievable place. I've been going there for years to get my head straight. *Maryland* side of course. D.C. side is a piece of shit the way they got it going right now."

I didn't know what to make of him. He seemed nice enough and that's exactly why I thought I needed to be on my guard. *He knows and goes to Oxon Cove, regularly*? Things were definitely looking up.

"So that council resolution? Don't let it worry you—I know you and Luther can handle it. Just wanted you to be prepared for when Randy Weaver's goons get their hands on it. Seemed weird to me you'd never mentioned it in any of your press stuff—I realized you probably never saw it. You can play it both ways though, and I'm sure you will."

My awakening warmth and trust for him must have been apparent to him because he pulled his chair closer, tapped his fingers on the table as though picking up the beat of what he'd say next, and then he launched off in a new direction.

"Look, I'm here because you're wondering are you sure you're fighting for the right side. *Am I right?*"

I smiled acknowledgement of Luther's influence around town.

"Good, I'm glad we got that straight. What you're doing is *right*. That's it. The sum total of this bullshit deal is that Congress is fucking with us again. Let me tell you—we do need a new prison, but screw the bastards for wanting to put it on Oxon Cove, for dumping it on Ward 8. And for wanting to make money off the kids who are going to get locked away."

"You wanted to meet me to tell me that? I appreciate it, really I do." I laughed. "But I suspect there's more?"

"Well, yeah, there's more."

I took a deep breath. Of course there was more—a *Washington Post* reporter's time is slightly more valuable than gold itself. "How much more?"

"I have it from a good source that *Hizzoner* is supporting the prison."

James rubbed his chin, allowing time for the news to sink in. I detected a little twinkle of glee in his eyes; this was old school D.C. politics, not for the faint of heart.

"Come on. Oh, come *on*. You're joking, right?"

I refused to believe that the former Ward 8 council member, and three-time former Mayor, who continued to float the halls of the D.C. government buildings like an uneasy ghost of days long gone, could be *this* foolish and brazen in acknowledging his debts around town. I immediately thought of Damien—for a politician who had had nothing but the undying love and support of his community, this seemed like the ultimate betrayal. James watched me process the information and then turned his hands outwards, smiling; I silently conceded that I was now officially between a rock and a hard place.

"Linda—what did you really expect? Weaver, Roland, and our very own Mayor-for-Life. *The Ward 8 Holy Trinity*. About as concerned with the future of the community as they are their own pockets. Not a hard decision for them, just a harder fight for you guys."

I shook my head. "*How can he do this?*"

"He's calling a press conference and will be taking a walkabout to say that he thinks there's—oh, get this—nothing but snakes and rats down at the Cove, and the prison would be an *economic benefit* to the community."

"Yeah, well I have to agree with him about the snakes and rats, just not down at the Cove." I searched for a report in my briefcase. "Here, look at this. Antoine Ford at Princeton, completely *killed* the economic benefit argument for prisons in his study last year."

"Had a feeling you'd have your comeback, had a feeling you'd be on top of this." He paused, tapping lightly on the table again, weighing up where to go next. When he spoke his voice dropped; there wasn't a hint of the newshound left in him.

"Do you know what the odds are for me holding down my job and my marriage and for getting my kids through school?"

I hesitated. "Not good?"

"Worse than not good. You could make a fortune betting on me just for trying to live the life I want. Why do you think I took the crime beat? I'll never stray. I'll never fail at anything in my life because I *know* how it ends, when a black man fails. There is no room in this society for a black man to fail at *anything* he does. There is no second chance or trying again. Before you get a chance to try again, you're behind bars and a marked man—for life."

"You're with Luther, aren't you?" I said, understanding now what was really going on. "He's all about the *next* generation. He's done with this one. I don't entirely understand it. How you can be so certain?"

"He's exactly right, that's why. We can't let the next generation fail. They have to get it right first time around. All the hard work, all the investments we make in our community here on out have to be about the *next* generation. From the ground up—Luther's been going on about it forever. He's right. We need to start by making our neighborhoods safe and building a place where—plain and simple—kids get to be *kids*, on *every* level. Follow that trajectory. How do we protect our kids, educate them, nurture them, build a community that is for and about *kids*, so that they grow up knowing they can and will be different from the last generation? I don't know exactly. But I can tell you one thing for certain—not by building a fucking *prison* in Ward 8."

He finished the last of his second beer. "You keep doing what you're doing. And don't let the *Close to Home* bullshit get to you."

"It's not *bullshit* James. How can you say that? There are young kids in prison right now, who deserve another chance, who should have another chance. You said so yourself. They probably won't get that chance. Not if they're dumped in Ohio with no one to look out for them. This is not bullshit. If I'm struggling with it, if I don't have Luther's convictions, it doesn't make it bullshit. How can you say that?"

"Bosnia, you know? I was there. I cut my teeth as a journalist in hell on earth. UN Peacekeepers stood by while blood ran in the streets because they weren't *allowed* to help. UN Rules of Engagement bullshit. I watched people die, I watched people kill, I watched people *do nothing*. Wasn't till NATO bombed the shit out of those fucking Serbs that the massacres stopped. And there are *those* in this world who'll tell you *America had no right* to go in and save those Muslims that no one gave a fuck about. *America saving Muslims*. That makes a great story don't you think these days?! But half the former Soviet fucking Union thinks we should have let the Serbs finish the job. *Wasn't our war to fight*. You worried this isn't your war? You think you should check the *rule book* to make sure you're on the right side? Let me tell you, there is a *side* that wants you to believe that it was O.K. to wipe out Grozny in two days. I was there—made Bosnia look like a fucking tea party. There is always a side that makes doing the right thing *look* wrong. There may not even be a right or wrong—life is never, ever that simple—but you, right now, are doing the right thing. That I can tell you."

He looked up at the waiter who had arrived with an undisguised air of disgust at the sight of all the food he had ordered. He chose to ignore the slight and nodded his thanks to the waiter.

"When a *prison* is being built next to a *school*, on a *park* for fuck's sake, you get on the side that wants to stop that prison. Figure the rest out later."

I sat back as the waiter placed my food in front of me.

"Good. I'm starving. Let's eat," he said. He picked up his fresh glass of beer, and placed his first forkful of food into his mouth at the same time. Just watching him made me wonder if I was going to be able to keep up with him over lunch. He confirmed my fears by stopping for a moment to admonish me for not digging in quickly enough, and then he launched into a story about growing up in Ward 8. In no time at all, it was me who was interviewing James, I was the one eager for quotes and tales that could be re-told. The more he opened up, the more I mined him for information about what it was really like to grow up East of the River, to have achieved success and stayed home. Four generations of his family had lived blocks from his house, doors always open, a constant flow of people in and out of each other's homes. He was very funny, we laughed a lot; his life seemed abundantly full of love and good times. And gunfire at night. Not always, but a familiar enough sound, each time followed by a mad rush to see who might have been involved. And friends who had passed before their thirtieth birthdays. His world was the world I worked in, I knew the street names, I knew my way around, I had helped and gotten to know many residents there. But the life James described was simply unknowable to me.

After a while he slowed down, the food and the beer draining much of his energy, slurring his speech, transforming the powerful force that blew into the restaurant just an hour ago.

"Shouldn't drive," he said matter-of-factly.

"No, probably not."

He gave his keys a resigned shake and replaced them in his jacket pocket; after tossing a few bills on the table he took me by the elbow and lead me outside.

"Walk back to the office?"

"Sure," I said, although I felt a mixture of disappointment and relief that James asked me to do this. It didn't fit with the picture that he insisted I preserve of him as a successful black man who had beaten all the odds. The *Post* was many blocks away and we filled the time with very few words as we walked. He started to make his way awkwardly up the steps and then he turned.

"My neighborhood," he paused, "doesn't need a *goddamn prison*." His voice was nothing more than a strained, dry whisper. He waited a moment for his head to clear; I could see the haze of alcohol wash over him until he said simply, "D'you understand?"

He reached over and shook my hand. "It was good to meet you. Real good. Tell Luther, hi from me." And then he was gone.

Yes. I understood. Because the doubt that had plagued me, since Luther sent me those reports about the prison population in America, had at last taken its leave. How did I ever allow myself to even consider the possibility that a prison might be good for Ward 8, good for the prisoners and their families, good for the community? James had achieved the greatest success possible as a man, as a journalist, and yet he carried it with him; Luther carried it with him; Anita carried it with her. Each one, in their own way, was still being asked to carry it, despite having risen up and having made something of their lives. James half-destroyed by it, Luther consumed by it, Anita never free because of it. It was the *certain* knowledge that there were *still* those wielding significant power in America, from the leader of the United States Senate on down, who firmly believed that poor blacks didn't deserve better than a prison. That black boys and girls born into the statistical certainty of never graduating high school, should be neglected and ignored until they could be swept away, out of sight, into ever more prisons and that others should make a *profit* off their broken lives. 900,000. 900,000. 900,000. Wasted lives. Human beings locked up. Behind bars. Caged. African Americans—who are only one sixth of our population—but half the prison population. Right and wrong. An easy choice if I followed my heart, an easier choice now that I had my facts straight.

I sat on the steps of the *Washington Post* building—its place in history seemed to fill the air about me—and I called Luther on his cell but reached his voicemail.

"James is—he's great. Thanks Luther. Thank you."

That night as I read to Sandra, she was full of questions. I think she always knows when I'm not really with her, in the moment together—that even though I may be reading to her, I'm distracted. Asking me a barrage of questions and not even listening for the answers is her way of drawing me back; she was deliberately funny and cute, utterly irresistible, placing her soft little fingers on my head and turning me to face her every time I absentmindedly looked away. Eventually we abandoned the book we were reading and made up stories together. This was her favorite activity; she had won me. We cuddled and laughed and traveled far away to a magical, invented land of ours. And then the phone rang. We listened to the message on the answering machine from Andrew, the Legislative Director for Baucus's office. He may as well have been an evil King come to wreak havoc on the land. Sandra screwed up her nose at the message; she knew what it meant, and she tried to stop me from getting up. I told her I needed to tuck her into bed and call Andrew back. She protested the hurried kisses and quick hugs that I gave her before I pulled the covers up and turned out the light. We had spent the whole evening together, playing board games after dinner, we read for nearly an hour, but still I was left with the feeling—my constant companion—of never having enough time to spend with my child.

I called Andrew back; the latest *Childhood Lead Poisoning Prevention* hearings took place earlier in the day, and I was eager to know the outcome. I had kept my promise to Rafael. I had followed the glacially slow progress of the bill and hosted several campaign organizing sessions. I helped him craft a thoughtful testimony for the hearings, describing the impact of lead poisoning on his niece's quality of life, and presenting his perspective as a doctor and research scientist. Heavy, impressive stuff. But I wasn't able to attend the long-awaited hearings, the first step to getting the bill passed. I was holding out for, half-expecting, good news from Andrew. He wanted to know if I had heard what happened.

"Guess who played bait and switch at the lead hearings?"

"Sorry, I was swamped with work today, and I've just spent the past two hours playing about a thousand rounds of *Rat-a-Tat Cat*."

Andrew brushed aside my personal life. I wasn't offended; he was likely pumped with adrenalin that could only be worked out of his system by re-hashing the gory details of his day. A really bad day as it turned out.

"*Brightwood*. He used the Landlord Association's bill."

"What happened?"

"Baucus at last got to introduce his bill. But Brightwood had already lined up enough council members to table Baucus' bill and hear his *Lead Abatement is a Waste of Money,* bill instead. We got a hold of the Landlord Association's lobby materials—they had a model bill—Brightwood's is word for word, almost identical. They didn't even bother to change it. At least it didn't pass. *Nothing* passed. We're back to square one."

"How'd Baucus take it?"

"You know what he's like, he never gives up. He's having a meeting tomorrow morning, 8:30, here. He wants to get tenants and landlords together to start talking again right away."

"8:30? Can't make it. Sorry. But go ahead and send me the info, and I'll take a look, get you my thoughts."

Moments after I got off the phone with Andrew, Jonathan called.

"How'd this happen?" I asked him.

"Today, all so fast, the hearing was a madhouse. The place was packed. Tenants thought they were finally going to be heard. Baucus was taking hell from them, for selling out, because half of them didn't realize that he didn't even know what had happened. Brightwood's sitting there like a peacock all proud and smiling, because he doesn't need his bill to pass, he'd already killed Baucus', and that's all he wanted to do in the first place."

"I take it you'll be at Baucus' meeting tomorrow?" I asked.

"I can't, I already have a breakfast meeting on the Hill." He paused. "Richard will be there for *Homes First*."

"That's O.K., I already told Andrew I can't make it."

I suspected Jonathan was weighing up whether this was true or not, disappointed that he had not better trained me to set aside personal differences for the cause. I tried to convince him that I wasn't merely trying to avoid seeing Richard.

"Really Jonathan, I can't make it."

"O.K.," he said. "It is what it is."

The emails and faxes came through for the next half hour, and I reviewed them, marked them up, took notes and worked hard to prepare a package for Andrew for tomorrow's meeting. I pulled out my lead campaign files and reviewed them; we were not using our best weapon, the data on the spread of lead poisoning across the city. It was Worthington's committee we were up against, and she was sitting on the second worse affected ward in the city. No one wanted to personally attack her, or the landowners in her ward, because everyone was afraid of Roland, so we had all avoided using the Ward 8 data. But a while ago, Charlie from Park Service had shared news with me about an ongoing investigation over at DOJ into Roland's violations of the federal lead abatement regulations. Charlie's insider there had provided him with confidential memos and a sealed indictment against Roland. We had never discussed using the information before now. I called Charlie; he already knew what had happened at the Committee hearings. He made a few calls and got back to me.

"You can use the documents," he said. "Go get that bastard and all who support him."

I couldn't possibly fax or messenger any of the Justice Department documents to Andrew. It had been made clear to me that they were for Andrew and Baucus' eyes only; I had to personally ensure that no one else saw them. So I finished putting the package together, and drove to Andrew's house on Capitol Hill.

"Baucus didn't want to go this route, you know," Andrew said, as he skimmed through the confidential material. "He's known about all of this for a while. He wouldn't even let me put a call in to Justice. To him, Sheila's a colleague, an elected official, no matter how complicit she is in any of Roland's affairs."

"Don't worry about it, there's no mention of her in these papers. She'll come out clean. It's the descriptions of his properties that you'll want, and DOJ's findings just confirm the research you did about lead poisoning in Ward 8. It'll make your negotiations go a whole lot smoother, that's all."

When I returned home and went to bed, I lay awake thinking about what I had done that night. Driven across town past midnight to avoid the slightest chance that I might run into Richard had I instead gone by Andrew's office to drop the files off in the morning. It is what it is.

A few days later Rafael called me for an update me on the lead bill. Not surprisingly, the very existence of the Justice Department's documents acted like a plumber's snake tenaciously tunneling through a clogged drainpipe full of crap; the legislative agenda of the Health and Human Services Committee significantly shifted on matters relating to childhood lead poisoning. Rafael was delighted at the progress we were making at last.

"Do you have some time to get together?" he asked.

"Of course, what's up?"

"Can we meet—" he paused, and then laughed. "I don't know how to put this delicately."

"Rafael," I spoke carefully, since I couldn't begin to imagine what he meant to ask me, "*What* do you have in mind now?"

"Well, I've lived in D.C. twenty years or more, and I've never been the other side of the Anacostia River. What do you say I fix that before I leave?"

I was relieved at the simplicity of his request; Rafael was not asking me to take on another worthy, hopeless cause. But then his words truly sunk in.

"Leave? *Leave* what?"

"D.C. Marguerite and I are moving back to Houston."

Another friend bites the dust. What is it with this town? No place else I've ever lived, have I had to say this many goodbyes. Between Ian and I, we could cry us a river of goodbyes, which it seemed, was what Rafael had in mind.

"Could we go to Anacostia Park, maybe have lunch by the river?"

"No, no, we can't, because you, Rafael—*you* can't leave. You are my one, token Latino friend."

Rafael roared with laughter. "Linda, you are wicked, you know that?"

"I'm sorry, but you *can't* leave. I haven't the faintest hope of ever improving my Spanish if you leave. And you know how bad my Spanish is."

"Aren't you even going to ask me why? I accepted a fantastic job at Baylor—they're ready to start clinical trials! Let me tell you all about it when I see you."

"Rafael, I don't want to do this to you, but I have to. If you leave, who'll watch over your kids at the stables?"

"Ah, now you are successfully tugging at my heartstrings."

"Well thank God for that, so don't leave. *Think of the children*."

"That's another favor I wanted to ask of you. Will you come with me to say goodbye to them? And, there's a party at my aunt's house—for Marguerite and me—a sort of engagement and going away affair."

"Rafael, I *hate* goodbyes, and by my count you're up to three already. How many more do you have in mind?"

"Well, you're right. There is one more. Marguerite and I also want to get together with you and Ian before we leave."

"So you're determined for this friendship to bleed slowly and painfully to death it seems. Nothing can save us now."

"Please, Linda, your drama is too much for me! So when can we go to the River?" he asked again, and I reluctantly, begrudgingly agreed to meet later in the week for lunch on the banks of the Anacostia River.

OF WHAT CAN BE ACHIEVED
BEFORE NINE IN THE MORNING

*Thou shall not be a perpetrator; thou shall not be a victim
And thou shall never, but never, be a bystander.*
                                                    Yehuda Bauer

Vernon Frederick greeted us in the lobby when we arrived at his offices on 16th Street and lead the way to the elevators. We rose to the top floor where the reception area, flooded with natural light, and giving out onto views of the city and the Potomac River to the west, housed an enormous art gallery. Luther, Anita and I were momentarily, uncharacteristically, speechless.

"I collect art," Vernon announced as we stepped off the elevator. "Children's art. Children who are talented, troubled, and who could use the money to turn their lives around. What I don't do is buy the work of cosseted artists who don't need me to help pay for their paint. Take a look. They're good."

Luther threw me a glance to say, what have we gotten into here? I shrugged and we dived in; starting at one end and working our way around, we carefully inspected the different pictures. Had Vernon not already told us, I would never have known that children painted the pieces before us. They were, for the most part, magnificent. I could see from their descriptions that the paintings had come from all over the U.S. Frederick's bank had determinedly forged its way into underserved communities, where other banks wouldn't go unless told to, unless mandated by law; his acquisitions told something of the story of his success in willingly venturing out across the country.

Luther and I came up in front of a painting of two boys leaning on their bicycles and eating popsicles. The canvas was probably as large as 15 x 20 foot, a wall of summer colors and heat; one of the boys, doubled up with laughter, looked almost as though he were leaning out of the picture towards us, larger than life.

"I love it," I said, "hey Anita, look at this one."

As I turned to her, I saw that she was looking directly at Luther, and what passed between them was unmistakable and difficult to witness.

"Mr. Frederick," she said, "Thank you so much for sharing your collection with us and for taking this meeting."

He took her cue. "Call me Vernon, please. Let's go into the conference room, this way."

As I followed Vernon, I glanced back and saw that Luther was still in front of the same painting; he nodded to Anita to go ahead without him. I caught a glimpse of him forcing his fist against his mouth. I understood now—his shock at having been taken off guard. Losing someone suddenly, in a way you never expected, were never given a chance to prepare for, makes it forever after impossible to know what might suddenly detonate inside you to send the memories and grief showering down all over again. Better that it happens when you are alone, because once the pin is released, there is no holding back the emotions that explode as intensely as the moment you stood at the side of the grave, trying to imagine the person you once held in your arms, now lying in a box, set in the newly turned earth before you. For Luther, this gallery, this meeting, was no place to attend to his brother's memory. He would have to fight with everything he had inside him to force away the loss of having once been a part of two boys, two brothers, laughing on a summer day.

I called Greg on his cell while Vernon's assistant tended to our coffee and drinks. He was uncharacteristically late for the meeting. Just as I was considering how we might discuss the complexities of financing the Windsor takeover without him, he was at the door.

"Good to see you again, Vernon," Greg said, warmly shaking our host's hand. "Apologies for my being late, no excuses worth telling." He spun one of the conference chairs towards him and as he sat down, he said, "Look, sorry Vernon, but Luther needed to be elsewhere. He won't be joining us today."

Vernon turned towards the lobby with a puzzled look on his face and was clearly disappointed, but he didn't pry. "Shame. I hope he'll catch up with me later."

Anita and I both fell back in our chairs; the news knocked the wind from our sails. But Greg was already picking up the slack and he launched into the meeting by reporting that the Mayor had at last, put Windsor on his Affordable Housing shortlist for city financing. Later, Greg told me in private that this was his reason for being late. The Mayor's decision came down to the last minute. He continued to reject Greg's advice until he reviewed the latest polls; only then did he understand that endorsing the tenant takeover of the largest apartment building East of the River was probably his only hope of winning back support in the neighborhoods there. The news was just what we were hoping for. No banker in his right mind, no matter how committed they were to serving low-income communities would take Windsor on without the city's sponsorship. Vernon would have assumed that the government would back the project when preparing his risk assessment; he would not have called today's meeting otherwise.

"So," Vernon said, "Tell me Linda, why we shouldn't be encouraging the Windsor residents to take their *Section 8* vouchers and go elsewhere?"

I was not sure why he directed this question at me. I didn't want to think that it was because I was the only white person in the room, but I was having a hard time thinking of any other reason right now.

"Section 8? *Section 8*? You want me to review the benefits of Section 8?" I asked, giving myself time to gather my thoughts, and clarify that I hadn't completely misunderstood Vernon's intentions.

"Would you?" Vernon asked politely, reminding me entirely, at this moment, of my thesis supervisor in grad school. Never one to tire of flogging a dead horse.

Greg looked at me with a mischievous grin. Anita meanwhile was barely hiding her disdain at the suggestion that Windsor residents should take their housing vouchers and go elsewhere.

"Well, I don't know. I can't speak for the residents, but many of the low-income Windsor families have already had that choice for a while—if they qualify for Section 8, which only some do. I mean, if their means are insufficient, so they can—well, it's essentially a voucher system—go elsewhere. But they didn't need to—uh, go, elsewhere, anywhere else—because Windsor was a great property. It is a great property. Well-managed, reasonable rents. It's just that now that it's going to be sold, in this market, there's no real choice right now. Where would they go? And it's my understanding that the residents in this case, want to stay. In their homes—Windsor Apartments—I mean."

"Your understanding?" he asked.

"Anita has carried out surveys. We included them, in the materials we sent you?"

"Yes."

He got up and walked over to the dry erase board on the wall, just by the floor-to-ceiling picture window. Poorly placed, if you asked me; it was hard not to stare at the spectacular view just beyond it. I could see parts of the Georgetown University campus, the tip of the golden dome at the heart of Georgetown, I could even make out a few boats going by, way out on the river. Greg nudged me, and pointed me back to the board. Now I knew I was back in grad school.

Vernon was silent as he quickly filled up the board with a series of numbers and graphs. When he was done he talked us through them.

"The richest one percent of this country now earn twenty times the average household income in America; thirty years ago it was ten times."

His hand moved across the board.

"Look here, median household income, has stagnated over the last ten years, around $46,000. So ten times that is 460,000. Twenty times is 920,000. That's the *widening gap* people talk about."

His hand moved down the board. Now I noticed the elegant palette and brush cufflinks and the tailored shirt, the handsome suit and carefully knotted tie, and then my eyes settled for the first time on Vernon's face. He was not particularly attractive in any conventional sense—his jaw was a little too large, his soft, gray eyes almost too deeply set—but even in his mid-fifties he looked like a college kid. *Energetic*. Smart, in control, full of understanding, full of knowledge. More than in control. In power.

"The poverty rate meanwhile has stagnated. We're still hovering around 12.5 percent of the population at minimum. Now of course, we have immigration to attend to and poverty might occasionally come with donated computers and clothing today, so let's remember to put it all in perspective shall we? But *poverty*, as I'm sure you all know, is still defined as roughly $17,000 annual income for a household of three. Not much money left over for crayons and paint brushes."

More facts, more figures, and then he summarized for us.

"So we've gone from 12 percent of the population in poverty, versus the top one percent at $460,000 or more, ten years ago, to the same 12 percent at the bottom, versus the top one percent at $920,000 or more, today. And right here, let's focus on this, shall we? The *median* is still stuck at $46,000."

While my head was starting to spin from this unexpected economics lecture—it was still only 7:35 in the morning!—I was acutely aware that Vernon must have slotted us in at 7:00am, at short notice, for a reason, and that could only mean he had already made up his mind on Windsor. Good or bad, a decision was what we were looking for today. If he rejected us we could move swiftly on to the next potential backer; hopefully by then we might also have a decision from the Housing Authority in hand to help us along. If he had decided to back us, then I guessed he wanted us to be clear about his motivation; he wanted us to know that his intentions were entirely honorable. Unless the whole *meet you personally in the lobby/children's art gallery tour* was merely some clever ruse to help land himself a Housing Authority partnership in a hot, emerging real estate market.

It was my experience that people in positions of power such as his—people who have earned every moment and dollar of their success—are fascinated by, maybe even obsessed with, statistics and facts and figures. They do not like to see them manipulated, explained away, or altered to win arguments. They like to study them in their purest form, and draw on them for personal direction. Vernon, it seemed, had remained emotionally and physically tethered to his childhood growing up in the projects in Chicago. Although he graduated from the Wharton Business School and had a CEO track career at one of the nation's largest banks, he chose to break away and focus his personal and financial future on the most economically depressed, minority neighborhoods in the country, opening his first branch just blocks from where he grew up. He had built an enormously successful business for himself and proved that high-risk investments in the nation's poor could work and were a vital part of narrowing the wealth gap.

"So, what now?" Vernon said, after wiping the dry-erase board clean.

Hmm, could be a sign of good office etiquette, or we might be in for *more* statistics? I found myself thumbing my empty coffee cup, wondering if I might just stand up now and quickly refill before the next economics lecture. Much as I admired his thoroughness, I already spent an unhealthy chunk of my life reviewing the economics of poverty in the United States, and at this hour, I just really needed another coffee. I thought to save myself by offering to top up everyone else's mugs. Greg smiled at the unfortunate transparency of my non-altruistic gesture. Vernon however, seemed to approve of my impromptu coffee break because it had apparently renewed his energy for what came next.

"You came here today to convince me that the Windsor tenants can meet the down payment and are committed to making their mortgage payments. Right? Well, what I want to know is, anyone here care to define my liability?"

Wow, this is definitely worse than grad school. I cannot function before nine in the morning. It is against my religion. I never, ever signed up for classes before 10 am, no matter how much I loved the subject, or the professor. Right *now*, I should be mindlessly deleting emails, reading the Post online and thinking about what to have for breakfast.

"Your liability is what you'll pay, if we fail."

Luther had joined us. Relief flooded over me, not just because I was less of a target for Vernon now, but for Luther himself. His being there to make a real connection with Vernon was personally important to Luther; this was part of his dream to bring new investors—who did not first require that the current residents be cleared out—East of the River.

Vernon nodded approval of Luther's response. "You see for *me*, that's just it. We can put an exact number on the cost of tenants defaulting on their mortgage payments, we can assess the risk involved in having to repossess property and repair damages incurred by problem homeowners. I know I might well take on felons and drug dealers and possibly even a convicted murderer, along with hard-working honest families, by investing in Windsor. So what I want *you* to do is to think of the liability I take on, and that you take on, if we fail to significantly improve the quality of life of each homeowner *after* the takeover." He sat on the conference table, at ease now. "My bank is hoping to generate a new customer base East of the River. If we don't move beyond homeownership, towards generally improving the standard of living, then honestly, what will we have achieved?"

Vernon moved back to the board.

$17,000

$46,000

$960,000

"Got that?' he said. "So what's my average liability per household currently, at the existing poverty level?"

"Thirty odd thousand?" I offered.

Vernon looked at me as though to say, *ah, so you are awake.*

"Exactly."

"I don't—" Greg looked lost.

"What I'm looking at is not how much it will cost me to invest in a tenant takeover of Windsor, I'm looking at how much it will cost me to move all the tenants from the lowest household income to—*at the very least*—the median income. I'm not talking about closing the wealth gap overnight or anything bold right now, this is about raising the most basic standard of living and investing in the future of the next generation. You can start by telling me how you intend to get the kids living in the Windsor apartments to graduate High School?"

Luther's and Anita's faces lit up and Greg, I knew, was fighting every impulse to text the Mayor that we had sealed the deal with Vernon.

Anita stood up.

"May I?" she asked, moving to the board.

She summarized the plan that we had all been working on for the past few months. This spoke directly to what Vernon was getting at. Anita focused on the budget—our assessment of what it would cost to provide on-site services at Windsor apartments after the takeover. Some of the funds we had raised were already designated for this program. Through the Citizens Group we aimed to establish a daycare center, a fully-staffed after-school study hall and library, provide internet access in all the homes, and with a modest medical office in place, hire a registered nurse, full-time counselor and maybe even a part-time doctor and dentist. These services would first be made available to the residents, and afterwards, if feasible, to the surrounding neighborhood. We were still developing our goals for job training and placement. We had studied similar community plans across the country and in the city, and our goal was to learn from our own program and replicate and improve it for other communities East of the River.

Vernon asked no questions until Anita finished her presentation, and then he turned to me again.

"How much exactly have you raised?'

Ah, *now* I got it. He thought as the campaign's fundraiser, that I spent my life at elegant art gallery openings and fabulous gala dinners with wealthy funders, and therefore I was a force to be reckoned with. If only this were true. Mostly I wrote lengthy, dull grant applications and raked through my emails or waited patiently by the phone, for good news. My instincts couldn't have been further off target this morning; his choosing me was not a matter of race after all. Perhaps I could chalk that one up to sleep deprivation. Should I have shattered his illusion of my role in all of this, convinced him that I was truly but a foot soldier in Luther and Anita's army? No, what the hell, that day I felt like garnering a hefty pat on the back for all my efforts. Someone as formidable as Vernon thinking I was important was deliciously flattering, the least anyone could do for making me talk about *Section 8* at 7:00 in the morning.

When I went on to announce the latest budget figures for this particular program, Greg exhaled deeply. I realized Anita had not yet told him of the gigantic windfall from the WWW conference call. It had all happened so fast, and I was still awaiting final confirmation. Maybe I shouldn't have presented it as a done deal, but something told me WWW wanted this as badly as I did, and she simply never failed to get what she wanted.

"So this is looking real," Vernon said finally.

It all took us a moment to grasp that he was not talking about our community services program. Vernon had just given us his word that his bank would finance the Windsor Apartments tenant takeover. *My God*. I now knew what it felt like to float on air. I couldn't believe it. The excitement was bursting out of me, rippling across my skin like a fever chill. Greg got up and shook Vernon's hand, we all lined up to personally shake the man's hand, and then we were all back out on the street—Greg, Anita, Luther and I. I looked at my watch: 8:27am. I'm not even at my desk at this time, most mornings. I'm often in the car singing goofy songs with my four year old on the way to school. And if I were at my desk, I'd *still* be trawling through emails, reading the *Post* online

(O.K., maybe by now I'd have moved onto the *New York Times* or *Access Hollywood*) and wondering what to have for breakfast. So *this* is how the for-profit world works. I could get used to it. Moving obscene amounts of money around before most not-for-profits have even opened their doors.

"Go on Greg," Luther teased, "Tell *that* to the Mayor."

OF TIME SPENT BY A RIVER

*How can anyone anywhere love
these half-broken figures
bent under the sky's brightness?*

                                    Yusef Komunyakaa

Rafael and I sat eating our lunch together at a picnic table under a grand willow tree, its curtain of long-leafed branches drawn around us like a private screen from the heat and the bugs, and we watched the shadowy, dark waters of the Anacostia River flow gently passed us.

"I think I have this whole situation figured out."

"What situation?" he asked, in between mouthfuls of egg sandwich.

"You and Marguerite, Houston, the clinical trials, going home to your Dad. It's all come together."

"You mean my life? Well, yes, that's what I've been hoping for all this time."

"So, you wouldn't be expecting a Rafael or Marguerite junior anytime soon would you?'

Rafael blushed. Very cute. Very busted.

"When? I mean if you're going to make me go all the way to Texas to visit you, I think I have the right to know."

"In the spring. Come on, Texas is not so far."

I allowed some time for the news to sink in. Mommy Marguerite, Daddy Rafael—tiny, pink baby feet. *Love* that.

"All you ex-pats are going to bankrupt us, you know," I told him. "Ian and I travel across this country, visiting friends, and sure, it's great to see what lies out there beyond the beltway. But we *have* noticed that our friends rarely make the trip back to D.C. once they've left. Why is that exactly?"

He shook his head. "That's why I wanted to come here today, take a drive around the neighborhoods here—see it all before I leave. If I'm completely honest with you, Linda, I never took D.C. into my heart. Maybe that's why so many return to from wherever they came and then never look back on the city."

"Except for the kids at the stables. They are going to rip your heart out and stomp all over it when you say goodbye to them."

"Yes, they will."

He stood and gestured for me to walk along the river with him.

"Having a father in your life, there's nothing like it. Most of those kids will never know what that's like. You know, I went through most of my life ignoring my father and just when we fixed our relationship, I left to study and work and build my career. Well now the baby's coming I have to go home and show him that I've succeeded. Not just in my work. With my life. I want him to see for himself that his son now has all that he ever wanted for him, and that it's all because of him."

Rafael didn't need to say much more. I already knew the journey of his life. When he was fourteen, living in a depressed working-class neighborhood so far outside of Houston, that he would take two buses to go into town with his friends, his father suffered a near-fatal car accident. He had never regarded his father as anything other than the man who dutifully went to work each day at a newspaper press to be able to provide food and clothes for his family. Their relationship had been limited to questions about his school grades, the Astros and occasionally about the need to use condoms. He never knew that his father was a thoughtful, emotional, well-read man who spent hours reading at the public library and could recite whole passages from the works of his favorite authors, Lorca most especially. After the accident, when Rafael went to search his father's things for keepsakes to bring to the hospital to encourage his recovery, he found his father's notebooks, filled with quotes and thoughts about his life, about Houston and its mix of cultures, about Rafael and his two younger sisters; he was astonished to discover that he did not know his father at all. He was unaware until then of how deeply his father loved his family, and how precious their small, rundown house was to him. In one of the notebooks, he found sketches of a new house that his father was dreaming of building. He had written out estimates for the costs, and was saving to realize his dream. Rafael wondered how he could not know his father better. Was it his indifference, or his father's love of solitude that had kept them apart? While his father seemed to want so much from life, he was struck then—a teenager convinced that his path in life had already been carved out for him—with the realization that he, Rafael, wanted exactly nothing from life.

In the several months that followed until his father fully recovered, Rafael was saved from himself. He started to pay attention at school because he now understood that if he were to set out on a new road in life, he would have to acquire the qualifications one by one, that would allow him to take another step, and then another step, forward. Watching his father's painful but ultimately successful recovery, made him eager to grow up. His friends were changing every day, some becoming more serious about the future, others consumed by hopelessness. Rafael became a watcher like his father. Watching his old friends run with the girls, and experiment more boldly with drugs and alcohol he felt a growing revulsion at the predictability of the life course they were blindly following. Yet he knew that nothing would have shaken him from his own empty path had a car not skidded in the rain and struck down his father. He had learned that he could mess up his life and then try to fix it, or he could try to get it right the first time.

When Rafael told his father he wanted to go to college, his father hugged him harder and closer than at any other time in his life. He took any job he could find to save money, and he started taking extra courses to prepare for college. By then he was sixteen, and not immediately able to give up the lifestyle he had going with his old friends, so it took him until he was twenty to graduate high school with enough extra credits to be accepted into a half-decent state university. But it was enough to set his life on a new course. He never looked back, not until he was a Professor in molecular biology at the University of Maryland, heading up his own lung cancer research lab, and wondering how he might begin again to tend to those who loved him.

"So you're really leaving?" I asked Rafael, at last.
"I'm afraid we are, yes."

"Don't worry, we'll pass the damn lead bill without you."

"I'll be checking in on you to see that you do."

We watched an egret skim across the river and swoop back to the bank not far from where we stood.

"Come on," I said suddenly, "I want to show you something. Something that's not so nice about D.C., and maybe you'll miss it less, or maybe not."

I drove us back across the river and then back over the river again, this time on the Benning Road Bridge. Rafael laughed and waited patiently for me to explain. I stopped the car and put my hazards on—we were parked in the barely existent break down lane—and I saw him start to silently question my sanity.

"This is were we get out. Come on."

We scrambled down the bank to the river and I pointed to a sign.

"Welcome to the Middle Ages," I said, as Rafael read aloud the wording on the rusted metal sign at the water's edge.

I had only known Jonathan for a few months when he asked me one Saturday afternoon, in the late fall, to meet with him again. He told me to park on the Benning Road Bridge, and he added, as an afterthought, to wear good shoes because we were going down to the river. *He's crazy*, I thought—the rain fell in torrents outside my window. I asked him if perhaps it was dry where he was, but he laughed and said no, not at all, and he again insisted that Ian and I meet him right away.

We pulled up and parked behind Jonathan's car. The rain rushed along the road and spilled over onto the curb; wide rivulets coursed through the slick mud banks, down to the churning water below. It was difficult to find a footing as we eased our way down to the river, sliding more than walking to keep up with Jonathan. We stopped finally on a small mound of firm ground just beneath the bridge, where the ground was not yet soaked by the relentless rain.

"This is the Anacostia River when it rains."

He had to shout to be heard above the roar of the cars racing through the rain on the bridge above us. A foul stench filled the air; raw sewage gushed from an open pipe just beside us, directly into the river.

"This is what the United States Congress thinks of the Anacostia River and the people who live next to it. This is one of the outflows for the Capitol itself. That's the personal crap of our esteemed Senators and Congressmen coming our way, into our river, every time it rains."

As Ian and I started to back away, part of me feeling as though Jonathan had gone too far by bringing us here, he turned to me.

"I want you, Linda, to think about this every time you sit in one of those negotiations on the Hill about *funding* and *resources* and you are told, there just isn't the money available, to help the District. That D.C. can't have a vote just *yet*. This is a RIVER! You hear me? A RIVER! And that is *human sewage* going right into it. Take a good look at this. Now take a deep breath and remember this smell. *This* is the Ancostia River when it rains."

I remember looking at Ian and thinking of our recent camping trip in Shenandoah. We hiked all day and arrived hot and thirsty at a gleaming, silvery mountain stream. The burst of cool, fresh air passing across the trail alerted us to the water even before we heard or saw it. As I set up the tent, Ian pulled out the filter and pumped water into our bottles. We gulped down the icy water, slaking our thirst in an instant. Then we splashed our faces, and sitting on rocks at the river's edge, soaked our feet and listened for a while to the sound of the water tumbling past us. Now as we stood, side by side, soaked through, shivering, looking down at the Anacostia River, its waters seemed tortured by comparison: filthy and dark, foul smelling and unable to offer refuge of any kind. Ian placed his arm around me, rubbing me to keep me warm and he kissed me.

"Always something new with us," he whispered, and I knew what he was saying. Moments before Jonathan called, we were curled together on the sofa reading and sharing coffee and cookies—our normal, boring and deliciously cozy, rainy Saturday afternoon ritual. But since we had moved to D.C. and I had met Jonathan, there had been whole new worlds to discover, many of them far from beautiful.

Lightning struck over the water and thunder broke immediately afterwards, directly above us. The storm unleashed a driving rain that pelted us hard, even in our shelter under the bridge.

"We should go," Jonathan said.

We made our way silently, save for the sighs that came with the effort needed to scramble back up the bank of sodden mud and reach the top. When we finally arrived, dripping and iced through to our bones, I turned to say goodbye to Jonathan and saw that he was already at his car and getting in. Just before he closed his door, he leaned out and waved us away.

"Go home," he told us, both of us knowing full well that when we returned to our homes to change and warm up, this river would again lie between us.

Later that day I surfed the web and quickly discovered that D.C. had sewer overflows all over the city. There was even one at the bottom of my street that flowed directly into Rock Creek. This explained the awful stench that often arose near the clock tower entrance as we walked with Sandra, on our frequent visits to the Zoo. And there are others that flow directly into the Potomac River, where people fish on the weekends and the city's rowing teams practice. Raw sewage flowing into the rivers in Washington D.C., the capital of the United States of America. Even the White House sewage flows unchecked when it rains. It seemed so impossible, so thoroughly mediaeval—surely not here? I felt the same way when I later found out that the residents of D.C. pay taxes, but still don't have a vote in Congress. Not here? Not in *America*? Yes here. Another veil lifted.

As I told Rafael the story, I think he knew what I was trying to say. Jonathan showed me that it isn't always beauty that moves us to love. The trip down to the river had enraged Ian and I, ignited our souls. And I had, in that instant, fallen hard and fast for the city, felt bound to its future forever.

"O.K.," I said to Rafael, "Let's go have some fun. Then you'll never forget today, and you'll never forget D.C."

"What do you have in mind?"

"Negra Modelo's in Rock Creek Park."

"Isn't that illegal?"

"And?"

We called Marguerite and she patched Ian in on speaker-phone and we demanded that they join us; we were so persuasive that they both managed to sneak away from work early. Rafael and I picked up food and drinks at Eastern Market, and had cold beers ready for them when they arrived at the park.

"Well," Rafael said to us as we all lazed on the grass, recovering from our feast, "Two goodbyes down, two to go. Maybe goodbyes aren't so bad after all."

OF THE LINES WE LEAVE BEHIND

for you are the
daughters of women
who detached their wings
repaired them
and passed them on
to you
that you would fly

Gloria Wade-Gayles

How do I tell Ian? I was on the web, reading the results of the school lottery, and I reluctantly sat back from the string of numbers on the screen, which refused to match the numbers I had in my hand. *How do I tell Ian?* We were allowed to apply to three out-of-bounds schools and Sandra did not receive a place at any one of them. The effort we invested in selecting the perfect three schools now seemed utterly pointless for such a game of chance. All those open houses and meetings with principals, the time we spent carefully reviewing test scores; it was just a routine to make us feel a little more in control. The annual lottery was merely a parade of good intentions, both the school administration and the parents, eager participants. The best schools in D.C. no longer had any spare out-of-bounds places and everyone knew it. The lottery allowed the school superintendent to say that the system had given kids in failing school districts a *chance* at a different school and allowed other parents to say, we really did want our kid to go to public school—*we did try.* We already knew that Sandra had not received a place at the brand new charter school at the top of our street, nor at the bilingual charter school two blocks over; there were no lucky numbers for us at any of the school lotteries. All that was left was our neighborhood elementary school. This was where my courage failed me. This was where I decided to forget about my meticulously honed beliefs and principles and take the road I never thought I would take. The private schools we applied to, as a desperate precaution, had come through for us.

The reality seeping in, the numbers unchanging before me, I recalled now the bitterly cold, fall morning when I drove Sandra to a local testing center to take the *WPPSI-111* pre-kindergarten exam. Ian refused to come, leaving for work extra early that morning—his way of protesting. Not before telling me once again how he felt, not before asking me once again not to take her. I somehow managed to quarantine my own doubts, scrape the thick ice off the car, and to drive Sandra to the three hours of word, writing and block games through which her every move was recorded and graded. Not that I didn't hate myself for taking her. *WPPSI-111*—the very name puts me in mind of children swirling around in gigantic test tubes with enormous litmus sticks declaring their pH to be high, low, or—the ultimate failure—perfectly neutral. Testing four-year olds to decide their future may have seemed absurd to Ian and me, but surprisingly, I discovered that this was not so for all parents, some of whom bounded gleefully into the testing office, ready to expose their progeny's brilliance. As I sat in the waiting room watching sweet, little kids disappear innocently into the unknown passageway to their futures, Sandra soon to follow them, I reassured myself that in the end, there was no way Ian and I would ever send her to private school. Now this seemed inevitable.

I called Ian at work. He was devastated, livid, that a spinning cage full of numbered balls had decided our child's future for us.

"We cannot do this," he told me. "We can't send her to private school. I don't give a damn about the money. It's just wrong. I told you we should never have made her take that damn test."

"Ian, please," I pleaded with him. "Please, don't let's do this again." The quarrels we had when the school applications were due had upended our lives for weeks on end, and very nearly torn us apart. "Please just *trust* me."

"No, I *don't* trust you, because you *want* her to go to private school, and I don't. I told you, all along, there is no way—" But then he hesitated, the confidence escaping slowly from his overblown conviction, the full meaning of the lottery results sinking in; he had never allowed himself to consider the high likelihood that we might completely fail to find a half-decent public school for Sandra. "Maybe we should look at houses again."

I could hear the defeat in his voice already. We had a binder full of real estate listings; we had grown tired of walking through homes we couldn't even afford to imagine ourselves living in. He retreated to safer ground.

"I have to get back to work," he said, once again in control. "We'll talk later."

But we didn't talk later; we argued, viciously. For weeks afterwards, we debated back and forth and Ian was angry with me, as I'd never known him to be before. We were used to being on each other's team, yet in that time we flipped back and forth from offense to defense, one against the other, no back up. Catherine wouldn't get involved; her only contribution was to occasionally take Sandra to the playground so that Ian and I could argue freely. Ian was determined to send Sandra to the local elementary school, and I wouldn't even consider it. Not after I visited the school and saw the dilapidated state the building was in, the peeling paint in the cafeteria, the barren room not fit to be called a library and the buckets collecting rainwater falling through the leaking roof. Not after I saw the *bars* on the windows. Not after I saw the unimaginably abysmal test scores.

"I won't send my child to a school like that," I told Ian. "I *can't* do it. I don't care how well intentioned the teachers and parents are. The school is failing *in every way*. It's *falling apart*. I can't do that to Sandra."

"That's *it*?!" he exploded. "Because of a bunch of completely *meaningless* test scores, a leaky roof, a crappy library, you're going to support an education system that you know goes against *everything* we believe in?!" He headed off my only remaining defense, "And please, *don't* tell me you only want her to have what you had!"

I tried again to explain to him how it was that my convictions were left in the dust when I stood inside our neighborhood school. As a child I went to the kind of school every parent dreams of, with engaged, smart teachers and the finest equipment available. We had a cavernous library with endless rows of books and private study areas, bright, beautifully organized classrooms and state of the art music and science labs; in all the rooms, there were huge picture windows overlooking the courts and competition level playing field outside. I looked out at the sky and the seasons shifting before me and I learnt to observe the world outside, not just the one inside my classroom. It was unthinkable, unimaginable to me that Sandra would look through wired windows, or worse still, bars—that there may not be any windows at all—as she contemplated those same seasons, as she learned to take the time to listen to her own thoughts and ideas, to let herself wander uninhibited through her imagination. I didn't even attempt to talk about the test scores. I knew what Ian would say. Our child was unlikely to have any problems with the standardized tests. *We will be there for her*, he would say; *we will be vigilant. We aren't the ones who need to worry.*

"Linda, you are being ridiculous. I don't care what state the building's in. I don't care about the windows. You can tell me all you want that it's a bad school, it's a failing school, that the test scores are the worst in the city, and you know what? I'd *still* say, let's send her there. Because we're not going to check out of her life once she's in school. She is going to be O.K. no matter where she goes. I want her to go to our neighborhood school."

Ian believing that it was not the school's failings but my own, which stood to jeopardize Sandra's future—that somehow I wasn't dedicated enough to her cause—didn't sit well with me, but then again, I wasn't being totally honest with Ian. I had another motive for sending Sandra to private school, one that I didn't fully understand or entirely have control over. But I found it impossible to explain that motive to Ian—the guilt I carried over the two roads that David and I traveled down as kids, and how this relentlessly drove my everyday choices for Sandra.

David and I started out well enough, on the same path in elementary school: I was just one year older than him. We were both idyllically content kids—popular, carefree, yet each in our own way, enthusiastically studious. We looked forward to school each day; no one ever had to drag us out of bed to go. But when it came time to enter middle school, our lives diverged entirely, irreversibly. I was accepted at the local private school, where our sister had gone a few years ahead of us, but David wasn't. After that—I'm the first to admit it, and he never forgave me for it—I was somewhat oblivious to what happened next to him. I was too busy growing up and surviving my own new school to care. While I learned to adapt to and even came to enjoy, the obsession my new school had for discipline and hard work, his self-confidence and moral compass, so carefully cultivated at our elementary school, were rapidly shattered by the violent, disruptive code of conduct that dictated survival at the local public school. He floated between self-loathing and anger, the emotions piling one on the other, until he found, at the age of fourteen, a way out. Such a depressingly pathetic cliché, but then the truth often is. First cigarettes, then marijuana, very quickly alcohol and cocaine. And I never knew. I thought he was just having a hard time learning to be mature and responsible, that he should just *pull himself together,* but I had no idea what he was going through. He tried again, to get into my high school, and he failed, and in his own way he bore that failure with him—the debilitating mixture of regret and rejection—and the deficient schooling that he was left with, always.

As I tried to define what it was I really wanted for Sandra, I realized that my own education could have been different. I looked back on all my childhood years spent studying, how much I resented the torrent of exams and tests, and the pressure to excel in everything I did. But I survived, I came out O.K., better than O.K.; I did well for myself. Only after he died, did I reluctantly consider the possibility that David may not have survived the pressure at my school, either. His choice perhaps was only ever, not enough or too much schooling; his problem was that he didn't fit here or there, and there was nowhere else for him to be as he walked the path from boy into man. Still, it could not have hurt David, or damaged him, to be kept tethered to books the way he was diminished, and in the end, destroyed, to have spent his teenage years away from them, just trying to stay alive. And that's how I came out wanting Sandra to have what I had, wanting to protect her from my foolish dreams and Ian's naïve idealism.

"She *has* to go to private school," I told Ian. "We have no choice." As I said the words, they were dry and coarse, and yet almost sweet in their finality—*no choice.*

Ian of course knew that David was behind my resolve; he understood that I filtered every major decision in my life through the gray light of David's death. Whether or not he resented this other force in our lives was hard for me to determine; he had never yet risked telling me so. What Ian couldn't know—I barely understood this myself—was that I was hoping perhaps to even make amends to David by sending Sandra to private school.

The final deadline for holding Sandra's place at the private school arrived. Ian was all out of ideas for now and he capitulated, purely because I had worn him down. This was not a campaign I was proud of winning, this would be chalked up as one I would much rather have never fought. As I filled out the forms and wrote out the first check to Sandra's new school, he was about to leave the room, but instead he turned back to face me.

"You know, don't you, how far this kind of money could go at the public school. You know what an impact we could have made as parents there." To be certain that I knew he blamed me, not the city's school system, not even bad luck, for our situation, he said, turning away, "If you could only be bothered."

The fight, even worse, the decision, burnt us badly. We barely talked for weeks after, and as the new school year approached, the excitement of Sandra starting Kindergarten was overshadowed by Ian's distrust and disapproval of her new school. I took the photo of the two of them, standing holding hands at the school entrance, and I saw myself, beginning my journey into adulthood, on the steps of my new middle school, all those years ago. I thought, I wish David were here. Then—as a little girl, not used to standing alone, because we had always gone to the same school together, because we had always taken our first day photo together. And now—for him to have seen that I had chosen something better for his niece.

For months afterwards, Ian and I continued to talk about moving to a better school district. And we would come back to the list we drew up when I attended over thirty school open houses a year ago. In a city of half a million people, there were perhaps a handful of schools that met the nationwide standards for test scores. A handful of schools whose buildings were worthy of welcoming the city's children through its doors.

A handful of schools that managed to excel, and go above and beyond the ordinary expectations of public schools, and they were—nearly every one of them—in Northwest D.C., nestled in the very white, middle-class, often wealthy, neighborhoods of the nation's capital. We were for the most part, priced out of these neighborhoods even if we could convince ourselves to want to live in any of them. We had placed our best hopes in our local charter schools. We passed one that was flourishing, every day on our way to dropping Sandra off at private school; its doors stood wide open to children from across the city. I couldn't resent the charter school for such a noble gesture—at last the barriers of race and class were starting to tumble—but I couldn't help thinking that Sandra, a little girl growing up less than two blocks away, should have had a place there.

The détente began with Parents Night, at Sandra's new school. At the last minute, Ian called from work to say he'd be there. We heard a lecture in the state-of-the-art auditorium about all the experiential learning programs offered at the Kindergarten level. We had a chance to see some of Sandra's work, to see how well she was already writing and the astonishing progress she was making in math. We met with the teachers, and the abundant assistants. We walked around her classroom. We counted eighteen chairs. As we wandered the halls and took in the stunning artwork and complex science projects of the upper grades, Ian pulled me aside and kissed me.

"I'm sorry."

"Me too."

"She'll be O.K. here, won't she?"

"Better than O.K."

"God, this school is so—" He searched for words as he surveyed again the panorama of creativity and color around him, a celebration of childhood covering the halls. "It's *bursting* with life."

And this was how we were afforded the privilege of worrying less, of knowing that our child would be well prepared for the world outside as she grew into adulthood. Through choosing to cast aside our preciously guarded principles and beliefs and by doing what we believed would be best, not for us, but for our daughter. Surprisingly, I found myself worrying most about having disappointed Ian, not about whether I had chosen well for Sandra, or the unforgivable hypocrisy of my choice. Ian fully expected me to fight on his side, and I had let him down. As he watched me work long days and late nights to build the campaigns for Luther and Anita, I know he wondered how I could fail to place the same effort and determination into building a half-decent neighborhood school. And he told me through the distance he placed between us, his diminished interest in my work, the lack of patience he displayed with me, that he perhaps now believed in me a little less.

I decided to confide in Anita about the fights Ian and I had over Sandra's schooling; she was a mother, she would have faced the same crisis when her daughter went to school, although I had no way of knowing whether she could afford the luxury of even considering private school. She had unexpectedly accepted my offer to come to my house one afternoon, just as the tail end of the summer drew away from the first chill days of autumn. We sat in the back garden, under the warm, golden light shed by the star magnolia, its once bottle green, glossy leaves turning to yellow and gently drooping, preparing to fall. We were reluctant to head inside just yet, so we sipped hot tea to ward off the cold and used garden rocks as paperweights to hold down our work spread out before us; the papers lifted and fell with the occasional breeze rustling over us, punctuating the silence. After a while, Anita looked up from her work and asked me whether we should think about getting dinner ready, and I took the opportunity to tell her what had happened with Sandra and Ian.

"Honey, you do what you gotta do," she said.

I tried again, determined to engage her. She was uncharacteristically harsh as she regarded me, her tone just shy of a scolding.

"If you're looking to me to *judge* you and tell you what you're doing is wrong, you can just forget that crazy notion right now. It's not for me to judge you. By the look on your face, seems to me Linda, you've already passed sentence on yourself. But this isn't about you. It's about Sandra. So just let it go, and move on."

As though to reinforce the point, she again took up the testimonies that we had been working on and started to read silently. I couldn't begin to know what was really going on in her head. Whether she judged me but would never say it, whether the question was too loaded to talk about over tea on a sunny October afternoon. Whether she refused to say what she might really be thinking—that I could afford the choice, so any conversation we might have together was just a waste of her time? Did it really matter anyway, what Anita thought? I guess I'd been hoping she would exonerate me—tell me a mother has the right to do what's best for her children, no matter what. But even Catherine had refused to do this. "It's between you and Ian," she had said. I had to accept that I'd made a decision I would never be entirely content with, even as it continued to fester between Ian and I. Forever after, his pride and disappointment fluctuated over Sandra's new school. As he saw it, we had laid down our own bricks and mortar on the wall that divides the city. I knew he was right, of course I did, but Sandra's education was simply not a campaign I wanted to fight on a daily basis over the next thirteen years.

The sun had begun to fade and the air turned unrelentingly chilly. We brought our work inside and took over the dining room table; we had many more hours ahead of us before Luther joined us to review our strategy for the prison hearings. While I continued to worry over what Anita really thought about Sandra's schooling, I could tell she had moved on by the way she settled in and acted as though nothing had changed between us. I admired her for this. Perhaps it was a necessary survival quality; perhaps it was the definition of politeness. Whatever it was, I respected her immensely for it. I had not yet learned to do the same—to let go quickly, to allow myself the grace of forgiveness.

As we poured over another draft of talking points on my laptop, we received a call from Kadija who had just heard that the new and final date for the Zoning Hearings had been set. I could hear Damien cursing in the background as he read over the list of people Randy Weaver had lined up to testify. As Jonathan's intern, he had worked closely with Kadija over the past few months and they formed a strong team together. He was devastated to learn of the former Mayor, Edgar Brook's support for the prison, but luckily for all of us, this merely fuelled his determination to shut the prison down. He had become a boy on a mission.

"The Zoning Commission has never seen *anything* like this," Kadija said. The city had to rent a bigger space for the hearing because so many people signed up to testify. Can you believe it? We may have broken the record!"

The excitement filling Kadija's voice celebrated the effort that she and her Conservation Club colleagues had invested in the campaign. There had been lit drops at Metro stations, phone banks, mailings, more lobby visits and press conferences and endless organizing meetings. The coalition of civic groups and activists that Luther and Anita were able to pull together from D.C. and Prince George's County, added to Kadija's on the ground organizing, had created an extraordinary force of will to oppose the prison in Ward 8.

"And guess what? Weaver *still* can't pull it together. We still have more people signed up."

"You've done a fantastic job, Kadija," Anita told her, "You too Damien. You should be real proud of yourselves. This is great news."

Before hanging up, Damien asked if he and I could meet one-on-one for me to help him prepare his testimony.

"You just miss me, right?"

"You kiddin' me? Jonathan's a way betta boss'n you'll eva be."

"Really? Why's that?" Anita asked, her curiosity peeked.

"Cos he's *black*."

Before Anita, who's disapproval was already etched into her face, or I, could even think of a response, Damien burst out laughing and said, "Na, cos he's *payin'* me to do ma job now. I ain' jus' a volunteer no mo'. I'm a *Policy Associate*." Damien pronounced the title as though he had just been made President of the United States. I remembered that feeling well, my first job; having a title—*Retail Assistant*—had made stacking shelves seem vital to the national economy. *Policy Associate*. Ready and willing to save affordable housing and build better communities, wherever needed. Good luck to you.

"Yeah, well I got you that job, Damien."

"Na, you jus' wanna'd t'ge' ridda me."

"You got that right."

"I'm gone."

"Good, go, I'll see you Friday."

"Friday."

I started preparing the salad for dinner when Anita came into the kitchen to join me. She watched intently as I sliced the vegetables, and

I thought maybe she was about to tell me something about herself. I sensed she was worried, troubled.

"Why did you leave *Homes First*?"

When I didn't respond, she asked again, this time more boldly, "What happened to make Linda Thurston leave *Homes First*?"

The manner in which she pronounced my full name, juxtaposed with *Homes First*, in a way I hadn't heard the two spoken together in over a year now—I was surprised how inseparable the four words still seemed. Something like having been on a High School sports team and all the hours of team practice, riding the team bus, losing, winning, and knowing that nothing will ever feel the same way again.

"Many reasons," I said. "Mostly, I'd been thinking of coming East for a while and you presented me with the opportunity."

She weighed my answer, and I could see clearly that it didn't begin to satisfy her. But then she headed down a path I couldn't have anticipated.

"What about *WWW*?"

I'm not sure I understood what she meant by this. I stammered my confusion back at her. "*WWW*? What does she—?"

"It's just very curious to me why she's been such a help to us. You saw Vernon's reaction at the meeting, when he heard she'd gotten her hedge fund ladies on board. Why'd she let you go, if she values you so much?"

Half regretting, half validating my decision to leave, I told her, "Jonathan always said you can't fight what's outside if you're fighting on the inside."

"Were you?"

"Fighting on the inside?"

"*Were you*?"

"Yeah. We were."

"Think about it. I'd like to get this sorted out before we get in any deeper with her."

I made up an excuse to go upstairs and I retreated into my study to think over what Anita had said. Her astute and almost prescient approach to organizing had simply unveiled my own concerns over WWW's overeager desire to assist us. When I returned, with some random files in hand to make a show of having searched for something important, I shared with her my misgivings about the new funders' conference call.

"It's just that I need to know, Linda, before we bind ourselves any further to this powerful, munificent woman, what her *motivation* is, and whether she'll still be around once she's paid off whatever debt she now owes."

Whatever pleasant intimacies we may have shared in the name of friendship this evening, she wanted instead to get to the heart of this problem. She needed an answer now, before Luther arrived. And if we were to plough through another several hours work, I needed my head clear, so I slipped upstairs again to my study and called Catherine. I told her of Anita's reservations about WWW. She took her time to process the information and of course, because she is Catherine, she asked for more.

"How much?"

"How much did her uber-richistanis magic up for us?"

"Spill."

"$750K over 2 years. Plus all the new referrals of course."

"You're screwed," she said. "Utterly, totally screwed."

There was no slow dawning; the truth burst open like a multi-hued sunrise on fast forward.

"I've been paid off, haven't I?"

"Yes, you have."

We were pretty quick to unravel the now painfully obvious sequence of events. Richard went to WWW as soon as I gave him the documents. She set in motion a process to protect the organization and the only way to do that was to protect Richard too. They must have moved money around leaving no trail behind, using all of his well-honed methods to make everything look legitimate. Except that I had already raised my concerns with Jonathan. Realizing how serious the situation was, he must have confided in the Chair of the Board—WWW. And they must have worked together to make the whole problem disappear. And then it hit me—like a fly to honey, I had walked into WWW's trap.

"Catherine, it was *her*! *WWW* sent me those documents. She knew I'd have figured out what Richard was doing eventually, because it was my money he was tapping into. She *knew* I'd make the decision to leave before I'd ever expose *Homes First*."

"Sorry babe, more importantly, she knew you'd never betray Richard." She gave me little time to recover from this particularly painful observation, before hammering home her point. "Damn, she took a huge risk giving you those files, but then again your fucking annoying reliability has always been your biggest weakness. As Richard well knows."

Richard. The well-known expert at getting people on his side, before they even know that sides exist. That way when the fight starts, he has them exactly where he needs them—in his corner. That's where I was when the budget documents landed in my lap. WWW knew that, of course she did. That's where, despite all that I now knew, I still stood.

"And what about Jonathan?" she asked. Her profession had taught her well to trust no one.

"Oh, come on," I said angrily. "He's all I've got left to believe in."

"No," she reconsidered, either to protect me or because she refused to believe him capable. "I don't think he knew everything. They must've shielded him from the mess." And she added, as though speaking it aloud would make it so, "Jonathan's the only good guy in all of this."

"But he *did* know," I confessed to her. I recalled the look he gave me when I revealed to him what Richard was up to, his silence when I said I was leaving. "I just don't know how much."

She didn't say a word now. I waited for her to make this one better; if there was any forgiving Jonathan, she would think of it, but she didn't speak. It would be for me to make my peace with whatever Jonathan did or didn't know about what Richard and the Chair of the Board had done.

"So anyway," I was eager to change the subject, "I've only another minute, but how's BDJ?"

"He's almost BDY, we need to stop calling him BDJ."

"Is it really *a year*? Come on, you've survived a whole year with a Bible-thumping, red state LA?"

"Well, one who happens to give a damn about the *earth that God gave us, I might add*."

"I know, I know, he had you at, '*I might add*.' Very gentlemanly. Very sexy. Come on, how is it really?"

"He's so *earnest*, it's adorable in him—not annoying like you."

"Thanks."

"We're still seeing each other nearly every day. And I'm not sick of him yet. I even like talking about my work with him."

"When have you ever talked about your *work* with a boyfriend?"

"There you go. I'm in too deep. He calls himself a *conservationist*. He doesn't like the word *environmentalist*. He claims there's a whole new movement out there, people who believe in Creation Care. I told him I don't care what he calls it, as long as he wants to save it, protect it, and clean it up. So, I went all the way."

"You told him that you *love* him?"

This *is* all the way for Catherine. She may be an outwardly flirtatious, raucous, sexy young woman but as I well knew by now, deep down she was insanely protective of her heart, soul and body. She shared none readily.

"Did he?"

"He did."

"*Wow.*" What else can you say when a die-hard, agnostic environmentalist has met her match in a die-hard, Christian conservationist?

"That's great news. Great news for the environment, at least."

"And your friend's everlasting happiness?"

"Just an added bonus. O.K., give me the quick version and I'm outta here."

Her steely armor fell away as she proceeded to gush about BDY. I was not used to this new, soft, sappy, blissfully in love Catherine, but I could get used to it, I was sure. In my head I already pictured the engagement party, wedding, the works. I promised her we would meet soon to perform a full BDY performance review, but reminded her that for now I needed to return to Anita.

I sat for a moment at my desk after I hung up, and I fretted about how to tell Anita what I knew about WWW. When I joined her again in the kitchen, exactly where I left her, she had the presence of someone who was waiting, as though at a doctor's office or a train station. She would not let this go. I'd known highly principled organizers before, who would not think twice about turning away a half million-dollar grant, if it comes from an unethical source. It doesn't matter how hard you plead the case that the money could transform people's lives, allow the organization to grow and hire new staff, open a new field office, they'd still reject the grant. As a fundraiser, I knew how hard it was to find money that had not been birthed of someone else's pain and suffering, so I respected that Anita sought to know the money's provenance and the expectations that arrived with it. I never imagined that we would draw closer to each other by discussing her organization's funding, but as I wove the story out for her, she told me, "You lost so much, didn't you? I always wondered what force could possibly have been strong enough to drive you from *Homes First*." She didn't press too hard when I told her there were parts of the story that I simply couldn't share. We agreed that we had no real reason to refuse WWW's assistance, but we also recognized that she would consider her debt to me fully paid, given the generosity of her grant; it would not be as easy, next time around, to tap her for funding.

"I didn't just leave Homes First, Anita. The timing was right, but I chose to work with you and Luther."

"I've wondered about that," she said. "People who run have a tendency to keep running," she said. "Right on past whatever's good for them."

Later that night, after dinner and a lengthy, exhausting work meeting, Luther, Anita and I collapsed in the living room. Apparently BDY was not the only one who had managed to meld love of Jesus with love of the earth. The particular tale that Anita now shared, about the day when her daughter (who was around five at the time) thought *Jesus* was at their front door, stemmed from our discussion of how impressed we all were with Kadija's work. Luther, Anita and I were in fits of laughter as she spun out the story.

"She said, Mama, Mama, come quickly! *Jesus* is here!" In between abbreviated breaths and more laughter, Anita assured us, "I promise you, that is *exactly* what Michelle said! She came running into the kitchen, screaming, *Jesus* is here, *Jesus* is at our *front door!*" She stood up to relate the next part of the story. "Michelle took my hand and led me to the door and there he was." Anita walked an imaginary Michelle to my front door and pretended to open it. "The man *did* look a lot like Jesus. Tall, thin. Long, dark hair, down to his shoulders. Deep, brown eyes. He had a baggy white shirt over these baggy pants—you know, everything but the halo. And when he spoke, it was like his voice melted into you like honey. And of course, just like all the rest of them, he was white." She crumpled into the sofa and continued with an affected serious tone. "How'm I supposed to tell Michelle, that's not *Jesus* sweetie, that's just an *environmentalist*?"

We all laughed hard and then Anita sighed, exhausted from the telling. "She was five years old. Nearly broke her heart. I told Kadija the story when she asked me if she should take the job with the Club. She was worried that they would have a hard time with her faith. And I told her that after I got to know him—that man who just showed up at my door—I learnt he wasn't particularly religious, but he *lived* the way Jesus lived. *Worrying* about how everything little thing he did affected everyone else around him. So I told her to take the job with the Club, that the work they do is mostly good work."

"Yeah, really," Luther joked, "I'm sure Jesus would get really bent out of shape if he knew we all didn't recycle."

He cast the evil eye on me as he said this. He had not forgiven me for saving the butcher block paper from the trashcan, and for my many, many other even less subtle references to his abundantly wasteful lifestyle. In his mind, he really did have better things to do with his life than to remember to recycle his beer bottles. Lucky for me, and more importantly the planet, Anita was starting to set him straight on that level.

"Jesus has become an excuse, I think," she said, her tone suddenly shifting, "If we let the earth go to hell, don't worry about it, the *next* life will be better. Everyone going on and on about the next life. I don't believe that was what Jesus intended. I think he wanted us to make this life good, in every way."

It was unsettling sometimes, the way Anita's faith lay underneath all that she said and did; it made her seem suddenly older, more responsible, it could drop a line between us at the most unexpected moments. Her sincerity was admirable; it flowed freely but it could change the conversation in an instant. I noticed Luther shift uncomfortably; he tapped the arm on his wheelchair parked next to him by the sofa. I knew that he did this when he was eager to wrap up a meeting and leave, but he appeared to change his mind; he laid his hand by his side and leaned forwards.

"Oh come on, Anita, not this again," he said, his voice thick with anger. "It's so *easy* for whites if blacks believe in Jesus, so easy for the rich if the poor believe in Jesus. They can go on ignoring us, let our communities rot away and they *know* we'll just go right on believing in Jesus, hoping he'll save us. And they have all the bases covered, if not now, in this world, then don't worry, in the next one. After we're all just a pile of dust."

An unmistakable pall of embarrassment and disenchantment flashed across her face as she regarded him. I couldn't imagine what had set them off tonight, their normally unified front before me seemed suddenly to dissipate before my eyes. I suspected that this was a conversation started elsewhere and left unfinished, and that soon I would be a mere spectator. Perhaps we were falling victims to our growing trust for one another. I hadn't failed to notice that of late we had more regularly and readily exposed our once private troubles to one another.

Anita decided to take the high road, letting Luther's allegations pass and continuing with her story. "So this man is standing at my door, and Michelle is just going crazy now, she's saying, *Jesus! Jesus*! I love you Jesus! I had to kind of move her away and I said to him, *can I help you*? And he said, I swear this is true, *I was about to ask you the same question*."

She smiled at the remembrance, but Luther snickered, rolled his eyes and looked away.

"He worked in our community for three years. He set up a little office, helped us stay in touch with what the Hill and the City Council were cooking up. Raised all his own funds. Never took a cent from us. This was maybe nine, ten years ago. He helped us so much when no one else cared about what was happening over here. And then one night, he was out drinking with some of the folk he'd been working with. And he made the mistake of telling one of them that he was glad they were friends now after all those years, or something like that."

Luther looked directly at Anita, and then looked away. Only now did I realize that he had heard this story before.

"Everyone laughed, and then someone said, what makes you think we're *friends*? Something like that, or maybe they told him to leave, at least that's what we heard."

Luther finished the story. "Our very own do-gooder packed up his family and left and we never saw him again. Last we heard he was working in some community in Louisiana, trying to get the chemical plants to clean up their act. Something like that."

They exchanged a glance that told me more than they wanted me to know. I wondered how long it took Anita to forgive Luther for scaring away her hard-working activist with a heart of gold—I was just guessing here—just for being white, and for getting too comfortable in the community.

"And it doesn't bother you that your daughter thought Jesus was white?" I asked. Now that the mood had swung open the doors to honest discourse, it seemed as though tough questions were expected.

Anita turned her eyes from Luther and fixed her gaze on me, as though weighing up my intent by asking such a question. "That's not important. How can it be? Jesus is the son of God, and God has many faces. It's of no matter to me." She must have read that I was completely perplexed by this answer, so she qualified it, speaking a little too forcefully, and I was certain she was really addressing Luther again. "It just doesn't *matter* today. We all have our own image of Jesus. The blacks in this country, we have our own liturgy now, our own pastors, we worship by our own rules and we sing to our own hymns. We've breathed life into the gospel. Blacks believe because we choose to believe, not because anyone tells us to. No one *tells* me what to believe. What matters is that because we believe in Jesus, we strive to do his work. God's work. *Good work*."

Anita seemed satisfied with her answer. She expressed little vulnerability; her conviction was impressive. But Luther answered her as though lecturing third grade students.

"Everyone knows that this world is a mess and that we need to fix it. We don't need Jesus to tell us that. I didn't sign up to do God's work when I decided to try to heal our neighborhood. I decided that I care about my fellow human beings enough to want to help them anyway I can. Half the time what we're trying to fix is all the damage that's already been done *in* God's name. Not just here, all over the world. And you *know* it."

Anita said softly, "Luther, come on now. We—"

"Jesus is *white* because someone chose to put a human face on God," he said dryly, wearily. "Jesus, the son of God. Aren't we all supposed to be God's children? Why give *God* a human face at all? This is a world full of people believing in different Gods. You really think making God's only child white and male, is going to solve the problem, and bring us all together as one big happy family? That's *exactly* the problem. What works for some people is never ever going to work for others. There are a thousand versions of Christianity out there trying to decide who Christ really is and how he supposedly wants us to honor him. Christian fundamentalists are getting some of the most evil bastards this country's ever seen elected to government in school PTA's, city councils, all the way up to Congress, because they *believe* that Jesus wouldn't want health care for the *poor*, they *believe* that taxes are *evil*. God has become the poster boy for being a selfish, greedy bastard, and for ramming suffering down other people's throats in this world, and all of your kindness, Anita, and all of your goodness, is never going to change that."

Now she stared at him—I knew exactly what the look meant—for letting her down so completely. I saw it the day I told her that I wasn't sure we could protect all the residents of the Windsor apartments, that some might fall by the wayside, that otherwise we would have to fight too hard for the few, and might risk losing the whole campaign. It took me some time to appreciate that for her, there was never any question—it simply wasn't our choice, who to save and who to turn out on the streets.

"I, personally, have *nothing* to believe in, except doing right by my fellow man," he said, defiantly. "And that comes from my heart, and I don't need anyone to preach it to me."

Only then did I realize that this was not a new debate for them; this was not a friendly post-dinner exploration of faith and what motivates people to help others; this was a burgeoning war depleted of any hope of compromise, even as they pressed on, defending their positions.

"Whether you think Jesus is the son of God, or just a good man who fed the poor with his own bread and fish, doesn't matter at all. Maybe for some he has become a symbol of selfishness. I don't understand it, but others are free to believe what they want. But if he helps *me* be a better person, that's all that matters, isn't it Luther? Can't we agree on that? That's one path that *does* unite us all."

"Is it? Is it really all that matters? I took the bus up 16th street the other day. It's been years since—since—I had to go that way." Luther faltered and I wasn't sure why, but Anita's face softened suddenly. "And I'd forgotten—all the churches and synagogues and mosques and temples in this city! Seventh Day Adventist, 19th Street Baptist, National Church of the Nazarene, Catholic, United Methodist, Bahai, Hindu, Nation of Islam. The Mormons and their fairytale castle. There's Reform, Conservative *and* Orthodox Synagogues. And the Mosques—I don't even know the different ones—Nation, Sunni, Shiite? I have no idea. Why don't people of the same *faith* even pray together anymore? You tell me why there are all these endless places and ways, for blacks, and everyone else, even for men and women, to worship *separately* on the Highway to Heaven. How can that possibly be O.K. with you, that we are all so *divided*?"

"My faith is my home," Anita replied, her voice firm but full of forgiveness. "It's who I am. It doesn't divide me from everyone around me, it teaches me to love them, no matter what. Even those who have no faith."

I was torn apart by the escalating conflict between them, my own feelings falling everyplace in the midst of theirs, my own long, fruitless search for God as unsatisfying and confusing as the mess dividing them. I no longer even belonged inside their conversation and I felt certain someone was going down hard if the fight continued.

"You know what?" I said, "I'm beat. I have so much work to do tomorrow. O.K. if we finish up for the night?"

"Great idea," Anita said, getting up. She tried to help Luther with his wheel chair but he brushed her off. I helped her gather their papers, laptops, and coats and then I saw them to the door. Luther insisted on getting into Anita's car without any help from us, so she touched my arm and we stayed back.

"I'm sorry, Anita. Really, that was a stupid question. I didn't mean to offend you. I love that you know what you believe—I wish I could feel the same way. I always assumed Luther was like you. You're so strong in your faith, I figured he must be too."

"Luther is—" she said. "He's going through a lot right now with these campaigns."

We watched as Luther struggled to open the car door and get in by himself, sliding into the passenger seat and hoisting his useless legs into the car. I didn't see anyone's God—white, black or other—queuing up to give the man his brother back, or make him walk again. His wheel chair was left suddenly empty on the sidewalk, as he closed the door with a slam so that we would know that he didn't care if we talked about him, and he didn't want to overhear us. He must have already known that Anita would confide in me. That they loved each other as they'd never loved before. That he feared that her faith would force them apart, and she feared that his lack of faith would turn her away from God. I didn't know how to respond. I loved them together. They were strong, brave and funny and they made you feel as though you had found a place in the world where your heart beat louder and stronger just for being near them.

Anita started to go down the steps then turned. "I used to be so afraid for Michelle, it used to tear me up. Just wanting to keep her safe. Never mind the rest you worry about. And then I realized—as mothers, we take our sorrows and turn them into gifts of love for our children. All we can hope for is that their sorrows will at least be different from ours. That's our best work." She kissed me goodbye. "Don't worry about Sandra."

I watched as she got into the car and I saw her take Luther's hand as she leaned in to kiss him, tears streaking his face.

That night as I waited up for Ian to return home, I realized if we are all so divided, it is not merely because we have been forced apart by circumstance, religion and society. It is because we aren't the same, and we never will be. Luther and Anita were as different as any two people can be, and yet they were somehow bound together. We aren't the same, any of us, not in our skin color, our beliefs, our fears, or our dreams, and we don't *need* to be the same. We don't need to get in on any one faith, one concept of God, or one belief system. We just need to get out, find each other and take each other just as we are.

Ian took one look at me when he got home and said, "Forget it, you're not going to solve whatever it is tonight," before leading me, his arm tight around me, to bed.

OF THE END OF THE ROAD

The flames lighted up the tin soldier. As he stood, the heat was very terrible, but whether it proceeded from the real fire or from the fire of love, he could not tell. Then he could see that the bright colors were faded from his uniform but whether they had been washed off during his journey or from the effects of his sorrow, no one could say.

The tin soldier melted down into a lump, and the next morning when the maidservant took the ashes out of the stove, she found him in the shape of a little tin heart.

Hans Christian Andersen

Rafael and I drove up through Rock Creek Park on a breezy October morning and we were silent, for the most part, as we gazed at the colors cascading down on us from either side of the road. The trees closest to us had already fallen under autumn's baton and formed mysterious harmonies of gold, ochre, scarlet and umber; the larger trees and those deep in the woods still resisted and held onto their brilliant green, summer foliage. The creek, running perfectly clear that day, its surface sparkling with reflected fragments of the sun's unhindered light, mischievously switched sides as we crossed bridge after bridge before disappearing for good to the north, as we headed west. The park was offering us a perfect symphony to honor the conclusion of another long, sweltering hot summer in D.C.

The oppressive, code red days were behind us now. *The government advises you to stay indoors today! Avoid driving! Ride your bike!* (*Ride my bike indoors?*) For today, the air was divinely clear, like nothing we had experienced yet this fall. I inhaled it, head out the window, mouth open to the wind, as Rafael pressed on the gas and drove too fast up the steeply winding road to the stables, the thrill of a perfect day in the park too great to resist. Relief now for the dread that was building for what would come next. Although I had already said my goodbyes at the stables once before, I knew back then that Rafael was staying on to tend to our adored little friends who had so profoundly touched our lives. Now it was his turn to turn away. I tried to comfort him with the knowledge that he likely would not have continued volunteering at the new riding facility anyway, but he scoffed at the notion. Had he stayed in D.C., the new site, if anything, would have been even more convenient to his College Park lab. My other efforts at consolation all seemed to make little impact on his mood, so now, all out of ideas, I let the wind rush over me, and I tried not to think about how he would get through this particular set of goodbyes. Instead, I remembered how twice a week we used to drive this same road together to volunteer at the stables, and how the kids and our friendship helped us heal when we were about as broken as two people can be.

When we arrived at the office, a few of the staff were sitting around reviewing the day's lesson plan. They all looked at Rafael as though he had just returned from a funeral, likely because he wore a shockingly grim face that no one there was used to seeing. This was not the Rafael they knew—the one who routinely ignored schedules so he could have more time with the kids, and who happily admonished the staff for being too serious about lesson plans. Arlene, the program director, who worked closely with him over the years, accidentally kicked her chair over as she stood to hug him, and then she tearfully struggled through a *Thank You* speech on behalf of all the staff. I thought maybe Rafael would now want to tender his goodbyes to the children by himself, but he nodded to me to join him as he left the office.

As we walked along the stalls of privately owned horses, he casually stroked the one or two who greeted him as we passed, and then we made the turn towards the block of program horses. These older, less impressive looking, creatures recognized his voice and several came to his call. He gently rubbed their necks, nuzzled closely with his favorites, and slowly worked his way around the back of the stables to a separate run of stalls where the very best of the program horses, and his most beloved of all, were kept. A sleek, white, barely dappled, mare came forward at once as he approached and reached her head far out over the stable door to touch him. He talked to her in Spanish—his secret love!—and then he reluctantly backed away, and we made our way towards the barn.

As we entered the dimly lit, cavernous building, leaving the chill air and dazzling sunshine behind us, the barn's pungent odor of sawdust, manure and sweat, greeted us, and it took a moment to get used to. We stood together taking the barn in: the carnival of worn out jumping poles and obstacles carelessly abandoned by the last class, the immense back doors gently creaking to and fro as the sunlight strobed through the worn wooden panels, and the flocks of sparrows darting manically about the cathedral high ceilings, preparing for winter. We both loved this place deeply, profoundly; it was a place where miracles happened.

My eyes fell to the railing where I stood when Rafael came over one day and told me that Arlene needed our help with a new kid. The child was autistic and had never spoken, and was so far refusing to come out and meet the horses. As we stood discussing how we were going to work with her, who would lead, who would side-walk, Arlene pulled the saddle from the horse's back. *This* is how you're going to work with her, she told us, *bareback*. She instructed Rafael to fetch the little girl while she maneuvered me into position at the horse's side. When he returned, he didn't hesitate as he tossed the little girl up onto the horse's back before she could even acknowledge her fear. She sat there for a moment stunned, her comically tiny legs reaching stiffly forwards, since she couldn't begin to bend them around the horse's huge body. We walked circles around the barn, Arlene leading, Rafael and I on either side, the girl bobbing happily up and down to the quirky gait of Andrew, one of our gentlest—but let's face it, laziest—horses. Rafael was so stunned that he had managed to get the little girl on the horse, and so afraid that she might slip off Andrew's enormous bare back, that he barely said a word while Arlene and I nervously talked incessantly. We tried to encourage the girl to stroke Andrew, showing her how, and she did try briefly, stopped, tried again, and then realizing that she liked stroking him, kept her hand flat against his back for the rest of the ride. Suddenly, at the end of the class, as Rafael carried her back down to the ground, the girl said, "*Annoo*." Her first word. Right there, she spoke, as though she knew she had to get the word out before the class ended. The beginning of speech for a scared, little girl while Arlene, Rafael and I were unable to speak— stunned into silence. The girl always rode bareback after that, with the three of us to guide her. For a while *Annoo* was a little orphan word, repeated often, but with nothing to keep it company or help it grow, until another morning at the barn, with the girl's parents waiting at the railing, when in an explosion of confidence and excitement, more words followed and there was nothing after that, to hold them back.

Rafael's kids were waiting in the classroom, off to the side of the arena. He took a moment to observe them from where we stood; they were rowdy and anxious, the rooky teaching assistant was having a hard time calming them down. He made his way passed the wheelchair ramp and entered the classroom. A chorus of '*Rafael!*'s rose from the kids, and they quickly swarmed around him. It was not going to get any easier, and I was not sure I wanted to watch. He launched into a story to ease them down gently. It was the tale of a boy who at last finds something he has always been looking for, but he is given a choice before he can keep it. He must leave his best friends behind if he is to keep that most precious thing that he has always wanted. Rafael told the children, "I think I can, at last, start to make a whole lot of very sick people better, and that is what I have always wanted, but first I must leave you—my best friends—behind."

Some of the kids did not really understand and they simply laughed and asked Rafael to tell another story. Others remained quiet; they sensed something was wrong, but had no words to tell us what they were feeling. Still others understood, and these kids stared at Rafael in disbelief, some with tears staining their soft, black cheeks. *Rafael is the boy. Rafael has found what he is looking for. Rafael is leaving. We are not what Rafael is looking for.*

He moved around the classroom saying goodbye. One by one, he talked to the kids, hugged them, made special hand gestures that only they understood; he used simple words, even used the horses names to communicate with some of the kids. Eddie got extra time alone with him, outside the classroom, in the tiny hallway, where they could acknowledge how this particular friendship would truly end. Rafael the scientist, eye to eye with modern science's limitations; his heart was likely shredded now. I stepped outside and breathed deeply in and out, the ecstatic pleasure of filling my lungs with the pure, clean, fall air crowned with a lengthy exhaled sigh of relief; then it hit me hard that the inability to do the same was just what would take Eddie from us.

When Rafael emerged from the barn he was badly shaken up, his face the color of fear. I started to walk us back to the parking lot but he turned, went back inside for a while and then waved one last time to the kids, both hands raised, before he left and reluctantly joined me where I waited by the car.

"I was wrong," he said, his voice rough, irresolute, "God, and *how*."

I tried to make out what he meant but he didn't answer me, started the car and pulled quickly away from the stables. During our descent through the park, I thought we might fill the time with funny reminiscences of the horses and the kids, but he remained silent, and after a while I simply stared out at the blurred colors of fall, and no longer even tried to make the leaving easier.

OF FRIENDS AND FAMILY

We had dreamed away the day, he in delirium, I in reverie.
David Bradley

I wished I could just take the money and run. Not to Mexico or Hawaii, I wasn't thinking of doing anything wildly illegal, dishonest or stupid. I just wished sometimes that our funders would hand over their money, let me do my job, and every now and then drop by for a nice chat over coffee about how radically the world had changed as a result of their good fortune and generosity. But instead, every dollar I brought in for our campaigns came with the unavoidable tax of having to write progress reports. I was swimming in monthly, quarterly, semi-annual, annual and biennial, reports and proposals, a definite indicator of our campaign's healthy bank account, but I really would rather be changing the world than writing about it. Anita, Luther and I planned to hire new staff to expand our work in the community. Personally, I couldn't wait to offload all this report writing onto someone else, and get back out in the field. But until then, for just about one week of every month, reports and proposals took up all my time.

I sat in Anita's living room, waiting for Damien to show, while reluctantly working on yet another draft of our progress report for the Southeast Redevelopment Foundation. Each board member had submitted very specific, very dreary requests for further information about the Windsor project. I knew that these caring, thoughtful, very important people were justifiably asking to know exactly how their *30K/3yr* grant was being used. But still, I couldn't help it if I was anxious to get my head and heart fully focused on the upcoming Zoning Commission hearings. Unbelievably, with no one around and pitiably few distractions—I couldn't possibly drink any more coffee—I was close to finishing my work, when I heard an eruption of voices in the hallway outside. Only after I repeatedly keyed in *Control/S* on my laptop—second nature; the modern equivalent of protecting the homestead, I suppose—did the commotion command my full attention. I could hear Anita's voice, strained, yet soothing and calm, and one, maybe two female voices yelling over her. Before I had a chance to make out the other voices, the door was flung open and a teenage girl and a young woman entered with Anita.

"Wha's *she* doin' here?" a girl shrieked, pointing at me. She stood over me with her finger inches from my face, her other hand curled around her hip; her pose was ugly, vicious. Her lips were puckered in disgust; she demanded a response from me.

"I'm Linda. I'm, I'm—working with Anita."

"Oh, *Linda*, Mama told me about you," the other young woman's face brightened with recognition. She stood back, as though wanting to introduce herself but conflicted about how this would look to her friend. Now it seemed obvious to me that this was Anita's daughter, Michelle. For one thing their appearances—especially their gorgeous, dark, oval eyes—were so similar, they could easily pass as sisters. But it was the way they held themselves, with their shoulders set back and their backs drawn taut, that struck me, an inherited trait or a learned skill, passed on mother to daughter. After a moment, Anita, her face taut, anger stealing the softness from her eyes, excused herself and led the two girls into her bedroom.

As they closed the door behind them, I got up. I wasn't sure what to do since Anita didn't ask me to go, but she couldn't possibly want me to stay. I looked down at my notes and wondered if I should maybe leave my work there and take a walk. *Why did that girl threaten me like that? Why the hell was Anita so embarrassed?* I saw it, the way she looked at me, before she went into the bedroom. I looked at my notes again to see if I shouldn't first finish up the section I was working on, then take all my stuff, and leave. Maybe I could meet Damien in the hallway and head over to Luther's place instead? I couldn't decide, all I could think about was the conversation rising like an unpredictable squall from the bedroom, ripping through the serenity of Anita's apartment, and hurtling its way towards me.

"You are *fifteen*, Felice," Anita said, her voice alarmingly tense, irate. "I have known you since you were a bump in your mama's belly. You are like a little sister to Michelle. You should show us some *respect*, young lady!"

"You wan' me to keep any fuckin' job jus' coz iss a *job*! You ma Mama's friend, not mine! I won' do it! I don' care how many frenz you hadta talk to. I *won'* do it."

"What *will* you do Felice? *What?*" Anita was trying hard not to lose her patience, trying to get through. But although she could command a whole roomful of people, she was not even beginning to reach that small, ferocious girl.

"I can fin' ma *own* job! An' I will! I can fin' ma own job! I don' need yo' help. I don'! An' as fo' *you*—" Felice flung open the bedroom door and turned back to confront Michelle. "You stupid *bitch* fo' tellin' her!"

She ran from the apartment, slamming the front door behind her, leaving her words reverberating around us: the threat, the promise of failure.

I watched her leave and now knew the lay of the land. Still standing, I gathered my work and files together quickly, the *sh-sh-sh-shing* of the paper, my every move, filling the now silent room. I pulled my jacket on and started to move towards the door, but not before I heard Anita say softly,

"That baby doesn't stand a chance without our help. Michelle, what are we going to do?"

As I walked towards the elevator I saw Felice standing, repeatedly slamming her hand against the down button, cursing and crying. She looked so tiny now, maybe just five feet, skinny, even gaunt.

"Bitch, are you *followin'* me?" she yelled when she noticed me at last.

I didn't reply, which unexpectedly infuriated her even more.

"Wha's the *matta* with you? Why ain't you sayin' nothin'?! Wha's the *fuckin' matta* wi—"

"When's the baby due?"

"*Anita* tell you? She woulda, tha' *ol'*—" She stopped herself as her rage started to lose some of its force. I saw some kind of realization flash across her face, her eyes instantly brightened with tears.

I pointed to the bump in her tiny frame. "She didn't need to."

Something snapped as she looked down at her belly, as though she was fully taking in for the first time what it really meant. She backed away from the elevator. "I gotta go," she said, the tears now streaming down her face, and she turned and ran back to Anita's apartment. Banging on the door, she shouted, "Anita! Anita! Michelle! Iss *me*!" and I watched as she disappeared inside, Anita's arms drawing her in.

I was considering whether I should try to find Damien or wait for him, when I realized that the elevator was broken—it wasn't coming— and this was probably the only reason Felice was safe with Anita right now and not spinning out of control on the streets outside. I set my things down on the hallway floor and sat leaning on the wall.

I couldn't help feeling disturbed by the sudden exposure to such an intimate moment in a stranger's life. I closed my eyes and the faces were still there, refusing to be forgotten, beginning with the time I volunteered at my local community center, through all the years at *Homes First*; people forever milling around whose lives were raw and exposed and on display for the whole world to see. In an average week, I would help AIDS patients fill out medical benefits forms, help a runaway teen find temporary shelter, give drug addicts Metro passes to get to their rehab clinics, and attempt to steer an assortment of young and old working poor away from flaky, unreliable gigs into better jobs or HED and training programs. And always, the search for a place for people to stay the night, a week, whatever we could get them. Shelters at capacity, transitional housing facilities maxed out, and more names added to housing waiting lists. God, now that I thought about it, I spent a huge number of hours filling out government forms for clients who just couldn't bear to write in tiny boxes about the unexpected, messy, unorthodox path they had taken through life, and that had led them to our door.

At *Homes First*, Richard's clients had drifted in and out filling our days with their truly bewildering worries and troubles. We were responsible for human beings who had been stripped of all the expected comforts of life in the United States, or maybe they never even had them in the first place. We tried to first find them shelter, food, clothing and medicine, and then worked on building a new life for them. So there was little we didn't know about them in the end. As we filled out the endless forms, their anonymity unraveled before us.

Name
Current/ Last Address
Date of Birth
Place of Birth
Marital Status
Name of Spouse
Name (s) of Dependants
Emergency Contact 1
Emergency Contact 2
Last Place of Work
Last School Attended

And on and on the questions went. With each came a little discussion with our clients, and slowly their life story unfolded, allowing Richard or me to devise a plan to help them. No more guessing games after they met with us. I would look out at our waiting area sometimes and ask myself, *How complicated is that young man looking at the pictures in National Geographic—how damaged is he really? And that family—two little girls in matching sweaters and their mother, the worry etched on her face—why is it that they have nowhere to go?* It would be so easy to judge them until you filled out the forms, and their lives stared back at you, in black and white, the colors of their lives, of missed opportunities. The intake volunteers would ask us, do we really have to fill in these forms? Do we really need to know all this about the clients to help them? Good questions. Better question, what *more* do we need to know? Do they have any friends or family who can help them? Was their family life unsafe or unstable? Have they held down a job for more than two years? Do they know how to read and write?

Richard was great at his work because unlike me, he knew how to put his feelings in store; there was never any risk of his becoming emotionally stranded, so he got the job done, quickly finding the resources to help someone. Me, I would linger with each client, listening to their life stories, even the truly crazy, or embellished ones, and when it came time to finding them help, I was lost sometimes, with them, trying to make sense of it all. Why anyone's life should be so hard. The forms made it easier to stick to the job in hand, but I never forgot anyone, their names and faces still floated freely in my mind. It was just as well that I found campaign work, its human element offering a more diffuse emotional experience, far less of a daily punch to the stomach than Richard's work.

Felice's predicament was really nothing new to me. Maybe that's why she reacted the way she did. We both knew, in the instant that I asked her when the baby was due, that it was O.K. for her to turn and run. Felice, terrified and still just a child, needed Anita to survive. Chaos reorganized by starting back at the basics. What's your name? Where do you live? Where are you going now? *Do you have family or friends who could help you?*

As I contemplated all this, I suddenly saw Damien come in through the fire escape door. He looked startled to see me.

"Damien hi, I was waiting for you, I thought maybe we could go to Luther's place."

He didn't look at me; he looked at the floor, and didn't say anything.

"Oh, no. Damien—"

I stopped myself before I said it—*not you*—because I couldn't quite believe this, I couldn't put this one in its place. You're not supposed to mess up if you have people there for you, and Damien had an army of people there for him. I didn't want to believe he had proved all those people right—the ones who wanted him to fail—the ones who wanted to build him a prison, reserve his bed ahead of time and make a profit off of locking him up. He leaned by my side against the wall, and I realized now that I couldn't look at him either. I didn't want to judge him, I wanted to be calm and understanding, but I didn't understand. I didn't understand. How could he do this? Not Damien. She wasn't even sixteen—she was still a kid! *Not Damien*.

"It's not me," he said quietly, "it's Theo."

He shrugged away my mercurial loss of faith in him, and started to make his way to Anita's apartment, his head low to his chest, his arms awkward at his side, every bit of his playful swagger, every part of him that shone, vanished. Every part the boy with the world at his feet now made into a man whose path had already been decided for him. Even if he succeeded, as hard as he was working to succeed, he would be expected to carry his friends and family with him. I wanted to go after him, and apologize for doubting him—say something to comfort him for what he must be going through—but I remained where I stood and watched as he disappeared into Anita's apartment. *Do you have family or friends who could help you?*

The bus moved slowly across D.C., struggling through rush hour traffic. I sat staring out of the window, watching the sun starting to set over the monuments, my favorite time of day on the Mall. I couldn't get over seeing Damien. And thinking that it was *him*. He didn't seem to care, he had bigger problems on his mind, but maybe he would care, when he finally thought about what I said to him. He might never comment, but he would still know that I didn't yet believe in him completely. My mind fell to Theo—it wasn't so shocking to me that he would have been so foolish as to get a girl pregnant. Unlike Damien, who had immersed himself in a new world, extricating himself from all that could distract him, Theo lived life on the fringe of change. While he strived to excel in school and stayed late to take extra courses in computers and graphic design because he believed this was his ticket out of poverty, I knew that his home life was hell. I knew that he cared for his mother, who was an addict and rarely around, and his little sister, whom he mostly raised by himself. I knew all of this because Damien had confided in me about Theo. That he should have found comfort elsewhere, even that he failed to take precautions, I understood. Even had it been Damien, even then, a part of me would have understood, that the deck was stacked, the dice biased, and that the game they played had never, ever been fair. Still, I had hoped, and wanted to believe, that Damien and Theo had started to write their own rules and that for them, winning was no longer quite so hard.

Back at home, I found Ian and Sandra dressed and standing by to go to Rafael and Marguerite's party. Sandra looked adorable in a crimson red flamenco dress that Ian had bought for her, for $10, at the top of our street.

"You don't think it's offensive, you know, buying into stereotypes?" Ian asked me, as I looked Sandra over and planted a kiss on her head. She was wedged between us, and her head turned as each of us spoke, as though gathering signals from orbiting satellites.

"What? That you've dressed our daughter as a flamenco dancer to go to a Latino party? No you're not buying into stereotypes at *all*, baby."

"Come on, I just thought it was cute. You know, in Rafael's honor."

"It is cute, and offensive, and Rafael and Marguerite will love it, and be very honored, so come on, let's go!"

"I never know with you. You're so sensitive about not hurting people's *feelings*." This was said with generous sarcasm and ridicule, his hands floating back and forth, Haight-Ashbury style, "It's hard to keep up with."

Damien came to mind. "Trust me," I assured him, "I'm no expert. Let's go, this *lovely* young lady has a party to go to!"

We did not have far to go. Rafael's aunt lived a few blocks from us, on an unusually narrow section of Park Road, where the buildings crouched low over the uneven, dirty sidewalks. Sandra, roughly two feet closer to the pavement than Ian and me, commented cheerily about the things she saw as we walked.

"Look Reeses wrappers! What's that? R-e-d- B-u-l-l? Look, it has a picture of a *red bull*! Something smells. They're cooking something over there! Can we go and see?"

We made our way passed a group of Latina women selling steaming, hot papusas and fresh, sliced mango from picnic coolers, in front of a rundown cash-checking store. The apartment we were looking for was next door, directly above a small laundromat with a dirty, decaying storefront, its windows protected by a mess of bars and steel mesh. The noise and odors, even the darkness of the street, followed us as we climbed the stairs. As soon as we entered the upstairs hallway, the cloying smell of bleach and fabric softener, and the weary light from a small, cracked fluorescent fixture permeated the tiny space. We pushed back the door and looked inside the apartment. The way Rafael had described his nights of drinking and singing with his relatives there, I had imagined a colorful kitchen of terra cotta and hand-painted tiles, complete with chillis and garlic hanging from the walls, and a vast living room with warmly hued walls and carpets, and abundant wicker furniture. But instead, the apartment was small and cramped, and the kitchen was barely that, a tiny galley with just enough room for two or three people to stand; Rafael's success had evidently not filtered through to his extended family.

I couldn't help but notice right away that the walls were covered ceiling to floor with family photos and religious icons—gold leaf Virgin Mary's and wooden crosses. Some of the crosses looked homemade, with shiny, plastic Jesuses glued to them, glue showing; others were miniature works of art, mostly of the Virgin Mary with the baby Jesus in her arms, or intricate portrayals of the suffering of Jesus on the cross. I immediately thought of Anita and Luther and wondered if they had found a way to reconcile; Anita and I had not spoken of the argument since that night. I set the worry for my friends aside when Ian tugged at me to follow him into the apartment.

The living room had very little place to move; just a narrow passage along the edge of the coffee table that allowed movement in single file to and from the kitchen. As Ian, Sandra and I slowly progressed towards Rafael's aunt to greet her, people all around us made the effort to shake hands with us from where they sat on the sofas, chairs, windowsills, radiators and floor of the living room and from the two small bedrooms. Rafael's sister, the mother of the little girl who was sick from lead poisoning, got up from her chair to embrace me and said, "You are very welcome here. Your family too."

Rafael was late. Always late. My Spanish passed for conversation enough to make jokes about him always being late. I was not expecting the response to his arrival when he did finally walk through the door; the volume of noise soared, men laughing, women laughing and clapping hands. Beer bottles were passed urgently about, hand to hand, and Rafael's aunt was suddenly over here, over there, laying out platters upon platters of food. This was not only a celebration of Rafael and Marguerite's engagement, but also I suspected, of any event that warranted a visit from Rafael. At least it seemed that way to me—he was a hero returning to a very eager and grateful crowd. He graciously tasted and praised his aunt's food, and joked and laughed with everyone around him. Ian and I could barely hear or understand a word of what anyone was saying which only amplified the sense of how separate we were from this world that existed a stone's throw from our own house. In the midst of the chaos someone turned the music on, volume up high, and then Marguerite arrived. Rafael immediately spotted her and put down his beer. He walked over to her and led her into the melee, holding her hand in both of his, with the air of a man who would never make the same mistake twice; he would never lose her again. The music pounded, the voices rose up and the smell of the lavish feast filled the air; the little apartment and all the people in it intoxicated me. Ian and I tried hard to conjure up whatever Spanish we knew to make conversation with the people crushing around us. Sandra sat on the floor playing checkers with another little girl and they had—in the way that children often do—created a separate world for themselves that seemed to keep at bay the towering, noisy giants around them. Perhaps I had had too many beers; it helped my Spanish, but not my ability to stand, so I found a place on the arm of one of the sofas, next to a third or fourth cousin. We struck up a conversation and I discovered that she loved carpentry—she had to shout the words, *working with wood!* until I understood her—and was learning it from her father and brothers. I yelled at her, over all the noise, to *start your own business!* She looked at me as though I had fallen from space—I thought she was twenty-five, but she was only fourteen, and still in school. We laughed long and hard at my mistake. I had told a girl that she was a woman and unknowingly rocked her world. She was so proud to be treated like an adult that I worried she might quit school the very next day and take my stupid, drunken advice. *Stay in school!* I told her, and she laughed and reminded me again that she was *only fourteen!* Rafael suddenly emerged from the crowd, turned the music down, but only a little, and announced that not only were he and Marguerite getting re-married, but that his niece would soon have a cousin, bringing more clapping and shrieks of congratulations. Everyone around us tried to squeeze a way over to Marguerite and the confusion yielded yet more laughter and shouting. Rafael's aunt put her arms around him, kissed him and whispered to him as the music started to pound again. I watched her as she moved away, and disappeared into the kitchen to fetch more food—how could there possibly be more food? She reappeared with an enormous sheet cake, iced with Rafael and Marguerite's names inside a decoration in the shape of Texas, and every inch glazed in red, white and blue. The cake started to blur ever so slightly and then ever so *not* slightly. *Oh God, I am so drunk.*

Ian and I watched Rafael and Marguerite cut the cake and feed each other the first piece, the talk of wedding dates and babies and baby clothes swirling all around us. Then suddenly I was quite certain that I thought I saw—I think the baby Jesus just *winked* at me from one of the paintings. I was now just a little afraid at what I might see next, if we didn't leave right then and there, before another friendly relative handed me another beer to toast the happy couple. Ian grabbed a hold of my hand and we slipped out of the apartment clutching onto Sandra who begged us over and over to stay. I stumbled happily, drunkenly, onto the gloomy, dark sidewalk and soon I was doubled over laughing.

"Hah!" I told Ian. "We *did* it! We left without saying goodbye!"

"I am *ssso* drunk!" Ian blurted out. "That was one hell of a party!"

Sandra squeezed her way between us and took both our hands. "I'll get you home. Just don't let go of my hand."

That's my girl, the five-year old designated walker.

Just then we heard a window grind against its swollen wood casement from somewhere behind us, and a familiar voice shouted out our names. We looked back and up the street towards Rafael's aunt's apartment.

"Hey! Ian and Linda, *and* Sandra!" Rafael called. Marguerite leaned out of the window with him. "Come see us in Texas—we'll miss you! Oh, and *Goodbye!*"

"Bastard," Ian said under his breath.

"Total," I whispered back.

The little street we walked on now was dimly lit and eerily quiet after the party. I wasn't so drunk that the thought didn't come to me as we made our way through Columbia Heights in the midnight hours, that there were plenty of people in this world who would be terrified to walk this way at night. *What* I asked myself is there to be afraid of? What are we all so *afraid* of? God could take me now and I would die a happy girl.

ANITA ALONE

When God had made The Man, he made him out of stuff that sung all the time and glittered all over. Then after that some angels got jealous and chopped him into millions of pieces, but still he glittered and hummed. So they beat him down to nothing but sparks but each little spark had a shine and a song.
Zora Neale Hurston

Anita saw the light reflecting off the wheelchair's wheel, and she knew that Luther would fall. She watched as he tumbled from the chair and fell sideways onto the basketball court, bracing his fall with his left hand, and covering his head with his right arm to deflect another blow. And then she saw a boy turn on Luther and kick him as he lay on the ground. By the time she reached him, with Damien at her side, he was back in his chair, dazed and silent. He refused to speak to her, refused help from the medics, refused to give a police statement, refused, as she walked alongside him back to his apartment, to take her hand.

Earlier that evening, Luther and his friends had been playing their regular game of Friday night pick-up basketball with a large, loud crowd watching. A few families had brought blankets and food; the high school kids and Windsor Apartment residents were out in full force. The ball moved lethargically up and down the court, both sides blocking any chance of a play for the first ten minutes or so, but for Anita, who had come tonight to watch for the first time, the game was thrilling. She and Luther had never discussed the argument at Linda's house, but it had somehow cleared the air between them and since then they had been spending all their free time together. She had even accepted his offer to come and watch him play tonight although she had never cared for basketball. She was surprised to find herself enjoying watching Luther on the court—she liked how the other players fully integrated him into the game; he didn't seem to be at any disadvantage at all. That was something to see, even as they playfully cursed him out every time he took possession of the ball.

She was chatting with Michelle, looking away, when one of the players made a break and landed the first basket. She missed the shot, but that first goal seemed to unlock the gears on the whole game—she could feel the swell of energy rising in the crowd. The players now moved more swiftly, the ball exchanged hands almost too quickly to keep pace with, and the score started to build on both sides. The noise in the crowd and from the court escalated; more spectators arrived and settled in, and very soon Anita and Michelle were too excited to talk, and watched intently as the players raced back and forth.

The fight broke out just beyond the court, about forty feet from the entrance. The sounds of a group of teenage boys, two of them yelling at each other, drifted over to where Anita was sitting; at first she couldn't distinguish them above the noise of the crowd. But then there was no mistaking the epithets that caused a cold fear to rise swiftly inside her: *nigger, bitch, ho, nigger, nigger, nigger.* She turned away from the court, to where she was certain the words were coming from, but she couldn't see anyone behind the concrete wall framing the entrance. Anita took her daughter's hand, holding it tightly, and reluctantly turned back to watch the game. The shouting suddenly stopped. Anita felt her shoulders fall with relief. But then as she watched Luther wheel at full speed down court, a group of about six or seven boys rapidly spilled onto the court. They shoved and pushed each other; it seemed playful enough— as though they were just joking around—until one of them pulled out a knife. He stabbed the player who had just run past with the ball and yelled, "*She not yo girl, she a bitch!*" Then he screamed at Luther. "*Nigger, I said get outta ma way!*"

Luther lunged at one of the teens but the boy turned so quickly to punch him that he was unable to block the blow. Anita started to run to him when someone shoved her aside, and yelled at her.

"Don' go'n there! *Stay outta there!*"

It was Damien. He had to lean over Anita to restrain her from running onto the court and she watched instead as Luther's friends lifted him up and helped him back into his wheelchair. The sound of sirens tore through the air, police cruisers and ambulances pulled up one after another, blocking the street, and seconds later, twenty or so officers and medics swarmed the entrance to the court. And then, there they were. Two black youths, hands cuffed behind their backs, being led away across the court in full view of everyone at the game. Anita felt horrified, sickened, watching them—grinning at the notoriety and celebrity of their moment on the court. She took a long look at the two young men as they were forced into the police cruiser parked across the street. There was her cousin staring back at her, as though to say, I've gone and done it again. *Help me*. She saw in that instant—in the act of their being taken away—the violence, hate, stifled spirits and rage of boys too broken to become men.

She watched the ambulance pull away with the injured basketball player, the one who had been stabbed first, repeatedly; his blood now stained the entrance to the court. As she waited with Michelle for Luther to be seen by a medic, she noticed a police officer leaning over to collect the knife from the ground, and place it an evidence bag. Evidence enough to lock at least one of those boys up for a very long time.

No matter the calmness of any given day, it seemed to Anita that the violence in her neighborhood ran as an undercurrent ready to break through with the slightest change in course. Just one small group of youths, wild enough, high enough, mean enough to go looking for trouble could leave a wide swathe of destruction in their path, their victims seldom hurt or killed for a reason. Three-foot coffins and sweet little kids lying like angels in silk, an eighty-eight year-old granddad, high school football stars or a twelve year-old girl. All *defying* reason. Anita's heart had been wounded so many times growing up in her neighborhood, that she felt tonight as though her heart might just give in, that it quite possibly could not take anymore strain. For the first time in her life she asked herself if she were strong enough. For all of this.

She knew intimately the foundation of neglect and violence that had been set to make those kids what they were. She thought she had seen something of her cousin in one of the boys that night, as they tumbled jostling onto the court, arguing loudly, before the knife came out. And then she had seen his unmistakable face staring back at her from the cruiser. The very first time Anita's cousin was arrested, he had been caught shoplifting. The store pressed charges and he was fined and given community service for twenty hours. He read to a first grade kid in his school for two hours a week, for ten weeks, and then went out and broke into a friend's house to steal his CD's. This went unpunished. His mother was drinking herself into oblivion while he was out looking for his first gun. He settled on a toy gun and held up a woman outside a department store in Silver Spring. Somehow, the D.C. and Maryland police did their work and he was picked up for this and sent to juvenile corrections for five months. Just out, he graduated high school and finished writing a songbook about being a misunderstood black youth, before securing his first real gun and getting arrested for assault with a deadly weapon. His father, whom he hadn't seen in ten years, came to visit him in jail, but they had nothing to say to one another. He had pinned high hopes on his father's visit but there were to be other life-changing reunions in his cards. When he got out again, he spent a few months working as a plumber's assistant, and then helped rob a house in LeDroit Park; his old friends had flocked to him to beg money from him while humiliating him relentlessly for working too hard. He was picked up again and thrown in prison for another three years, but got out early for good behavior. He had just recently come to live with his stepfather in Anacostia, with a promise to study and work for a trade certificate. He may not have had a functioning mother, his father may have been gone from his life but he did have people like Anita and his stepfather always struggling, fighting to keep him straight and safe. It just wasn't enough when all around him were the kids, the ones he'd known his *whole* life—a potent bond of survival between them—getting high, defining themselves by the crimes they had committed, and pretending to be men by fathering children they hoped never to see grow up to be just like them. How could anyone help him now?

Luther was lying awake in the dark when Anita entered to check up on him. After he stubbornly refused to go to the hospital, one of the medics on the scene had given him two codeine tablets that had long since worn off.

"Come sit with me," he told Anita.

There was a storm of emotions building inside her and she was afraid to talk. But she did as he asked, and she joined him on the bed. He was breathing heavily as he looked at her.

"Why do you believe in God, Anita?"

Anita knew all that resided in his question. She knew that he had disarmed himself for her, opened himself up and allowed only her into his heart, no one else. He both trusted and loved her, she knew this. But she also knew that her resolute faith in God terrified him, believing as he did, that it lay between them and would tear them apart. Years ago, when they first met, she encouraged Luther to seek counseling at her church. The priest he met with tried to convince Luther to see his survival as a sign that God had a plan for him. He nearly never forgave her for this, certain as he was that losing his brother and being bound to his wheelchair, were unmistakable signs that God, if he even existed, had long since checked out on the world he had supposedly once created. *Why do you believe in God, Anita*? Did she still believe that God had a plan for Luther? Was the stabbing tonight in the plan?

Anita took Luther's hand and they sat silently for a while. At work each day, she had been visiting the church sanctuary, although not always to pray as she used to, but simply to feel closer to God. What she saw tonight, what she felt tonight, was the hand of God pushing her away, forcefully, deliberately.

"Maybe, I think, God is the spirit in me that keeps me going, no matter what. I believe completely that Jesus is a guide for us on earth—how to live our lives. But I can't tell you if I still believe in a God who watches over us and protects us. I wonder if we haven't been left after all, to do that for ourselves. And for each other."

Luther laid his head back on the pillow.

"So you do doubt."

"Sometimes, yes I do. Sometimes."

"That's enough for me. I'll take it."

He leaned towards her and pulled her close, and she lay beside him until he fell asleep. Not long afterwards, she went to the kitchen and stayed up reading her bible. It was not easy for Anita to find even the slightest whisper of God in its pages that night, but still she did not give up.

OF ENTERING THE UNKNOWN WORLD

But in the very heart of it I catch myself bracing a little, as if in fear of being tricked. As if to really believe in it will somehow make it vanish, like a voice waking me from sleep.
Tobias Wolff

Anita greeted me at her door and showed me in. I could tell something was up, and I waited for her to tell me. But she didn't tell me, in fact she made a big effort to pretend that all was right in the world, so I went right ahead and asked.

"Is is Felice? Is she O.K?"

"Felice is fine."

"O.K. How was your weekend?"

"O.K."

"How's Damien holding up?"

"*Damien*? Damien wasn't hurt."

She got up as though she had somehow slipped up, and walked to the kitchen where she began pulling down mugs and setting the coffee pot up.

"*Hurt*? Who was hurt?"

Anita, reaching for the milk, told the fridge that Luther was hurt in a fight.

"*Luther*? *Luther* was in a *fight*?"

And this was how I found out what happened here on Friday night. While Ian, Sandra and I were raving away at a party on the other side of town, Luther was getting stomped on and one of Damien and Theo's classmates was stabbed. The whole fight, I now discovered, was over Felice. She had been sleeping with several boys and at least one of them was under the impression he was in an exclusive relationship. When he found out he wasn't, and that Felice didn't even really know who the father of her child might be, the boy went after one of Felice's many boyfriends. Had Theo been there he might have been the one in the back of the ambulance.

"How's the boy?" I asked warily. "The one who was stabbed?"

"He's not safe yet. He's in an induced coma to stabilize him."

If the boy dies...what if he dies? The boy's classmate will be tried for murder. I thought about my high-school classmates. They're librarians and teachers, nurses and politicians, carpenters, financial planners, research scientists, doctors and electricians. They're refugee camp workers and community organizers. None of them spent time in juvenile detention centers unless it was as counselors. Not one of them is a convicted felon that I know of. I couldn't even begin to imagine one of my classmates dead, and another classmate accused of their murder.

"How's Luther?"

"I'm alright, I'm here," he said, pushing himself through Anita's front doorway and swinging his chair around to face us.

Luther insisted on working on the Windsor Apartments campaign. I suspected he didn't have the stomach to concentrate on the prison campaign and outline arguments against building a prison in the neighborhood. There were at least two local boys whom he would be happy to see locked up right now.

It's hard for any of us to admit that there may just be evil people in this world—people who were born to fight, hate, rape and murder. We probably all want to believe that circumstances alone can explain what makes someone a criminal. But one cold hard look at the evidence settles that issue for good. There are in fact prep school rapists and upper-class pedophiles. And a whole host of vicious murderers and brutal dictators who defy both explanation and forgiveness. Luther perhaps understood this better than any of us, but it did not diminish what we were trying to do together. We weren't pretending that criminals and crime don't exist, and wouldn't always exist. We simply hoped to extricate the kids who were in danger of going down a path of crime or failure, because it seemed to them, in their tender, naïve, impressionable years, to be the only choice available; these kids did not need a brand new prison in their neighborhood. Today though, our purpose was less clear for all of us, especially Luther. It had been made muddy by neighborhood kids—kids whom he knew well, whom he watched grow up—throwing him from his wheelchair and kicking his soul to pieces.

So instead of working on the hearings, which were now less than ten days away, we worked on the tedious business of reviewing financial spreadsheets and individual loan agreements for each of the Windsor residents who had requested the right to stay and be part of the takeover. Vernon had asked us to do a thorough risk analysis on the loans and a revised cost analysis for the community support center we were hoping to open after the takeover. As part of this process, we reviewed resumes and rap sheets. And I have to say I was on the mat now. Between what had happened to Luther—I couldn't help staring at his swollen, bruised face—and the criminal history of some of those we were hoping to make homeowners, I was fighting hard right now to restrain what welled up inside me, and to persuade myself that I was still doing the right thing.

I stayed long past dinner, not to socialize, but simply to be near Luther and Anita. I didn't want them to think that I felt awkward because their lives were complicated, or that anything may have changed between us. I knew what it was like every time David O.D.'d. Friends who didn't know how to behave staying away, exactly when I needed them most. The three of us didn't talk much. We merely focused on our work and said very little. Finally I gathered up my gear and kissed them both goodnight. Anita saw me to the door and followed me out to the corridor.

"That was good. We got a lot done. Thanks."

"Are you really O.K?"

"We'll get through. We have to, don't we?"

Later, as I stepped outside the apartment building, the street was quiet and dark; fear unexpectedly stirred inside me, though I wasn't afraid.

LUTHER ALONE

You move towards her outstretched arm
  a little slower than shy,
As if you'll have need of a sober witness,
  as if this is where you know
The experiment ends, and memory dogs
  'round the corner

Cornelius Eady

Luther closed the door behind Anita; she was upset, but he insisted on being alone tonight. He wheeled across the apartment to the balcony's edge and looked out over the river, towards the downtown lights. They glittered like a miniature milky way, swirling just above the horizon. As he tried to make out the individual landmarks, using the Washington monument as his starting point, he was startled by the unwelcome recollection of a night, years ago, when he was returning home from school with his older brother.

They lived in Columbia Heights back then, with their mother and her boyfriend, a sadistic drug-dealer who was kind enough to the boys, but thought nothing of attacking their mother with a broken beer bottle. Every night after school, Luther and his brother took a chance and tried to take the quickest way home, through the park. Meridian Hill, in those days, was a dark, frightening place. Dealers, prostitutes and a collection of heavily-armed, aimless gangs prowled the trails and hid out behind the fountains and stone walls, their presence a painful mockery of the intricacy and beauty of the landscape and gardens. That night, Luther and his brother ran as fast as they could, trying to make it out of the park safely, when gunfire suddenly tore through the air. Someone came up behind them, terrifyingly close, and the boys scrambled to get away. They moved silently, edging their way along the sidewall of the park, until they heard the footsteps turn away. They took off running, looking back one more time to be sure they were safe. They ran right into her. *Serenity*. An enormous, impossibly smooth, white lady in her flowing dress. She sat glowing, even in the shade of dusk, with the slightest smile on her face. She was cracked all over, graffiti scrawled across her marble skin—her perfection flawed—but she remained still, while all around them, the park rattled with sounds that were startling and frightening to the two boys. As the darkness settled around them, *Serenity* gave them cover while they caught their breath and tried to decide on the best way out of the park. They edged slowly down the path they had just taken, this time keeping their backs to the stone wall towering over them. They eventually reached the side entrance for Sixteenth Street, and emerged onto the sidewalk, stunned and relieved to be alive. Not yet out of danger, they tore downhill two or three blocks and crossed over to Fourteenth running back up the hill, now two blocks east of the park. They didn't stop running until they were home, where they found their mother, barely conscious, lying on the floor. That same night, eleven-year-old Luther packed his family's few belongings, helped his brother dress his mother's wounds, emptied his savings out and stuffed them in his pockets, and eventually flagged down a cab to take his family back across the river to Anacostia. And he never looked back, never regretted what he had done, until years later when the violence he so feared sought him out once more.

Luther was not given to revisiting the day that he and his brother were shot. His memories of the shooting were, in any case, not his own; they were born of witness accounts of what happened. He learnt to remember being shot and seeing people scrambling away from him to find cover, he could even recall hearing himself scream at the sight of his bloodied brother collapsed beside him, and yet he knew that these were fictional memories. What he never failed to remember was that when he eventually did regain consciousness days later, at the hospital, he was immediately aware that a huge part of him had been severed away. And although the doctors told him the sensation was probably because he no longer had feeling in his legs, he already knew he had lost his only brother. This part of his life he remembered clearly, he didn't need witnesses to tell him what it felt like to have his heart clenched tightly in his chest, to be barely able to breathe, until he forced his mother to admit that his brother had died.

Now Luther sat on his balcony, looking across the river and staring at the lights towards the western part of the city, wondering why it bothered him so much that Linda had insisted on staying late tonight. That's where she lives, he thought—on the other side of the river—away from all this. What could she possibly understand of his life? What did he know of Meridian Hill Park? She had once told him that she loved to run there, and to have picnics near the fountain, on Sunday afternoons. She even said, *Oxon Cove should be like that*, a place where people go to play soccer and frisbee and walk their dogs. He felt the cool night air gather around him as he wheeled himself back inside, awkwardly struggling to close the glass sliders. *Serenity* is a white woman who doesn't know a damn thing about life.

Luther finished his beer and happily threw his beer bottle in the trash before gathering some of the papers from the day's work session to review in bed. As he read Linda's meticulously written notes in each file, he was jolted by the realization that she may already know how much he doubted her, and that nonetheless, she had stuck around. He wondered if he wasn't beginning to do to both Anita and Linda what he had always done to the people who had tried to be close to him. Find any excuse to make it stop. The crushing sense of losing control. Wanting to be together even while wanting to be elsewhere, alone. Linda had stuck around; she'd invited him into her home. *That other one, the one who ended up in Louisiana. I forced him away.*

His thoughts fell to Anita. *God, I wish she were still here, now.* When they first met, Luther lived off the lasting scent of the evenings when Anita would drop by his apartment to talk about their campaigns. The surprise visits lifted his spirits and even as she demanded more work of him, he leaned to her more, accepted more responsibilities, imagining that these were gifts of her love for him. Now she was really his and was willing to give him all the space he needed, even to wrestle with God. That kind of love was unknown to him. It provoked feelings inside him that were unpredictable, hard to comprehend—what he would now do for Anita, the compromises he was already considering, the parts of him he was willing to give up. He knew suddenly, that this time, he didn't want it to stop. Any of it. Linda—a new and unexpected friendship. Anita—the love of his life.

Luther heard his front door lock turn and he watched Anita enter. She stood in the doorway.

"Don't be alone, Luther. Not this time."

"Come, babe. I'm so glad you're back."

OF REMAINING SILENT NO MORE

I rapped. I rapped hard. I rapped harder than I'd ever rapped in my life. I took all the skills I'd picked up rapping with those penitentiary philosophers out on the yard and threw the whole handful at the parole board... I meant every word I said. I was changed. I knew it, and I wanted to make sure they knew it.
Nathan McCall

I thought this day would never come. *The Zoning Hearings*. No last minute postponement. No venue changes. No Commissioners called away on urgent business. I spoke to the clerk, talked to Baucus' office, Greg, everyone I could think of, and they all said, *yes*, the hearings are going ahead, starting at 7pm tonight.

I made the first call that would activate our colossal phone-tree, and soon I was slogging through, calling people at work, at home, on their mobiles, urging them to show up tonight. The repeated cancellations had tested the devotion of our volunteers—they became irritated, some infuriated, by the number of phone calls they received in recent weeks, every time we thought the hearings were happening, every time we called to cancel—and we had surely lost some support. But most of the people I reached in person were utterly relieved to hear that their chance to speak out had finally arrived, and they eagerly made their designated calls to keep passing the message forward. The word spread out over the morning, reaching across the city—the culmination of more than a year of preparation for this one day. I gave Anita and Luther regular updates and we stayed in constant contact with Ward 8 and Prince George's County leaders. Kadija and Damien held down the phone banks, and we all spent the rest of the day cranking through the contact lists and confirming our speaker attendance list. We cast our net and dragged over and over again for anyone who had not yet been contacted in person. All the work we did would be measured by the number of activists we turned out tonight, by how long we could keep the opposition testimonies flowing. All that mattered tonight was our message, that these testimonies would hammer home over and over again—Parkland not Prisons/Schools not Jails. Make it stick, make it work; leave the Zoning Commission no other choice but to say no.

I packed up my slide projector, laptop and papers and headed over to Luther's apartment. My cell phone signal vanished as soon as I took the escalator down to the Metro and I realized there was nothing more to be done until I reached Anacostia. It felt odd to be suddenly free of any responsibilities, with the hearing less than three hours away. I should be frantically doing something, shouldn't I? What? My testimony. I pulled it out, but I couldn't bear to look over the words again. Every time I tried, my stomach caved, a combination of resentment that we had to do this at all—invest this much effort in stopping a proposal that never should have seen the light of day—and anticipation that I was about to have my day in court. I closed my eyes, rested my head on the window and dozed off, as the train swayed its way across the city. When I awoke, one stop before Anacostia, there had been a staggering demographic shift in the train's riders. How does that happen? We board the train as an integrated nation and we exit as a segregated one? I walked along South Capitol to the Windsor Apartments and I didn't see another white face until I was downtown again, later that night.

"What *is* it with you whities?' Luther asked, as he opened the door.

I could see that his TV, always on in the kitchen, was set to Channel 8. He and Anita must have been watching City Council meeting re-runs, presumably seeking inspiration for tonight.

"Think you could you ask your crew to clean up a little? Even *bathe* maybe?" he teased me.

I knew of course what he was saying. In the black community, activists very often dress as though they are going to church when attending a meeting—the women immaculately clad, nails polished, hair swept, sprayed and gelled into position, the men in suits and ties. They are representatives of something great and significant—their neighborhood, their community. *White* activists on the other hand...lanky, unwashed hair comes to mind. Ripped jeans. Lots of weird braided bracelets. And as Catherine always likes to point out, a certain *scent*. But it's hard to talk about things out when you're part of that world. That you don't know why the universal dress code for white activists is the predictable, forlorn look of an unkempt student lost in a daze ten years into their, still as yet undefined, PhD thesis? Occasionally the dismal wages of social justice work afford such appearances. But mostly it's that peculiar blend of guilt and conviction that bears heavily on the conscience of many white activists, that for some reason, gets buried under poorly chosen, often hideous, guises of humility.

Luther had decided to lob this grenade at me just before the long-awaited hearings, hoping no doubt, to let off some steam. I was happy to play along.

"It's a little late for me to ask our activists to shower and change before tonight, don't you think? Should have done that when I had them on the phone earlier today."

Luther laughed, and Anita, impeccably dressed in a Ghanaian-style embroidered green, red and ocher tunic and flowing black pants, not a stray hair to be seen, did a twirl to show off her outfit.

"We were just having a laugh." Luther informed me, "at those guys on TV."

I caught sight of a grunge kid pouring his heart out at a council hearing on the state of the city's schools. We all watched a little while, and he was actually very convincing, poetic even, except he wasn't a kid at all as it turned out, but a High School science teacher. He talked eloquently of missed opportunities and the need for change. But hell, he should have worn a suit.

"Very funny guys, come on, we've got work to do," I scolded them.

They had made their point. If you believe in accepting people as they are, than you cannot believe in asking them to conform to be heard. But as an organizer it's too easy to turn out concerned citizens who look like they just woke up from a bad dream to discover they missed the 60's and didn't get to go to Woodstock. Far harder to draw outrage and attendance at hearings from the wealthier members of the community—liberal or conservative, white or black—whose voices would be more readily listened to, merely for being rarer. We had struggled hard to convince lawyers from Foxhall and doctors from Georgetown, to come downtown and tell the council that they also wanted more affordable housing in the city, and that they too believed that Ward 8 deserved better than a prison. But such activists rarely testify in their elegant suits about the need to invest in the future of black children, preferring instead to put in a discreet phone call to an old buddy on the council, or to have lunch with a former law school classmate on the Hill. Or simply to write checks to keep the campaigns alive. The reality was, we needed them, however they chose to participate in our campaigns, but it would be nice, every once in a while, to have them actually show up at the hearings.

I found a moment to call Ian again, and I could hear that he was relieved, nothing short of ecstatic, to know that this day had come at last.

"How's your testimony?" he asked. "You didn't make any last minute changes I hope."

"I think it's done, I'm going to go with what I have. It's a little emotional, but then again, so am I. I just can't believe they didn't cancel again."

"Been a long road. You guys are going to kill this thing."

"How's your testimony coming along?"

"I think I have only one thing to say really—what the *fuck* were you guys thinking?"

I laughed. "Think you could tone it down a notch?"

"O.K., so listen to this. I'm going to work the idea that aside from throwing lives away, we're wasting money. Every year a black man spends in prison, you could have paid for his college education twice over, with change to spare. I just found that out. Something like *60K*, a year. Why didn't you use that, Lin? You never even mentioned it."

"Ian, we can't—"

"After four years of prison, a black kid's not paying taxes any time soon, and he's already cost taxpayers upwards of 240K. After four years of college, he's paying Uncle Sam some decent change and we start closing prisons, instead of building new ones. I'm going with that. That's my testimony."

He waited for my endorsement. I waited to be sure he was finished.

"Only I wrote it all out. You know, so it'll sound incredibly eloquent, and heartfelt."

I hesitated still.

"Well?"

"We didn't use it because it can be taken the wrong way. The *cost* of the black man in prison. Could take us down the road of make them pay for themselves when they're in prison. The social commentary gets fouled when you make that argument, that it's better for the taxpayer to get it right in the first place."

"What? No, it doesn't. How did you—" Ian was irritated; as an MBA, he was on ground most familiar to him, so he had little patience for my balanced argument approach. "Lin, the economics of a *jailed* black man makes no sense at all. What's wrong with saying that?"

"I know that, you know that, but there are people out there who will tell you that if a black man is in jail it's his own damn *fault*, so make *him* pay the price, make *him* work for the privilege of food and lodging. To hell with all the reasons he ended up in jail in the first place. Your logic is good, it's great, it's just hard to package."

"Why do you do that? You're so concerned about understanding the other side's arguments, you dismiss whole realms of discourse, just so's not to offend. Why do you care, when they don't? These guys are having a conversation about the *money* they are about to lose if they don't get to build another new prison, and lock up another 2,500 blacks, and you're sitting there trying to understand their perspective and avoid taking them on."

"I'm, we're—Luther, Anita—trying to encourage our activists not to sound like that, like *money* is the issue. We're trying to keep the message simple, that black kids deserve better, not because it costs society too much money if they fail, but because it's wrong for society to *allow* them to fail in the first place, to go on *forcing* them to fail. It's a moral issue, not a financial decision."

"Money is the *only* issue here, now and always. I have no problem putting *money* on the table tonight. It's the only language the other side speaks. There used to be a time, Linda, when locking up black people and making a profit off them, was called *slavery*."

I was moved, really moved by Ian's passion. "But they're not our target—Randy Weaver and the prison company. The Zoning Commission is."

"You want them to walk away from a multi-million dollar proposal that's being presented as an economic boon to Ward 8, I hope you're not just going to talk about how blacks have the right to go for a walk in the park and to learn algebra too? How about how blacks have the right to their own slice of the American pie too?"

"*That* you can say, just don't come off like some white guy who wants to educate blacks to save himself some wasted tax dollars."

"My incredibly naïve little friend, I know you're going to find this incredibly hard to believe, but there really are people out there who couldn't give a *fuck* about blacks, and if those bastards come on board your ship just to save themselves a pretty penny, then you've done your job, either way."

As I hung up, Ian's words stayed with me. As far as I knew, Anita, Luther and I hadn't done our jobs unless our simple, morally impeccable message alone persuaded others to change their minds. This was admittedly, far harder than ingeniously manipulating every angle of the issue to please a bunch of bigots, but we wanted others to join our ship because they wanted to travel with us, in the new direction we hoped to take. Otherwise this whole journey, this whole campaign, began and ended at the dock. Maybe I was naïve, but I imagined that it wouldn't take long before people started jumping ship again if we couldn't all agree on where to go next. Ironically, I now pictured Ian showing up for tonight's hearing in his elegant, dark charcoal suit and green shirt, with perfectly coordinated tie. He was, I now realized, that rare activist that we had courted hard—the businessman in a suit who cares enough to testify—but he would be speaking a different language from all the rest of us. He would abandon heart for economics, if that was what it took to be heard. Strange that I had only ever thought of him until now, as someone like me, who believed that right and wrong are carved in your heart, and that this alone requires you to act, when all along, perfect logic had driven Ian forwards. Perhaps this was why the school fight lingered with us. Sending your child to your local public school makes *perfect sense*. Anything stands in the way of that, as far as Ian was concerned, you just deal with it. You make it work. It had little to do with feelings of the heart. Knowing this now, I admired him even more profoundly.

Luther nudged me. "Take a look *around*. This is something else."

His face was radiant with pride and anticipation; his unremitting resolve to protect his community had paid off. We had gone from a mere rumor to this—the chance for the people in his neighborhood to defend themselves, on their own terms, against the latest whimsy of the United States Congress. We were seated before a committee of District of Columbia officials; there would be no Senators from Mississippi or Congressmen from Virginia and Maryland telling D.C. what to do in this meeting. The auditorium was full to capacity. Uniformly gigantic fire marshals, with D.C.F.D. emblazoned on their broad backs, resolutely guarded every door, preventing anyone else from entering. I was afraid to use the restroom, or go in search of food, for fear of never being allowed back in. Anita read my mind.

"No one is allowed to leave their seats, so buckle-up and let's have some fun," she said, "And Linda, don't even *think* about using the candy machines."

We were by now, veterans of lengthy hearings and meetings—council, zoning, planning, Mayor's office, committees, sub-committees, HUD, Hill. It didn't really matter where we were; Anita and I had the same approach. We always brought abundant loose change and small bills and scoped out the nearest and best vending machines before each meeting started. We were the only two outsiders allowed to use the best candy machine in the D.C. council building, hidden away in the DPW committee staff room. I came upon it by accident, years ago, when I was looking for a DPW staffer's office and instead hit pay dirt in their staff room. I was just getting my coins lined up to buy a packet of very creamy, fresh-looking cheese crackers when the staffer walked in on me.

"Linda, hi. Err, this is our *staff* room."

Message clear, but not too obnoxious. Still, definitely not enough to warn me away.

"Janice, hi. This is the *best* vending machine in this entire building! I know, I've tried them all. How come *DPW* has its own machine?"

She laughed. "Chair works us 24 hours a day, so the staff's non-stop munching. High turnover of snacks, nothing ever goes stale." She came over and pointed to the machine. "I'm the vendor liaison. Posh way of saying I get to ask him what he can put in here. The protein bars and juice were my idea."

"Wow. This machine could save people's lives. Really. At one in the morning when I'm ready to pass out, and I still haven't given my testimony to the sub-sub-sub-committee hearing on lead abatement, I mean, I could come here and be *saved*."

"I could turn a blind eye, I suppose, if I ever see you in here again."

Best day of my council-building trudging life. This beautifully kept, well-stocked machine, and my new-found friendship with its protector, meant that forever after, I would know the feeling of pushing the flap back and reaching for the prize in the DPW staff room. How many times did I hold my breath, as I put my coins in the fun little slot, or my dollar bill sneaked its way in through the perfectionist bill scanner, waiting for the thud, thud, *buddum* of success? No more for me, the cremated peanut butter crackers and mushy KitKats of the public machines, located in the swampy, basement utility room, next to the *furnace*!

We understood each other fully, right away. It was a great meeting. Janice and I worked well together for years afterwards, and spotted each other many quarters, until she left town to take a fabulous job in San Diego, for which she has never been forgiven, by me, her friends and family, the DPW committee staff, or the entire city. Janice: another ex-resident of D.C.

I had already located several new and bountiful machines in the building where the Zoning Hearings were being held; student campus buildings boast premium vending machines, and Anita and I had been looking forward to an opportunity to get away.

"Why don't you two ever pack your own food?" Luther asked. "Stop running around like you're starving orphans and pack your *own* food."

He did have a point. Inside his briefcase was the stuff marathon runners dream of: protein bars and power shots (weird little packs the size of a quarter that he ripped open, and sucked on, to extract the disgusting-looking, sticky goop inside), Gatorade, vitamin water, and always a chunky deli wrap, and always, a banana. Luther, as ever, came prepared, and as ever, did not appreciate drama.

"We'll be O.K., thanks." Anita took care not to insult him; at this moment, it appeared as though he would be our only candy machine for the long night ahead and we were hoping he would share.

"Just be nice to—" I started to say, but a commotion of shouting and singing started to spread through the auditorium. From where we sat, near the front, I could look back and sweep the whole audience, and I soon realized it was coming from the busloads upon busloads of people who recently arrived together, the last to make it inside before the doors were closed. They wore matching t-shirts with the slogans, 'CLOSE TO HOME! BRING THEM HOME!' and made so much noise that the Committee Chair issued a threat to evict them. The fire marshals started to move en masse towards the group, and they sat down and quieted down.

Luther leaned in to me. "*Amazing* what $10, a chicken dinner, and a t-shirt can buy these days."

The imported prison supporters took their every cue from none other than Randy Weaver himself, who waved his hands to gently stroke the air around him downwards, as though he were conducting an orchestra through the last movement of a magnificent opus. He drew out the moment, allowing the noise to subside only fractionally with each motion of his hands, and finally the crowd fell silent.

Luther whispered to me that he had sent someone out from our team to conduct interviews as the astroturf got off the buses. "They're from Virginia, for the most part. And they don't have a clue what this is about. Weaver sent his goons out to do round-ups, and this is what they got. A whole bunch of people, happy to have a warm meal in their stomachs, money in their pockets, and a chance to shout out loud."

"Don't worry about them, Zoning will see straight through them," Anita said. "I want to know what the real prisoners' families have to say."

Luther surveyed the crowd once more.

"Look around. We did good."

It was true. If Weaver had resorted to the desperate last-minute tactics of a paid lobbyist, it was because we had succeeded in turning out a tremendous force of dedicated volunteers for the hearings. The testimony list was heavily weighted to our opponents' side, but as Luther predicted, and as we soon saw, most of those listed either don't show, or stood to say something painfully insincere—noticeably rehearsed and paid for—their heads turned frequently to Weaver's coaches for affirmation.

"I think your honor, tha' we should, err, keep the prisoners home. Close to home. Err, bring 'em home."

One by one, they blundered through their statements, and looked clearly relieved when they got to sit back down. Nearly two hours into the hearings, Weaver's men returned to round up the astroturf and take them home. Everyone was relieved to see them released, and the fire marshals were then able to admit authentic witnesses, for both sides, who had been patiently waiting for a seat inside the packed auditorium. Now the real business of debating the prison at Oxon Cove could begin.

The prisoners' relatives rose, one by one, and made their way down to the speaker's table to tell their stories. An elderly African American lady got up from several rows behind us, and shuffled cautiously to take her seat in front of the commissioners. Her voice faltered as she shakily struggled to state her name, and to tell us that she lived in Oxon Hill just across from the cove, in Prince George's County. Emboldened by having survived this first ordeal, she now lowered her mouth to the microphone.

"I'm here fo' my two sons and fo' my gran'son. My sons is *both* in prison in Ohio, an' I look after my gran'son, because his Momma work all day and *all* night long. I haven't seen my sons in mor'an a year. My grandson in't seen his Daddy. Such a *lo-ng* way to go. I support the prison. I do. See, I jus' don' know how much longer I can be missin' my sons. An' without me, what can they do up there to change and make a *new* life for thesselves, without me, and their family aroun' them? Tha's why I *support* the prison."

After she sat down, another grandmother, and yet another, rose to tell of the burden of having brothers, sons and grandsons locked up in prisons far away. Of long, arduous bus rides for visits cut short at the whim of a prison guard. Of being the only hope of rehabilitation for these otherwise forgotten men. So many grandmothers raising grandchildren whose parents lived out their days behind bars.

A young woman took her seat at the table. She immediately seized the auditorium's attention as her voice rumbled softly through the speakers and out over the crowd. Her skin was Nubian black, soft and smooth, her hair a shiny midnight blue-black cascade of curls framing her face. Her entire demeanor—her posture, her cream-colored suit and dark brown silk shirt—warned of her purpose in being here tonight: to be listened to, to be taken notice of.

"My husband did what he did and it was wrong, but it was a mistake, and his sentence was a far greater injustice than the crime he committed. And now he's *three hundred* miles away from us. From his family. We want this prison so other families don't go through what we're going through. I should be able to see my husband. My children should be able to grow up seeing their father more than once every six months. We should be able to do that, at least that, now that he's been taken from us."

Gnawing at my gut, day after day, this was what I feared the most—not losing, but being face to face, all evening long, with the other side. They were mothers with sons and daughters in prison; they were children with fathers and mothers in prison; they were wives with husbands in prison and husbands with wives in prison. They were brothers and sisters, of prisoners. They were grandparents with children and grandchildren in prison. They were all black. I wouldn't be even a half-decent activist if I didn't at least *try* to understand the other side's perspective. I didn't merely understand it. I got it. I believed it. I wanted them to win too. Just not here, and not now. Not at Oxon Cove. Not at the pleasure of a bunch of old, white, frat boys on the Hill. Not without D.C. deciding what's best for D.C. But still this was not enough to stop the clawing inside, the need to know that I wasn't walking on others, by being so determined in my own path. Being right was not enough. It never is. There are always others who will fall if you endure. The Randy Weavers; the Senators from Mississippi and Ohio who happily abuse their authority in Congress—let them fall; they will readily stand again. But not these families.

At the end of the day, this was probably, for me at least, the most humbling and confusing part of this whole fight. I had called it many names—the elephant in the room, my Achilles heel—but knowing that there were black men for whom a prison near their homes and their families might have offered new possibilities for reform, and a better way of life once released, this hung heavily in my heart. It didn't stop me from believing that the prison shouldn't be built in Ward 8, it was just that Luther and Anita had refused to admit to me what they knew deep down, that this prison would never be built in D.C., if not in Ward 8.

Pennsylvania and Ohio were already lined up to scoop up the contract from D.C., and would likely spar energetically for the honor of building another private prison. Cast off so far away, the prisoners who ended up there would have to try to make it without the support of their closest and most trusted supporters. *Do you have family or friends who could help you?*

Hours of testimony from prisoners' families dragged on, and the Zoning Commission decided finally to shut the hearings down at 1:45am. The following night we returned again and slogged through even more testimony from those who supported the prison. Our time would come, but not until our hearts were filled with the lives of those who were left behind when African American men and women were sent away and locked up. Not until we could have no doubt of the burden we would lay at the doors of the prisoners and their families for opposing the Ward 8 prison.

After I sat down, the room filled with applause. People stood all around me, cheering. Luther clapped and pumped his fist in the air; Anita clapped with her hands pointed towards me. "Yes," she said. "Yes." Her face was pure relief and joy. She leaned in to say something to me, but I couldn't hear her, or any of the other people who crowded around us to congratulate me. Everything around me had fallen into silence. I stared at the slide picture, up on the giant screen, next to the Commissioners— Kumar with his arms and legs stretched out in full leap across the water, ready to splash right into the Cove. He was jumping for joy, he was laughing out loud. He was the very image of what it means to be free. Captured in that single frame. Blown up for all to see. Did I speak for him? I did. And I know in my heart I did well. Nothing I had done before this night had ever felt the same. Suddenly the silence in my head broke. The Zoning Commissioners were calling for quiet but the crowd kept clapping and started chanting *Ward 1 for Ward 8, Ward 8 for Ward 1.* I couldn't believe it. As an activist you could spend an entire weekend trying to come up with a campaign slogan like that, and here the crowd had invented it and given voice to it all of its own. Tonight we were truly *one state*, effortlessly crossing rivers and ward boundaries. We were through acting as though our future was not shared, as though some of us were better because we were white, or better because we were black, or better because we lived east of the river or better because we lived west of the river. There are few times like this when in black and white, you at last see what we share, and set aside what divides us.

The Chair of the Zoning Commission rose to calm the crowd. When she at last restored quiet in the room, she asked me a question about the Environmental Impact Statement. I heard the question but I couldn't even open my mouth to speak. I was finally coming to terms with what I had done. *I had taken down Randy Weaver.*

I had taken down Randy Weaver. It happened in an instant. After I had finished presenting my testimony, the room erupted in applause and the crowd was instantly on its feet. I spoke of the history and prevalence of environmental racism in America, of the opportunities denied black children in D.C. and across the nation. I had suggested jokingly we build the prison on parkland in Georgetown—that too would keep the prisoners close to home, wouldn't it? But we would never do that because we all understood that children need schools and parks, not prisons. I presented slides of the Cove, of Ward 8 children playing and old men fishing by the water; of bald eagles and spring wild flowers. Of a world utterly different from that proposed by the United States Congress. Utterly different from the slides previously presented by Randy Weaver showing state of the art lock-down methods and security fences. And then, once I had finished, and the crowd had quieted down and returned to their seats, the Chair asked Randy Weaver if he had any questions for me, and he had said, "Just one." Randy Weaver had asked me one single question.

"Would the young lady please tell us what *Ward* she lives in?"

The Race Card.

I looked over at Weaver and I was face to face with the Race Card.

I didn't immediately answer. I took my sweet time. I spoke slowly, so that I would not be misheard.

"I'm *very* proud to say I'm from *Ward 1*. If the United States Congress decided tomorrow to steal parkland from the kids of *Ward 1* to build a prison there instead, I would hope my fellow citizens in *Ward 8* would come together *as we have tonight*, to oppose their decision."

The '*yes's* and '*uh-huh's* broke free, the entire room was again on its feet. The chant. *Ward 1 for Ward 8, Ward 8 for Ward 1.* A river vanished between us. Weaver was speechless. The Race Card—his favorite card—that he once used so effectively to protect his community, before he started slumming for private prison companies, had burnt up in his face.

I had testified. Not for the first time, not for the last time, but I now knew what it *means* to testify. To have tapped into my heart and soul, forced a confession of fear and hope from deep within me. To have been moved until I shook, I shake still, even thinking about that night. Kadija answered the question from the chair about the EIS. She answered the next question after that, and the next. I didn't take any more questions because I couldn't hear anything but the silence that had once again descended on me. And the sound of my beating heart. *I could hear my own heart beating.* When I returned to my seat next to Luther and Anita, they both hugged me and congratulated me, but still all I heard was the silence. All that was left behind for having testified. I had torn out from its roots what had been growing inside me, since the day I stood in Anita's apartment for the first time, and presented it to the world. The tree of knowledge. And it had left behind empty earth for me to begin again, ready to plough over and replant—the silence waiting to be filled again with knowledge and truth—the next campaign.

Luther noticed that something had passed over me, and he placed his hand on my arm.

"That was something to see. No one ever shut Randy down like that before."

He waited for me to answer. "Why didn't you tell me about the slide show? How long've you been working on that?"

I thought of all the trips to the Cove. I'd sit for hours and watch the light change and the birds and animals come and go. I watched people walking or jogging along the path or others set their fishing tackle out and quietly wait to catch a few catfish for dinner. The bald eagle on the sand bar always eluded me when I tried to photograph him. I often rushed home to upload the photos, convinced I had got him, and then there he was—a large brown and white blur across the screen, or half a wing missing, or his head at an angle that made him look like a dull, nondescript brown bird instead of the pride of America. I had to rely on one of Charlie's photos for that part of the slide show. The others were mine though, a study of what it was we were trying to protect, an attempt to understand what might truly be lost. As the photo collection grew, so did my love of the Cove. This too I unearthed and lost tonight, the secret of my deep, profound love of the park.

"I feel the same way," Luther said. "Now that I know the Cove, now that Kumar plays there. I feel the same way."

The night passed slowly, the testimonies against the prison building one on the other, a now impenetrable wall, and I already knew that there could be no exit strategy for the Zoning Commission. Just after midnight, Luther's name was called. I looked over at Anita. She looked exhausted, her head leaning to one side, but she was completely focused on Luther. We both knew what he would say; we had both listened to and read his testimony many times over. As he held onto the microphone on the table in front of the Zoning Commission, I saw that his hands shook a little. Luther had come to understand that this prison proposal was more than a mistake—an amendment that slipped by unnoticed—more than a little mischief from the old boys club on the Hill. It was a knife twisted in a wound that had barely healed.

"Freedom can be taken away. I'm not sure it can ever truly be returned," Luther began.

"It can be quickly stolen, but never quickly restored. Freedom for blacks in America wasn't merely taken away, it was never there in the first place. We *arrived* here without freedom. So how do we set about rebuilding what we do not even know? If the black community is in disarray, if we are struggling to keep our sons and brothers and more and more of our *daughters* and *sisters* out of prison, it is because we are still learning how to be free. Without knowing from where we came, before our freedom was taken away, how do we figure out where to go?

Our only certainty is that we have been *hated, incarcerated* and *abused*. Is that what we build from? Then we must seek to be loved, free and comforted. Isn't that our only compensation? Our only hope?"

Luther turned away from the Zoning Commission to face the audience. He scanned the faces from Ward 8, people he had known all his life. These were Luther's brothers and sisters, every last one of them. He turned back to face the commission.

"Then why does Congress propose that we build more prisons while our schools are falling apart? Why has our neighborhood been neglected and allowed to fall into poverty and crime that is now so deeply embedded, it seems impenetrable? Why do we look out at a filthy, polluted river, made that way by the federal government itself, and by corporations and people far upriver, over whom we have no control? Why do we watch now as our homes fall into a path of development that we have *no* stake in? Where do we begin, to start, to take back freedom we have never known?

I can tell you that we can start by saying, no to prisons and yes to schools. Two million Americans behind bars is enough. Nine hundred thousand black men and women behind bars is enough. We can see, despite everything that we've been taught to believe about the civil rights movement, that our freedom has *not* been restored. Wrongs have *not* been righted. Not yet. Not when I can't vote for my own Senator and my own Representative in Congress because a D.C. with a vote, will be a majority black state. Not when a racist from Mississippi still has the power to build prisons for our next generation of black youth, in the heart of the black community. Not when National Parkland is good enough for whites, but not for blacks. It is a *slow* process restoring our freedom because it has been so utterly, completely taken away. But we can do some of the work tonight. D.C. voters are here from *all over* the city to ask you to vote for what's good for Ward 8. What's good for the African American community. And what's good for us, first and foremost, is to be free."

Luther leaned in closer and he finished, with the classic, clipped directive of a veteran fighter.

"Members of the Zoning Commission, I urge you to vote against the proposed prison in Ward 8 at Oxon Cove."

As he sat back, the room was again on its feet, and now there was pushing and shoving as friends moved forwards to congratulate Luther. The evening was over, whether the Zoning Commission decided to proceed or not was irrelevant, because a jubilant, spontaneous celebration of Luther's testimony, of all our testimonies, of having stood up to Congress, of having set a stake in the future of Ward 8's kids, was breaking out across the packed room. Over the loudspeaker the fire marshals made announcements about exiting the building safely, but no one was going anywhere just yet. We swirled through the crowd, Luther, Anita and I, greeting activists and extending the moment, any way we could. It was not until much later that I understood that the feeling we so eagerly held onto was that of having done enough, just by bringing these people together in one room—people who might never otherwise have known each other, now greeting each other as friends.

Suddenly, the Chair of the Zoning Commission surprised everyone by making an announcement that the evening's proceedings were not yet over. She battled against the noise and confusion long enough to settle everyone down. And we did continue, into the night, until just before 3am. We made several trips to the vending machines, even Luther's stocks were depleted; we were weary, dry-skinned and blurry-eyed, but we all understood that if we finished the testimonies tonight, then the Commission would be free to arrange a vote as soon as possible. A decision would at last be made on the Ward 8 prison. The air was charged with emotions now pared down and honed to the purest expectation of success.

It was Damien's turn to speak.

"I'm here tonigh' as a high school studint to tell you that I don' need a *prison* next to ma school. I don' need to be reminded that I'm fightin' the odds *every day* by tryin' to stay in school. I'm one of only fifty-five percent of kids in ma community that will graduate high school this year. I'm one of the few's gonna get inta college. I *beat* the odds. *Same* odds those *for-profit* prison execs over there is usin' to predict I'm gonna need a prison cell soon. Well I *won't*. I have a full scholarship and I'm gonna graduate college. I'm not the one you need to worry 'bout. My frien' Theo, he's my *best* frien'. We started on this campaign a year ago. We travel' all over togever. We met wiv church groups in Prince George's county, we wenta Metro stations all ova D.C. We been everywhere we could, givin' out fliers an tellin' people about this prison. An' a whole bunch of them are here tonight, 'cos they all *know* iss a bad idea, and 'cos *we* got the word out. We got people here from D.C. *an'* P.G. 'cos they all know—iss all black and iss mostly poor people when you get to our neighborhood, bu' we *don'* have to accept what Congress is tryin' to do to us. We can say *no* to this.

Theo's the one you should all be worried 'bout. He's the one tha' jus' found out he's gonna be a Daddy. An' he hardly been in school since. You wanna build him a *prison* so he know he can jus' go ahead right now an' *give up*? I wan' him to know he done somethin' right. Tha' all them weekends and nigh's we wenta meetings and we stood talkin' to people, *this* is what it was fo.' Tha' *we* can stop this and *we* can prove to *usselves,* that we get to decide what's right for our community. He'll get back to school. Luther'll make sure o' that! But iss upta *you* to make sure he don' have to look out the window at a prison, and make him think his life's all over already.

Las' thing I wanna say. I lived in Ward 8 ma whole life. We don' even have a supermarket, and you wanna build us a prison? My school is fallin' apart and you have the money for a prison but you don' have the money to fix ma school? You really expect me to believe tha'? Because I don'. I *don'*. I'd like to tell you again, I'm a black boy who is gonna go to college. An' when I come back, I'll be back here in fronta this same commission with plans for cleanin' up our river and our creeks, and fixin' our parks. I'll be askin' you to support programs for kids to spend mo' time outside, not stuck behind bars. Not *locked up.* Tha's a *promise.* An' when I see you then, I hope you'll say *yes* to *that.* Thank You."

When Damien sat down, after the room burst into thunderous applause, I made my way over to him. He had brought us home safely. There was no question in my mind now that we had won.

"I'm sorry, Damien."

He shoved me playfully. "Forget it. All you was feelin' is what I'm feelin' for Theo. He ain't got the right to let us down like that. Forget it. Look at this. Look at what we did together."

Anita, Damien, Kadija and I now stood together exhausted, bewildered, arms loose on each other's shoulders, Luther before us, holding Anita's hand, watching the tumultuous celebration going on around us. We had created this—this force of humans making their mark on an infinitesimal moment in the history of the world—to change what could have been. Out of six billion people on the planet we may have altered and quite possibly improved the course that a few thousand will take in their lives. And we had each given up a whole year of our lives to do that. It seemed so worthy and insignificant a victory. Even now, I am incensed by the arrogance of the amendment that started all this. An exclusive, miniature club of lawmakers adding their hands to such a degrading slap in the face to one of the poorest African American communities in the nation. A decision they had no right to make, for people they would never know.

We were all worn out and yet at the same time keyed up, frenetic, just shy of crazy with excitement at having made it this far. At being able to go home and wake up knowing that the decision was finally out of our hands. This was a high from which none of us would come down any time soon. It was a peculiar feeling. Knowing without a doubt that we had given up the very best part of ourselves and that a year ago we didn't even know each other. But I had to let go and go home. I protested Luther's suggestion that we go back to his place and crack open some beers. Tempting as the offer sounded, I longed for the comfort of home. I said my goodbyes and walked out to catch a cab. The air was cool and refreshing at first, but as I waited, first a few minutes and soon fifteen minutes passed, and the cold swirled around my ankles and a chill rose in me. So I decided to start walking home, rolling my slide projector behind me, playing back over and over in my head the testimonies and highlights of the night, hardly noticing the rumble the wheels made against the sidewalk in the quiet night. Somewhere around Dupont Circle I found a cab. The driver, an African American, asked me what I'd been doing out so late. What *am* I doing out so late? Coming home from a meeting.

"Oh," he said, "The prison! I heard about that. Whose idea was that? A *prison* in Ward 8?"

Just as I got out he asked me if I thought we'd won.

"I think so, I hope so."

"Well, that's a change."

OF THE LINES WE DRAW

The shadow is what we think of it; the tree is the real thing.
Abraham Lincoln

Just a few nights after the marathon Zoning Commission hearings, I awoke in the night to the phone ringing and slipped downstairs to take the call. I found myself saying, "Yes, I'll come. I'll come right away," only because it was Danielle who asked me. Afterwards, I dropped the phone next to me on the sofa and sat back. 2:40 in the morning. "I'll be there as quickly as I can," I had told her, but now I couldn't move.

It occurred to me, as I drifted in and out of sleep, that perhaps I knew too well the adrenalin rush of night calls—of someone loved feeling trapped, or lost, because of paths mistakenly or unexpectedly taken. It seemed that as my friends and I inched our ways on in life, every turn brought new pressures and changes that we weren't able to reference by experience. We were explorers navigating a new world of rapidly shifting extremes, learning as we went, how to handle the uncharted territory of modern male and female relationships, the infinite poles of poverty and wealth, the surging and receding tides of religion and race, and the foreboding fragility and vulnerability of the planet. These were journeys that we had thought we were well prepared for when we set out bursting with idealism and confidence, ready to rock the world, having graduated from the best universities in the world, at the end of the twentieth century. And we'd done our best for the most part. We were all trying to do some level of good, but it too often seemed as though we were floundering against a massive storm of misery that as yet showed no real signs of abating. Whatever our successes and joys, we held onto our having tried, but most of all, to our having been there for each other.

Now I stood in the kitchen, cold as always, and the chill made me gather myself inwards in every way, expecting the worst from going to see Richard. But I either took this chance or faced a lifetime of regret for never having gone. So I finished getting dressed, made some coffee for the road and wrote a note for Ian. He would understand—he would be worried, but he would understand.

I turned up the heat in the car and rolled down the windows to let the fresh night air in. I tried hard to focus on the barely lit road ahead, clicking my high beams on and off when I passed the occasional car. I could smell the musty water in the blackened marshes, the thick, pungent scent conveyed by the wind as I sped along the parkway. I watched the old oak trees arched over the road—gigantic, grand forms against the dark sky—disappear in a blur past the car. Each pair had somehow grown together with time, as though they were always meant to meet in the middle of the road, although they would forever stand their ground on either side. Separate yet together.

What is there left to salvage? There is nothing worse than those urgent, fatal, last words that are spoken at the breaking apart of a profound love or friendship. When Catherine and I once fell out over a staggering lie that severed the once perfect understanding and trust that existed between us, we had to rely on blind faith in forgiveness to save our friendship. Because there was no accepting or explaining deception of that kind. I never thought we'd get through it. But then months later, we unexpectedly found a way to move on. The betrayal lies between us still, never quite resolved, but we have learnt to live with it, and to expect of each other that we will more cautiously guard our trust because of what was almost lost. With Richard it was different though. There were so many lies.

All around the lake house, the exterior lamps were triggered by my arrival and their silvery light danced across the water and shot soft white streamers into the quiet, infinitely dark sky. There would be no slipping in quietly. I stepped out of the car, my every move amplified by the gravel driveway, an intrusion on the secluded haven, and searched for signs of Richard. Danielle greeted me instead. She looked pale and exhausted under the lantern at the front of the house. She hugged me, thanked me for coming and went back inside. I watched her turn the hallway light on and then off again as she disappeared upstairs, not even stopping to talk with Richard. Perhaps I had been the most stubborn in my belief in him, and she was counting on this, in asking me to help him now. If she only knew that my stamina and willingness to forgive him had merely left me the most familiar, and now the least accepting, of his faults and whims. I considered for a moment that Richard was inside, and I was out here—that we were still apart for now—and I hesitated to disturb this balance that I'd at last come to accept.

So instead of heading in after Danielle, I stopped still to look around, taking in the old house, the weathered porches and sagging windows, the well tended garden, the lake front with its beach gently sloping away, an open invitation to the water. All were as familiar to me as my own home. This lake house, his grandmother's home, had been a magical place for Richard and his friends for so many years—full of laughter, music and intimate conversations that transformed us all. Now the silence seemed almost distressing, the only relief came from the light whispering wind on the water beyond the shore. I turned and walked briskly into the house, into the living room, and was surprised to find Richard fast asleep on the sofa.

I hadn't been back there in more than a year, yet as I dropped down and sat on the floor beside Richard, I anticipated the familiar contour of the sofa against my back and the coarse texture of the hand-woven rug on my legs. Right there, by the middle cushion, was where I so often sat up all night with friends in this room. I knew the touch of the brushed cotton sofa cushions against my outstretched arm, could feel again my hand in Ian's and the way the cushions moved when we would hug or laugh. We had both been good friends to Richard, sharing life's upsets and thrills together and surviving strongly bound to each other. So many nights passed into dawns over beer and bottles of wine, giant coffees spiked with whiskey, mellow herbal teas, fire circles and sleeping bags under the stars.

And phone conversations. Hours of effortless, thoughtful, funny, uncomplicated phone calls that left us feeling as though we simply wanted to call back again, right away, and keep going. Once he called me from a rental car while driving north along the Pacific coast highway. Every now and then he would pull over so that I could hear the ocean and it seemed at times that I could almost taste the salt air as we talked. I was in the office, imagining the arc of the coastline below him—steep, golden cliffs falling away to white sand and the vastness of water beyond. He had been away for two weeks and he called, he said, because he had work to talk about. We developed one of our best campaign strategies over the course of that phone call, as he drove towards Seattle. After the new Mayor had taken office, the comprehensive rehabilitation program, for addicts in transitional housing facilities, had been suspended. We volleyed ideas back and forth to come up with a plan to keep the program running while the Mayor's pick for the Director of the Department of Health found his feet. And then all of a sudden Richard had said, "It's so good to hear your voice." And I had replied, honestly, easily, "Yours too."

I had been missing our phone calls for nearly a year. I couldn't stop myself, no matter what; I longed to hear the sound of his voice again.

There was nothing I could do except wait for Richard to wake up. I lit the stove, put the kettle on and searched for tea. I found the tin of dried mint, and recalled clipping whole bunches from the edge of a mountain trail, several summers ago, while on a hiking trip with friends. We were days into the remote wilderness of the Rocky Mountains and the mint had been a welcome surprise. The smell of mint, as we broke the stems, floating over the trail, and later the tea around the campfire, flooded back to me now. It is the scent of magnificent friendships.

"Lin?" Richard had found me half asleep in the kitchen with my head resting on a warm mug of tea.

He shook me gently. Slowly I pulled myself up to face him as he knelt on the floor beside me.

"Are you O.K?

"I'm O.K." I tried to steady myself from the weight of sleep. "Danielle asked me to come."

"Danielle?"

"Yeah, she was worried about you—because of your grandma. I'm so sorry, Richard. Danielle drove here from Philadelphia tonight to help with the funeral arrangements. She called me on the way. She's upstairs, she's gone to bed."

We waited. We had to choose our words carefully.

"Lin, I know this is hard, but I'm so glad, I'm so happy you're here."

The last words that passed between us were bitter, fighting words—words that drew lines in the sand and left little room for reconciliation. I watched tears swell in Richard's eyes; he swallowed and set his jaw to stop them. It was so hard for me to discern anymore what was real pain to him and what was a moment's remorse that would pass and scarcely be considered again. This felt real though. This felt painfully familiar and real.

"How could you do it?" It was hard for me to get my words out; they sat so heavily in my heart. "I wish I didn't *know* Richard—all the things you've done. I'd take you back in a second."

"God, I've missed you. Honestly, I don't know what else to say. It's killing me, your being gone."

This was familiar territory for us. Richard seeking to sift through the debris of relationships that he had destroyed, me helping him to rebuild—but we were not accustomed to searching for pieces of ourselves amongst the ruins.

"I need to go outside," I said, suddenly flushed with panic.

I sat on the bottom step of the porch and looked out at the lake. I slowly took in the water and sky, barely differentiated, and the occasional flickering of lights from boats shifting on their moorings across the bay. This was a landscape so familiar to me, that even with the veil of night I could make out the shoreline across the lake—it lingered in my mind, refusing to be forgotten, drawing on the part of me that was reluctant to let Richard go. I ran my hands through the damp sand and looked way up, far out, searching the sky. Stars almost touched the horizon in the perfectly dark sky when Ian, Sandra and I had slept in our tent in New Hampshire, just a few months ago. Now the stars were higher up, swirled in the same vastness of the milky-way, but far fewer were visible, and each less distinct then they had been across the perfect canvas of the White Mountains. *I want to go home to Ian and Sandra.*

Richard leaned on the kitchen doorframe watching me.

"You and I, Lin, we've facilitated reconciliations for people who completely disagreed, even hated each other, but this, *us*, we can't save?"

When I was silent, he surprised me and I think himself, with what came next. He drew his ace, forcing me to acknowledge what was really at stake here tonight. His voice was angry and raw.

"You had *needs* too. You wanted me to be David, to fill his shoes, and I never signed on for that."

He had pried open the place in my heart that he knew I always listened to. David was the part of me that struggled to rest and live contentedly. I needed to admit my role, and perhaps allow Richard to feel less responsible, for where we were now—he did deserve that—but I was simply unable to find the words. Nothing came to me but the massive silence of losing David.

When David died, my friends, even Ian, fell away for a while, unsure how to be around me in my grief. But Richard and Catherine were there for me. It was what intricately bound them both to me, to be forgiven always, no matter what, I once believed, just for being by my side when I needed them the most. It was only a matter of time, working side by side with Richard every day, before he started to fill the void that David had left behind.

"I was a more perfect brother though, wasn't I?" Richard said. "I didn't get *high* and fuck you over every time you needed me. And I'm here, now."

I couldn't even look at him, because what he was saying was unassailable—that I had wanted him to be what David never was. Only in my heart was David ever a brother who didn't hurt me, disappoint me, or taunt me with the bitter disdain that he crafted out of the confidences he readily extracted from me. Before Richard decided to plunder my program funds, he had never hurt me in any way; he was at least consistent in his love and consideration for me, even as he hurt so many others around him. This was why I stood by him for so long; David was never so kind.

By my early withdrawal, Richard must have understood that he had pushed too hard by bringing David up so soon; he said nothing more, while my silence merely built inside me. I looked behind me hoping to see that he had backed away, but instead he stood, arms folded, willing to give me more time. I was unexpectedly comforted by this; we were still there for each other.

The birds scattered around the trees in the back garden, now eerily lit by the approach of the new day. They had been there all along;

I only now let their song in as Richard's words ricocheted in my head. *I was a more perfect brother. Every time you needed me.* I listened to the mourning doves coo and watched the robins hop across the damp, dark lawn, frenetically pulling worms from the soft ground. The song sparrows awakened; their enchanting warbling thrust boldly into the stillness of the morning. Soon the cedar waxwings would begin flittering and chattering noisily in the giant, old mulberry tree. I breathed in deeply. It was all so perfect, except for the two of us.

I gathered some gravel from the driveway, passing it hand to hand, allowing the finest pieces to fall through my fingers; I reached for a stick to break into tinier and tinier pieces until there was nothing left but a pile of twigs and crushed bark.

"That was unforgivable, what I said," he whispered. "I'm sorry."

I turned again to face him and leaned slowly back on the railing for support.

"You *were* better than David. You *are* better than David. That's why what you did—it's just impossible for me to forgive. I had expectations of you that I never had of David. That's probably unfair to you, but then you're right, you were always there for me. And I'd come to need that and to trust you, completely."

He set his eyes on mine, waiting for more. I couldn't allow the intimacy between us now, I knew it would undo me, and yet I was unable to look away.

"There was this one year with David. It was really great, perfect even. He had a great job, a sweet girlfriend and his life seemed to be heading where he wanted. He was *clean*, which is kind of what mattered most."

I said this and yet remembrances of all the other years of David shutting me out, of finding him wasted, enraged and terrifying—or morose and suicidal—flooded back.

"We had fun that year. We'd talk about our dreams and ideas. We had so many ideas, the way you and I always did. You were the *best* of that *great* year, Richard. You were the brother I always wanted."

Relief flooded his face, a smile breaking open; it was so unlike him to unveil his emotions so readily. My own fears resurfaced at the thought that he might yet convince me to back down, and I added, viciously, my tone unkind and unforgiving, "Except when I was scraping your friends off the floor or trying to shelter Danielle from all your lies."

"Lin, all it is—is that I'm still trying to figure out what I want. Why could you accept that in David and not in me?"

"I tried to accept you the way you are. I tried. I covered, I even *lied* for you, for years, Richard. I'm just not willing to do that anymore. You've changed. When I met you, you were a brilliant, fearless organizer. People wanted to join you in making a difference. You were the fucking *Pied Piper*! What happened? *Don't be a stranger*—remember we promised each other that? That we'd try to be there for anyone who needed us, that we'd always be honest. We'd never lie to each other? But these days you're a stranger to everyone, especially to me."

He pushed off from the back door and walked towards me, never taking his eyes off mine. He sat close to me and then suddenly he turned his head away, as though ashamed or afraid, I couldn't tell which.

"The past few months have been unbearable. Sometimes, I'm laughing with friends at a party, my mouth dries up and I feel the loss of us so intently that I, uh—" He angrily wiped tears away from his face. "I have to close my eyes, and remember how you said to me that day, when I was driving on the Pacific coast highway, that you—that you missed the sound of my voice. I want to be that man again. The one you once found room for in your heart. I—" He took his left hand in his right, pressing the thumb and fingers of one against the palm of the other, his signature way of being wholly honest with me. "Fuck, this *hurts*. I thought I could tell you this, why can't I tell you this?"

I had always known that Richard loved me, and I had always denied that he loved me; his telling me now couldn't possibly hurt us.

"It comes down to loving you, anyway you look at it. You sort of became a habit—thinking of you, wanting to spend time with you. There's nothing sinister to it. It was just what we were, that I could hold onto. Something of you I could have." He waited. "You asked me to try and explain. I'm trying here."

I wish I weren't so certain that there was no going back with Richard. I had to fight hard, otherwise he would have won me back just for loving me.

"Can you forgive me?"

I wanted to. I knew I couldn't. "Did you place so little value on Ian and Danielle's love for us? Danielle took you back, every time you betrayed her, she stayed with you. And Ian believed in us, in you and me, and what we did together at work, every day. How could you ever think—"

Richard's eyes flooded with tears. He understood that I wasn't backing down.

"Tell me this?" he said, "Where does it come from? Your *conviction* that everything is going to be O.K., when everything is *not* O.K., is never going to be O.K.?"

There was pure fear in his words; this was the tone Richard reserved for speaking a shade of truth that he rarely exposed. I recognized it because it was the only reason I had borne his lies all these years.

"I want your determination. Where does it come from—your ability to believe and go on working, with such awful misery all around you? Doesn't it ever strike you that all of your commitment, and your optimism, and that bottomless well of self-righteousness that you draw on, is all just a *wasted* effort?"

He was drawing me back in, reawakening the feelings that had blossomed and faded, blossomed and faded through all the seasons of our friendship.

"When I was in Africa—do you have *any* idea how impossible it is to measure success out there? You have to talk and think about Africa like it's just another country, otherwise you can't even get your head around what Africa means—what all those countries, individually, mean—in terms of human suffering. We counted the number of new patients we were getting AIDS medication to—roughly 200 a day—out of the *20 million* people who have AIDS. I know what you would have said, Lin, if it had been you working out there. You would have sent me one of your darling emails: Arial, 11 point, exclamation marks all over the damn place.

Richard-
We're making great progress! You should see how lovely the people are!! We got AIDS meds to 200 new patients today!! More later – got to go!
-Linda

We both laughed at this. It was true. He knew he was reaching me; he smiled, his eyes light and clear. He wanted me to be on his side again.

"You used to encourage me *every* fucking day Lin. I'd be so angry at how little we were getting done at *Homes First* and you'd come in my office and you'd convince me that what we did mattered. Now I feel like none of it matters, because every day there are more and more people walking in and asking us for help. And we just can't. We can't. We don't have the money, we don't have the resources."

This was the conversation that had flowed continuously through our eight years of friendship and work—how to stay focused, how to keep going, how to be there for one another when disillusionment came knocking at the door. He was trying to tell me that our work together was not yet done, so how could we possibly give up on each other now? So deliberately, to show him that I could, I stood and walked away to my car, leaned against it, my arms folded tightly on my chest to keep the cool air and Richard out. He got up and came straight towards me, in every way determined for me to hear him out.

We looked directly at each other again, by his design once more, and it was hard for me to understand how we had come to this. What unraveling would have to take place for us to go back to that perfect summer when we met campaigning against the downtown shelter closings.

"Anyway, before you go. My cousins are selling the house."

"The house? God, I'm sorry."

"Yeah, if I want to save it, I have to buy them out. I understand where they're coming from—it's an opportunity for them to see more money than they'll ever know in this lifetime. So while you're busy saving the land over there," Richard pointed across the water towards Oxon Cove, "can you find me the 2.4 million dollars this land is now worth? So I can buy my family off and save the only thing I know *absolutely* how to love in this whole world?"

The house, precious enough to Richard's friends, was where his family had celebrated their most intimate and enduring times together. It had been their gathering-place for love and reconciliation and laughter, his grandmother standing strong against whatever worldly forces conspired to drive them apart. Marriages in trouble had been saved here, engagements announced, SAT results and college admissions letters opened at the kitchen table; the sweetest and most bitter of life events had flowed through its doors.

"I'm sorry Richard, Your grandma was always good to Ian and me."

"We had good times here."

"Your family might come around. You're very persuasive when you want to be."

"Trust me, *$2.4 million* is more persuasive. Grandma paid $8,000 thirty-five years ago. Its money for nothing."

He smiled, watching me, reading me, and must have known I was getting ready to leave, despite this latest news. I started to say one last thing and he cut me off.

"I know what you're going to say. Call the Nature Conservancy, right?"

I had to laugh. He was right.

"Yeah, well I'm meeting with them in two weeks—turns out this land has quite a story to it and there's a cohort of enviros and civil war buffs all lining up to help. My *only* hope at this point."

"So you're finally running a campaign again. Back where you belong." I dropped my hands to my sides. "The only thing that keeps me going, Richard—the *only* thing—is those little victories. Doesn't matter how hard you have to work for them. They're all that matters."

"And there was I thinking, it's the people you work with," he joked.

"You were—"

"Didn't you feel it too? Come on, Lin."

I was suddenly relieved to be speaking so openly with him at last. This exposed, we were compelled to explore the shared territory of our relationship once again, but this time, utterly uninhibited. Maybe we would get to the fraud, Danielle, maybe we could make it all the way back to us. I pushed away from the car and took his hand and we sat back down on the porch steps. This was what we were trained to do—dig ourselves out of trenches to seize the land being fought over.

"You want to know what it felt like, all those times when we talked for hours after work, or we were together in a meeting, or we sat out here after one of your parties? It felt good to be close to you—I'd be lying if I didn't admit that—but that's *it*. There was *never ever* going to be anything more than that." This was the question I had long been waiting to ask him: "How could you let yourself believe that there could ever be more?"

"God Lin, it was everything I ever wanted to spend time with you. There were times I thought we might get there, have a shot at being together. I hoped for it, I just kept hoping."

"What about Ian? How can you act like our love doesn't exist?"

"Oh, I *know* it exists." he laughed. "It's what I'll never have."

I couldn't exactly remember at what point in our friendship, Richard had started to confide in me about his affairs. I only knew that he waited until he was certain that I cared enough about him to be sympathetic. And now looking back, I was alarmed that I ever let him convince me he meant no harm.

"Richard you *live* for falling in love with, and being with, every woman who comes your way. I would have meant nothing to you."

"But you did feel something? You've never admitted that to me before."

"You've never admitted to me that you wanted to be more than a friend."

It was gone, the threat swirling around us that could have in a second, had we acted on it, shattered our worlds. So I told him what had been bearing down on me ever since I left *Homes First*.

"I never wanted to leave. I wanted us to always work together, not just because we were so good at what we did. It meant everything to me that we'd always be in each others lives."

"I never expected everything to come apart this quickly," he said quietly.

"It has amazed me to watch you tear it all up—*Homes First*, Danielle, that last intern. She was just looking for someone to be her friend, maybe a lover, and you had to promise her the earth and nearly kill her with grief when you left." I took up a handful of sand. "Like all the rest of them," I said, almost to myself, as the sand escaped with a rush through my fingers.

"Like you? Because with you I swear it was different. I don't think you realize how deeply I loved you."

"You had no right to love me that way. And don't you think I loved you? In a different way, but just as deeply?"

"You think I choose to be here right now?" He leaned away from me and turned to look at me, so that I felt closer and further away from him than ever. "I don't know, after all these years we've known each other, how to be apart from you," he said.

This was what I had been thinking, all the time. How can I be apart from Richard? How can I possibly let him go? I got up and he followed me silently back to the car; this time he didn't hesitate as he swung open the door for me to get in. I took this to mean he was ready for me to leave, and for it all to be over at last between us.

"I slept with her for her *money*. Danielle knows it. *You* know it."
"What?"

He towered over me. I had rarely felt the difference in our height in all the years we'd known each other. The twelve or so inches that separated us, now they were augmented, terrifying—Richard forcing me downwards into myself, as he watched, waited, demanding my response.

"You slept with our intern for her *money*? I know this is Washington, Richard, but for God's sake, we lost the whole fucking Congress to a bunch of self-righteous warmongers and thieves because the President fucked an intern. Things go wrong in Washington and they go wrong quickly and badly. Her Dad could have *destroyed* you with one phone call. He could have shut *Homes First* down. Phoney tax fraud, anything. A bogus audit. He could have pinned anything on us. Jesus, he might even have uncovered what you did. You thought you could manipulate *him,* as well as her?"

"You still don't understand do you Lin? I was fucking *desperate* to save that program. Do you honestly think I would have transferred your funds if I weren't? When her Dad wrote us a check for 75 grand it made it *worth* being with her. It's all over. And your program funds. We didn't—it wasn't illegal."

"You're *unbelievable*. You're still trying to justify—"
"She meant nothing to me."
"Yes, I know, but did you ever stop to think about what *you* meant to her?"

Before I knew it, I headed towards the lake again. I was searching for something, I didn't know what, but the water that was once dark and infinite, now stirred softly and glimmered, as the sun began to find its strength. I was drawn to this awakening, to the reassuring emergence of the shore and tree line across the lake, just as I had remembered them.

Richard followed me over and stood silently next to me.

"I can't go on living by the standards that you set for us, even as colleagues, let alone as friends. I'm so *lost*. Standards you change every day. You believe your work justifies what you did. You know I can't accept that." I turned to face him. "If we aren't ethical in the way we handle money, in the way we treat each other, in the respect we show for others, what's the point of what we do, Richard? You go up to the Hill and you come back and complain about lobbying, graft and corruption and not being able to find funding for anything worthwhile anymore—and meanwhile you're screwing someone for her *money* and because her dad's on the right committee? You're moving my program funds into your account by messing with time sheets and unrestricted donations. And because all that saved the program, that makes it O.K. for you? Does it *really* Richard? Make it O.K? For her, for you, for Danielle, for *Homes First*? I can't believe we're back here again—you and me—Richard. You asking me to fix everything. I *can't* fix this."

I couldn't prevent the memories from flooding back now, of running with Richard's dogs here, swimming by moonlight with our friends, lying on the sand at night with the warmth of a summer day still at our backs. I pictured us sitting with our plates full of exquisite foods, prepared by all the houseguests, the tastes never ordinarily found together but blending beautifully. Ian laughing and throwing me another beer, always with a book, reading to us, entertaining us, as we drunkenly begged him to read more. And Richard sitting close by, Danielle curled into him, relating hilarious stories about his time in Africa or his lobbying antics on the Hill. The best of friends, the best of times.

I walked away from Richard one last time. When I got to the car I watched him walk slowly up the steps onto the porch and then he was back inside the house. I remained there a while longer in the disappearing silence of the morning, the prelude to the day's commuter traffic building on the parkway, an early flight out from National soaring overhead and the birds now in full song. I couldn't help thinking—even as I felt rage inside me for all that he had done—that I wanted him to come back and find the words to allow me to believe in him again.

The loss of us, and what we were, I thought I was prepared. Nothing could have prepared me for that. As I drove back home I searched frantically on my iPod for the one song I had to hear right then. The iTrip blanked out as I spun through the artists' list and I knew I should have been focusing on the road but I couldn't stop until I found the song. I tapped the iTrip and it flashed back on. I pressed play so hard that I turned the iPod off. At last I clicked it back on and the music started to rise, filling the car, first the guitar solo, then the voice, begging me to believe. The music flooded and burned, my friend lost, the love leaving me. Only those words, only that hopeful, sorrowful song could force me to bear the hurt.

You were here/ Always here/ For me

I pulled over to the side of the road and looked out at the Potomac River and watched downtown Washington waking up, the office lights so bright in the night, disappearing into the oncoming light of the new day.

We killed our days in pain and laughter/ pain and laughter
Tomorrow I'll be here/ I'll be here/ For you
You were here/ For me

This was the song that David gave me the last time that I saw him, before he left me for good, no tomorrows.

Ian greeted me at the door, his voice hoarse, his face haggard and pale; I doubted he had slept much while I'd been gone.

"You O.K? I waited for you."

"Did you know?" I asked him.

I leaned on the back of the sofa, he leaned on the bookshelf, and we faced each other.

"To you babe, it was a good n' honest brother-sister thing, but to him—well, it was pretty obvious to everyone around what he wanted from you."

"So why didn't you mind? Why weren't you jealous?"

"Of what? That someone else admired you? That you liked him, that you loved him? So what? I know how you feel about us, what the hell else matters?"

Hearing Ian say this with such ease in his voice, with complete conviction, just confirmed for me how simple life really is when you know whom you love. He led me out to the back garden to the hammock, where he had laid out blankets and pillows. I slipped into the hammock and Ian was soon by my side. It was morning already, the last traces of dawn were gone; I threw a blanket over us—shelter and protection for what we were together. The garden was spectacular at this time of day, luscious and green, the flower and herb beds a brilliant wash of colors and scents. The hostas that bordered the trees and lined the edges of the path stood like guardians, tall and brave, ready to meet the sun, their strength renewed by the cool night and an early morning shower under the sprinklers. Giant drops of water remained on their broad, gray-veined leaves, reflecting tiny patches of the pure, blue morning sky. All here was refreshed and vigorous, prepared to take on the new day, so different to the weariness flowing through me. As the sun began to warm us, I tossed the blanket on the ground and a quick rush of cold air passed over us as it fell. Ian had been waiting for me to settle. He nestled into me and I lay my head on his shoulder.

"Everyone's well-intentioned in your mind, even when they fuck up. It makes life easy for me. It's how I know you'd never betray me. But it doesn't make it easy for you. Because people lie to you all the time."

I knew that he meant David, Richard, even Catherine.

"What about you and Richard?"

I couldn't help but ask; I was not the only person who had lost. He ran his fingers through my hair, he played with a curl, twisting and untwisting it. He looked exhausted; while I navigated my way through the end of a friendship, he lay awake imagining what it must have been like. We lived in a different world now, one where a large part of the last eight years of our lives had to be rearranged and forgotten.

"I want to believe that we were friends, that I wasn't used."

That he left off here, told me of the confusion and loss that he too had to contend with. We fell into silence, our thoughts our own, allowing ourselves to be drawn down into the hammock, at last finding rest together. Sometime in the late morning, I woke up parched and disoriented, with the full sun on my face. Ian was long gone and he had left me the iPod by my side, with a note under a rock, by the hammock.

Gone to work. You have been a good friend.

I got up and went inside to drink for a long time, cold water straight from the tap, until I was refreshed and my face dripping. Now I laughed, with complete joy, perfect happiness, at the thought of Ian.

"You look like hell," Catherine said.

"Thanks, you look lovely."

"What happened?"

I wanted to tell her, but I couldn't speak. I played with the sugar packets on the table, making concentric circles, pink sweetener, white sugar, pink sweetener. Once Catherine had added the milk and sugar to her tea, playfully stealing one of the packets from my work of art, she settled her full attention on me, and nodded for me to begin. I took cautious sips from my coffee, avoiding having to speak. Catherine smiled expectantly, thinking perhaps how fun this was going to be, to deconstruct what had happened with Richard and to enter into our private world. Secretly delighting in the story and its recounting. We were in that moment, two friends sharing intimacies about another friend. I wasn't sure how I felt about this, and I recalled that she didn't keep her promise—Catherine had assured me that Richard and I would find a way back to each other.

"It's O.K.," she said. "Let's change the subject."

Nothing came to me. I waited for her to say something.

"Just tell me," she said, her voice gentle and careful, "is it—*over*?"

"Yeah." My eyes flooded, but I rubbed them to force the tears away, and I succeeded with remarkably little effort. Catherine must have noticed this; she of all people would have understood its significance.

"God, you really did it. I thought you two would figure it out."

We sat in silence until Catherine got up to go the bathroom. I didn't want her to leave just yet.

"You said this wouldn't happen. Did you really believe that?"

"I did actually. You and Richard not being you and Richard—it just doesn't seem possible. I can't believe it."

This is what everyone had said. Greg would not forgive me. He wanted me to do whatever it took to forgive Richard. He had even offered to have a bible reading with us together, and I tried not to laugh at the suggestion because somehow I knew he wasn't joking. But he didn't know, no one really knew, all the harm Richard had caused lately; that his past vices had been surpassed by more recent transgressions of impossible magnitude. Somehow it seemed that even Catherine, with her hound's ear to the ground, still knew little of the *Homes First* funding situation—it had been well concealed and was now buried. It was easy for others to say *forgive* when they did not know what exactly must be forgiven. People used to say that to me about David and I did forgive him repeatedly, consistently, letting him tear away a part of me every time, until there was nothing left of me to demand forgiveness from. Ian knew this, because he lived with my erratic grieving, the moments when unexpectedly and inexplicably, I felt lost and untethered, without David. He was the only one not demanding that I *forgive* Richard.

Catherine returned from the bathroom and she stood over me.

"I won't let you do this. I *despise* Richard, I hate him. I think he's a total bastard, as you well know. But you two need each other. I won't let you *do* this. Why won't you tell me what happened?"

I loved Catherine. I really did. We were the sisters we each left behind in our hometowns, filling the roles they once played for us. I looked up at her now as she waited expectantly, wanting to help me strategize a path back to Richard and I was chilled by the memories that surfaced of my sister and me. *All those times and places with my sister threatening, demanding, pleading, that we give David another chance.* In cafes just like this one; movie theaters, while we waited in line to buy tickets; bus trips to places I couldn't recall even as the ride itself remained as real as if it were happening now; phone-calls across thousands of miles; changing rooms as we tried on clothes we had carefully selected for each other; even my office with the door closed, hoping no one else would hear. For Mom's sake, for her sake, for David's sake; she convinced me occasionally that it might even be for my sake.

"...reconsider."

And here was my friend Catherine, whom I loved and trusted, asking me, as my sister always did, to *reconsider*. This was the one word I heard, because if I acquiesced, the flood-gates for reconciliation would have been opened.

"No."

I had longed to say this. To close the door. To slam it shut. To turn away the monster clawing to come in and reside with me. David. Richard. Turned away at last. I was safe and free.

"Lin—*come on*—it's been, what? Nearly ten years? You cannot just shut him out of your life like that. He wants to try and fix things. Give him another chance."

"No."

She sat back and a slow smile turned one corner of her mouth. She took my hand across the table, and said, "Good for you."

"Not negotiable," I confirmed, and my friend was for once, delighted to lose.

OF MOMENTS IN TIME

We are living in a time of unbearable dissonance between promise and performance.

Marian Wright Edelman

The children sat tight together on the hard benches lining both sides of the hay wagon. Even more kids sat cross-legged on the worn, wooden floor. Two National Park rangers were squeezed in among them, playfully passing their large pointed hats around and letting the kids try them on. Slowly the wagon pulled away and with squeals and shrieks of laughter and happiness, the first group of kids left on a great adventure around Oxon Hill Farm. We started to load up the next wagon, when an Americorps volunteer arrived to tell me that the walking tour of Oxon Cove was ready to go. I waved to the kids and made my way over to where a large group of volunteers stood waiting for the walk to start. We set off together, a multi-colored reflection of the work we had done to make this day possible—young and old, black and white, all eager to see Oxon Cove for themselves. The sun shone down, warm and brilliant, as we slowly meandered our way through the fields of mown grass and down the long path that led from Oxon Hill Farm to Oxon Cove. As we approached the D.C. side we started to fill trash bags with the litter we found choked up in the grass and trees, and lining the gravel path along the creek. We collected soda cans, plastic bottles, grocery bags and potato chip bags and hundreds of cigarette butts. It was a perfect fall day and as we walked, we left behind a more perfect landscape to celebrate it. Once we reached the little bridge, the whimsical tribute to this idyllic cove, we paused and stood together to look out over the water. Our thoughts were not on the prison, not on what had been stopped, or what could have been here. Our hearts were full with what had been saved.

We had not expected the Zoning Commission decision to come in so soon. The picnic, walks and rides today were meant to be a rally, to bring even more attention to the prison campaign, so that even if the Zoning Commission let us down, we would already have the momentum to go to the next step. But earlier in the week we received the news that the Zoning Commission had reached their decision, to unanimously reject the proposal to build a prison in Ward 8, at Oxon Cove.

So there we all were, celebrating, with a lightheartedness and sense of relief that had made me feel, for days now, as though I in my own way, had been set free.

By the time we got back from our walk to the picnic area on the Maryland side, our numbers had swelled still further. I wandered around the crowd in a daze with Luther, Anita, Charlie and Damien. All we could say to each other, to anyone who stopped to greet us and congratulate us, was some variation of how we couldn't believe it was all over.

"Can you believe this?"

"I can't believe this."

"This is unbelievable."

There were people from all over D.C. and Prince George's County, all relieved to have come today, knowing that the fight was over. Kids from the Windsor Apartments and the local Boys and Girls Clubs played baseball and horseshoes; elders from church groups stood together and greeted each other with exuberant words of praise—"*God is GOOD!*" and "*Jesus is our Lord. He don't never EVER let us down!*"— that rang out around us, as though a miracle had occurred, right here, on this very day. Local activists from Ward 8 and Prince George's county exchanged campaign stories and told Randy Weaver jokes, while Conservation Club, Earth Corps and Americorps volunteers walked through the crowds making sure everyone was well-fed and happy. Even the prison reform and low-income housing advocates had set aside their usually weighty concerns, and now pounded each other, and Damien and in his friends, in a volleyball game. As I stopped at last to sit under one of the giant oak trees to catch some shade, I looked slowly around me, and all I could think was, I *can't* believe this. We'd gone from Anita's apartment to this.

Two gigantic cakes were cut and speeches followed. We had won.

A few weeks later, the glow of that perfect day having faded a little, I got a call from Andrew. I thought, even though it had been a while, surely he's calling to talk about Oxon Cove. We had some beautiful coverage of our celebration rally in the news, and some of the outlets were still running the story, as they watched to see if *Reform and Corrections Inc.* would appeal the Commission's decision. But instead he was calling about the lead bill. I had all but forgotten about it and dreaded hearing his news. But while Andrew was frantic once again, this time it was in a happy sort of way. He called to tell me that the bill had finally made its way out of committee, through countless more revisions and negotiations, and was coming up for a vote before the full council. With Roland and Weaver both looking like yesterday's news, and Edgar Brooks at least temporarily out of favor with his base for having supported the prison, the city's council members seemed to be breathing a new kind of air, one no longer rank with fear. Andrew and I had a lengthy chat about the bill and its strong prospects for survival and I promised to dust off my testimony from countless hearings past and drop in on the council meeting. The truth was, I really had nothing much to do just now.

I had been frustratingly out of sorts since we won the prison fight, at times even low. I thought it would be good to use the extra time on my hands to make the rounds and catch up with friends whom I hadn't seen in nearly a year, but my heart just wasn't in it. I needed to hear them tell me *'you rocked the world!'* but they mostly acted as though nothing much had changed, which of course nothing much had. Andrew calling me now to ask for advice on how to stop lead poisoning in children— something that should have happened *fifty* years ago—didn't do much to brighten my mood. Even the Windsor campaign, looking so healthy, and chugging along on the road to victory suddenly seemed to me, to be too small a step; we were turning tenants into homeowners, but we had a long, long way to go before we could start rebuilding lives.

The only other commitment I had going on that week was the candidate interviews for the new organizing position we had created, and it had been strangely comforting to see myself in the eager, young, white things who'd shown up, ready to help make a difference. The truth was we were looking to hire an African American. Of course we were. What did that say about the chance Jonathan took on me? But Luther was not

Jonathan, and he was adamant. I'd given up trying to tell him that the wage we were offering was barely livable and white candidates more often had the back-up resources to fatten a non-profit paycheck. He simply threw my own truth back in my face. When I couldn't afford to live on what *Homes First* was paying me my first year there, I had taken a second job.

"So he'll take a second job," Luther said bluntly, in response to my suggestion, that we pay more to attract more African American candidates.

Of course I had to ignore, or simply accept Luther's assumption that when we hired, not only would the candidate be black, but also male. That would be Luther's own private way of doing God's work.

As the lead hearings approached, I pulled out my old files to review the history of the legislation, and it struck me as nothing less than embarrassing that so many council members had worked so diligently to repeatedly kill the bill over the years. Once again I forced myself to look in on the issue from the other side. But as hard as I tried, I couldn't see how anyone in their right minds could stand in the way of protecting children from avoidable harm and forcing building owners to maintain their properties in good condition. It seemed absurd not to support the bill, but I would need a better argument than that. So I buckled down, and took a long look at the cost analyses. I was thinking of Ian; he believed in taking control of the money on any issue. In this case, we'd need to prove that landlords couldn't afford *not* to do the abatement. Between the existing federal regulations and liability, both of which had finally taken some prominent landlords down, it seemed pretty obvious to me at least, that D.C. needed to update its laws, and fast. The deeper I got in, the more I found my anger rising and ultimately settling on Sheila Worthington. She *supported* the prison; she *opposed* the lead bill; she tried to *quash* the Roland slumlord investigations. Sheila Worthington sold out her own community time and again, forcing Luther and Anita, and now Damien, to fight their own council member, just to survive. I was suddenly aware for the first time, how different this past year would have been if Worthington had been a true leader, if she had done what was best, not for herself, but for her community.

I looked at the photos in my study, slowly and carefully. I had made myself a new gallery of moments in time. Kumar jumping into the water at Oxon Cove. Luther, Anita and Vernon Jordan, and all the Windsor Apartments residents, standing in front of the building's marquee. Damien in our favorite café in Eastern Market, killing math sheets. Theo holding his baby boy. The two cakes iced with the words Parkland not Prisons/Schools not Jails. Baucus introducing his lead bill. Delegate Marlowe speaking on the floor of the House. Charlie in his Park Service uniform, holding an evidence bag full of something gross-looking. Catherine on the phone at work. Rafael and me standing either side of Eddie, sitting bareback on *Annoo*. Rafael in his lab in Houston. Ian testifying at the Zoning Hearings with Randy Weaver, head in his hands, in the background.

I was ready. I called Luther and I told him we weren't being tough enough on Worthington.

"Whoa there, Lin, what's all this about?"

"We need to go after Worthington, tomorrow, in the lead hearings."

"What? *No*, Baucus will never agree."

"Forget Baucus. You're an independent operator, everyone knows that. This is our chance to launch a campaign for a new council member. We're two years out, the time will fly by. It doesn't matter if we don't have a candidate yet. We need to start undermining Worthington, now."

"*We?*"

"*You,* Luther. *Anita, you,* it doesn't really matter who does it. You know exactly what I'm saying."

"What has *gotten* into you?" Luther was half mocking, his usual confident self, and this infuriated me.

"We need to make a change in Ward 8 and East of the River, Luther. Something *real*. Permanent. A black leader who *leads*—your whole big dream. Not just another campaign to stop another fucking prison and save another fucking apartment building from going condo. Not just another council member phoning it in for 80K a year."

As I said the words, I regretted them. Luther was the last person on earth I should be lecturing on how to save black neighborhoods. I thought he would throw it back at me, but he said softly, "You're right, Linda. But this is a whole different ballgame."

"I know that."
"No," he said. "You don't know."

I didn't have the heart to go to the lead hearings. I didn't think I could listen to anymore bloated rhetoric about why the cost of lead abatement is just too high; how it would force landlords to increase their rent and force low-income residents out of their homes; and tacitly, not explicitly of course, how it's not *that many* kids who's lives were being destroyed. I found myself heading over to *Homes First*, and I sat outside Jonathan's office, waiting for him to finish up a meeting with Kadija and Damien. We arranged to have lunch together and over the next hour or so we laughed about the prison campaign and Jonathan teased me for being so melancholy.

"You're just missing your *baby*. Campaign's all grown up and left home and Mommy's all at a loss about what to do next."

"Yeah, maybe it's some of that," I conceded, "but what about the Congressmen who signed the bill in the first place? And how are we going to get the parkland back? And cleaned up? And what about our vote in Congress? And Jonathan—*for God's sake*—what are you going to do about *Worthington*?"

Three black faces stared at me.

"You want to take Worthington out?"

"Well, why not? She doesn't exactly match up to the challenge of being the council member for Ward 8."

Jonathan taught me one more lesson that day. "*We* get to take her out. You can't be seen or heard. As for representation for D.C., eat your heart out."

I trusted Jonathan. I trusted Kadija and Damien. We were all smart enough to know that we had just thrown our hats in the ring. If what I was being told was that white was bad for black politics, but good for the statehood vote on the Hill, that was O.K. with me. As long as now we were talking about some real change.

"O.K. That's fine. I know backstage. I'm good at backstage."

"Did *Luther* put you up to this?"

Damien answered right away. "Luther's been wantin' this all along. Anita's *finally* on board. We can't wait any mo'. Everythin's come togever wiv the prison an' Win'sor. Worvington's jus' made it easier. Made *usall* take notice."

This was a circle Damien couldn't wait to widen.

After lunch, I made my way over to Anita's apartment as part of my ongoing commitment to avoid the lead hearings. She didn't seem at all surprised to see me and opened the door wide, to allow me to wheel my bike in.

"There's something I want to show you," she told me, as soon as I'd taken off my helmet and gloves. "Come with me."

We entered her bedroom and she led me over to a worn, but well-preserved antique roll top desk. I didn't notice it the first time I was here, nearly a year ago, when she had encouraged me to take a look around her apartment. She carefully unlocked the tambour and pulled out one of the delicate drawers inside. She moved backwards, cautiously, away from the desk without turning, and I came around to look at the drawer in her hands. Inside I saw tiny glass jars of what appeared to be different flavor jams.

"*Jam?*"

I looked again, and noticed this time a handful of small tubes of paint, the metal casing on most badly deteriorated, the labels torn; dried pigment had collected where it once oozed from the tubes.

"*Paint?* You paint?"

"My great grandmother did. But these are mostly my mother's paints."

"Your great grandmother, she painted the girl?"

She nodded. I remembered now. "And your Mom did the irises."

She sat on the edge of her bed with the drawer carefully balanced on her lap. She motioned with her head for me to join her. I sat beside her and was touched by the gesture and this new intimacy, the way she had so purposefully invited me into her sanctuary.

"My great grandmother, Alice, grew up a slave, on a farm in Virginia, outside of Richmond. It was a terrible place—I've done my research on it." She paused. "Nana Alice and the master's little girl were somehow friends. The girl was good to her. She gave my great grandma some of her colors and papers and paints. Nana Alice continued to draw and paint, so over the years the girl brought her materials, and sometimes they painted together. Of course, all the girl ever saw of my great grandma's work were pretty scenes of life on the farm. Horses, fields, the big house."

She took up one of the tubes of paints and turned it over in her hands.

"Look at that—*Vermillion*. Such a beautiful word, don't you think?"

I took the tube from her and held onto it.

"Nana Alice never showed anyone her slave paintings. She painted them in secret and hid them away. She told my mother that some of them were too painful to look at, but she had to record what she saw. Think of what she *really* saw, when she wasn't sketching horses and trees. What she saw in the fields, in the town, at the market. Later, when she fled the farm with her family, she took only that one painting. She rolled the canvas up tight and never let it go, not until they were safe to the north. You can still see the cracks in the surface where the canvas was damaged on the journey."

"That was the only painting she took?"

"She wanted to leave those nightmares behind. But the painting—it's her. It's Great Grandma Alice. She was nearly sold, nearly separated forever from her parents. There was some kind of commotion in the marketplace the day she stood on the block, and the sale was stopped, and the family kept her. She stayed on the farm until her friend married and moved away, and then she escaped."

I closed my eyes and pictured the painting I had stood in front of so many times. That beautiful girl is Great Grandma Alice. I looked at the tube of paint in my hand. Vermillion. *Vermillion*. It spoke of such sophistication in such a savage world.

"Do you know Linda, what I read recently?"

"Mm-mm." The words I might have said seemed to disappear as they breached my lips.

"Elie Wiesel—"

"Yes." *Yes, I know who Elie Wiesel is.* A man who has tried—devoted his life to trying—to understand our world. A world of vermillion, cabernet sauvignon, doctors, bridges, farmers, lace, airplanes, computers, antibiotics and flutes; of war, slaves and genocide; of God. These are the words fighting to come out, trapped inside me. The vast, incomprehensible swirl of man's boundless humanity, compassion, creativity, faith, inhumanity, cruelty and destructiveness.

"He *said*—" Anita lingered on the word; she looked down at the paints in the drawer on her lap. Perhaps she too was thinking of vermillion and human auction blocks.

"He said, that the survivors of the holocaust believed, *that if only they told their story, the world would change.* These paints—her painting—is how my great grandmother told her story."

I took the drawer from her and laid it carefully on the bed. Then I lightly took her hand in mine and we sat like this for a long time, reluctantly reflecting on how insufficiently the world has changed. Anita, I know, looked at her Jesus icon with his brilliant gold halo, while I looked at the blank blue wall in front of me.

Later I biked home thinking of Anita and the slave girl, and it struck me, as I walked in the door, how much shorter the ride home seemed that night.

OF ALL THAT CAN BE REBUILT

There is no stoppage and never can be stoppage,
If I, and you, and the worlds, and all beneath or upon
 their surfaces,
And all the palpable life, were this moment reduced back
 to a pallid float,
It would not avail in the long run,
We should surely bring up again where we now stand,
And as surely go as much farther, and then farther and farther.
                                                Walt Whitman

Today I sleep in late and awake to find the house empty. Ian has taken Sandra to school. I take my coffee and cereal out to the garden and write out various To Do lists for an hour or so. I'd been contemplating where to go next with my life and work, and once again, Jonathan stepped in to guide me. I'm going to keep working with Luther and Anita, but now we're really going to start shaking things up. I call Catherine to invite her and BDY over for dinner and she is delighted to hear that I'm out of the doldrums.

"You were *no* bloody fun these past few weeks. What's got you so happy again?"

"Politics," I tell her.

"*No*, I don't believe you. You've already found another campaign? What happened to I need time off, *blah, blah, blah*?"

"*Real* politics. Election campaigns. Local and national."

"That's shark-infested, piranha territory—are you sure you want to get involved?"

"I don't think sharks and piranhas co-exist, do they?"

"Somewhere in the world, I'm sure they do."

We both laugh as the words roll out, "Washington, *D.C*!"

After talking to Catherine I feel strong enough to call Andrew. The lead bill was killed. I knew it would be, I just couldn't bear to be there, to watch someone like Baucus be defeated. Worthington voted against. I try to reassure Andrew, telling him Worthington's voting record will speak for itself in two years time. But there's not much hope of consoling him now, since he has to immediately contemplate his next moves. My next call is to the DC VOTE campaign. I arrange a meeting with their Campaign Director. I happily stay on the phone for the rest of the morning and take a first shot at a draft campaign strategy for an, as yet, unidentified Ward 8 candidate for the next election. Luther and Greg I am sure, will be happy to fill in the blanks. They each have whole Blackberrys full of up-and-coming black activists.

I'm back in the game, but before I lose myself to my work again, I have to take on a house project that I've neglected for far too long. A few weeks ago, Ian and I met with a contractor about fixing the exterior kitchen wall; we had noticed holes in between the brick, and pools of sand and mortar at its base, near the rose bed.

"What do you think?" Ian asked the man.

"I can fix it, make it good as new. Should be roughly $22,000, based on square foot, but I can do it for twenty."

"But it wouldn't be that much, right," Ian asked calmly, "because you wouldn't need to point the whole wall, just the loose parts?"

"Oh, I only do the whole wall. Best for the wall."

Best for the wall, best for you, not best for us. Ian and I had taken a trip to the 17th Street hardware store, and we met a man there who would save us $20,000, minus $18.78 for materials.

"Anyone can point," he told us, "if they have the patience and the time. Let me show you how."

So now I crouch low, scraping away the old mortar between the bricks at the base of our kitchen wall. It starts to crumble quickly and suddenly a horde of giant ants scurry out from the joint I am working on. The bloated queen ant tumbles out. More ants follow. I sit back from my work and peer into the now substantial hole in the wall and realize as I do, that the brick itself is eroding; the wall is coming apart. When I think there are no more ants to follow, I proceed. More scraping, and more of the loose mortar crumbling and falling, like fine sand, to the ground below. I reach for my fine wire brush, not looking away from the hole, even for a moment, in case more creatures start to emerge. I brush away the last of the debris in the joint. Taking up my water bottle I vigorously squirt water into the hole, and watch as the parched wall gulps away the water and appears dry again instantly. I reluctantly leave the site and refill the bottle at the kitchen sink. Finally the tired old wall and joint is satiated. I can begin to point. My mortar sits in a bright red bucket at my side, coarse and thirsty. I ignore the instructions on the bag, and trust the instructions of the pro at the hardware store, who talked me through pointing as though I would be delivering a baby.

"Keep your mortar *dry*, drier than you think it's possible to work with. Take your *time*. This is painstaking, tedious work," he had said.

I reach the last section of the wall. I tried and tested his theory all day. A nice dry mortar (even drier than the paltry three pints for every 20 pounds of concrete that the bag recommends) will serve you well if you are patient with it, and coax it gently into well-soaked joints.

Ian surprises me by returning home early after his latest business trip is postponed; he appears from the kitchen, holding two beers.

"Well, I'm going to read the *Post*," he says, "while you save us 20 grand."

He tips his beer to mine and opens the paper. He is all bluff and no conviction. I know that he will shortly go upstairs and change, and join me, and we'll work together and get this done, and we'll have a damn good time while we're at it. It strikes me as I work, that evicting the ants and restoring the wall is not unlike the effort it has taken me to restore myself over this past year. Somehow, unwelcome thoughts and fears, sometimes overwhelming self-doubt, lodged with me and degraded my confidence, humor and worst of all, my conviction. First the mortar then the brick itself crumbled once there were unwanted guests in the wall. It is a blessing to scrape and wash this wall, and to point it back to health. Knowing that everything that matters is intact and can be restored has reaffirmed what has sustained me all along. That we each can be stripped down and rebuilt and make it through the coming thunderous rains of life.

PERMISSIONS ACKNOWLEDGEMENTS

Grateful acknowledgement is made to all the authors quoted in this book, and to the following:

Quote from "The Chaneysville Incident" by David Bradley, copyright ©1981 David Bradley, reprinted with the kind permission of the author.

Quote from "The Image" by Bunyan Bryant, copyright ©1994 Bunyan Bryant, reprinted with the kind permission of the author.

Quote from "I'll Fly Away" from *The Autobiography of a Jukebox* by Cornelius Eady, copyright ©1997 Cornelius Eady, reprinted with the kind permission of the author.

Quote from "Anointed to Fly" by Gloria Wade-Gayles, copyright ©1991 Gloria Wade-Gayles, reprinted with the kind permission of the author.

Quote from "Their Eyes Were Watching God" by Zora Neale Hurston, copyright ©1937 by Harper and Row, Publishers, Inc; renewed ©1965 by John C. Hurston and Joel Hurston. Reprinted by permission of HarperCollins Publishers.

"Justice" from THE COLLECTED POEMS OF LANGSTON HUGHES by Langston Hughes, edited by Arnold Rampersad with David Roessel, Associate Editor, copyright © 1994 by the Estate of Langston Hughes. Used by permission of Alfred A. Knopf, a division of Random House, Inc.

Quote from "potentially yours (for jeff cole)" from *fingering the keys*, by Reuben Jackson, copyright ©1990 Reuben Jackson, reprinted with the kind permission of the author.

Quotes from Dr. Martin Luther King Jr. are reprinted by arrangement with The Heirs to the Estate of Martin Luther King Jr., c/o Writers House, as agent for the proprietor, New York, NY. *Copyright ©1963 Dr. Martin Luther King Jr; copyright renewed 1991 Coretta Scott King.*

Quote from "The Poisonwood Bible" by Barbara Kingsolver, copyright ©1998 Barbara Kingsolver. Reprinted by permission of HarperCollins Publishers.

Quote from Yusef Komunyakaa, "Prisoners" from Pleasure Dome © 2001 by Yusef Komunyakaa and reprinted by permission of Wesleyan University Press.

Quote from "Makes Me Wanna Holler" copyright ©1995 Nathan McCall, reprinted with the kind permission of the author.

Quote from Toni Morrison, reprinted with the kind permission of the author.

Quote from "The Portrait in the Rock" by Pablo Neruda, from Pablo Neruda, Selected Poems, Edited by Nathaniel Tarn, copyright ©1970 Anthony Kerrigan, W.S. Merwin, Alastair Reed and Nathaniel Tarn. Published by Houghton Mifflin Harcourt Company.

Quote from "It's Not About the Bike: My Journey Back to Life" by Lance Armstrong with Sally Jenkins, copyright ©2000 Lance Armstrong. Published by G.P. Putnam's Sons, member of Penguin Putnam Inc.

Rainer Maria Rilke, excerpt from "The Future" from *The Complete French Poems of Rainer Maria Rilke*, translated by A. Poulin, Jr. Copyright ©1986 by A. Poulin, Jr. Reprinted with the permission of Graywolf Press, Minneapolis, Minnesota, www.graywolfpress.org.

Quote from "Firelight" from THE NIGHT IN QUESTION, by Tobias Wolff, copyright ©1997 Tobias Wolff. Published by Random House Inc.

Quote from "The Outsider" by Richard Wright, copyright © 1953 Richard Wright, renewed ©1981 by Ellen Wright. Reprinted by permission of HarperCollins Publishers.

Quote from Marian Wright Edelman, reprinted with the kind permission of the author.

ACKNOWLEDGEMENTS

My profound gratitude goes to Robert Bausch, for being an extraordinary teacher and mentor. Thanks to Susan Coll for advising me to "turn my book inside out." Thanks to my fellow writers and Bausch workshop groupies at the Writers Center, especially Jennifer Buxton Haupt, Peirce Howard, Joram Piatigorsky and Rimas Blekaitis. Heartfelt thanks to Reuben Jackson for encouraging me to pursue the dream, and for the daily doses of good music and poetry. Thanks to Eugene DeWitt Kinlow and Tonya Vidal Kinlow, for sharing Oxon Cove with me and for the journey we took together.

Thank you to Jodi Ferrier for visualizing what was just a notion and making it real.

Thanks to all my friends and colleagues who helped me to get to this point in ways they probably don't even know, but especially to Ingrid Flory, Greg Kidd, Jae-Jae Spoon, Greg Rhett, Sherri Owens, Jill Inbar, Amy Tinto, Linda McCabe, Lynne Cherry, Lynne Mersfelder, Don Lewis, Amy Kendall, Paul Bernstein and Julia Dworkin. Thank you Bardia, for the window seat where it all began.

Thanks Moira for always believing, for being survivors together, and for all the laughter and love.

Thank you to Sylvia and Lewis Whitman, for your boundless love and kindness, and to Gordon Whitman, Julia Paley, Isaiah and Natalia, Susan Paley and Zeke, for all the good times and silliness.

Thanks to my Mother and in memory of my Father.

And to Jim and Nicholas, thank you for making every day a miracle.

Made in the USA
Charleston, SC
12 October 2015